THE BAYERN AGENDA

"Hypercool. It's like the Golden Age of sci-fi got an upgrade, with all the big honking space cannons and some desert planet dry humour thrown in for the bargain."
John Birmingham, author of the Axis of Time series

"Highly recommended, snarky sci-fi adventure."
Joe Zieja, author of Mechanical Failure

"A twist-laden caper of intrigue and improv filled with dark humour and, uh, surprisingly engaging galactic economics."
Antony Johnston, creator of Atomic Blonde *and* The Exphoria Code

"*The Bayern Agenda* is exactly the dose of intergalactic espionage you need. Action, humor, and pathos, wrapped up in a plot that Le Carré would be proud of… Moren is one to watch."
Eric Scott Fischl, author of Dr Potter's Medicine Show

"Immersive, intergalactic spy-fi. Moren gives us a Cold War thriller with wormholes and anti-grav fields."
John August, screenwriter of Titan AE *and* Big Fish

"The action scenes, both on the ground and in space, show a focus on thoughtful planning and careful pacing. The characterization delves just enough into emotionality to give the characters realism without moving the focus away from fights, intrigue, and spycraft."
Publishers Weekly

"A great spy story, with tidbits of science explaining the intergalactic travel and even a hint of romance to come."
Booklist

DAN MOREN

The Bayern Agenda

WITHDRAWN

ANGRY
ROBOT

ANGRY ROBOT
An imprint of Watkins Media Ltd

Unit 11, Shepperton House
89 Shepperton Road
London N1 3DF
UK

angryrobotbooks.com
twitter.com/angryrobotbooks
In from the cold

An Angry Robot paperback original 2019

Cover by Amazing15
Set in Meridien and Futura by Argh! Nottingham

Distributed in the United States by Penguin Random House, Inc., New York.

ISBN 978 0 85766 819 6
Ebook ISBN 978 0 85766 820 2

Printed in the United States of America

9 8 7 6 5 4 3 2 1

To Kat,
you're my favorite.

CHAPTER 1

Loitering was an art form.

Especially when one was loitering with purpose. Simon Kovalic's gray eyes cast over the shelves with just the right mix of interest and vacancy. Not so bored that somebody would want to engage him in conversation, and not so interested that he missed what was going on around him.

He took in the antique shop in a glance, eyeing the few other customers on this frigid false night. Regulars, most of them, he guessed, with a sprinkling of tourists from elsewhere in the Illyrican Empire. Though why anybody would voluntarily choose to visit Sevastapol he had little idea; it wasn't as if *he* would be here if it weren't for the job. But he went where the Commonwealth told him to go, even if it meant going deep into enemy territory to a moon where even the nice parts didn't get far above freezing for much of the year.

Still, humanity – or the Illyrican portion of it, at least – had decided this rock was worth colonizing. Mineral deposits were one reason, but when it came right down to it Kovalic was pretty sure that they'd done it just because they *could*. Even in their pre-Imperial days, the Illyricans had felt they'd had something to prove, and what better way to do so than to tame a wild planetoid to their whims. It didn't really matter that it was a barren, snowy rock; it had a breathable atmosphere and temperatures that were within the habitable range – if only barely.

Through the thick, insulated windows Kovalic could see the snow hurling down outside. Blizzards were all too common on Sevastapol, and they were brutal and unforgiving; there were more deaths from exposure than almost anything else. Weather-related accidents were a close second.

Inside, however, it was perfectly comfortable; tapped geothermal pockets provided efficient heating for much of the populace. Kovalic had unwound his scarf and unzipped the parka he was wearing, stowing his balaclava and gloves in one of the coat's voluminous pockets. He raised his arm, the motion splashing a colorful display across the fabric which included the local time. Orbiting a gas giant gave Sevastapol an irregular day/night pattern; they were in false night, the sun itself down, but the light never quite extinguished as it reflected off the huge mottled planet that dominated the sky.

"'Scuse me," said a gruff voice, as a compact figure brushed past him.

"Not at all," said Kovalic.

The shorter man continued on, browsing a shelf of antiquated books, most with faded printed covers, others covered in moldering leather. He didn't seem to be reading them, though – mostly just staring glumly at the shelves.

"Anything?" murmured Kovalic.

"Not a thing, boss," said Tapper. "Quiet as my Aunt Mary's funeral."

"Wasn't that the aunt who wasn't actually dead?"

"Yeah, but she didn't want anybody knowing."

"Right. Well, stay sharp. It's almost showtime."

"I was born sharp."

Kovalic coughed to cover his smile. The general consensus was that Tapper was in his sixties, but nobody was sure exactly how old he was – even Kovalic, and they went back twenty years. But, despite the hair that had long gone steel gray and a face like a worn leather boot, Kovalic would have put him up against any operative half his age.

"Any of these good?" Tapper asked, nodding at the books.

"From a reading perspective or a collector's?"

Tapper shrugged. "Your pick."

Kovalic scanned the titles. "Definitely some classics among them, but I don't collect them. Ask Page."

"I don't get it," said Tapper, shaking his head. "These things just take up space. You can download any text you want. Why would you want to clutter up your home with these musty old things?"

Kovalic ran his fingers over the spine of one of the books. There was something tangible about it, he supposed: a connection you got with a physical book from turning its pages, that you didn't get from reading the same text on a screen. The idea that, for hundreds of years, the same volume had passed through the hands of countless others, linking all of them together in one continuous thread. Not that he had any intention of starting his own collection: they were a serious pain in the ass to move.

A sedate chime tinkled from the door at the front of the shop. He checked his sleeve again; it was just about time.

He nodded to Tapper. "Go mingle."

"Aye aye," said the shorter man, drifting off towards another corner of the shop.

Kovalic returned to perusing the shelves, taking his time before casually turning around to survey the display behind him. That gave him a chance to study the front of the shop and its occupants. Besides the shopkeeper – a tall, thin man, with tufts of gray hair that looked like they'd been glued on – there were a few other men and women scanning the shelves with the hungry looks of collectors searching for a find, and a couple who were poking about in the furniture section of the shop, wearing bright new parkas and exclaiming about each new item. Those would be the tourists.

Then there was the new arrival.

Bundled up as the figure was, about all Kovalic could tell was that it was a man – a short, stout man with a ruddy nose protruding over a subdued plaid scarf. Rather than a parka, he wore a sleek wool overcoat; more elegant than functional in the brisk Sevastapol weather. That made him a man concerned with appearances, especially when combined with the wide-brimmed felt hat pulled down tightly on his head. As disguises went, it was amateurish at best, unnecessarily conspicuous at worst.

The man walked past the shopkeeper, who was too busy reading from a thin volume held at arm's length to notice. He made his way stiffly towards the back of the shop in a manner so painfully casual that it practically shouted LOOK AT ME, I'M STROLLING, NOTHING TO SEE HERE.

Kovalic tried to avoid rubbing his forehead, and stared instead at the wall of books. He'd known going in that their contact wasn't trained for this sort of thing, but the general, Kovalic's boss, had deemed it an acceptable risk, given the man's stature and the value of the information on offer. Then again, the general didn't have to sit here and watch the worst tradecraft this side of an espionage vid.

As the man got closer, Kovalic's eyes narrowed. Something was off. The way the man was moving was *wrong*; his steps were wavering, unsure. Like he'd been injured. As if on cue, he clutched the side of the bookcase nearest Kovalic, his gloved hand gripping the wood as if his life depended on it.

Hefting the book in his hand, Kovalic opened his mouth to speak his part of the sign/countersign when he was interrupted by a mumble from the man in the hat.

"It was the... worst of times..." The voice was strained, hoarse, as if each word were being dragged out of it. The man was leaning heavily against the bookshelf. All the hair on Kovalic's neck stood to attention.

Kovalic reached over and tugged the scarf down, recognizing the face that he'd seen in the dossier: wrinkled, pale, and jowly. But the man's complexion was flushed, like he'd spent too long in the cold. Sweat beaded on his forehead, and his eyes had gone glassy. They met Kovalic's briefly, but there was no recognition there – they were empty and unfocused. The man swayed briefly, then started to crumple. Kovalic stepped over quickly, easing him gently to the floor.

"Shit." He pressed his fingers to the man's neck. There was a pulse, but it was thready and irregular.

Tapper, having seen something was off, made his way back over to his boss.

"What the hell happened?" he asked, his eyes flitting between Kovalic and the man on the floor.

Kovalic shook his head. "It's Bleiden, all right, but he's sick or something." His gut clenched. He supposed that it could have just been bad luck: maybe he'd gotten the flu that was going around. Maybe he'd eaten some bad shellfish. Weird coincidences happened all the time.

Then again, Kovalic had found himself rather attached to his life over the years, and part of what had kept him alive had been sweating the small stuff. He glanced up at Tapper.

"See if this place has a first aid kit."

Tapper nodded and headed towards the front of the shop. A few of the other customers were now eyeing them curiously, though none had made a move to intervene.

His eyes alit upon a tall, dark-haired man who was watching the scene with studied disinterest. Snapping his fingers, Kovalic got his attention. "You. Gimme a hand."

The man looked almost surprised to be addressed, then reluctantly made his way over and crouched down by them.

"How's your field medicine training, lieutenant?" Kovalic murmured.

The man's expression morphed from confused to sharp so fast it was a wonder it didn't give Kovalic whiplash.

"Rusty at best, sir," said Aaron Page. "Is he wounded?"

Kovalic patted the man down, checking for any obvious sign of injury, but, as he'd suspected, there was nothing. "I'm thinking poison."

Page's eyebrows went up at the conjecture. "But that would mean…"

"…that he was compromised. And that they knew we were coming."

Tapper chose that moment to reappear with two things: a small dingy looking medkit that might have been new when the sergeant was young, and a troubled expression. "Uh, boss? We got company." He jerked his thumb back at the windows.

Of course – he should have known there'd be another shoe.

"Uniforms?"

"Armed response troops, with a few plainclothes running the show."

Kovalic sucked in a breath through his teeth. "That'll be

Eyes. Well, shit." He'd hoped they'd managed to fly under the radar of the Imperial Intelligence Services, but with his luck he clearly shouldn't be buying lottery tickets anytime soon.

Tapper gestured at the shop. "Boss, this place is a kill zone. We gotta move."

Page had taken the medkit from Tapper and unzipped it, and was now rifling through the contents. "Without knowing what they dosed him with, I'm not sure which antidote to administer."

Kovalic rubbed his forehead. Saving Bleiden would be ideal, but at the moment even getting themselves out of here was starting to look like a tall order. "Lieutenant, talk to me about options, and make it quick. Sergeant, see if there's a back door." He nodded towards the rear of the shop, where a path snaked between two bookshelves. IIS wouldn't be dumb enough to leave an exit uncovered, but if there was any chance of getting his team out of here, Kovalic needed to know the lay of the land.

Tapper disappeared towards the rear of the shop while Page pulled out a vial and an injector. "It's mostly bandages and ointments, but there is a dose of epinephrine that's only a few months past its expiration date. If whatever they gave him triggered anaphylactic shock, that might help."

Well, if it didn't, he'd probably be dead anyway. Kovalic nodded to Page, who locked the vial in place and, without much in the way of ceremony, stabbed it into the man's thigh. There was a *click* and the man jerked.

Kovalic looked over at Page. "How do we know if it wor–"

The man gasped and convulsed, his eyes springing open as he tried to sit up.

Grabbing him by the shoulders, Kovalic held him steady. "Easy there."

The man's gaze swung wildly, seizing upon Kovalic. "Are you... Conductor?" he wheezed.

Protocol had gone out of the window by this point, so Kovalic just nodded. The man's hand came up and gripped Kovalic's arm tightly. His voice was strained again, and he fought to get each word past clenched teeth. "Eyes... watching me." His grip curled Kovalic's parka sleeve, insistent, and the colors of the display flickered and warped. "Important... meeting. Bayern. Three... days. Per–" Suddenly, his eyes rolled back into his head and he started convulsing again. White foam leaked from the edges of his mouth as his face twisted into a pained rictus. After a moment, he went limp.

Kovalic put a finger against his neck, but this time there wasn't so much as a faint pulse. Gesturing to Page, they gently laid the man down on the floor. Kovalic closed the blank eyes and let out a long breath, hand over his mouth.

Tapper caught Kovalic's eye from the back of the shop and jerked his head. There was an exit, then. He also raised five fingers and pointed them towards the rear. Five men watching it, probably waiting for the order to breach. Kovalic waved him over.

"Shit," said Tapper, glancing down at the body. "He didn't make it?"

Kovalic shook his head. "But he gave us something – we just need to make sure it doesn't go to waste."

"What's the plan?"

"I'm thinking we need to give the abort signal," said Kovalic, raising his sleeve and tapping an icon on the display. A burst of static exploded directly into his earbud, eliciting a curse.

"Too late," he said, tapping it off. "They've already set up a jamming field."

Tapper shook his head. "Not good. Standard portable jammer has an effective radius of about twenty-five meters."

Kovalic peered at the wall behind them, measuring in his head. "That easily covers the whole shop. And getting out of its range is going to mean fighting our way through whoever's out there."

"So, maybe we don't go through," said Tapper, pointing a finger at the ceiling. "Maybe we go up?"

Kovalic looked up. The shop occupied the ground floor, but the building was at least four or five stories tall. Not quite high enough to get them all the way out of the jamming field, but it didn't need to be – there ought to be a comm array on the roof that they could hijack to boost the signal. He didn't like the idea of being trapped on the roof, but it was better than walking out of here and into the Illyricans' hands. He glanced at his sleeve; it had been five minutes since Bleiden had come in, and Eyes surely had the place surrounded by this point. They had to move now.

"Did you find a set of stairs back there?"

"Not quite. But I think I've got something."

Kovalic turned to Page. "Keep an eye on the situation here. Let me know if it looks like they're about to breach." The lieutenant acknowledged with a tip of his head. Kovalic followed Tapper to the rear of the shop, which turned out to be a small storeroom with a side door that looked like it hadn't been used since the founding of the Illyrican Empire.

"Jesus, would it kill them to send in a building inspection team every once in a while?" said Tapper, kicking at a soggy cardboard box filled with decaying books. Slivers of paper launched into the air, fluttering to the ground like dying moths.

"We'll have to come back and enforce the fire code some

other time. Talk to me about this exit."

"Right," said Tapper. "That door lets into a side alley, which feeds into the street out front, but there's also roof access via a fire escape – I caught it on my recce earlier. They're using standard breach tactics, stacking up right here." He nodded to the wall to the left of the door. A workbench sat against the brickwork there; they each took an end and managed to shift it away from the wall, disturbing a cloud of what was undoubtedly valuable antique dust.

Wiping his hands, Kovalic rifled through his pockets, but they were empty aside from his backup comm unit. Weapons were a liability more often than a benefit in these types of missions, though he was wishing he'd reconsidered that stance right about now.

Tapper, meanwhile, had produced a fist-sized tube from his satchel and had set about drawing a rectangular outline in some sort of white substance onto the brick wall.

Kovalic blinked. "Do I even want to know where you got that?"

The older man chuckled. "You know me, boss. Always prepared. I know a guy around these parts who owed me a favor, and he just *happened* to have a spare tube of detpaste going to waste. Imagine that."

Kovalic opened his mouth, then snapped it shut. Some people collected books. Others collected high explosives. Who was he to judge?

"Carry on."

Finished with the outline, Tapper peeled an adhesive tab from the rear end of the tube, slapped it on his sleeve, and gave Kovalic a thumbs up.

Kovalic nodded and ducked back into the front room. At some point, the shop's other patrons had begun to catch on to the fact that something was amiss – except for the shopkeeper, who had remained engrossed in the text he was studying and who, Kovalic was becoming increasingly convinced, was hard of hearing.

Instead of browsing the wares, the rest of the customers were eyeing Page, who had taken up a spot near the door, but clear of the windows just in case IIS had deployed sharpshooters. Though he was leaning casually against the wall and staring off into the middle distance, that seemed to have just made the rest of the shop's patrons even more nervous. They'd huddled together, watching him, and every time one of them so much as shifted their weight, Page's eyes would snap to them and he'd give a curt shake of the head.

Kovalic cleared his throat and addressed the room. "Ladies and gentlemen, may I have your attention?"

Half a dozen gazes shifted to him, so he put on his best calming smile.

"This is an IIS security action. I apologize for the inconvenience, and we'll have you on your way in just a moment. In the meantime, if you could just seat yourselves against the far wall?"

Quite a few of them blanched at that announcement – nobody really *liked* the Imperial Intelligence Services, but that didn't extend to questioning or disobeying them. That was way too much heat for the average law-abiding citizen. Although none raised an argument as they shuffled over to the indicated wall.

Tapper materialized at his shoulder. "We're ready to go."

"Good," said Page, joining them. "Because they're coming in."

"In that case, exit, stage right." Kovalic gave a last look over his shoulder at Bleiden's body, lying limp against one of

the bookshelves, and his lips thinned. But there was no time
to linger on regrets – they had bigger problems. He looked
up and pointed a finger at Tapper. The sergeant touched a
blinking icon on his sleeve and there was a deep bass *thump*
that rattled the antiques on their shelves.

Yanking open the door to the back room, they darted in.
Particles of dust were floating everywhere, but, with the
exception of the giant gaping hole in the wall, it was hard to
say whether the back room was actually in worse shape than
before. Wind and snow whistled in from the makeshift door.

The three men clambered over the rubble that lay in the
threshold of the new door, finding themselves in a narrow
alley between two tall buildings. In addition to the debris
from the explosion, there were five armed response troops
scattered about: two of them were down and not moving,
apparently flattened by the explosion, while one was
staggering to his feet. The last two had their hands clapped
over their ears and were shaking their heads slowly. Carbines
hung from slings over their shoulders, and pistols were
holstered at their waist alongside a standard issue pair of
grenades. Their heads were swathed in helmets, balaclavas,
and goggles.

Kovalic pointed Tapper towards the one who was trying
to get up. The sergeant jogged towards him, then dealt
him a swift kick to the head that knocked him back to the
ground. Page had already closed the distance to one of the
two standing members of the team, delivering a knee to the
gut that doubled the trooper over, followed by a sharp elbow
to the back of the neck.

The last was standing against the opposite alley wall;
he'd started to regain his balance, and when he saw Kovalic
coming towards him he fumbled for his carbine. But he was

clearly still reeling from the explosion's concussion, and as Kovalic's hand came around – still clutching the hardcover book he'd been perusing earlier – it clipped him just under the chin, slamming his helmeted head back into the brick wall with a satisfying *thunk*. Not enough to knock him out, but it would at least ring his bell. Kovalic gave him a kick to the ribs, just to make sure he'd stay down.

Tapper had already liberated the weapons of the trooper he'd downed, slinging the carbine over one shoulder. He'd also grabbed a comm unit, and was starting to collect the grenades from the other troops as well. Page had likewise stripped another fallen trooper's equipment, checking the magazine on the weapon before locking it back into place.

"They'll localize the explosion any second," said Tapper. "We'd better make ourselves scarce."

Kovalic looked around: the alley dead-ended here, but, as Tapper had said, there was a metal fire escape on the side of the building – so at least the fire code hadn't been wholly ignored. The last flight was retracted, but with a short jump Kovalic pulled it down, clanging loudly to the ground.

"Go," he said, gesturing at Page and Tapper. The two didn't need any further encouragement as they scrambled up the ladder, Kovalic following close behind.

It was five stories to the top, navigating stairways that switched back and forth upon themselves as though they were sailing ships taking advantage of prevailing winds. Snowflakes bit at Kovalic's face, which had already started to numb from the cold. Reaching the top, he swung himself over the small lip that ran around the edge of the roof.

The roof itself contained an extensive collection of venting pipes, an emergency exit, and – Kovalic let out a sigh of relief – a comm array. Page was already ripping the cover off its junction box. As Kovalic joined them, Tapper took up position at the top of the fire escape, waiting for their pursuers.

Kovalic hoped to be long gone by the time they showed up.

"Stay low," he muttered to Tapper. "Eyes probably has snipers on the surrounding rooftops. No reason to make it easy on them." The curtain of snow around them made it hard to even see the adjacent buildings, but in a sniper's thermal scope they'd stand out like a parade float.

Tapper gave him a dry look. "Not my first dance, boss."

"Fair point."

"Just go get us our ride home."

With a nod, Kovalic went to join Page at the comm array. The younger man had a multitool clenched between his teeth as he twisted a pair of wires together; he looked up when Kovalic arrived, and took the tool out of his mouth long enough to say, "Two minutes."

Running a hand through his snow-covered hair, Kovalic glanced over his shoulder at the fire escape. Two minutes might be pushing it, depending on how fast the rest of the shock troops figured out where they'd gone. That meant the three of them would have to hold the roof while waiting for pickup, which was made easier by the fact that they had the high ground, and much, much harder by the fact that they were severely outnumbered.

"Do what you can."

Page didn't bother to respond, just delved back into the mess of wiring. Kovalic returned to Tapper, who was at the top of the fire escape, sitting with his back against the low wall.

The older man gave him a searching look as he sat down.

"What do you think, cap? We're in it this time, for sure."

"Come on," said Kovalic, nudging the sergeant. "We've been in tougher spots before."

Tapper pursed his lips. "I can think of maybe one," he admitted. "But I wouldn't exactly put it in the win column."

"Hey, any fight you can walk away from."

The sergeant gave a noncommittal grunt and checked his purloined weapon again.

Sighing, Kovalic looked up at the sky; between the city lights, the blizzard, and the false night, the sky had turned gray with tinges of pink. On a clearer evening you'd have a nice view of Yalta, the gas giant that Sevastapol orbited – its rings were spectacular. Certainly a hell of a lot pleasanter than a snowstorm.

"Boss." Tapper's hiss broke his train of thought. The sergeant caught his eye, then nodded towards the fire escape. "They're in the alley."

Kovalic looked across the roof at Page. "How's it going?" he called softly.

Without turning around, Page held up one hand with a single finger extended, then returned to his work.

"We're going to have to buy him some more time," said Kovalic, grimacing.

"I was hoping you'd say that," said Tapper. He hefted two of the grenades that he'd taken from the downed response officer below, then pulled the pins on both and lobbed them casually over the wall. Distantly, Kovalic heard them clink to the ground, followed by an exclamation of surprise that was cut short by a pair of explosions that echoed back up to them.

Leaving Tapper to watch the fire escape, Kovalic crossed over to Page, keeping his head low. "Page?"

The younger man pulled a circuit board from one slot, slid it into another, then slammed the junction box closed and handed Kovalic his own sleeve, which he'd peeled off and attached to the box by a pair of jury-rigged wires. The display rippled and blinked but showed a solid signal.

"Good work, lieutenant," said Kovalic. He punched in a code and opened the channel, patching it to his earbud. "Skyhook, this is Conductor. Copy?"

A buzz of static flooded the channel, but a moment later a somewhat broken-up voice cut through. "Copy, Conductor. Three by three."

"Roger. This is an abort. Repeat: abort. Immediate extraction required at source coordinates."

"Confirm abort."

"Sigma nine seven five."

"Confirmed. Skyhook en route, ETA three minutes."

"Best news I've heard all day. Heads up, the EZ is hot."

"Acknowledged, captain. See you in a jiffy." The comm beeped as the link was disconnected.

Kovalic looked up at his two teammates, but both of them had heard the conversation. "Three minutes to hold?"

Page raised his eyebrows. "Not going to be easy."

"When is it ever?" Tapper said.

"Hey," said Kovalic, with a shrug. "It could be wor–"

A shot pinged off the brickwork just behind him, sending shards flying in every direction.

"Down!" All three men hit the deck.

Kovalic rolled over to look at Page.

"High-caliber sniper rifle," the lieutenant said, cool as a frosty beverage on a summer day. "Impact point suggests it came from over there." He nodded in the direction of the next building over. There was a hiss and a sizzle, and Kovalic saw a shower of sparks cascade from the junction box, which had apparently caught part of the sniper round. Well, they wouldn't be making any more calls.

"We're going to need suppressing fire when Skyhook gets here," said Tapper.

"Congratulations. You've just volunteered."

"And I wondered how I always end up with the best jobs."

Kovalic looked over at the fire escape. Tapper's grenades had evidently thrown them into a bit of a disarray below, given that nobody had tried to come up and over yet. Still, they couldn't count the rest of the armed response troops out of the fight. The net was being drawn fast.

Which was fine, as long as they weren't in it when it closed. Bleiden's intelligence might have been scant, but it was going to live or die with them.

"Two minutes. Page, hold off the sniper. Tapper, on three, suppressing fire into the alley."

"Copy that," said Tapper.

Sucking in a lungful of air, Kovalic steadied himself. "One... two... *three*."

Page lifted his weapon, and sent a series of bursts in the direction the shot had come from. Simultaneously, Tapper and Kovalic popped over the low wall and fired down into the alley, the shots singing against the bricks and metalwork. A few muzzle flashes signaled return shots, but at this range and angle they were little more than blind fire.

After a few seconds, all three men slid down with their backs against the wall again.

"How long on the clock?" Tapper asked.

"Minute and a half," said Kovalic. "We should be able to see him." He scanned the sky in the direction that he was pretty sure was south, but the storm made it hard to see more than a few meters off the roof. The snowflakes kept flying into his eyes, refracting what little illumination there was from the streetlights below and the one flickering star above.

Star?

"Heads up! One o'clock high!"

Tapper and Page's heads both swiveled to follow Kovalic's glance.

"You sure that's him?" the sergeant asked.

"If it isn't, then we are in a hell of a lot more trouble."

As the light came closer it resolved into a pair of points – two headlights – blinking rapidly on and off, in a very specific pattern. The whooshing noise of the engines was audible now, reaching them at a delay, given the craft's speed.

"That's him," said Kovalic. "Sergeant, the signaling laser if you please."

Tapper fumbled in his bag, then pulled out a small device about the size of a pen, and flicked it on and off rapidly, in the same pattern that the ship had blinked its lights. The headlights blinked again in confirmation.

"Suppressing fire again," said Kovalic, circling a finger in the air. "Let's keep the area clear for him. One… two–"

He never reached three, as a brilliant column of light descended from the heavens, piercing through the gray veil of snow and striking the incoming ship dead center. A fireball ignited in the sky, sizzling through the snowstorm. A moment later the sound of the explosion and the accompanying shockwave hit, blowing back Kovalic's hair even at this distance.

And then, in its wake, a sound of emptiness so loud it almost threatened to deafen him.

"Holy shit," breathed Tapper. "I thought the fake transponder–"

Kovalic swallowed, his mouth suddenly parched. "They must have found out from Bleiden." Though how *he* knew, Kovalic couldn't imagine.

From below came indistinct shouts and the rattle of feet on metal.

"Boss," whispered Tapper, "they're coming. We need to go."

Go? Go where? Their escape route had just been blown out of the sky. If IIS had identified the ship before destroying it, they'd have all the IDs his team had used to get on planet. Which meant they needed new ones – and that meant time. And a place to hole up.

He took a deep breath. Roll with it, he reminded himself. First things first: getting off the roof.

"Page," he said, catching the lieutenant's eye. "How far to the next roof?" He nodded in the direction opposite from where the sniper had taken his shot.

The younger man shrugged. "Three meters, but it's down. Doable." More challenging, it meant jumping the alley where the troopers – and their many weapons – were currently hanging out.

Kovalic nodded at him. "You first. Tapper and I will cover for you."

Page didn't question the order, just nodded and got to his feet. Crouching, he got some distance from the edge of the roof and then looked at Kovalic expectantly.

With a nod, Kovalic raised one finger. Then a second. Then a third. At the third finger, Page took off, sprinting for the edge of the roof. As his foot planted on the low wall, Tapper and Kovalic swung their guns over the side, and fired off a few bursts towards the alley.

There was at least one *thwack* as a round struck home on body armor, followed by a grunt and a clatter as the trooper hit the deck. Out of the corner of his eye, Kovalic saw Page land and roll on the opposite roof and then spring up again, flashing them a thumbs up.

"You next, old man," said Kovalic.

Tapper looked like he wanted to argue, but years of taking orders won out and he just gave a silent nod, then followed Page's example. This time there were plenty of rounds flying upwards, but with both Kovalic and Page providing cover fire from opposite sides of the gap nobody had time to draw a bead on Tapper. The sergeant didn't stick the landing quite as gracefully as his compatriot, but Page helped him to his feet and the two waited for their commanding officer.

Kovalic rolled his neck, and then tightened the cinch on the gun's strap. He crept towards the same place Page and Tapper had started their run, and took a deep breath. Then, counting silently to himself, he pushed off and sprinted all out to the edge.

The scariest part of making a jump was that moment of commitment: planting a foot and pushing off, floating over the void. As long as you didn't hesitate, you'd be fine. You just had to trust that you'd make it. It had to be automatic, instinctive.

Kovalic didn't think twice as his foot went down and his leg muscle tensed, sending him up and off the edge of the roof, arcing over the alley. He saw the roof of the neighboring building in front of him, and relief washed over him as he realized he'd make it with room to spare.

And then the biggest bee in the history of the universe

bit him right in the shoulder, sending surprise and, shortly thereafter, stabbing pain through his whole torso. A split-second later he dimly registered the crack of a rifle report. Then he was just falling.

CHAPTER 2

Elijah Brody pulled himself up through the cockpit opening, grabbing the ladder rung above him.

"That was one hell of a ride, doc," he said, climbing up to the catwalk that led into the simulator.

Dr Barbara Thornfield stood, arms crossed, her typical appraising look married to barely-contained irritation. Her hair, which just brushed the tops of her ears, had once been blond, but it had taken on a paler, whitish cast with age. The wrinkles around her mouth were quirked in the grimace Eli had gotten to know all too well over the past six months, and her pearlescent fingernails drummed on the sleeves of her white coat.

"You're dead, Mr Brody. Again," she said. "I could speculate about the causes, but let's just go with the obvious ones: you disobeyed a direct order, not to mention risking your own life and the mission in three different ways."

"Only three?"

"This isn't a laughing matter, Eli."

"How were the vitals?"

Her lips pursed at his evasion. "Mostly stable. Elevated as expected during the confrontation, with a couple of blips here and there. But I'm more worried about your judgment.

You were reckless in there."

Eli shrugged. "It was just a sim. There wasn't any real danger."

"We have simulators for a reason – to train you for real life situations."

"But if you *know* it's a simulator, you're never going to react the same way," he said tiredly. They'd had this particular argument at least a dozen times over the past six months, with neither prepared to budge an inch on the subject. They could both probably perform each other's lines by this point.

Dr Thornfield sighed. "Eli, the kind of trauma you've seen – watching your friends and comrades killed in front of you – it doesn't just go away, even after five years. You've made a lot of progress in the last six months, but my job is to evaluate your fitness to fly for the Commonwealth of Independent Systems, and right now..." She shook her head. "I have concerns."

"Look, doc. I'm not a soldier any more – haven't been for five years." The slaughter at the Battle of Sabaea had seen to that. "I'm just a pilot. There is a difference."

"You flew into the side of a frigate. Pilot or soldier, you're just as dead."

OK, that's fair. But it was upside down! Well. I was upside down.

"I'm just saying, I *felt* a lot better. Minimal panic response, pretty much no nausea." He jerked a thumb back towards the simulator. "I couldn't have done half of that if I'd felt space-sick. And as far as taking orders goes, well, I'm just a civilian, doc."

The doctor threw up her hands. "And you'll do as you like. I know. Well, I think we can say we're done with our session for today." She turned and started down the ramp to the hangar floor.

Eli trailed after her, unzipping his flight suit and peeling off the sleeves. He let it fall loosely at his waist. It had gotten plenty warm in the cockpit, especially after the shooting had started, and the cool air in the hangar was refreshing. Regardless of his criticisms, the sim was pretty good at fooling his body, if not his mind, into thinking he was actually flying a ship.

But he was starting to feel that itch between his shoulder blades. The same one he'd gotten after his first months of intensive simulator training at the Illyrican Naval Academy almost a decade ago and, before that, back when his Aunt Brigid had first taken him up on her short-haul flights.

"Come on, doc. I'm ready to take a trainer up. Just a couple quick laps around the airfield. I'll have it back before dinner."

"Dinner is ten hours from now."

"So, is that a yes?"

Dr Thornfield shook her head. "I just don't think you're ready for that step yet, Eli."

Frustration bubbled up in his chest. "When the hell am I going to *be* ready, then? We've been at this for six months and… I need this."

Her head tilted slightly. "Why do you think you need this?"

Eli scuffed his shoe against the floor, waving his hand at the hangar. Besides the simulator there were a few actual ships present, mostly for maintenance. He could hear the buzz of pneumatic tools and the clank of machinery, smell the faint whiff of fuel. His blood sang with it.

"This is torture, doc. It's like plopping a kid down in a candy store and not giving him a taste. This… This isn't where I *belong*."

One white eyebrow arched. "Where do you think you belong, Eli?"

He stabbed a finger skywards. "Up there."

"Uh huh. And where are you going to *go*?"

Eli opened his mouth to respond, too late realizing the trap he'd burned right into. "What?"

"Simple question: You've got a ship. Where do you go?"

She wants me to say "home". "Somewhere... that's not here."

The look she gave him was skeptical, knowing. "Not a lot of options, as I understand it. You betrayed the Imperium at Sabaea–" she held up her hands to forestall Eli's protest, "–on moral grounds, yes, I understand. But then you defected to the Commonwealth – and last time I checked, your home planet of Caledonia was still firmly in Imperial territory."

Not that there was much reason to go back, frankly. Eli had run as far and as fast from the planet as he soon as he could. He'd come to the Commonwealth of Independent Systems because of a promise of a future from the covert operative – and, he'd started to think, possible friend – Simon Kovalic. *Then again, Kovalic promised a lot of things. And then he dumped me here for six months and didn't look back.*

Dr Thornfield's expression softened. "I know it doesn't feel like it, Eli, but you are making progress. Slowly but surely. We'll meet again next week." She waved a hand and a sharp smile flashed like a shooting star. "Try not to let your recklessness get the better of you before then."

Flipping her a mock salute, Eli turned to head to the locker room. Next week and next week and next week until his hair was gray and his reflexes were shot. Everybody was just keeping him in a holding pattern, and that was dangerous, because when he didn't have anything to occupy his attention his thoughts gently settled to the bottom of his stomach.

"'Not ready yet,'" he fumed. Teeth clenching, he delivered a sharp kick to a loose bolt on the floor that had made the mistake of getting in his way. It skipped and skittered across the hangar floor, bouncing off a pair of shiny black boots.

Eli looked up, an apology on his lips, then stopped dead in his tracks as he recognized the man to whom the boots belonged.

"Good day, Mr Brody. A word?"

He was an old man, slim with a fringe of white hair around his ears and the back of his head, and an equally white vandyke beard and pointed mustache that stood out against his bronzed skin. A hawkish nose and narrowed eyes gave him the air of a predator, despite his otherwise grandfatherly appearance. He wasn't stooped, but he leaned on a handsome black wooden cane with a gold-colored pommel.

Eli had met him twice before, both times in the company of Kovalic, and though he didn't know the man's name it was clear that he was Kovalic's boss. Despite that, he spoke in the cultured accents of a high-born Illyrican, a fact that made Eli's head spin. What was a member of Illyrican nobility doing ordering around an elite Commonwealth military team when the two superpowers had been at war for most of Eli's life? He wore no insignia, just a navy blue military-style jacket over a white shirt and black trousers.

One thing Eli had concluded: he was certainly not a man to be trifled with.

"Uh. Hi," said Eli, not quite sure how to address him.

"You remember me."

"You're a hard man to forget – I don't believe I caught your name, though."

"No?" said the old man. "A shame."

They stood there in silence for a moment, then Eli caved.

"Uh, what can I do for you?"

The old man gestured with one liver-spotted hand. "Walk with me?"

Eli looked around; the maintenance crews were going about their business – none of them were paying the slightest attention to the two of them, though in some cases that looked like a very deliberate sort of not-paying-attention. Giving the old man a cautious nod, Eli fell into step with him.

The man moved slowly, with an awkward stride; Eli detected the faint whine of servomotors as he moved. Prosthetic legs, he realized, trying not to obviously look down at them.

The old man caught the glance anyway, and smiled. "Lost them years ago. Had these prosthetics custom-built – they were top of the line at the time, but I'm afraid they haven't aged well." He chuckled. "I could say the same about myself."

Eli gave a polite cough-laugh in response.

"You're probably wondering exactly what I'm doing here, so let me be direct: I need your help, Mr Brody. We have a situation on the planet Sevastapol."

Eli frowned. "That's an Illyrican colony."

"I'm aware of that," said the general dryly.

"What kind of situation?"

The old man raised an eyebrow.

"I've seen the sorts of situations you deal with and just in case it's slipped your mind, I'm not a soldier."

"I don't need a soldier. I need a pilot."

"There's some dispute on that score, too," said Eli, jerking a thumb over his shoulder.

"Yes, I've read Dr Thornfield's reports."

He's read… Eli's head snapped towards the old man. "Those are supposed to be confidential." *Why am I even surprised?*

"I don't agree with her conclusions," continued the man, ignoring Eli's comment. "Seems to me you've made quite a bit of progress in these last six months. We've been keeping tabs on you."

Eli shook his head, trying to take it all in. "Who the hell *are* you?"

The old man stopped and turned towards Eli, fixing him with an appraising stare. "The real question, Mr Brody, is how do *you* feel. I need a pilot who can handle whatever's thrown at them, and I've seen your records – all of them. I think that's you."

"This is crazy."

"All you have to do is go in, pick up some passengers, and come back." He paused. "There's just one condition."

"I thought you were being direct. Call it what it is: a catch."

The old man shrugged. "If you like. Thanks to your defection from the Illyrican Empire, the Commonwealth currently has you classified as a 'strategic asset.'"

"Yeah, I know," said Eli, rolling his eyes. "I can't even leave the planet without seventeen forms filled out in triplicate."

"Indeed," said the old man, having the grace to look slightly apologetic. "My fault, I'm afraid. But I also have a solution." He produced a tablet from under his arm and handed it over.

Thumbing it on, Eli skimmed through the text onscreen, then blinked and read it through again, more closely. Then blinked again. "What is this?" he said, looking up at the old man, and then back down at the screen.

"Exactly what it looks like," said the old man. "An officer's commission in the Commonwealth military, lieutenant rank. Which, if I'm not mistaken, is roughly equivalent to your former standing in the Illyrican Navy."

"I told you: I'm not a soldier," said Eli, holding the tablet out towards the old man.

The man raised a hand, palm out. "I'm afraid without your agreement, I can't fully brief you on the mission."

"Then I don't want your job."

"I think you do."

"What makes you so sure?"

"For one thing, it gets you out of here," said the old man, waving a hand at their surroundings. "I can sign off on your medical records. No more simulators. No more focused therapy sessions. But even more to the point..." There was a slight hesitation before the old man spoke again. "It's Captain Kovalic's team on Sevastapol. And they've run into a spot of trouble."

Eli froze, the tablet still held in his outstretched grip. *Six months*. It had been silly to think that Kovalic and his team had spent it sitting around, twiddling their thumbs – he'd seen them in action, and only an idiot would leave them on the bench when there was a war on, cold or otherwise. Even from his meager interaction with the old man, Eli felt pretty comfortable in his assessment that Kovalic's boss was far from an idiot.

That said, Sevastapol was behind enemy lines and Kovalic, Page, and Tapper were stuck there. He eyed the screen again. *I don't* owe *him anything. Not really.*

Even he didn't find the argument terribly convincing.

"Why me?"

"You've worked with Kovalic before – he knows you. And, as I said, I've read your file. I think you're the right man for the job."

He wasn't sure exactly what it was, but there was something the old man wasn't saying – some other hidden catch, some ulterior motive, something that wasn't clear.

"So, what, you want me to just fly into Illyrican space, pick up a team of special ops soldiers, and stroll away, nice as you please?"

They'd reached the hangar's exit, and the old man gestured to Eli. "After you, Mr Brody."

The warm wind ruffled through his air, even as the humidity started him sweating. Sitting on the tarmac directly outside was a hovercar with tinted windows; a woman leaned against the hood, but she straightened up when they emerged.

Her dirty blond hair was pulled back into a businesslike ponytail, focusing the attention on her face: elegant and pale-skinned, with high cheekbones, a slender nose and wide, expressive blue eyes that were on Eli from the moment she saw him. She stood at ease, hands clasped behind her back. Just a couple inches shorter than Eli, she was tall for a woman, with a wiry build that might be unwisely mistaken for slight.

"Mr Brody, this is Lieutenant Commander Taylor of Naval Intelligence Command. She'll be leading the operation to Sevastapol."

"I haven't agreed yet," said Eli, glancing at the commander, whose face remained impassive.

"Of course," said the old man.

"What other idiots have signed up for this mission, then?" Eli asked, looking around. He sensed more than saw the woman tense.

"It's just Commander Taylor – and you, of course, if you agree."

"Funny."

"I'm serious, Mr Brody. It was hard enough getting one team in – a smaller group stands a far better chance."

Eli's eyes darted from Taylor back to the old man. "This sounds like suicide – no offense, commander."

Her eyebrows twitched upwards, accompanied by a quirk of her lips. "None taken." Her voice was pleasant, but deeper than Eli had expected, with a posh timbre that spoke of years of expensive schooling. *She'd better be full of surprises if she intends to make it back alive.*

"So what the hell is this all about?" Eli asked.

The old man nodded to the tablet that Eli was still holding limply in one hand. "I know you're not content to sit on the sidelines, Mr Brody. Even after everything you've been through, you still want to make a difference. Well, this is how."

Even if it means signing away my soul. He raised the pad again, staring at the letter of commission that would shove him right back into the military hierarchy he'd already run away from. *I never really wanted to be a soldier. But somehow, I keep getting dragged into it.* But he couldn't deny the way it made his heart thump – with fear, sure, but also, much as he hated to admit it, with a jolt of adrenaline. *Aw, to hell with it – I'm done sitting around.*

With a deep breath, he pressed his thumb on the indicated square. The screen flashed as it captured his thumbprint, and he stifled a gulp as he saw the text "Lieutenant Elijah Brody, Confirmed" appear. *I guess there's no escaping some things.*

He handed the tablet to the old man, who tucked it under his arm and waved a hand at the car. Taylor opened the rear door; the three of them piled in.

The hovercar pulled away from the hangar and Eli cast a last glance over his shoulder at the building that had been more or less the entirety of his world for the last half a year.

"So," said Eli. "I'm pretty sure I was promised some details."

The old man cleared his throat. "We may be an informal organization, *lieutenant*, but let's stand on some ceremony, shall we?"

Eli glanced at the commander, who couldn't quite hide the smile from her lips, then back at the old man. "Uh, I'm pretty sure I was promised some details... sir?"

With a roll of his eyes, the old man shook his head, but plowed onward. "A few weeks ago we were alerted to the existence of a high-ranking member of the Illyrican government with an interest in... making a change in his living situation."

Eli raised his eyebrows. "You mean defecting?"

"Quite. Captain Kovalic and his team were dispatched to Sevastapol to facilitate the defection, but it seems as though it didn't quite go according to plan."

"And what's so important about this particular defector?"

The old man nodded to Taylor. "Commander?"

Taylor leaned forward, elbows on her knees. "Albert Bleiden is the Illyrican Empire's Permanent Undersecretary for Trade and Commerce. My department at NICOM has been running an investigation in which Bleiden had been flagged as a person of interest. We think he could shed light on some unsettling ties between the Imperium and the Bayern Corporation. The general got in touch when the SPT moved to secure Bleiden's defection."

Bayern? As in the biggest company in the known galaxy? "What kind of ties?"

Taylor shrugged. "Given the Corporation's interests and Bleiden's position, almost certainly financial, but the details are a bit scarce. We were hoping that he would be able to fill in the blanks."

Eli raised an eyebrow. "Financial? Seems a bit out of Kovalic and his crew's area of expertise. Don't you have a team of special ops accountants?"

Taylor's look was the kind one would give a precocious third-grader. "People get mugged for pocket change all the time – we're talking trillions here. You think people wouldn't kill for that?"

"The worry," the old man put in, "is that combining the Bayern Corporation's resources with the Imperium's bald-faced ambition would be an... undesirable state of affairs. That makes uncovering the links between the two – and whatever information the defector has – paramount to the safety and security of the Commonwealth."

Eli eyed the two of them as his position became slightly clearer. *You needed a pilot on short notice, and lucky enough, my calendar was pretty open.* "So, what's the situation on the ground?"

"Touch and go," said the old man. "What we know is that shortly after the arranged meet time, Captain Kovalic issued an abort code. Moments later, a light transport matching the registration of their ship was shot out of the sky by Sevastapol's orbital defenses."

Shot out of the... "Uh, no offense, but this mission is sounding a little less cut and dried than that initial pitch. Sir."

"Welcome to the service," Taylor murmured.

The old man's smile took on a shade of the grim. "I told you I needed a pilot that could handle whatever was thrown at them. I hope I'm not mistaken in my assessment, lieutenant."

The hovercar slowed to a stop, and Eli frowned. They hadn't gone through a perimeter gate, so they were still on the base. He glanced out the tinted windows and saw that they had pulled up next to a sleek, if somewhat used-looking transport ship, its hull pitted with micro-abrasions and streaked with carbon-scoring. A maintenance crew was finishing what looked like final takeoff preparations, detaching fuel lines and umbilical cables.

"I take it I don't have time to pack a bag," said Eli.

"We lucked out: this intelligence is only twelve hours old. That's about as fast as it could have gotten here from Sevastapol. We don't know what the status of Captain Kovalic's team is, but if they're going to have any hope of escaping – or, for that matter, surviving – I need you on your way six hours ago."

"That's great," said Eli, eyeing the ship again and doing some quick calculations in his head, "but even at best possible speed, the fastest we can make it to Sevastapol is probably another twelve hours. Not to mention clearing the relevant wormhole gates – no small thing if Sevastapol is locked down. And, oh yeah, those orbital defenses you mentioned." He glanced at Taylor and thought he even detected a flicker of concern on her face at the list.

The old man smiled. "I knew you were up to the challenge, Lieutenant Brody. As to your concerns, don't worry: I have an idea that should make this considerably easier." His blue eyes glinted as he opened the hovercar door, and the sound of engines powering up roared into the compartment. The old man shouted to be heard over the noise. "There's more than one reason I wanted you on this mission."

Oh. Great.

INTERLUDE

Outpost SD73, The Badlands, Earth – May 23, 2397

The private's ears were ringing.

The concussion shell had hit ten meters away, but the radius of its effect was at least twice that. From his place at the top of the ridge, he watched, frozen in horrified fascination, as the shockwave flattened the grass in front of him like an invisible wave, then knocked him off his feet, sending him tumbling down behind the emplacement.

He shook his head and managed to crawl to his feet, the grass hot under his hands despite the cool of the morning. The knees of his fatigues were torn and grass-stained from his slide, and somewhere he'd acquired a gash on his upper right arm. Still, other than the high-pitched whine in his ears, he was more or less unhurt. He pulled himself to the top of the ridge and looked over.

The lieutenant had not been so lucky.

His commanding officer had been standing ahead and in front of the emplacement, on the grassy slope – exactly why, the private wasn't quite sure, except she had evidently overindulged the previous night. The private had seen the flask that had been passed among the officers before they were all sent out to their emplacements. Then there had been the lieutenant's bloodshot eyes this morning as she'd stood on the hill, hurling abuse at their adversaries, even though they couldn't have possibly heard a word of it.

He wasn't sure if it were chance or deliberate aim, but the concussion shell had landed squarely next to the lieutenant. Even from his position atop the ridge, the private could see the blood streaming from the woman's nose and ears. There was a chance she was alive, but even if she was she'd never be the same again.

A hand suddenly descended on the private's shoulder and he started and spun around, but it was just the third member of their emplacement team, a middle-aged sergeant whose brown hair was already starting to turn gray. His mouth moved, but all the private could hear was the ringing. Pointing at his ears, he shook his head, and the sergeant frowned. The older man took him by the shoulders and turned him around, then pointed at the lieutenant and then at the two of them.

Dirt loosened by the concussion shell's impact shifted under their feet as they picked their way down the hill. They crossed the ten meters to the lieutenant quickly, grabbed the woman by her armpits, and dragged her back to the emplacement.

The private wiped his palms on his trousers. He'd never touched a dead body before – and he was certain now that the lieutenant *was* dead – and he felt the overwhelming urge to scrub his hands.

"She was a bleeding idiot," said the sergeant. Relief flooded through the private at any sound making it through the ringing in his ears.

The older man stared down at the lieutenant, a disapproving

look on his face, then gave the private a bleak smile.

"But I guess she was our idiot." Hard brown eyes swept him from head to toe. "How old are you, son?"

"N-Nineteen," the private stammered.

"Goddamn if they don't keep getting younger," muttered the sergeant.

The private straightened up. "This isn't my first engagement," he said stiffly. "I was at Salinas."

"Salinas?" said the sergeant, raising an eyebrow. "How long?"

Scratching at his cheek, the private evaded the other man's gaze. "Evacuated on the third night."

"Before the whole place was drop-bombed from orbit."

"Yeah."

"You even fire a shot?"

"Maybe one."

"Hit anything?"

The private didn't reply.

"Well, for fuck's sake," said the sergeant, throwing up his hands. "They send me up here with a greenie and a drunk. Who the hell did *I* piss off?" He looked up at the sky. "And to top it all off, *that*." He jerked his chin at a point behind the private, who turned to follow his gaze.

The morning haze had begun to burn off, revealing the huge ship that hung miles overhead. Its massive engines glowed in the atmosphere, the waves of heat shimmering like mirages. It bristled with gun turrets and the gaping mouths of fighter bays, all of it topped off by a coat of crimson paint. Letters were stenciled, what must have been tens of feet high, on its bow, though they were still hard to read at this distance. The private lifted the binoculars on his belt and swept them across the prow.

"The Hammer of God."

"Modest, ain't they?" said the sergeant. "That's a dreadnought – there's a dozen of them in the fleet, all told, and ain't nothing we've got that can stand against them."

The private lowered the binoculars, gaping at the sheer enormity of the war machine. The ships had appeared suddenly only a few weeks ago, barreling from the outer reaches of the solar system straight towards Earth. All attempts at communications had been met with puzzling silence, but when an outpost on Saturn's moon Enceladus was obliterated with little fanfare, Earth had scrambled to mobilize what little space-based defenses it had.

It didn't look like it was going to be enough.

A lump rose in the private's throat. "How are we supposed to fight monsters like that?"

"Hey," said the sergeant sharply. "None of that. They may put on a good show, but don't forget they're human."

"Bullshit. How could humans do *this*?" said the private. He waved a hand and it encompassed the ship, the hill, and even the lieutenant's body.

"People do awful things, kid. Out of anger, fear, pain... In this case, I think it might be all of the above. The crims think we failed them – and maybe we did – but when they sucker punch us, that doesn't mean we don't punch back. You get me?"

For a moment the private said nothing, then he let out a breath and nodded. "So, now what?"

As if in answer, a loud whirring issued from behind them, and the two men turned to watch a boxy shuttle glide in for a landing behind the ridgeline, about twenty meters away. The grass around it flattened in the wake of its repulsor fields. The two men exchanged a glance, but the ship was clearly one of their own; they made their way down the hill.

A hatch in the side slid open, a ramp descending and planting almost viciously into the dirt. From the darkness inside, a woman appeared – dark hair, average height, a bandage on her right cheek – and waved at them; her rank insignia pegged her as a corporal.

"Hey," the woman yelled over the shuttle's engines. "One of you Lieutenant Carlin?"

The sergeant pointed a thumb over his shoulder. "LT's dead," he said.

"Shit," said the woman on the shuttle, pursing her lips, then shrugged and continued. "We're here to evacuate you."

"Evacuate?" the sergeant echoed.

The corporal looked back and forth between them, her eyes widening. "You haven't heard?"

"Heard what?"

"Beijing fell this morning."

For a moment, everything seemed to go quiet: no thrumming engines, no whistling shells in the distance, not even the chirping of a bird.

"Holy shit," the private breathed.

"Pretty much," said the corporal. "We're pulling back."

"Pulling *back*?" shouted the sergeant. "To *where*?"

The corporal leaned out of the shuttle and pointed towards the sky.

The sergeant's face morphed into an expression of disbelief. "You're joking."

The corporal shook her head. "I don't give the orders, sergeant, I just relay them. Speaking of which…" She gestured at the ramp.

Looking as though he'd dearly like to punch something – or someone – the sergeant gritted his teeth. He cast a look over his shoulder. "We gotta get Carlin's body," he said. "We'll be right back." Tapping the private on the shoulder, he motioned him back up the hill.

The private wasn't looking forward to dragging the lifeless body of his commanding officer – *former* commanding officer – anywhere, but he guessed the sergeant wouldn't indulge his squeamishness. And, morbid as the thought was, he kind of hoped someone would do him the same favor were he in the lieutenant's position. He shuddered.

Once again, they each took an arm, pulling the body towards the waiting shuttle. They'd covered about half the distance when a loud whistling filled the air. The private looked up in alarm: he'd already heard that whistling once this morning, and the result hadn't been pretty.

The sergeant had heard it, too, and unceremoniously dumped his portion of Lieutenant Carlin's body into the dirt. "*Down!*" he yelled, hitting the ground and covering his head with his arms.

For some reason – he never could figure out why – the private didn't react as fast. He even turned and caught sight of the angry, burning red star hurtling towards them. It wasn't until the last moment that he thought to throw up his arms.

For the second time that morning a shockwave bowled him over, sending him sliding across the grass. He thought he glimpsed the shuttle being flung away in the instant before he briefly lost consciousness.

When he came to, he was on a boat in the middle of the ocean, bobbing and weaving unsteadily, and trying not to lose his lunch. A blurry face swam into view over him – the sergeant, who was urgently mouthing something. His eyes tried to focus and failed, though he managed to divine that he wasn't on a boat, but a shuttle – *the* shuttle, he realized as his wits came back to him.

His head lolled to one side, and through the transparent viewport he saw the waves of grass rippling and then tilting crazily to one side as the shuttle lifted off. The body of Lieutenant Carlin was still there, too, splayed like a chalk outline. From the corner of his eye, he saw the sergeant draw back a hand and then felt the stinging slap across his face. He blinked again, this time pretty sure he could make out the words the sergeant was saying. It looked a lot like…

CHAPTER 3

"*Wake up.*" A slap caught Kovalic across the side of the face.
The room spun slowly into focus. Sparsely furnished, it looked like something out of an Earth history book depicting life in the pre-spaceflight era. There was a crude table and chairs that appeared to have been fashioned by someone with a less than comprehensive knowledge of woodworking, and a pair of lamps that had stepped right out of a museum; even the walls themselves seemed to be built of hewn wood, the chinks filled with some sort of pitch or mortar.

Addled as he was, Kovalic almost wondered if he'd somehow slipped through a temporal vortex into the past, but the face above him – and the hand readying another slap – was all too familiar.

Instinctively, Kovalic threw up his right hand to block the slap – or at least he tried, but when he made to move that arm, pain lanced from his shoulder across his chest and back, convincing him that it maybe wasn't the smartest move.

Fortunately, Tapper seemed to have realized he was conscious, and refrained from giving him another wake-up call. Peering at him, the sergeant raised his eyebrows expectantly.

"You awake, then?"

Kovalic swallowed, trying to work some moisture into his mouth. "Where the hell are we?"

"A farmhouse about twenty klicks west of the city."

"Farmhouse?" Kovalic's head spun. They were on... Sevastapol?

"One of those little dachas the cityfolk build to feel like they're in touch with their rural roots," said Tapper, with a roll of his eyes.

"Well, this guy is certainly not in touch with his ability to make furniture," said Kovalic dryly.

The smile on Tapper's face was genuine enough, but Kovalic had known the man long enough to see the relief beneath the surface. "Glad to have you back, boss."

Kovalic wiggled his fingers and toes, testing the rest of his body. Bruises and cuts, certainly, but the only thing that really hurt was his shoulder. His memory flashed suddenly, as though hitting play on a vidscreen, and he remembered the bee stinging him in mid-air.

"Sniper?" he hazarded.

Tapper confirmed with a nod. "Page got him almost immediately."

Another image sprang to mind: he'd hit the edge of the roof right in his chest, then held on for dear life as Page and Tapper had hauled him over. It was the last thing he remembered, and even that was a bit fuzzy.

He tried to squirm around to look at the extent of damage, but his neck protested so he settled for catching Tapper's eye. "How bad is it?"

The sergeant shrugged – a measured shrug. "Not too bad," he said. "You lost a decent amount of blood, but I think we've managed to stabilize you. Scavenged some blankets to keep you warm." He jerked a thumb over his shoulder, and a smile crinkled his face. "Page found a hatchet in the shed and chopped up one of those ugly goddamn chairs just in case we needed to make a fire. I don't think I've ever seen him look so happy."

Kovalic chuckled. "Sorry I missed it."

Tapper's smile faded. Back to business. "Anyway, we managed to get out of the city pretty quickly – you've only been out a few hours. Page hotwired a hovercar and we hightailed it out here. But it ain't going to be long before the crims put two and two together."

Pressing his good arm against the floor, Kovalic struggled upwards until he was slumped against the wall, and shook off the slight vertigo. "Resources?"

"You, me, Page," said Tapper, ticking off on his fingers, "the hovercar – although we had to rip out its transponder, so the second anybody sees us we're getting reported – and the guns we took off the armed response team. Oh, and the hatchet," he added.

"Pretty good, considering," said Kovalic. "Hell, compared to that job we pulled on Theros, we're practically packed for a picnic."

Tapper nodded, but the levity didn't reach his eyes. "How we getting out of here, boss?" he asked quietly. "With Jens gone, we've got no way off planet."

Jens. He winced at the thought of the big, bluff, blond man who'd piloted them on half a dozen ops, always with a grin and a ready joke. He'd seemed solid. Dependable.

Kovalic closed his eyes and saw the flash as the laser punched right through the ship, like a knife through a wet paper towel. He'd been assured the transponder code they'd purchased – at some expense – would keep them clear of Sevastapol's orbital defense network, but, as with the mission itself, it appeared their information had been faulty.

His eyes slid open again. "We'll have to do what we always do," he said. "Make it up as we go."

There was a click as the latch from the front door caught, and Page slipped in. The lieutenant looked unflappable as always, though Kovalic thought he could detect a slight note of reassurance from seeing his boss up and at it. Then again, perhaps that was just the blood loss playing tricks on him.

"We've got to go," said Page, without preamble. "Patrol ships coming in from the east."

Kovalic sat up straighter, and Tapper swore under his breath.

"The good news," Page continued, "is that I found a garage underneath the house, with a small truck."

Tapper and Kovalic exchanged a glance. "Remember New Karachi?" Kovalic asked.

"Just what I was thinking," said Tapper.

Glancing back at Page, Kovalic struggled upwards. "Lieutenant, think you can get that hovercar's guidance system online?"

Page nodded briskly. "Not a problem. But the second it shows up on the grid, they'll be all over it."

"That's kind of the idea," said Tapper.

The next few minutes were a blur of activity, as Page left to get the hovercar set up, and Tapper and Kovalic – though, thanks to his shoulder, mostly Tapper – assembled their gear and hauled it down to the garage.

The truck in question was really more of a jeep, and, like most of the rest of the house, Kovalic found himself doubting that it was as sturdy as the historical object it was meant to resemble. But it started when they hacked the ignition, and that was good enough for him. They slung the weapons in

the back, making sure they were loaded and ready, in case –
well, *when* – they ran into resistance.

As they worked, Tapper voiced the inevitable question.
"Where are we going?"

Kovalic grunted as he checked the magazine on a carbine
with his good hand, bracing the weapon against the side of
the jeep. "Our best bet is to get on a legitimate flight out of
here – either on a commercial spaceliner or on a cargo ship,
if we can find one that'll risk smuggling us out. If we try to
hijack a ship and fly it out of here, we're going to get blown
out of the sky by those defense platforms."

"Security's going to be high at the spaceports. More to the
point, you're not going to get very far bleeding all over your
shoes," he said, nodding to Kovalic's shoulder.

"Fair point," said Kovalic. "Cargo ship it is."

Tapper swung into the driver's seat and transferred his
comm control to the in-dash holo display; clearly the owner
had been willing to sacrifice some historical accuracy in the
name of modern convenience. Kovalic maneuvered himself
next to the sergeant, even as Page appeared from the door to
the house and hopped into the backseat.

"Hovercar's ready to go," said Page, pulling out Kovalic's
backup comm unit. "I can start it up from here and do some
limited maneuvering, but we'll be lucky if it doesn't crash
into the first tree it sees."

"Just keep the patrol ships' attention for as long as
possible," said Kovalic. "Tapper, any hits?"

"If we double back towards the city, there are plenty of
warehouses on the outskirts," said Tapper, pointing at the
map on the holoscreen. "But we also run an increased
chance of road blocks."

"Is there anything that's *not* back towards the city?"

Tapper panned around the map, then shook his head. "Sevastapol's not very well-developed outside of its urban areas – any further and we'll mostly be contending with frozen tundra."

"In that case: Page, we'll need to send the car west – once the patrol starts following it, we head back east. Like ships passing in the night."

"Right into an iceberg," Tapper muttered.

"I'm starting to think we need a morale officer," said Kovalic. "Page?"

"Ready, sir." The lieutenant was cradling the comm unit in his hands.

"Give 'em the rabbit."

Page tapped something on the screen and outside they could hear the faint sound of repulsors coming online, then fading into the distance. "This thing doesn't have a radar strong enough to detect the patrol ships," said Page without looking up. "So we're going to have to take a risk on when to go."

"Give it a minute," said Kovalic. "If they're going to bite, we should know pretty soon."

Huddled in the jeep, they all lapsed into silence, the only light the glow from Page's display washing his face in the blue-white tones of the drowned. Kovalic strained his ears, trying to catch any hint of response from the patrols, and did his best to ignore the throbbing in his shoulder.

Thirty seconds. Forty-five. One minute.

Nothing.

One fifteen. One thirty.

Tapper and Kovalic exchanged a look in the dim light, and the sergeant started to shake his head when something pinged the edge of Kovalic's senses. He held up a finger and closed his eyes to concentrate. It was faint, but there it was: the sound of engines high in the sky. It was hard to tell which direction they were heading, but they seemed to be getting quieter, not louder.

"Page?" he murmured.

"Still going," said the lieutenant. "No contact yet."

"Sergeant," said Kovalic, "I think it's high time we get out of here."

"Yes, sir," said Tapper. He tapped a control on the dash, triggering the garage door. With a screech and rattle of machinery, the mechanism slid upwards, curlicues of snow swirling through the opening. Kovalic pulled his parka tighter around himself as the cold seeped in along with the snow. It was already a bit brighter; false night wasn't long, especially at this latitude, and it would be sunrise soon. Which would just make it that much easier for the Illyricans to nail them.

Tapper reached out to turn on the jeep's headlights, but Kovalic grabbed his wrist with his good hand.

"Can you run dark?" he asked.

The sergeant hesitated. "On an unfamiliar road, with the crims on our tail?"

"Pretty much."

A grin spread across the sergeant's face. "I can damn well try." He threw the jeep into gear and pulled out into the thick crust of snow, the heavy tires crunching through the white stuff with nary a slip. Impressed with the jeep's performance, Kovalic revised his estimate: whoever's little getaway this was had clearly had a thing for historical authenticity, if not for taste.

For his part, Kovalic could see little in front of them, even once his eyes adjusted to the dark. A bower of trees covered most of the road, adding to the darkness, and snow whispered across the windscreen and up and around the three of them. Every time they hit a bump in the road – and they hit plenty of them – Kovalic found himself thrown upwards a couple inches, only to slam back down into the thinly padded seat. He started to worry his arm wasn't going to be the only part of him in need of medical attention.

But there'd been no sign of patrol ships yet. He looked back at Page, and the man spared him a brief glance and shrugged. "No interception on the hovercar," he yelled over the sound of the jeep's engine.

That was less reassuring. Then again, it had taken longer than he'd thought for the patrols to change course to follow the decoy, so maybe they were just being cautious. Still, something was giving Kovalic goosebumps, and it wasn't just the cold of the Sevastapol pre-dawn.

Tapper swore suddenly and wrenched the wheel to the right, narrowly missing a dark shape that Kovalic suspected was a tree or similarly immovable object, though it whizzed by too quickly for him to identify it.

"Sorry," Tapper called. "I can't see more than ten feet in front of my face."

"Maybe you need glasses, old man."

"Only if they've got night vision."

Kovalic gripped the jeep's dashboard as they hit another nasty jolt and he wondered how long before they'd lose a tire or break an axle. The jeep had already surpassed his expectations, but there was well-constructed and there was able-to-withstand-breakneck-speeds-on-a-dark-bumpy-road.

Suddenly, the jeep passed out of the darkened woods and onto the clear, wide open tundra. The blizzard had already faded, and the sky was lit with dancing auroras of green and red, caused by the magnetic fields of the gargantuan blue-gray Yalta, itself rising in the eastern sky. On the horizon, Kovalic caught the haze of pink from the city – they were getting closer to the outskirts. It also, thankfully, meant the ride had smoothed out.

"Almost th–" Tapper started to say when a large predatory shadow swooped overhead, making Kovalic instinctively duck. The sergeant hit the brakes and cut the jeep's wheels to the left, sending it into a sideways skid that only through luck didn't become a barrel roll. They came to a stop half-off the road.

A second later, the sound of engines at full burn caught up with them, but the ship had already passed overhead. It turned its nose back towards them and begun to lower itself into their path. Bright floodlights snapped on, bathing the jeep in harsh white light. Kovalic squinted and reluctantly raised both his hands.

"I don't suppose either of you can reach those grenades in the back seat," he murmured.

Even as he said it, another shadow rippled overhead, followed again by the whine of repulsors. Kovalic's heart sank. Taking out one patrol ship would have been hard enough, but two?

He sighed. "Belay that last, sergeant. Hands up, everybody."

The second ship came back around for another pass, and Kovalic frowned. There was something not quite right about it – actually, there were several things. The shape of its silhouette was wrong; it was sleeker than the patrol ship. And the engine pitch was higher, too, like it was straining at the seams. Plus, it was just hovering in the air, fifty meters or so above the first ship. As Kovalic watched, a sliver detached itself from the ship – an entry ramp lowering, he realized – and a figure appeared on it, leaning out over the edge to the point that it was almost parallel to the ground below.

The figure was carrying something, too.

"*Down*," snapped Kovalic, ducking his head between his knees.

A sound that could only be described as a *fwump* filled the air, followed by the sizzle of fat hitting a hot skillet, a heavy crunch, and the groaning of stressed metal. The floodlights that had been trained on them blinked out, as though extinguished by the pinch of a giant's fingers, and the only sound that was left was the engines of the second ship.

"What the hell just happened?" hissed Tapper, swiveling his head towards Kovalic.

"No idea," said Kovalic through gritted teeth, clutching his shoulder. "But I think I'd like to buy those guys a drink." He lifted his head back up to peer at the scene.

Whatever the second ship had fired at the first had caused it to completely collapse; it had crumpled to the ground and was now lolling to one side, smoke funneling from the engines. It wasn't on fire, though, nor did it look to have been damaged in any way beside its impact with the frozen tundra. Given that its engines appeared to have been disabled and the floodlights had gone out, Kovalic guessed that the culprit was some sort of electromagnetic pulse weapon.

Meanwhile, the second ship was maneuvering closer overhead, banking slowly from side to side, making sure its prey was well and dead. The side with the ramp slid towards the jeep now, and as it got closer Kovalic could more clearly see the figure standing on it. She – he was pretty sure it was a she – was carrying what was, upon closer inspection, some sort of rocket launcher. Kovalic frowned: there was something undeniably familiar about her, even in silhouette.

His breath caught. "Tapper," he said, as calmly as he could manage, given the circumstances.

"Sir?"

"Exactly how much blood did I lose?"

A man's amplified voice, also strangely familiar, boomed into the night, raising the hairs on Kovalic's arms. "Looks like you fine gentlemen could use a ride. Perhaps we can be of assistance?"

Kovalic blinked, staring into the face of the similarly stunned sergeant.

"No way..." Tapper said slowly.

CHAPTER 4

The ship drifted closer, the ramp hanging only a couple of feet above the hard-packed tundra as the repulsor fields threw up tiny whirlwinds of dirt and snow.

"Sooner is better," the amplified voice said. "We've got multiple bogeys coming in from the west, so I wouldn't mind getting the hell out of here."

The lady or the tiger, as the old saying went. Well, Kovalic knew which one he'd choose, given the chance. "All aboard."

Tapper and Page swung themselves out of the jeep as Kovalic wrangled himself more gently to the ground, grimacing as the muscles of his right arm instinctively tried to perform some of their customary duties. Page offered an arm, but Kovalic waved his good hand and half-stumbled towards the hovering ramp.

The silhouetted woman had turned her back on them and was yelling something to the pilot, but it was drowned out by the sound of the engines. Tapper and Page both clambered onto the gangway, between them hoisting Kovalic aboard. From the end of the ramp, he could see that the tube the woman was carrying was indeed some sort of launching device, though it was somewhat smaller than a standard rocket launcher. He could also see a lengthy pair of steel cables clipped to a belt around her waist, which explained how she'd kept from falling off the ship. A pair of combat boots hid the cuffs of her cargo trousers, which were topped in turn by a mid-weight navy blue jacket.

The blond hair, though, was shorter than he remembered.

"Nat?"

The face that glanced back over the shoulder, cheeks flushed red with the cold, plucked something deep in his gut, a half-forgotten memory of an old life. She nodded at him and offered a tight smile that was more business than pleasure as she unhitched herself from the harness.

"Simon," she said, ducking her head in greeting. "Come on, we've got to go." She waved the three of them into the ship, slapping the ramp's closing controls as she passed through the upper hatch. Hydraulics groaned as it slowly levered up to meet the ship's hull. Once Kovalic and crew had passed through the hatch, that too slid shut with a pressurized hiss. When the hatch light shone green, she touched another button.

"Everybody's aboard. We're good." The intercom clicked off without an acknowledgement, and the deck shifted under their feet as the ship started to gain altitude.

Nodding to the cramped corridor to their left, Nat gestured for them to follow her. Kovalic exchanged a glance with Tapper, who shrugged and gave him a no-after-you wave. Page, meanwhile, looked blander than a slice of plain wheat bread.

The corridor ended in an open hatchway to the ship's small cockpit. Nat was already strapping herself into the co-pilot seat, alongside a lanky young man with a head of tousled brown hair and an expression of concentration on his face. He spared a glance at Kovalic, his face breaking into a smile that wouldn't have looked out of place on a millionaire playboy. At the same time he pulled back on the yoke in front of him and the ship angled sharply upwards, forcing Kovalic to flail and grab onto one of the compartment's other two seats with his good hand.

"Captain Kovalic," said the young man. "Good to see you again. How've you been?"

"Pleasure's all mine, Mr Brody," Kovalic grunted, as he managed to lever himself into the seat. "And I've been better."

Next to him, Tapper had strapped himself into the vacant flight engineer's station, while Page had folded down one of the two jump-seats at the rear of the cockpit.

"Sorry to hear that," said Brody. "But if you'll all just strap in and stow any luggage, we'll be under way shortly."

"Brody, you're a lucky son of a bitch that I can't reach you right now," growled Tapper.

"Welcome aboard, sergeant."

Kovalic rubbed his forehead with his good hand. "Where the hell did you two come from?"

Brody nodded at Nat. "Commander cracked the local Illyrican comm traffic. Figured you'd be making some noise, so we just followed the growls of frustration."

That answered just one of a long list of questions, but as Kovalic watched Brody flicking switches overhead, a more pressing one came to mind. "Let me just *inquire* – before we get blown out of the sky – how you plan to get by the orbital defense system."

Nat pointed through the cockpit's canopy, which showed a rapidly darkening skyscape, punctured by pinhole stars. "We've got a three-minute window on this vector, clear of both the defense platforms and the orbiting Illyrican battleships, thanks to a sympathetic technician at the ops center – and by sympathetic I mean 'doesn't mind having his bank account augmented.'"

Kovalic raised an eyebrow in her direction and she turned her hand palm up. "You know the general," she said. "Always have a plan B."

"Right. He doesn't always like to *share*, though."

"He seemed pretty intent on getting your team back."

"Well, we're expensive to replace."

Nat rolled her eyes, and turned her attention to a console in front of her. "One minute left in our window, lieutenant."

"Copy that, commander." Brody seized the throttle lever with his right hand and slammed it forward. The increased speed pressed Kovalic back into his seat, his shoulder feeling like it was pressed inside a rapidly closing vise. The ship rattled around them like it was on the verge of breaking apart.

Kovalic closed his eyes. "This thing going to hold, Brody?"

The pilot's hands wrestled with the yoke. "Don't worry; she's a good ship. We'll make it."

A loud series of crashes issued from the rear compartment.

"Though it's possible I may have forgotten to tie a few things down."

Sweat beaded on Kovalic's forehead, dripping down his temple. Here was hoping the general's frugality hadn't extended to their ride. He was glad he hadn't died on Sevastapol, but dying *above* Sevastapol didn't really improve on the situation.

"Breaking atmo... *now*."

The rattling dissipated as they passed the atmospheric boundary, and the cockpit was quiet, except for the whirring of equipment. Opening his eyes again, Kovalic let out a breath and clutched at his shoulder, which was insistently radiating pain into both his arm and chest.

"Commander, could you plot the rendezvous path?" said Brody, as he swung the helm around and cut over the engine systems.

"Coming up now," said Nat, as a dotted green holographic display was overlaid on the cockpit canopy.

"Adjusting course to follow."

Kovalic looked blankly out the viewport. "Rendezvous with what?"

"Well, our ride home, obviously," said Brody. "Sorry, did you want to stay?"

"You got another sympathetic operator on the Illyrica gate?"

Brody chuckled. "Oh no, we've got something *way* better."

"Why do I not like the sound of that?" Tapper muttered.

The ship sped through the vacuum of space, tracing the course laid out for them by the green dotted line on the canopy. A few minor spaceborne objects zipped past, deflecting harmlessly off the ship's magnetic field. As far as Kovalic could tell, they weren't heading towards any inhabited body in the system, but rather a wide open expanse of empty space. Just as he was about to ask exactly where they were going, he caught sight of an object dead ahead: a small, dark gray blob hanging amid the blackness. As they got closer, it resolved into a large, blocky shape that Kovalic recognized all too well.

Project Tarnhelm. The experimental jump-ship that just might be the most valuable object in the entire galaxy. No need for wormhole gates when you had a ship – the *only* ship – that could instantaneously zip anywhere else at the push of a button.

"He *didn't*," Kovalic breathed.

"You better believe he did." Brody shook his head. "No expense spared. I hope *I* merit this much next time I need rescuing." He reached over and touched a control on the ship's console. Out to the fore, a crack of light appeared in the side of the larger ship, widening into a bright rectangle.

"All right, everybody hang tight," said Brody. "The last time I tried this, I totally killed myself."

"What?" said Tapper sharply, his head shooting up.

Brody throttled down as they approached the opening, leveling them off by flicking the attitude thrusters with delicate touches of his fingers. His mouth set in a grim line as they neared, then his whole face relaxed with relief as they passed through it; rotating the ship 180 degrees, he set them down with a gentle bump and spun down the engines, leaning back and giving a deep sigh. Another touch of a control, and the hangar doors started sliding closed.

"I left the artificial gravity on, but we'll need a couple minutes before the bay's repressurized," he said, taking in his passengers. "Then it's home again, home again, jiggity-jig."

Waves of fatigue washed over Kovalic; suddenly he could barely keep his eyelids from drooping closed. He was about to surrender to the weariness, when a firm, dry hand seized his jaw. He blinked and found himself staring into Nat's blue eyes. Her brow furrowed. "How bad was it?" The question seemed to be addressed to Tapper, who was also looming over him.

"Through and through," said the sergeant, his lined face concerned, if a bit hazy to Kovalic's eyes. "But he's been running on adrenaline and fumes for the last hour."

"Does this thing have a med bay?" Nat asked, looking at Brody.

"Commander, this thing is basically a giant empty shell strapped to an experimental propulsion system. We're lucky it has bathrooms."

"In that case, we'd better get moving. And you," she said, her attention alighting back on Kovalic, "you stay with me. *Capisce?*"

"I love it when you get all romantic," Kovalic said woozily.

"Tapper, Page, help him up. Brody, lead the way to the bridge."

Kovalic didn't remember most of their walk through the ship; it was mostly a blur of gunmetal corridors and one foot in front of another. An indeterminate amount of time later a door slid open and he found himself led into the circular command center of the ship. Brody, who'd sprinted ahead of them, had already slid into the narrow pilot's couch that was sunk into the floor of the room. He flipped a series of switches and a deep rumbling began to vibrate through the deck plates.

"Get him strapped in over there." Nat pointed to an empty workstation as Tapper and Page walked Kovalic into the room. She took a seat at one of the other stations, bringing up a schematic of the Sevastapol system on the bridge's tactical holographic display. "Lieutenant Brody, looks like the Illyrican Navy's perked up: they've deployed a squadron of fighters from one of the carriers in orbit. They'll probably focus on the path to the gate, but if they see your ion trail, we're going to have some explaining to do. I'd strongly suggest that we be somewhere that's not here."

"All the systems were powered down to give us a low sensor profile," said Brody in a suffering tone. "I'm bringing them up as fast as I can, but it takes a few minutes to get the engine lit."

Having helped get Kovalic situated, Tapper and Page had found seats of their own among the other stations around the compartment's circumference. The vibration through the deck grew stronger as the engine continued to ramp up.

There was a ping from one of the consoles and Brody let out a breath. "Good thing we parked outside of Sevastapol's mass shadow. Means I don't have to wait to do this." He reached over and punched a glowing red button. "Hold on to your hats."

The engine rumbling died as weightlessness hit. For a moment, Kovalic floated gently against the restraints, a calm before the storm. Then sudden gravity, twice as strong as before, slammed him back into his seat like he was being sat down for an interrogation, and blackness seized him again.

CHAPTER 5

It was almost peaceful in the ward, Eli mused, as he leaned back in the patchily upholstered visiting chair. Most people hated hospitals, but he found something about them soothing. Maybe it was the sterile environment, or the air of detached, professional calm punctuated occasionally with minutes of rapid fire panic – not that different from piloting, come to think about it. He had let his eyes slide closed and raised his hands behind his head, allowing the rhythmic *beep*-pause-*beep* of the machines lull him into a pleasant, half-awake state. *I could use a nap.*

"Brody."

The voice wasn't loud, but it was sharp – startled, Eli twitched and barely managed to save himself from toppling all the way over, which probably would have sent a cadre of doctors and nurses bustling into the room. Instead, the chair slammed down hard on the floor and his eyelids snapped up like they were on springs.

Kovalic was eyeing him from the hospital bed, where he'd been propped up with almost as many pillows as if he were at a fancy hotel. He'd been changed into a standard blue patient gown, and the covers were drawn up to his waist. On most people it might look like helplessness; on Kovalic it just looked like he was biding his time. Even the sling on his right shoulder could have been a ruse, something to make an enemy underestimate him. He had a slightly disreputable look, thanks to his stubble, which had grown out a bit – there probably hadn't been much time to shave in the field – but somebody had seen to combing his short brown hair.

The all-too-familiar slate gray eyes didn't contain quite enough levity to be considered amused; mainly, he just looked tired. Sprinkled with a dash of surprise at seeing Brody. *Bet you didn't expect that, did you, captain?*

"Welcome back to the land of the conscious," Eli said. "It's very exclusive: they don't just let anybody in, you know."

"What are you doing here?"

Eli shrugged. "You blacked out when we engaged the jump drive; all those extra G-forces combined with heavy blood loss are a no-no, it turns out. Your bo… er, the general wanted somebody to keep an eye on you. And I guess I'm the low man on the totem pole." Despite his newly minted commission, he hadn't been asked to wear a uniform, but he still occasionally found his fingers at his collar, where his old Illyrican rank tabs would have resided.

"Lucky me." Kovalic cocked his head to one side. "The whole escapade is kind of blurry, but I have a vague recollection of Na… of Commander Taylor calling you *Lieutenant* Brody. Or maybe that's just a lingering nightmare."

Hardy-har. Raising two fingers to his temple, Eli gave him an ironic salute. "Lieutenant Elijah Brody, Commonwealth Navy, at your service."

Kovalic raised an IV-connected hand to his forehead and pinched the bridge of his nose.

"Headache?"

"Yeah, sure. That's it."

With a half-roll of his eyes, Eli settled himself more comfortably in his chair and avoided looking at Kovalic. Unfortunately, there wasn't much else to look at in the hospital room, which hadn't really been decorated for people who were, well, awake. So he ended up staring at the room's one painting, an abstract piece of pastel splotches and splashes that had probably been intended to evoke some sort of soothing feeling in patients, but just made Eli feel like somebody had murdered the Easter bunny.

"Hey, Brody."

"Yeah?"

"Thanks."

Taken aback – and a little bit reluctant to let go of his grievance that easily – Eli glanced at Kovalic, fully expecting an air of condescending sarcasm. But the look in his gray eyes was sincere, and as Eli met them, the older man ducked his head.

"Thanks for coming after me," Kovalic clarified. "That was an impressive bit of flying."

Eli gave a modest roll of his shoulders and pretended to buff his fingernails on his jacket. "Oh, you know, no big deal." *I only piloted a prototype jump ship – which covers the distance of half a dozen normal wormhole jumps in a matter of minutes – helped covertly take out an Illyrican patrol ship, evaded an orbital defense network* and *an Imperial battle fleet, and jumped home. Your average Thursday.*

"Look, I'm sorry you got dragged into this."

With a blink, Eli came to and found Kovalic still looking at him. "You're what?"

"You never wanted a military life. I'm sorry you ended up dragooned into service. I'll talk to the general and have him rescind the commission."

"Whoa. Not that that isn't big of you, but maybe it hadn't occurred to you that I did this for my own reasons, sparky." The offer was tempting, but, as the old saying went, in for a penny, in for a life of covert military action. Besides, there was no way in hell he was going back to Dr Thornfield and her simulator after what he'd just pulled off. *You're going to have to drag me away kicking and screaming.* More to the point, he was pretty sure he was done needing to be rescued by Kovalic.

Kovalic raised an eyebrow. "Come again, *lieutenant*?"

"Sorry. *Captain* Sparky."

Before Kovalic could return fire, the door opened and Commander Taylor strode in, looking no less composed than she had during the mission to Sevastapol. She was still out of uniform, wearing the same style of civilian garb that Kovalic and the rest of his team favored.

"Simon. Feeling any better?"

Kovalic raised his free hand and made a so-so motion. "I'm not going to lie – the painkillers help. How'd you get in, Nat?"

She folded her arms across her chest, and Eli thought he detected a note of warmness in her expression that he hadn't seen before. "As you recall, I still have *some* privileges. Plus, this is a naval hospital, so a lieutenant commander from NICOM has some pull."

"Still putting the fear of god into junior officers, then?"

Taylor actually smiled for the first time that Eli could remember, a flashing white arc that had an almost predatory glint about it. "It's a perk."

Eli glanced back and forth between the two; he felt like he was missing some part of this conversation, and something in the atmosphere reminded him of the moment on his homeworld right before a sandstorm kicked up. "So... you two know each other, I take it?"

"In a manner of speaking," said Kovalic. "Eli Brody, this is Lieutenant Commander Natalie Taylor–"

"We've met–" Eli started to say, but Kovalic trampled right over him.

"–my wife."

A succession of surreal images flashed, rapid-fire, through Eli's mind: Kovalic cooking pancakes on a hot griddle for Taylor, Kovalic mowing the lawn on a summer day, Taylor lounging on the couch with a drink at hand. None of them quite seemed to achieve the level of solid reality. All he wanted to do was blurt out "your *wife*?" but some part of him seemed to realize that would be inadvisable. So he went with the next best thing.

"Uhhhhh."

"Ex-wife," Taylor was already saying, her brow furrowed. "Finally got around to putting a thumbprint on those documents, have you?"

"Next time I have a minute."

Eli scrambled up out of his chair. "I should, uh, go and leave you guys to it."

Kovalic waved a hand. "Stand easy, lieutenant." He frowned as the rank left his mouth and shook his head. "And I'm not sure I'm going to get used to *that*. You're here on business, I take it, Nat?"

A shadow flitted across Taylor's face, too fast for Eli to analyze, but the commander's customary poise returned almost immediately. "Of course. The general sends his regards and wants to debrief you as soon as you're well enough."

Kovalic reached for the covers. "I'm well enough now. Let's go."

"Whoa," said Eli, raising his hands. "I'm pretty sure that the doctors are going to want a say in this one."

Kovalic fixed him with a stare. "It's not my first time being shot, Brody. Now, get a doctor in here and get me clearance to leave before I decide to fight my way out with you as a human shield."

"Righto. Sir."

It took some wrangling, but somehow Taylor convinced the on-duty doctor, a nervous young man by the name of Samuelson, to release Kovalic into her care. Still, the doctor insisted in putting his patient in a repulsor chair until they got out of the hospital. Kovalic wasn't happy about it, but Taylor insisted, taking up a position behind the chair and pushing him along the hallways. The captain crossed his arms and fumed silently, but Eli got the distinct feeling that Taylor was enjoying herself. Neither of them acknowledged his presence as he tagged along behind them.

A hovercar, twin to the one in which the general and Taylor had ushered Eli away for the mission, waited for them outside the hospital; the commander and Eli helped Kovalic into the back seat. Whisper quiet, it whisked them to the naval base's entrance and then onto the surface streets of Salaam, Terra Nova's capital.

Kovalic and Taylor shared the car's front seat, but neither of them said a word during the journey. Eli sat in the back, the child left to amuse himself while the grown-ups feuded, or whatever it was they were doing.

Kovalic's married. It shouldn't have shocked him, he guessed – lots of people got married. But somehow he'd imagined the gruff older man to be one of those "married to the job" types. Though, he supposed if he'd *had* to pick a spouse for him, Taylor pretty much fit the bill. They hadn't exactly become fast friends on the mission to Sevastapol, but he'd seen enough of her in action to know that she was at least as capable under fire as Kovalic. *Maybe they're both married to the job – which kind of sounds like, I dunno, double bigamy?*

The car pulled up next to an apartment block in a nice, if sterile, part of town and Eli caught Kovalic's perplexed look at Taylor.

"I thought you were taking me to the general?"

Taylor nodded up at the building, which stretched a good ten stories into the dark night sky. "He's upstairs."

Kovalic snorted. "Let himself in with the key under the mat, huh?"

They got out – Kovalic waving off any help from Taylor – and filed into the lobby, where a lift took them to the building's seventh floor. The inside of the place was no less bland than the outside: the hallway was a uniform off-white with soft, drab carpeting and nondescript doors fitted with small number plaques. When they reached the one marked 705, Kovalic raised his wrist to the reader panel next to the door. With a click, it unlocked, and they let themselves in.

Eli had been expecting that the apartment behind the door would be as dull as the rest of the building, and was surprised to find that it was nothing of the sort. Instead, it was a cozy one-bedroom unit, with a compact living room, galley kitchen, and a full-height window with a nice view of Salaam's twinkling lights. The walls were decorated with paintings in a twentieth-century style, along with one large fabric wall-hanging that, unless Eli missed his guess, was a Hanif piece. A sleek home audio system sat on a small cabinet, a home terminal on its partner; they flanked a small, artificial fireplace. It was homey, Eli decided, and in that no less incongruous with Kovalic than the idea of him in holy matrimony.

Ensconced comfortably on a rough-woven brown couch sat the general, one hand cupped around a tumbler of some sort of liquor. He raised the glass towards them as they entered.

"I hope you don't mind. I made myself at home."

"Please," said Kovalic dryly. "My home is your home."

The general gestured to a matching armchair, and Kovalic lowered himself gingerly into it with his good hand.

"How's the arm?" asked the general. Despite his solicitous tone, his eyes were narrowed, as if waiting to weigh Kovalic's answer against his own observations.

"Hurts like hell," said Kovalic. "But I'll live."

The general leaned forward, his joints creaking like a house settling in for the night, and his voice lowered to a more genuine register. "I'm glad you're in one piece, Simon." He spared a glance to Taylor and Eli, who had both remained standing – largely for practical reasons, since Kovalic had taken the only chair, and Eli couldn't imagine anything more awkward than plopping himself down on the couch next to the general.

"A job well done, commander, lieutenant. You have my compliments."

Well, great. That makes signing my life away to the military all worthwhile, then.

"But," the general continued, "if you'll excuse us, I'd like to talk with Captain Kovalic privately." His white eyebrows arched in expectation.

"Of course, sir," said Taylor, her back straightening.

Eli looked between them and started to open his mouth, but Taylor seized his forearm and gently but firmly dragged him out.

"I wasn't going to say anything," he protested, after the door had shut behind them.

"No, you weren't," said Taylor, taking up a spot leaning against the wall.

"So what now? Can I go home? Am I supposed to wait?"

Taylor shrugged. "We weren't dismissed, lieutenant, so we're staying right here until we're told otherwise."

"Have I mentioned how much I love the military?" Crossing his arms over his chest Eli sighed and leaned against the wall on the other side of the door from Taylor.

"So," said Taylor, eyeing him, "why exactly *are* you here, Brody?"

Damn good question. "Kovalic bailed me out of a couple jams," said Eli, jerking his head at the apartment door.

Skepticism was written all over Taylor's face. "You joined up because you felt like you owe him?"

It's a marginally less depressing answer than "I had nowhere else to go." "I guess. Why do most people join up?"

Taylor cocked her head to one side. "I don't know. Everybody's got their reasons. Personally, I think a lot of people are just looking for somewhere to belong."

Eli shifted uncomfortably, but if Taylor realized she'd hit a nerve she sure didn't show it. "What about you? Why'd you pick this glorious life?"

A faint smile crossed Taylor's lips. "I'm doing what I always wanted to do, Brody: solving problems, doing my part to make the galaxy a safer place. This is where *I* belong. Also, I'm damn good at it."

Can't argue with that. Must be nice to know where you're supposed to be.

With a sigh, his eyes drifted to the door, and he found himself wondering exactly what Kovalic and the old man were discussing in there.

The door clicked shut and the only sound in the apartment was the quiet rushing of the pipes behind the walls as someone else in the building took a shower. The general didn't say anything for a moment, just sat speculatively turning his glass in his hands. Kovalic shifted restlessly in his chair: he was tired, his shoulder was one big radiating ache, and his normally quiescent temper was rearing its head.

"Lieutenant Page and Sergeant Tapper gave me their preliminary reports while you were in the hospital. I was sorry to hear about Flight Officer Jens," said the general finally.

"Yeah," said Kovalic. "He had a family, you know."

"I'll send someone to inform them."

"No, you won't."

The old man looked up, nonplussed, and Kovalic held his gaze. "I was the commanding officer on the mission. I'll go."

For a moment the general looked like he was going to argue the point, but Kovalic's gaze didn't waver, and after a second he sighed and looked down at his glass, then gave a curt nod. "You won't be able to tell them the details."

"I know." He tried to keep the frustration out of his voice.

Lifting his glass to his lips, the general took a swallow, and then laid it down on the glass coffee table in front of him with a clink.

"So. What happened out there?"

"You tell me," Kovalic said, then snapped his mouth shut. "Sorry, sir."

Raising both of his hands, the general shook his head. "You have every right to be angry. The codes for the defense grid were genuine as far as I knew."

"That wasn't the half of it. IIS knew we were coming. Bleiden said they were watching him – he must have slipped up somehow. They poisoned him before he could get to us."

The general took his cane from its place leaning against the couch and rose with the mechanical whir and whine of servomotors. Leaning heavily on the stick, he limped towards the window. His shoulders slumped as he stared out through the glass.

"This isn't good, Simon. Bleiden would have been a highly valuable asset, especially in looking into the Imperium's links with Bayern."

"We may still have a chance."

The general looked back at him, eyebrows raised. "How so?"

Kovalic tilted his head. "Bleiden said something before he died – it's vague, but it's the best lead we've got. Apparently, there's some sort of important meeting on Bayern in three–" He ran the events back in his head, muddled by his injury, the rescue, and the hospital stay. How long ago had it been? "Two days' time."

Hope, sharp and bright, dawned on the general's face. "What kind of meeting?"

"That was pretty much all he had time to say before..."

The general stroked his chin. "Interesting. Whatever the Illyricans' agenda is when it comes to Bayern, it seems as though it might be coming to a head." His eyes went to Kovalic. "This is good work, Simon."

The praise did little to dispel the ashy taste in Kovalic's mouth. He rose and took another glass from the sideboard, awkwardly pouring himself a splash of bourbon with his good hand, then downing it in one go. It seared his throat on the way down, and set his stomach to roiling, making him wonder when had been the last time he'd eaten something that wasn't through a tube.

He paused, unsure whether to tug on a thread of his curiosity, but he hadn't exactly been holding back so far. "Sir, if I can ask: where did the intel on Bleiden come from?"

The general didn't meet his eyes, instead leaning heavily on his cane to peruse the lone shelf of knick-knacks in Kovalic's apartment. He picked up one – a porcelain penguin that, come to think of it, Nat had given him on a trip to Centauri – and turned it over in his hands.

"A highly-placed and very trusted source. That's all I can say."

Kovalic felt his grip tightening around the glass. "Due respect, sir, but I lost a man out there. It would have been nice to have the full story going in."

"And knowing the source of the intel would have changed the mission outcome how?"

He could feel his teeth sawing against each other, but he just clutched the glass, staring into it.

"Simon, he knew the risks," said the general calmly. "He was a soldier, like you."

"Yeah," said Kovalic, resisting the urge to hurl the glass to the floor. "Right."

They both stood in silence, the general once again gazing out into the night sky, and Kovalic staring at the world contained inside the tumbler. The idea of drinking himself into a stupor sounded irresponsibly appealing, he had to admit, but that nagging part of his brain that thought about consequences was being pesky again. He set the glass down on the coffee table, next to the general's. "So, what next?"

The old man combed his beard with his fingers. "The information Bleiden imparted, despite its unspecific nature, certainly merits further investigation. We've come this far, seems a shame to give up now."

Kovalic tipped his head. "Naturally."

With a nod, the general seemed to come to a decision. "The SPT will go to Bayern to find out exactly what this mysterious meeting entails."

No rest for the wicked. "Of course. When do we leave?"

The general hesitated. "I'd like you to sit this one out."

Kovalic blinked. "I'm sorry?"

"Commander Taylor has been seconded to our detachment by Naval Intelligence; she was already running an investigation into Bayern and the Imperium. I'm giving her command of the SPT for this operation."

"You're *what*?"

"She knows the ground, the players–"

"General, due respect, the SPT is *my* team. My *handpicked* team." His cheeks were flushed, whether from alcohol or anger he wasn't sure, but he found that he didn't care. "You can't just sideline me."

If the general was taken aback by his outburst, he didn't show it. His voice, when he spoke, was collected and cool– almost icy. "I most certainly can, captain. You are recovering from an injury and, if I may say so, a psychological strain as well. As *your* commanding officer, I get to make the call, and I say you are suspended from active duty." The coldness warmed slightly. "Besides, the team will be in perfectly capable hands with Commander Taylor – unless you have concerns about her capability?"

Kovalic's jaw clenched. Much as he might have liked to

challenge it, he recognized the urge for the petty impulse it was. There were no flies on Nat. "No, sir."

"Good," said the general, nodding to himself. "Commander Taylor, Lieutenant Page, Sergeant Tapper, and Lieutenant Brody will depart for Bayern tomorrow morning."

"Wait a minute. You're sending Brody too?" Kovalic said, his gaze snapping towards the old man. "He's not trained for this."

The general shrugged. "With you out of commission, the team is shorthanded. He acquitted himself well on the Sevastapol operation, according to Commander Taylor. Besides, he already knows the team and vice versa. And a pilot might come in handy, now that…" He trailed off, his mouth closing in a tight line.

Kovalic stiffened at the reminder of Jens's death. "It's a bad idea."

"Your objection is duly noted," said the general. "Now try and get some rest. I'll see myself out."

Taylor snapped to attention when the general hobbled out of Kovalic's apartment and Eli hastily scrambled to do the same, if a bit more raggedly.

"How'd he take it?" asked Taylor, her eyes darting to the door.

"About as well as you might expect," said the general. He continued on towards the elevator, Taylor and Eli trailing in his wake.

I have no idea what the hell they're talking about. This evening, the role of Third Wheel will be played by Eli Brody.

Taylor pushed the elevator call button. When the doors slid open, the general stepped inside and gestured for the other two to follow him.

"We'll do a mission briefing tomorrow morning," said the general as they descended. He tugged at his carefully trimmed beard as he looked at Taylor. "Send Lieutenant Page to my office early; I have a special assignment for him. 0830 should do. You, Sergeant Tapper, and–" his eyes slid to Eli, "–Lieutenant Brody can be there at 0900."

Me? Eli tried not to make his gulp too obvious. *This is what you signed up for, Brody. They say "jump" and you say "off which cliff?"*

The elevator chimed softly as they reached the ground floor, and they paraded out and across the lobby's faux marble surface, then let themselves out into the cool, but still humid, night air. A second hovercar, its headlights blaring white hot in the darkness, had pulled up behind the one that they'd arrived in. The rear door opened of its own accord and the general raised his cane in their direction as he entered.

"See you tomorrow, commander, lieutenant." The car pulled smoothly away from the curb, turned left on the cross street and disappeared.

The afterimage of the red tail lights shimmered in Eli's eyes; he turned to Taylor. "Well, that was fun. Thanks for letting me tag along."

Taylor sighed. "Anybody ever tell you you run your mouth off a little too much?"

"Only everybody."

Lips curved in a slight smile, a crack in the ice, and Taylor shook her head. "It's been a long day, Brody. I'll drop you home."

Eli glanced at the sky, which he fancied was already starting to show the dim streaks of light that presaged dawn. Public transit wasn't running this late – or early? – and his apartment in Heiwa was a long way out for an autotaxi ride.

Not to mention expensive. "Works for me."

Having shifted the car out of its self-navigating mode, Taylor drove crisply, precisely, always coming to a full stop at intersections, despite the lack of other traffic on the road. Her turns were sharp, smooth 90-degree affairs that didn't lag but weren't strong enough to throw Eli around inside the car. In short, it was hyper competent – the kind of driving you might expect from someone who had been trained and drilled in how to use a car just as they had any other weapon.

"You know the nav system could do all this, right?" he said at one point.

Taylor eyed him. "You let a computer do all your flying, do you?"

"Touché."

They didn't speak again for another few minutes. Eli drummed his fingers impatiently on the dashboard, trying to stifle the impulse to pepper the woman with questions. He wasn't exactly sure what was driving this need to know about Kovalic's domestic life, but he couldn't deny the fascination.

It's just too... normal. A part of him had almost been convinced that Kovalic was some sort of automata, a metal-and-silicon machine designed with a single-purpose efficiency. But it seemed that there was a human side to him after all.

"So," he said, unable to contain himself any longer. "How did you guys meet?" He regretted the cavalier tone almost immediately.

Taylor blinked, her eyes never leaving the road. "I'm sorry?"

"Uh. You and Kovalic."

Her mouth set in a hard line. "On assignment," she said shortly, her own tone inviting no further questions.

"Love on the battlefield, eh?"

"Are you this charming with all the ladies, Brody?"

Eli blinked. "Uh, I was just making conversation." *Because I get the feeling that if I were flirting with you, the only question would be whether you or Kovalic would put me in a chokehold first.*

"Do me a favor, and make it somewhere else. Or something else. Or, better yet, don't talk." It wasn't quite a growl, but there was some uncanny channeling of Kovalic in the way that she said it. Better, probably, that he didn't mention that as a fun fact.

The rest of the trip was conducted in funereal silence. Taylor navigated the car smoothly to his front door.

As Eli stepped out onto the curb, he bent down to look at Taylor. "I appreciate the ride, commander. Sorry about the... Well, sorry. I'll see you tomorrow."

The woman gave him a sidelong glance. "0900 at the general's office. Don't be late."

"Christ," said Eli, squinting at the sky, which was now conclusively taking on signs of light. "That's only a few hours from now. Can't a poor guy get some sleep?" He stifled a yawn.

"Duty calls, lieutenant."

"Well, tell it to try back at a more reasonable hour."

Taylor rolled her eyes and slid back into the car. And with that, she was gone, the hovercar's tail lights fading into the dark of night, leaving Eli Brody alone and wondering, not for the first time, what he had gotten himself into.

CHAPTER 6

She was pretty, the woman outside the general's office. *No doubt on purpose*, Eli thought. Not because the general seemed the type to surround himself with beautiful young things, but because at some point he'd likely calculated that a certain class of people were bound to be disarmed by a pretty face.

And damned if it isn't working.

Then again, she could also probably kill him six ways from Tuesday, using just the items she had on her rather sparsely equipped desk. Knowing the general, it seemed like one of the many qualities he'd insist on.

As though alerted to his thoughts, she looked up and smiled, her brown eyes friendly. "Sorry for the wait, commander, lieutenant," she said, nodding to Taylor and Eli in turn. She had one hand pressed to her ear. "The general is just finishing up with Lieutenant Page. Shouldn't be a moment."

It was 0907 by Eli's sleeve-comm. He freely admitted that he wasn't the most punctual person in the galaxy, but he'd been here for twenty minutes which he normally would have spent sleeping. At least the general's coffee was good. He took another sip from the disposable cup and glanced sidelong at Taylor.

Clearly, she was more accustomed to the military habit of "hurry up and wait." She sat on the edge of one chair, right leg crossed over left, peering closely at her sleeve. *Thumbing through the morning's communiqués, no doubt.* Leaning back in his own chair, he tried to take a surreptitious glance at her screen, but it was going to require being far more blatant than he had any intention of.

Sighing, he looked back down at his coffee and scratched at his chin. It had been a few days since he had shaved, and it was getting to the point where he'd have to decide whether or not he wanted a beard. Big decisions in the life of Eli Brody.

The front door to the anteroom opened and Sergeant Tapper, short and barrel-chested, strolled in, earning everyone's immediate attention. For Eli's part, he found it impossible to read the older man – his face was so lined and craggy it was hard to tell whether he'd had a rough night or a rough decade.

"Bloody hell," he muttered, looking at them. "Still waiting?" He nodded to the woman behind the desk. "Hello, Rance. We backed up today or what?"

"Good morning, sergeant," said the woman, leaning her chin on her hand. Her wide, relaxed smile suddenly threw Eli into doubt about the wholeheartedness of the one that he'd received. "Did Owen get the birthday present I sent?"

"That he did, lass," said Tapper, filling a cup with coffee from the tureen on the side table. He leaned against the wall and smiled as he stirred in a sugar cube. "Won't let it go, in fact. Jamie's worried that he's going to lose it, but I said it was pretty unlikely with the death-grip he's got on it."

Rance laughed, a deep, rich sound that made her eyes sparkle. "I'm glad. You'll have to bring him by again, sometime."

"I will at that," said Tapper, raising his cup. He glanced over at Eli and Taylor. "Long night, Brody?"

Eli grunted. "Early mornings don't agree with me."

"You call this early?" said Tapper, his eyebrows lifting as he took a sip of his coffee. "Christ on a crutch – pardon my language. Early was when the crims dropped onto Arcadia Planitia at 0430. This is practically tea time at the Centauri Plaza Hotel."

That earned him a bleary blink from Eli; Taylor smiled faintly, but didn't look up from her sleeve, and even Rance turned a laugh into a cough. *Some day,* thought Eli. *Some day that guy's going to give me an opening, and I'm not going to hold back.*

A light suddenly blinked on Rance's desk and she cocked her head, apparently listening to something on her earpiece.

Taylor had gone instantly – though not obviously – alert at the movement, letting her sleeve shift ever so slightly towards Eli. He risked a glance at it, and blinked at the paneled black-and-white line drawings and word bubbles.

Huh. Well, I guess I shouldn't be surprised she has a sense of humor – she was married to Kovalic, after all.

With a nod, Rance looked up at them and offered another all-too-genuine smile. "The general will see you now. Go right in."

Taylor stood, and inclined her head towards the woman; Tapper patted her shoulder as he passed her. Eli pushed himself up off the chair and followed suit, giving the general's assistant his best rakish grin. Or, at least, he *hoped* it was rakish – he'd be happy if it weren't sickly, given the state of his stomach. She returned it with the same smile as before; to Eli, it felt a bit like a last meal for the condemned.

He wasn't paying immediate attention to the room they

stepped into, so it was a minute before he took it all in.

It was packed to the gills. Mostly with books, which were piled on every available flat surface and filled a whole host of floor-to-ceiling bookshelves, but also with paintings, most of them classic landscapes and portraits that hung on every available span of wall, and finally with ornate furniture, including a pair of overstuffed leather armchairs and a matching loveseat, a heavy mahogany desk embellished with carvings of flowers and trees, and a green-shaded lamp that looked like something out of a twentieth-century detective novel. *Even just shipping all this crap here must have cost a fortune.*

The general wasn't behind the desk, as Eli had expected, but sitting in the leather armchair, set at right angles to the loveseat. Page was nowhere to be seen; Eli scratched his head and looked around. He supposed there could be another door hidden behind one of the pieces of furniture, but that would be... well... exactly like the general, from what little he knew of the man.

"Ah, good," said the old man, looking up at them. "Please, sit down." Eli waved for Taylor to take the other armchair, then took a spot on the loveseat. Tapper closed the door and leaned against it.

"Lieutenant Page has been given his orders," said the general. "Let's discuss your mission." He glanced at Taylor, then waved a hand, almost casually. "First, though, an operational matter: Commander Taylor will be in charge of the Special Projects Team for this assignment. Captain Kovalic has been placed on temporary leave."

Eli did a double take, his eyes scanning the rest of the room: Taylor, it was clear, had already known this. If there were anybody as shocked as Eli, it was Tapper, who pushed himself off the door with an expression verging on belligerent.

"Hold on just a minute, sir," said the sergeant, crossing his arms over his chest. "What do you mean the captain's on leave?"

"Precisely what I said, Sergeant Tapper." Though Tapper was standing off the old man's right shoulder, the general didn't crane his neck, didn't even turn to face him. "Is there an issue?" he said, as though addressing the room at large.

Tapper frowned, shifting his gaze between the old man and Taylor. For the first time, Eli saw a crack in the commander's veneer, as she gave the sergeant an almost apologetic look. With a shake of his head, Tapper leaned slowly back against the door. "No problem, sir," he said, his tone curt.

"Very well. Despite our setback in the Bleiden extraction on Sevastapol, we're continuing to investigate the ties between Bayern and the Imperium. Now, as this is Commander Taylor's show, I will turn the floor over to her." He opened his hand towards her.

"General," said Taylor. She leaned forward, her elbows on her knees, and took in each of them in turn. "Six weeks ago, my office at Naval Intelligence Command intercepted a batch of coded Illyrican signals in the Jericho system. In and of itself, there's nothing unusual about that: we skim all the traffic that passes through the Illyricans' relays in the bottleneck; I'm sure they do the same for us. However, unbeknownst to the Imperium, these messages used an encryption scheme that we had cracked two weeks prior. In particular, one of the messages pointed to Illyrican interests in Bayern – specifically, financial interests."

"Hardly a surprise," said Tapper. "Those bastards have their fingers in most monetary pies – so to speak."

"Quite," said Taylor. "That's why it got filed away at the time." She raised a finger. "But then, a few days later, there was another message, also bound for Bayern. And then another a few days after that. Overall, communications traffic between the Imperium and Bayern jumped four hundred percent in the space of a few weeks.

"This caught my attention, as you can imagine."

Taylor touched her sleeve: the room lights dimmed and a holographic display sprang into view, hovering in the space between the couch and the armchairs. In it was a simplified schematic of a solar system. As Eli watched, it zoomed in on the fourth planet, a mottled gray-blue world that he recognized as Bayern.

"NICOM doesn't have its own Bayern desk," said Taylor. "So I put in a request for the Commonwealth Intelligence Directorate's most recent situation analysis." She gestured at the screen. "As you are all aware, Bayern is the preeminent banking and financial hub in the known galaxy, a status it achieved thanks to its somewhat peculiar system of government."

"The Corporation," said the general, his eyes slitted. "A bizarre institution, to be sure, but one that seems to have served Bayern well enough."

"Indentured servitude, I call it," muttered Tapper from the back wall. "Making everybody on the planet an employee of a single huge company?"

Taylor shrugged. "They're employees *and* shareholders, and as such they ultimately dictate the direction of the Corporation. I'd argue the people of Bayern aren't any worse off than any number of other worlds – but that's a philosophical debate for another time. What *is* important is that the Corporation has enacted strict bylaws on confidentiality and data security. That's why plenty of other galactic corporations and even governments like to park money there.

"It's also why it's impossible for us to strong-arm the Board of Directors into giving us a peek into the Illyricans' finances. Both Bayern's Board and its Chief Executive have maintained that Bayern's stance on galactic conflict is strictly neutral. Picking sides is bad for business, you see."

There was a deep, ripping snort from somewhere in the direction of Tapper, but the rest of the room studiously ignored it.

"Despite that," Taylor continued, "the information Bleiden passed on to Captain Kovalic suggests that a meeting between the Imperium and the Corporation is imminent – less than two days from now." Here Taylor paused, her lips thinning. "We suspect that the Illyricans' envoy to this meeting was initially intended to be Bleiden himself, but with his death we're not sure who has taken his place. We do believe that the envoy is likely to meet with this woman." She touched her sleeve again and the planet vanished, replaced by a looped video of a statuesque woman with copper skin and iron gray hair standing behind a podium and smiling at the camera. She appeared to be answering questions in front of a large crowd, but there was no sound, so it was impossible for Eli to say. *Maybe she's doing a song and dance routine.*

"This is Senior Vice President Zaina Vallejo," said Taylor. "She's in charge of Client Relations – probably the closest thing Bayern has to a Foreign Minister – and she sits on the Board."

"In other words," the general said, "she's what you might call 'wired in.'"

"It's widely acknowledged that Vallejo has the full trust and confidence of Chief Executive Chakravarty and Chairman Petrovich," Taylor continued. "She's considered by many the third most powerful person in the Corporation, and a likely candidate for one of the top two positions in the next five to ten years."

"A power player," said the general. "Ambitious and cunning." He grimaced. "I know the type."

Eli looked around, not for the first time feeling like he was the one of the slower members of the class. "So, uh, what business is this of *ours*?"

Three pairs of eyes turned towards him, like spotlights on an escaping criminal. *I guess there is such a thing as a stupid question.*

Taylor glanced at the general, then back at Eli. "We can't run the risk that the Illyricans will sway Bayern towards their side."

"But you just said they don't pick sides," said Eli.

"So far," the general interjected. "But it's not impossible that the Imperium is willing to make concessions that the Corporation would find appealing enough to change their stance and lend their financial support. Those resources at the Imperium's disposal, well…" The general's eyes seemed to focus on something that Eli couldn't see. "The Imperium leveraged all the assets and natural resources at its disposal in the construction of its invasion fleets. It spent *decades* preparing to attack Earth and its colonies." He tugged on his beard. "But the destruction of Fifth Fleet at Sabaea dealt a significant blow to the Imperium's offensive capabilities. Then there was the incident with Project Tarnhelm – all that research and development gone up in smoke, their advanced prototype jump-ship…" He cleared his throat and tilted his head at Tapper and Eli, "…lost. Financially, those are substantial setbacks for the Illyrican war machine. A deal with the Corporation could fund a lot of new weapons projects and matériel, and that's something we can't allow to happen if we are to maintain the strategic balance." The general shook his head. "At this point, though, we simply don't have enough information."

Eli's pulse had quickened at the mention of Sabaea. He'd had a front row seat to that debacle – and, unlike the rest of his squadron, he'd been lucky to survive. The Illyricans hadn't exactly stopped occupying planets because they'd wanted to. *If there's a chance to stop them, sign me up.*

"Due respect, sir," Tapper put in, "but why us? Why not leave it to CID's Bayern station?"

"A few reasons. For one, Bayern station operates out of the Commonwealth embassy," said the general, but Eli could see the hesitation in the old man's eyes, "and thus their mission brief is more... passive. They aren't equipped to deal with this kind of operation. For another, well, let's be frank: I'm not exactly inclined to put my full trust in our colleagues from CID. They've proven, shall we say, *unreliable* in the past."

The general nodded to Taylor, who dismissed the holographic display and raised the lights once again. Eli blinked, his eyes tearing at the brightness.

"Your mission is straightforward," the general said. "Find the Imperial envoy, establish their purpose on Bayern, and, if necessary, disrupt it."

Yeah, what are the odds he'd send us if it wasn't *going to be necessary to disrupt it?*

"Commander Taylor will brief you more fully on your cover, but you'll depart within the hour. Any questions?"

Way, way too many to ask right now. Nobody else seemed to have any, though, so with nods all around Eli joined the sergeant and commander as they traipsed back into the general's outer office. *I think I may be out of my depth just slightly,* he thought, but he shoved the feeling down. *I can do this.*

"Well, that was fun," he said under his breath, as he gave a forced smile to the general's assistant.

Tapper clapped him on the shoulder. "You have no idea, kid. The fun's just beginning."

The knock on the door came again, even as Kovalic shuffled his way towards it, bleary eyed. It was before 1000 hours, and he'd still been lying in bed. Not sleeping exactly, but resting his eyes. He thought he might have logged a few hours of actual shut-eye last night, but it hadn't come without a fight.

He didn't bother looking through the peephole; there were a limited number of people who would knock on his door, and if it was a pair of wandering missionaries he thought he might actually be in the mood for an impromptu theological discussion. Instinctively, he started to reach for the door with his right hand, only to find it pressing against his sling. With a grumble, he switched and opened the door with his left.

Nat was leaning against the doorframe, a wry smile on her face.

"Simon."

Kovalic blinked. "Natalie."

"Invite me in?"

Stepping back, he gestured broadly, again with his left arm. "Please."

She strolled over to the couch and Kovalic kicked the door closed after her, suddenly all too aware of the fact that he was wearing a bathrobe – possibly, as he thought about it, one that she'd bought for him – slippers, and not much else.

"Uh," he said, "can I fix you some coffee?"

She cast her eye over to the small galley kitchen and raised a brow. "Do you actually know how to make coffee?"

"Well, I'll admit it's easier with two hands," he said. "But I think I can manage. Unless your tastes now run to those fancy gourmet espressos."

"No, still just black."

Kovalic busied himself at the counter with the coffeemaker and some of the instant single-serving cups, his back to his guest. "So," he said, "I'm sure you didn't come to watch me fumble around with a coffeemaker."

"It's got its appeal." There was an awkward silence. "Look," she said. "We didn't really get a chance to talk last night. Or while you were at the hospital. So I just wanted you to know that it wasn't my idea."

Kovalic clicked the cup into place and punched the button with somewhat more force than was required.

"What wasn't?" he said, feigning ignorance.

"Simon."

He stared at the coffee machine as it began to hiss.

"Simon, come on. Turn around."

Forcing his face into a pleasant smile, he turned and leaned against the counter. Instinctively, he tried to cross his arms over his chest and found himself hampered by the sling; awkwardly, he hooked his opposite thumb through its shoulder strap.

Nat had leaned forward on the couch, her elbows on her knees and her hands clasped. She wore an apologetic smile that made it all the way up to her blue eyes – had they always been that blue? – and slightly furrowed brow.

"I'm not trying to take over your team," she said. "I want you to know that. This is just…" she waved her hands, "…an unfortunate set of circumstances."

"Yeah, well, you got the house and the dog too." He regretted it the instant the words were out of his mouth.

The smile vanished, wiped away as though it had never been there, and was replaced with a face that looked like it had been carved out of marble: beautiful, but cold. "This isn't personal," she said flatly. "I asked the general for help looking into Bayern, yes, but I didn't ask to be in charge. That was his decision." She gave a shrug that, surprisingly enough, had an air of helplessness.

The reminder didn't make it any better. "Right," said Kovalic. The coffeemaker beeped behind him; he turned and found a clean mug on a shelf, then pressed the button to pour a cup. As it burbled full he stared at the white tiling on the kitchen wall.

"How's the arm?" Nat asked, her voice taking on a slightly lighter tone.

"It's fine," he said. Actually, it hurt like hell. The painkillers he'd been given in the hospital had helped somewhat, dulling it from red-hot-poker pain to dull bone-deep ache. But it was enough to mess with his equilibrium; everything was off kilter. Including this conversation. He picked up the mug and walked over to the couch to hand it to her.

"Good," said Nat, looking up at him. Not all the warmth had returned to her eyes, but they were less hostile than they'd been a moment ago. "Sit down." She patted the space next to her on the couch.

Reluctantly, Kovalic let himself drop into the space, though he put some more distance between the two of them. There was a faint scent of rosemary and mint that floated off her like an aura, and he wanted to be well outside its range. He rubbed at the bridge of his nose with his good hand and glanced sidelong at Nat.

"I forgot to say thank you."

"For what?"

He shrugged, an action that made him wince with pain. This time she saw it and started to open her mouth, but he barreled on. "For coming to get us. You didn't have to do that."

A faint smile crossed her lips again. "Even if the general *hadn't* made it a quid pro quo for this job, you know I would have."

"Yeah. Still. Thanks."

The smile was genuine this time. "You're welcome." She took a sip of the coffee and looked impressed. "Not bad for the pre-made stuff."

"Well, you know, I spare no expense. I'm home *at least* twice a month." He cleared his throat. "How is the house, anyway? Get that leaky sink fixed?"

Nat nodded. "Josh came over and did it."

Kovalic gave a disbelieving laugh. "Your brother fixed a sink?"

"He's got his moments."

"I hope it wasn't like the time he rewired the living room. It's a wonder you can't still see the scorch marks."

"Come on," Nat chided him, "it was all out of date wiring anyway. It needed to be redone. And, if I may remind you, he was cheap."

"Yes, we almost got our living room set on fire for just a case of beer. What a deal."

With a laugh, Nat took another sip of coffee.

"And Sadie?" said Kovalic. "You're not letting her get fat, are you?"

Nat laughed. "Much as she'd love to loll around in the

sun all day, no. The girl next door walks her when I'm away." She hesitated. "You should come by some time and see her; I know she misses you."

"Just make sure you show her a picture once in a while. Maybe when you feed her – positive reinforcement and all that."

"I'll take it under advisement." She glanced at her wrist and sighed. "I've got to run," she said. "Got a ride to catch."

Kovalic gave a tight smile. "Right."

Putting the coffee down, she put a hand on his knee and squeezed it gently. "Thanks for the coffee."

"Sure," he said. "Come by unannounced anytime."

With another smile, she stood and crossed to the door.

"Nat," he said, not looking up. "Just be careful, OK? You *and* the team. Tapper, you know, he can take care of himself. Page is good at what he does, but he needs a little... guidance, from time to time – somebody to remind him that he's only human. And Brody..." He shook his head. "He's a cocky son of a bitch, but he's got potential. Just make sure he doesn't get himself killed." He raised his eyes to hers. "They're your responsibility now. You've got to make sure they all get back alive." He felt his throat choke slightly on the last word.

Nat nodded, serious. "I understand. Don't worry. I won't let you down." She turned the knob and slipped out, letting the door click shut behind her.

Kovalic leaned back on the couch, then reached over and picked up the mug of coffee she'd left on the table and sniffed it. Still warm. With a shrug he took a sip, then put it back down and took a deep breath. He wasn't equipped for early mornings yet. The Novan sun, still on the rise, had suffused the room with a pleasant glow, and as he leaned back he found himself drifting off in thought. He trusted Nat, absolutely, but leading a team, being responsible for them, wasn't easy – take it from someone who knew.

CHAPTER 7

"Nova two-one-niner, this is Bayern Control. You have been cleared for landing on platform C-eight-five."

The voice was tinny over the cockpit's speaker, like the flight controller was talking through a can attached to a string. Eli reached out and toggled the transmission key. "Roger that, Bayern Control. Coming in on vector–" he glanced at the readout in front of him, "–one-one-five. Altitude 10,000 meters."

"Copy, Nova two-one-niner. You're clear all the way into port. Welcome to Bayern." They clicked off brusquely, without waiting for acknowledgment.

"Thanks, Control," Eli muttered to himself through gritted teeth, as he refocused his attention on the instrumentation and tried to ignore the faint pangs of nausea echoing in his stomach.

He'd been right, he thought, allowing himself a brief surge of triumph that almost managed to overwhelm his nascent shakes: The simulator was *nothing* like flying a real ship. *Take that, Dr Thornfield.* He hoped he survived long enough to tell her. There were so many subtleties the computer just couldn't quite reproduce: the way the deck randomly shifted as the ship bucked against the atmosphere's wind currents during the descent; the tension on the flight stick as he fought with it; even just the smell of the recycled air. It all played into making the experience a whole.

And making me sick.

He'd had no problems during the rescue on Sevastapol, but in retrospect he could tell that adrenaline had once again played a pretty big part there. There hadn't been time to stop and reflect, to think about what he was doing – it had been pure action.

The trip to Bayern was the total opposite. He'd piloted the ship all the way from liftoff at the Terra Nova spaceport, through two wormholes – from Nova to the Badr sector, and then on to Bayern – and to the landing. *Hopefully*. The autopilot had handled much of the dull, straightforward intra-system travel; really, when it came down to it, Eli had only taken the stick for takeoff, gate jumps, and landing. And frankly, the computer probably could have handled those as well, but he was never going to get his space legs back if he didn't try. All told, the trip had taken a little under twelve hours.

Of course, if they'd taken the jump ship they could have done it in less than two, but when he'd asked Taylor about it, she'd shook her head.

"The general cashed in quite a few favors to get it for the Sevastapol op," she'd told him. "Not to mention probably breaking several regulations in the process. It's back in the hands of the navy's sci-tech division. Besides, we play this one by the book, and that means a clean entry."

Clean entry, in this case, meant that the ship – the same lithe *Kestrel*-class light transport that they'd flown from the jump ship down to the Sevastapol surface – had been outfitted with a legitimate Commonwealth registration: the

Cavalier, out of Terra Nova. At least they'd let Eli pick the name; it was bad luck flying a ship with no name, and Eli was pretty sure they needed all the luck they could get.

According to the manifest, the ship carried no cargo, only himself and two passengers, and was simply providing transport from Nova to Bayern – all true.

Speaking of which. He keyed the intercom on. "Gooooood morning, travelers. This is your captain speaking. We're starting our initial descent into Bayern spaceport; should have you on the ground within half an hour." He skimmed the information on his display. "The temperature on the ground is a *balmy* 10 degrees centigrade, with a light rain coming out of the northwest. Local time is 15:37, and it's... Tuesday."

"Brody," came Tapper's voice from behind him, "if you don't shut up, I'm going to stuff you in your own airlock."

Eli blinked, still holding the intercom key. He cleared his throat. "Have a nice flight, everybody!" He clicked off. "Sorry, sergeant," he said over his shoulder, "didn't hear you come in."

"Well," said Tapper, throwing himself into one of the cockpit's other three chairs, "that may have been because you were blathering so loud." He scowled. "You woke me from a nap. A deep, *restful* nap, I might add."

And now somebody's cranky.

"Where's the commander?" Eli asked.

Tapper buckled himself in. "She's back in the crew lounge. Reading something or other."

"Just updating myself on Bayern's sociopolitical situation," said Taylor, as she stepped into the cockpit and sat down.

A light blinked on the console and Eli took the stick again, peering through the cockpit's viewport into the mass of swirling gray clouds. There wasn't much to see with his own eyes, so he flipped on the infrared overlay, which gave him a better, although grainier, view. He checked his vector guides again, but the *Cavalier* was a slick, responsive little ship, and there'd been no drift – they were still right on target.

"I trust you two have reviewed your cover identities?" Taylor said.

Eli had actually spent a decent portion of his downtime during the flight flipping through the dossier that Taylor had prepared, which was surprisingly lengthy for a person who didn't exist. Though, given the amount of detail that had been put into constructing "Elias Adler," it might raise certain philosophical questions about what existence really meant. The man had a bank account, his own business, and a reputation as a bit of playboy, which came complete with unseemly gossip and the rumor of illicit pictures. By comparison, Elijah Brody had officially been dead for almost six years – it wouldn't be hard to argue that Adler had more of a life than he did.

Tapper cleared his throat. "Yeah, about that. Why the hell am I a butler?" He glowered at Eli. "More to the point, why am I *his* butler?"

"You're not a butler," said Taylor, her voice taking on the tones of a schoolteacher gently correcting a student, "you're a valet. A gentleman's gentleman. Mr Adler's personal assistant and bodyguard."

"Oh," said Tapper. "Well, thank you, that's *so* much better."

"Lieutenant?" said Taylor.

"Uh, yes?"

"Any problems with your cover?"

No, I've always dreamed of being a successful businessman with a taste for the ladies. I just have no idea how to be *one.* "Uh, I'm kind of new at this," he said, keeping his eyes on the display in front of him.

"Don't worry," said Taylor. "Remember, my cover is as your PR rep. Just leave most of the talking to me. When in doubt, remember: less is more."

Right. The ship bucked and twisted in his grasp as he started their final descent; Bayern's primary settlements were in a rocky mountain range on the country's northern continent, and the wind shear at the higher elevations could be nasty.

His stomach dropped out from under him suddenly as a stiff breeze slammed into the side of the ship; behind him, he heard a half-swallowed gasp from Taylor and a not-entirely happy grunt from Tapper, but if either of them were prepared to make a comment about his piloting, they'd evidently elected to keep it until they landed safely.

When the computer signaled they were close enough, he brought up the repulsor fields and lowered the ship until the landing struts made contact with the platform. Tension bleeding out of his shoulders, Eli reached over and shut down the engines, the background hum fading away, replaced only by the sound of the wind whistling outside.

"Bloody hell," muttered Tapper into the relative quiet. "Couldn't the autopilot have handled that?"

Eli craned his neck, fixing the sergeant with a stare. "A precise landing onto a small, elevated platform during a high-speed windstorm? Probably." He grinned. "But it wouldn't have been nearly as much fun." *Plus,* he thought, with more than a hint of relief, *I needed to prove I could still do it.*

"I'm starting to understand why the butler always ends up being the killer."

"Boys, boys," said Taylor absently, her eyes focused on the tablet she'd produced, which had no doubt already hooked in to the Bayern planetary network. "Best make yourselves presentable. The docking authority says we have guests."

Tapper and Eli exchanged a glance.

"Guests?" said Tapper.

Taylor shrugged. "Mr Adler is an important Novan businessman. I'm sure the Commonwealth embassy has sent someone to greet him." She tilted her head meaningfully. "I suggest we not keep them waiting."

It was the work of a few moments for Eli to struggle into the traveling suit that Taylor had packed for him, a dark blue pinstriped affair with a blue-and-gold necktie. He ran a comb through his sandy, unkempt hair, trying to force it into a winsome look, and elected to leave the slight stubble on his face, in part because he deemed it authentic, but mostly because shaving would have taken too long.

Stepping into the ship's entryway he joined Tapper, who was tugging at the fit of his black jacket in irritation. The double-breasted piece was of a pair with the black trousers he wore, and contrasted sharply with the white open-collared shirt worn underneath. There was little to be done with the close-cropped gray hair, or weathered face, but Taylor had provided him with a pair of dark glasses, which completed the ensemble.

Looking up to see Eli eyeing him, Tapper shook his head and pointed a finger at his soon-to-be boss. "Not a word, kid. Not a single word."

Eli rubbed at his chin. "I think you mean 'not a word, *sir*.'"

"When this is over–"

"I wish I'd known you two bickered like a pair of five year-olds," said Taylor from the hatchway.

Turning towards her, Eli's protests died on his lips.

Sure, he'd noticed Taylor was attractive the first time

he'd seen her, but the air of cool professionalism that hung around her – and, more importantly, the fact that she'd been married to Kovalic – had the effect of making her one big, flashing "don't even think about it" sign.

But now he wasn't even sure if the woman in front of him *was* Taylor any more. From the elegant arrangement of her hair, twisted into an elaborate braid, to the tantalizing expanse of toned calf between high-heeled shoe and knee-length tan skirt, she was almost unrecognizable. Her face bore slight traces of makeup, enough to highlight the right features, and the short jacket atop the low-cut blouse ensured that Eli kept his eyes firmly glued to her face, avoiding even the slightest appearance of impropriety.

"Are we ready, then?" Taylor reached over and palmed the hatch control. With a hiss the door slid upwards, the entry ramp beyond it lowering to the tarmac. A gust of cold air swirled in, bringing a fine mist of rain with it.

Straightening her shoulders, Taylor marched down the ramp, leaving Tapper and Eli to trail in her wake. *Well,* thought Eli as the bracing blast of cool air hit him, *here goes nothing.*

The platform wasn't large – in fact, it was barely bigger than the ship, and it jutted directly out of a sheer cliff face. Eli wondered what he'd see if he peered over the railings at the edge and then quickly decided he was fine not knowing. Where the platform met rock, there was a large pair of formidable-looking blast doors. No sign of their supposed welcome party, but Eli couldn't blame them: it wasn't exactly a day for a picnic. The wind whipped at them as they stood on the platform. Whatever calm exterior Eli had been cultivating was quickly blown to shreds, and he could only hope that he didn't look half as bedraggled as he felt.

With little other option, the three trudged to the blast doors. When they got within about five meters, the doors began to grind open slowly. Bright light shone through, blocked only by the silhouettes of three people standing in the doorway.

"Remember," Taylor murmured, her voice barely audible over the wind, "let me do the talking."

In other words, "just keep your mouth shut, Brody." Following orders, right: he hadn't missed that part. But he gave an abbreviated nod as they pulled up in front of the welcoming party.

Two of them were women. The shorter of the two had dark skin, almost the color of volcanic glass, and equally dark hair swept into a braid no less complex than the one Taylor wore. She was dressed in a dark suit with a white blouse that bore a superficial resemblance to Tapper's bodyguard outfit. While she stood easy, there was something about her stance in which Eli detected just a slight note of wariness.

The other woman matched her in bearing, but nothing else. Tall and slender, she had yellow-gold skin and dark eyes that seemed to take them all in with an off-hand glance. Though she was also dressed in a two-piece business attire, she'd chosen a skirt, which showed off a pair of long legs ending in a pair of high-heeled shoes. Even Eli's untrained eye could tell her attire was the nicer and more expensive of the two.

Behind them stood the third member of their party, a broad-shouldered man in a dark suit, who was clearly meant to remain more or less in the background, despite an intense conspicuousness. He had a face that had taken a punch or two, but Eli guessed he was no stranger to returning them in kind. His attention had locked on Tapper, and Eli held back a smile. *Professional help.*

The dark-skinned woman was the first to step forward, extending her hand towards Eli. "Mr Adler? I'm Sarah M'basa, the Commonwealth deputy consul. Welcome to Bayern."

"Pleasure to meet you, Ms M'basa," said Eli, shaking her hand firmly, as he imagined a confident businessman would do. "This is my director of public relations," he said, gesturing to Taylor.

"Tara Mulroney," said Taylor, quickly seizing M'basa's hand with her own. "So nice to meet you." She dazzled the woman with a brilliant smile.

"And my head of security," Eli continued, jerking a thumb over his shoulder at Tapper. "Mr Tormundsen."

As M'basa's face turned towards Tapper, Eli swore that her smile missed a beat, but it might have just been his imagination. The Commonwealth official nodded to Tapper, who returned it silently.

"This is Amanda Wei," said M'basa, gesturing to the woman beside her. "She's a senior director of client relations at the Corporation."

The taller woman stepped forward and extended a hand. Eli shook it; her grasp was warm and firm. Wei's expression was far more impassive than M'basa's, though Eli couldn't tell if it was a personal or professional coolness.

"The Bayern Corporation welcomes you, Mr Adler," she said, her airy voice somehow floating above the wind. "I've been assigned as your personal liaison. If there is anything at all you need during your stay, please don't hesitate to ask."

"Thank you, Director Wei," said Taylor, again summoning that broad and somewhat alien smile. "Mr Adler is thrilled to have a chance to visit the Corporation, and he's sure that the discussions will prove to be most mutually beneficial."

"Of course," said Wei, her stolid expression not changing. "But business can wait until tomorrow. You've had a long trip, and no doubt wish to rest. We can handle anything you need to make your stay more comfortable. If you'd like to have access to funds, I can see to it that any currency is converted into non-voting shares."

Taylor produced a credit chip and handed it over to Wei, who bowed slightly. "Much appreciated, director."

Eli had gotten a high-level briefing on the Corporation's idiosyncratic treatment of money, but Taylor had also assured him that thanks to his VIP status and accommodations at the Commonwealth embassy, he shouldn't have much need for actual currency. The general had provided them with just enough to be deposited in the local bank as a gesture of good faith on the part of Adler Industries.

Wei pocketed the chip and gestured to the *Cavalier*. "I will see to it that your pilot is accommodated as well."

"Oh, no need," said Eli, with a casual wave of the hand. "I flew us here myself."

The widening of Wei's eyes was the first reaction Eli had seen from the woman. "Indeed?"

"It's a hobby. Don't worry: you'll find I'm fully licensed." He winked at her.

Taylor cleared her throat, taking Eli's upper arm in a surprisingly strong grip. "Mr Adler is a man of many interests," she said brightly. "But you're right; it's been a long trip, and we should *retire*."

Wei nodded, and gestured to the corridor on the other side of the blast door. "Please, come this way."

To Eli's surprise, the hallway was hewn from bare rock, shot through with occasional veins of black volcanic glass. The huge blast doors ground shut behind them, leaving them in an eerie silence, throughout which their footsteps reverberated, churchlike. Lit with illuminated strips fixed to the walls, the high arch of the ceiling stretched far above them into darkness.

M'basa's eye caught Eli's gaze and she smiled. "This is your first time on Bayern, is it not, Mr Adler?"

"Yes," said Eli cautiously. "I've always wanted to visit, but the opportunity hadn't presented itself until now."

"Mr Adler is a very busy man, with many obligations on his time," interjected Taylor, who looked a little miffed that she'd been relegated to the background. *Or is it Tara Mulroney who's miffed? I'm not sure I can tell where one starts and the other leaves off.*

"Naturally," said M'basa. "Running such a successful business no doubt occupies a significant chunk of the day. Still," she said, eyeing Adler with a speculative glance, "I would have thought his affairs would have drawn him here before now. But, I'll freely admit that my knowledge of the world of business is limited to what I've encountered in my job.

"But, as I was going to say," M'basa continued, "Bergfestung – that's the Corporation's headquarters or, as you might otherwise think of it, Bayern's 'capital city' – is carved out of an extinct volcano."

"Like the Tharsis Montes on Mars?" asked Taylor with a frown.

"Not quite," Wei said, stepping in with a polite laugh. "By comparison, the early attempts to make Mars habitable were quite crude. Then again, we've had a couple centuries to improve our technology. And, unlike Mars, Bayern's native atmosphere is quite breathable for humans. Still, you should find Bergfestung cool but comfortable, especially in contrast to Terra Nova."

Thank god for that. Nova's constant heat and humidity had started making Eli long for a trip to the arctic tundra.

They reached the end of the corridor, where a pair of smaller double doors slid open at their approach, revealing an elevator that easily accommodated them all . The milky white walls of the lift had a soothing, almost sterile feeling, unbroken except for a black glass control panel. Wei tapped an illuminated square and they began a smooth descent that made Eli think of their landing on Bayern, if only because the two were not in the least bit similar.

"How many people live in Bergfestung?" Taylor asked, breaking the silence.

"Approximately two million," said Wei. "Mostly in administrative and support services. The Corporation's chief manufacturing and agricultural concerns are located on the plains around the base of the mountain."

Eli almost let out a low whistle at the figure, but decided that it wasn't an appropriately Elias Adler reaction. Instead, he just nodded. "Impressive."

"The Bayern Corporation *is* the largest privately consolidated business concern in the galaxy," said Wei. There was no note of bragging in her voice, just simple stated fact. "It takes a great deal of personnel to ensure that it continues operating smoothly. I'm sure you of all people understand that."

"Oh, of course," said Eli, trying to inject a casual note. Wei's pronouncement had seemed almost suspicious – had he said something to make her doubt him?

Fortunately, he was spared from any further line of questioning as the lift's translucent white walls suddenly faded into complete transparency, timed perfectly to the car dropping into the main cavern of Bergfestung.

This time, Eli did let his mouth fall agape. The cavern was truly enormous, the biggest open enclosed space he'd ever seen. The lift car was attached to one wall and, while Eli could see the cavern's other side – which almost looked like a gray wall of clouds from this distance – he'd have been hard-pressed to make out any details over there. He wondered if there were people descending in lifts on the other side, staring back at them.

Glancing at the side walls, he caught sight of regular striations along them, suggesting that the cavern was not wholly a natural formation. When he peered down, that notion was reinforced.

Below them lay a city. Not a town, but a full-blown metropolitan center. Low-slung buildings of concrete and steel formed city blocks, divided by streets and boulevards and, to Eli's amazement, even parks. Lights winked below them, bereft of any rhythm or timing, a veritable discordant symphony of humanity.

Eli glanced over and saw Taylor's usually impassive face mirroring the wonderment on his own. Tapper, however, had barely shifted from the same flat, emotionless expression he'd been wearing since they'd gotten off the ship. Neither Wei nor her silent companion reacted, but Eli supposed they saw it every day. M'basa was somewhere in between the two extremes, though she smiled sidelong at Eli.

"I can't quite get over it either," she said in a hushed voice that wouldn't have been out of place in a chapel.

Eli shook his head. He could only think of one other thing he'd seen in his life that had evoked the same sort of feeling – the wormhole gates that connected systems for interstellar travel. Calling it man's triumph over nature was kind of a misnomer; nature was not there to be tamed or broken. It was more a sense of what man could accomplish in concert with nature – it reminded him of pictures he'd seen in textbooks showing Earth's old mills using paddle wheels to harness river currents for power.

"It's a hell of a sight," murmured Eli, shaking his head. They were still descending, a solid minute after they'd first entered the cavern, a testament to just how high up the landing platform had been.

As he looked back up, a glint caught his eye. A series of small squares were positioned around the cavern. *Mirrors?*

Some long forgotten tidbit from a science textbook floated to the top of Eli's mind. In order to approximate the planet's standard twenty-six hour day, they used a system of heliostats positioned on the upper sides of the mountain, combined with a series of specially bored shafts, fiber optic cabling, and these mirrors to provide sunlight inside the city. Helped keep the plants alive, and definitely had its benefits for the citizenry too: nobody wanted to feel like they lived in a cave, even if they *actually* lived in a cave.

The lift had finally dropped to the floor of the cavern, and the doors behind them whooshed open, letting them into a small foyer, lit in crepuscular hues. Unlike the rough-hewn caverns that had led from the docking platform, this had an unquestionably manmade look to it.

Wei turned to them. "I'll leave you here, in deputy consul M'basa's capable hands. I look forward to seeing you tomorrow."

Eli inclined his head. "The pleasure has been ours, Director Wei. Thank you."

Without a parting glance, Wei turned on her heel and left through a side passageway, her ever-silent security associate trailing in her wake. M'basa in turn gestured to a set of glass sliding doors. The three of them followed her through, exiting into what appeared to be a tunnel for ground traffic. At the foot of a short set of stairs sat a compact black hovercar, with the tinted windows Eli had come to associate with official transportation. While it didn't boast anything as tacky as the seal of the Commonwealth emblazoned on the door, Eli was pretty certain that anybody scanning the vehicle's ID would quickly discover that it was a protected diplomatic transport.

M'basa held the back door open, ushering them in. She herself slid onto one of the two facing seats. Without another signal, the car pulled away from the curb.

"So," said M'basa, turning towards them. Her face had lost the playful smiles of earlier, replaced instead with an all-business demeanor. "Now that we've gotten the pleasantries out of the way, would you like to tell me who the hell you are and what you're doing here?"

INTERLUDE

Earth Marine Corps Medical Frigate EMS Barton – May 27, 2397

Earth. It looked like a globe from the viewport of the frigate. Of course, it *was* a globe, just not one of those made out of plastic that hung in schoolrooms the world over. *The world over*. The private turned the phrase in his mind, eyeing it from an unexpected angle. It wasn't just any world, after all – for millennia it had been the only one humanity had ever known. For centuries after that, it had been the only one they'd visited. And for decades after that, it had been the only one they'd inhabited.

Now it was shrinking in the rear-view mirror.

"Sit down, kid," growled a voice. "You're making me nervous."

He turned to face the sergeant, who was leaning back in the chair, his feet perched on the corner of the hospital bed. The older man studied his face intently, then shrugged. "I've seen worse."

The private was going to make a sour expression, but just the memory of pain convinced him to let those muscles be. "A walk in the park," he managed, through clenched teeth.

"Well, the next time I tell you to get down, maybe you'll listen." The sergeant turned his attention to the vid monitor hanging opposite the private's hospital bed. Currently, it was showing a talking head on some sort of fleetwide broadcast, but the sound was turned down. It wasn't likely to be good news, anyway.

The private couldn't think of a response cleverer than a grunt, so he left it at that and hobbled back to the bed. The sergeant swung his legs down as the private levered himself back in, arranging the covers around him. He didn't try too hard – he'd learned from experience that the nurse would cluck his tongue at him when he came back anyway.

"They fixed your hearing, at least," said the sergeant.

"What?"

"I said they… oh, aren't *you* the comedian."

The corners of the private's mouth turned up. Bad as the burns were, they were treatable. According to the doctors he'd make a full recovery thanks to some time in a hyperbaric chamber and skin regeneration therapy. Restoring his hearing had been the more challenging procedure, requiring the insertion of specialized implants. Ear damage was notoriously difficult, and couldn't easily be repaired by regrowing his cells. Not yet, anyway. One of the doctors, a specialist, had told him there was great hope for advancements in the field – perhaps even especially now there was a war on, a thought that the private found unsettling – but not to get his hopes up. At the moment, he was happy he could hear anything, even if it was just the sergeant's gibes. He let his eyes close and focused on the sounds around him: the distant thrum of the frigate's massive engines, the regular bleep of the monitor at his bedside, even the somewhat raspy breathing of the sergeant beside him. They were each one of them rhythmic – soothing even. He'd just started to relax into a kind of waking restfulness when a rap at the door roused him.

"Pardon me," said a man's voice. "I'm looking for a..." he paused and there was the sound of tapping on a display, followed by a hesitant, "Simon V... Vy... a... ch–"

"Vyacheslav," said the private, in an attempt to save the man from himself. Opening his eyes, he turned his head towards the door. An olive-skinned man with dark hair and lieutenant's bars on his collar looked up from a tablet, his expression barely hiding the dismay as he met the eyes of the man in the hospital bed.

"Kovalic?" finished the lieutenant.

"That's me," said the private. "You'll pardon me if I don't salute. Sir."

"Uh," said the lieutenant. Clearly, this wasn't how it was supposed to go. "Of course. I'm Lieutenant Sen." He stepped into the room, tucking the tablet under his arm. "I've been charged with... Well, that is to say, it's my *honor* to..."

"Oh for chrissakes," muttered the sergeant from his chair, his eyes still firmly on the vid monitor.

"I'm sorry?" said the lieutenant.

"Nothing, sir."

"Right, well." He cleared his throat and launched into a well-practiced speech. "Private Kovalic, it is my duty – and privilege, yes – to bestow upon you this commendation for bravery in the field of action." Finished, he looked hopefully at the private.

The private raised an eyebrow.

"Oh, right," said the lieutenant, suddenly, pulling a flat box out of one pocket of his uniform. "This is the Earth Marine Corps Bronze Star." He snapped the box open, showing a

shiny bronze star surrounded by two olive branches. It
hung from a green ribbon with a thick gold stripe down the
center, flanked by two smaller gold stripes. For a moment, he
made as if to remove it, then seemed to realize that with the
private still in his hospital gown, there was nowhere to pin
it. Instead, he closed the box and set it on the bedside table.
Then, clearing his throat, he gave a crisp salute that was, so
far, the smoothest thing about him.

"Thank you for your service, private. Your planet
appreciates it." With a nod, he consulted his tablet and went
off to find his next victim.

The sergeant stood and reached over Kovalic's blanket-
swaddled legs to flip open the medal box. He let out a low
whistle. "Nice hardware, private. I'm sure they'll be back
with mine when that pencilhead finally works his way down
to 'T.'"

The private glanced at the medal, then looked away. Out
the viewport, where the planet was still diminishing in their
wake, he couldn't help but see the limp form of Lieutenant
Carlin lying on the ground, the grass rippling around her as
the shuttle took off.

"More like the Earth Marine Corps commendation for
stupidity in battle," he muttered. "And for what?"

"Oi," said the sergeant, his brow knitting. "None of that
now." He crossed his arms, eyeing the sullen man in the bed.
"You didn't save the LT, that's a fact, but you didn't put her
where she was, neither – that was her own damn fault. They
want to give you a medal for it, you say 'Yes, sir. Thank you,
sir,' and click your heels."

The private's mouth set in a disapproving line, but he
didn't say anything.

"Look," said the sergeant. "End of the day, you risked your

life for someone else, even if she was beyond saving. That's what that's for." He nodded at the medal. "It's a reminder of what wearing the uniform is all about."

CHAPTER 8

The uniform hung, perfectly pressed, in Kovalic's closet. It exuded an air of judgment that seemed improbable from a garment of cloth and metal, an implicit challenge.

He didn't wear it often – maybe once a year – and unfortunately, all too often for occasions like this. He'd unzipped it from its vacuum bag and let it air out while he was in the shower and changing the dressing on his shoulder. But now, standing in front of his closet with water dripping from his hair, he tried to meet its stare, with mixed success.

It had been two days before Kovalic had been able to roust himself. After Nat's visit, he'd spend the better part of the first day mildly inebriated, watching whatever came on the vidscreen in his apartment. Over the years, he'd learned that the end of many missions could be jarring – a dramatic plunge from the high of being in the field – and were thus best treated with something mind-numbing: bourbon, diluted with the latest celebrity gossip, sports scores, and dramatic vid series seemed to do the trick. The real key was not getting sucked in: twenty-four hours of recovery and then you got back on the horse. Like a controlled burn.

That might have been too many metaphors.

This time was different, part of his mind argued. This

time someone hadn't come back. He could take a little extra time, get a little drunker. But he'd seen what happened to operatives who embraced the excuse, succumbed to the temptation to numb themselves out of existence entirely.

Letting out a breath, he reached with a tentative hand to grasp the uniform's hanger. He cursed himself for his hesitancy: it wasn't as if the thing was going to shock him. It was just a uniform – *his* uniform.

In his line of work, he'd worn any number of uniforms from any number of services, including plenty of those from sides other than his own. But the one thing he *never* wore on a job was his own uniform. It was purely a matter of practicality: uniforms identified you. They told a story: which side you were on, what conflicts you had seen, even how long you'd been in service. All of those details, minor as they might seem, were too dangerous for someone in his line of work to give away. So more often than not, even when he was on assignment in Commonwealth space, he either stuck to civilian garb or wore a perfectly assembled uniform that still told a coherent, logical story – just one that was most assuredly not his.

But this *was* his – forest green trousers and a high-cut military jacket over a white shirt and black tie – and the story it told wasn't fiction but biography. From the Occupation War campaign ribbon to the Commonwealth Commendation for Exemplary Service that the general had wrangled for him after a recent mission, you could retrace the last twenty years of Simon Kovalic's life through the decorations on his dress jacket. He actually held distinctions from several services, including the now defunct Earth Marine Corps, in which he'd served for a grand total of three years before it was dissolved and replaced with its Commonwealth equivalent.

He reached out and fingered the worn green ribbon. That first commendation was one among many now, each with their own story to tell, but whereas some of them had faded over the years, that one retained perfect fidelity.

With a deep breath, he locked his eyes on the uniform, then pulled it from the rack, meeting that challenge it had laid down.

After all these years, and all these losses, was he still worthy of wearing it?

Two hours later, Kovalic stepped out of the small suburban house that Jens had shared with his husband, Mario, and their two small children. If there were any justice the day would have been overcast and rainy, but the sun was shining with its usual enthusiasm, and there was nary a cloud in the sky. Nova's climate verged on tropical in most of its habitable regions, so at mid-morning it was already halfway to sweltering. Part of Kovalic wished he hadn't decided to walk from the transit station half a mile away in full uniform, but he'd felt uncomfortable requisitioning a car, even for a perfectly legitimate purpose like this one.

Kovalic's lips pressed into a firm line. It wasn't the first time he'd had to notify the next of kin of someone who had died under his command. He'd only been able to provide vague information as to the nature of Jens' death – the mission was still classified – but he'd told Mario that Jens' sacrifice hadn't been in vain. He'd swallowed lies like those before, but the bitterness of this one had stuck in his craw. At least he'd been able to say with some truth that Jens hadn't suffered; he doubted the pilot had time to register anything before the ship had been blown out of the sky.

He needn't have worried about transportation, he saw,

as he started down the steps. A low-slung black hovercar was already parked out front, and standing before it was the general.

With a deep mental sigh, Kovalic strode down to meet the old man, who was leaning lightly on his cane. At least the general had opted to retain his usual casual outfit, a simple black tunic and trousers, rather than don his full uniform. And wouldn't *that* have caused a stir.

As it happened, the "general" part of his title was largely honorific, in recognition of his long years of service – albeit on the other side of the war. He held no official commission in the Commonwealth military; rather, he'd been appointed to his current post by the Commonwealth Executive itself. Thus, the only uniform in the old man's closet was the full Illyrican dress uniform – complete with a chest full of medals – that he'd been wearing when he defected, nearly six years ago now.

"Didn't expect to see you here, sir."

The general gave him a sharp look. "Flight Officer Jens was part of my team too, captain. And while you may have been the commander on the ground, I was the one who assigned the mission." He cocked his head to one side. "You, of all people, should know that I don't take loss lightly."

Kovalic's teeth clicked together. "Of course. Sorry – I've been a bit on edge since this whole thing, I'm afraid."

A weathered hand grasped his shoulder. "I think we all have," the old man said. "Can I offer you a ride?"

Kovalic inclined his head, and slipped into the hovercar. The general followed suit, closing the door behind him. In the typical efficiency that Kovalic associated with the old man, the car immediately peeled off down the street, without any need for direction or destination.

The old man sighed, and shook his head. "Terrible business, Simon. I *am* sorry."

Running his hand along the leather of the seat, Kovalic didn't respond. The interior of the car was posh, but not ostentatious. More to the point, the sound of the outside world barely registered inside the steel and glass cocoon. An explosion could go off right outside, and you might only hear a muted thump. It was easy for him to forget, sometimes, that the general was a hunted man, but he supposed the old man never really forgot.

"Truth be told," said the general, "I wasn't entirely forthcoming. Jens' death wasn't the only thing that brought me here."

"Oh?"

"Something's come up."

"That's... vague."

The general drummed his fingers on the armrest, as if having an internal debate, but finally appeared to come to a decision. "While I was at IIS, I spent some time cultivating a... personal intelligence network. Assets that reported not to a handler, but directly to me."

Kovalic blinked. "I thought the Executive required you to divulge all knowledge of operations as part of the conditions of your defection."

The old man cleared his throat. "Technically the deal stipulated that I had to reveal all knowledge of *foreign* operations – that is, those in the Commonwealth and on other independent worlds. That I did, to the letter."

Realization slid over Kovalic like the sun breaking through a thick afternoon fog. "You had a personal intelligence network *inside* the Illyrican Empire?"

The general offered only a modest shrug. "My concern

was the stability of the entire Imperium. You, of all people, should know that simmering resentment is practically an Illyrican pastime. It may be an empire now, but at heart it's still that lost colony that spent a couple hundred years believing it had been abandoned by Earth."

"It's a little harder to be sympathetic about that when it decided to channel its inferiority complex into a surprise invasion."

The general tipped his head. "Just so. But as the director of IIS, it was important for me to make sure that resentment stayed at a simmer – and that it stayed directed outwards. And while I did give up a few of the personal domestic assets that I thought might be of some use to the Commonwealth, there were a few that I, well, didn't."

"What exactly are you telling me here?" said Kovalic, pinching the bridge of his nose. He looked back at the old man. "You *still* have active intelligence assets inside the Imperium?"

"Mostly dormant," said the general blithely. "There are a few people with whom I correspond – discreetly, of course – in order to… keep my ear to the ground, if you will." The general hesitated. "Simon, I meant no disrespect by keeping this from you."

Kovalic didn't even want to consider how many laws that probably violated, or, for that matter, how the hell the old man had gotten messages back and forth across the border. Instead, he just rubbed his forehead. "OK. So you still have contacts in the Imperium. Why tell me this now?"

"Because I got a message from one of them this morning. A source codenamed CARDINAL. Highly placed, and very reliable."

"And?"

"The information involves Bayern and could potentially jeopardize SPT's mission."

As if to punctuate the point, the car came to a stop, and the general nodded at the door. "If you please, captain?"

With a frown, Kovalic opened the door and stepped out.

They'd stopped in front of a mid-rise office building in the commercial district of Salaam, an area mainly occupied by banks, white collar business, and law firms. The structure itself was utterly nondescript, an edifice of gray concrete and glass with no signs or other markings. Kovalic was already sweating in the Novan humidity.

"Sorry to drag you to the shady part of town on your day off," said the general as he levered himself out of the car and limped towards the building's entrance.

"I should have told you earlier, Simon." The doors whispered open and they stepped into the lobby. The security guard looked up at them, blinked at Kovalic's uniform, then apparently decided it would be wiser not to ask any questions, and looked back down at his screen.

The general led them to a lift and pressed a button for the top floor. They sped quietly upwards.

"As I said," the old man continued, as though their conversation had not paused, "most of my contacts were inactive. This one I have had regular correspondence with over the years, and while the reports were often trivial in nature, they did help paint a fuller – and, I must admit, at times more disturbing – picture of the scene on the other side of the bottleneck."

The lift let them out into a bland, carpeted corridor lined with frosted-glass doors. Kovalic followed the old man to the left; at the end of the corridor they swung a right. That led to an unmarked door; the general tapped a keycode into the panel beside it, then let himself in and gestured for Kovalic to follow him.

A small desk occupied the room, flanked on either wall by a pair of bookcases. A green upholstered chair sat across from the desk, and the walls were lined with diplomas for a "Doctor Tabitha Lestrade, Clinical Psychologist." Kovalic eyed one, then glanced back at the general.

"Who the hell is Dr Lestrade?"

"Hm?" said the general, looking up from where he was standing next to the right-hand bookcase. "Oh, a lovely woman. Works with delinquent youth, you know."

"She's real, then?"

"Oh, very real," said the general, with a smile. "She just happens to not be in on Saturdays."

"And she lets you use her office?"

"What? Oh. Well, she doesn't strictly speaking *know*," said the general, reaching behind the bookcase. With a click, the entire case swung slightly outwards, revealing a door with a fingerprint scanner.

"Really?" said Kovalic. "Behind the bookshelf? A bit cliché, isn't it?"

"She's hardly likely to try and move it, now, is she?" said the general. "Besides, sometimes the old tropes are the best."

He pressed his forefinger to the glowing scanner, and the door swung open, letting in a stream of light from the adjoining room. They passed through into what Kovalic immediately recognized as one of the general's many offices.

The number of offices that the man had sometimes astounded Kovalic; he wondered if there was one for every day of the week, if not perhaps every day of the month. The man certainly valued his privacy.

Then again, when people were actively trying to track you

down and kill you, it often paid to be a little bit paranoid.

"As I was saying," the general continued, closing the concealed side door behind him, "I do know that CARDINAL is absolutely reliable, in particular on this sort of information."

This room was somewhat smaller than the doctor's office next door, with just enough space for a simple desk and two chairs flanking it. A window looked out into the forest of skyscrapers; opposite it was another door.

"This CARDINAL," said Kovalic slowly. "It wouldn't happen to be the same 'highly-placed and very trusted source' that tipped you to Bleiden's defection, would it?"

The old man gave Kovalic a rueful smile as he seated himself behind the desk. "I suppose there's no point in trying to deny it."

"But you're not going to tell me who it is."

The general hesitated. "Not at the present time, no." He raised his hands. "I trust you implicitly, Simon. But this is a… special case. I can't risk compromising CARDINAL's security." A quiet ferocity had colored his voice, and Kovalic frowned. There was something protective about the general's tone that went beyond just the professional courtesy you gave to an asset. Something *personal.*

Kovalic might have pushed more, but the general clearly viewed the discussion at an end as he touched the glass display embedded into the wood. A holographic screen flickered into place hovering above the desk and a moment later, an amber light blinked on the console.

Frowning, the general tapped a control. "Good morning, Rance." The general's aide and bodyguard – she was never far from his side. "Messages?"

"None this morning, sir," her voice came over the speaker. "But… Deputy Director Kester would like to see you."

The general sighed, and leaned back. "I don't suppose you can put him off until after lunch?"

Rance's voice lowered. "I mean, he's here now. Waiting."

"Here? How the devil did he find this place?"

"I don't quite know, sir. But he says it's urgent."

With a raise of his eyebrows, the general sent a significant look at Kovalic. "Very well, send him in." He keyed the intercom off.

Kovalic glanced at the door and then back at the side entrance they'd come in through. "Maybe I should be going."

The general waved a hand. "No, stay. I want you in the loop on this. Besides," he said, making a sour face, "I'd rather not face Kester alone."

The office's main door shot open – any more force and it would have been slammed – admitting a man several years Kovalic's junior. He was dressed in a sharp, fashionable suit and his hair looked like it had been attended to by a staff of professionals. Clear blue eyes set in a brown face that had never quite lost the last of its baby fat went quickly to Kovalic, then dismissed him just as rapidly and focused instead on the general. Striding forward, he placed both of his hands on the edge of the desk.

"Now see here," he began. "Why wasn't I informed that you sent your team to Bayern?"

The general blinked, tilting his head to one side, and Kovalic felt his muscles tense.

"A pleasure to see you again, Deputy Director Kester. May I ask how you came by that particular piece of information?" The general's voice had taken on the mild tones that Kovalic had come to recognize as his most dangerous.

"Never mind how I came by it," said Kester. "As CID's deputy director of operations, *I* am your liaison for all operational matters, so why wasn't I briefed on this mission?"

The general steepled his hands. "There was no reason for you to be. This is an SPT matter."

Kester's expression shifted from anger to disbelief. "No reason? *No reason?* I have assets on Bayern – assets that your little crew of cowboys might put in danger."

"I'm sorry, but I can't help but think you're laboring under some sort of misapprehension here." Kester opened his mouth to speak, but the general continued as though he hadn't even noticed it. "I don't report to you. As the Special Adviser on Strategic Intelligence, any information I choose to share with you and the Commonwealth Intelligence Directorate is at my discretion, and should be viewed a courtesy – not an obligation."

"Operational control is *my* jurisdiction. That means all intelligence-gathering and special operations in foreign theaters are subject to my supervision."

The old man's white brows knit, not in anger, but in consternation, as though he couldn't comprehend why Kester wasn't understanding him. "As you may recall, Deputy Director Kester, I'm responsible directly to the Commonwealth Executive," he said. "*Not* to CID. If you'd like to check, I'm sure I could get the secretary-general on the line." He gestured to his console.

Kester looked briefly stricken, but Kovalic had to give him a hand – he covered well. Straightening up, he smoothed out his suit and gave the general a curt nod. "We shall see. I will be lodging a formal complaint about this matter with the director – who, in case *you've* forgotten, also reports directly to the Executive. I can't imagine he'll be pleased, especially after your little debacle on Sevastapol – the worst of times *indeed*. And I'm going to request an immediate recall of your team. Good day, general." He turned on his heel and stalked out of the office, this time doing his level best to slam the door in his wake.

Shaking his head, Kovalic leaned back against the wall and massaged his stiff right shoulder. "Nice guy."

The general was still eyeing the door, as though Kester might burst back through. "He's quite intelligent, I'm told – when his temper doesn't get the best of him. Ambitious, too." He shook his head. "But, right now I'm more concerned with how exactly he knew about the Bayern operation. That information should have been compartmentalized at the highest levels."

"You think we have a leak," said Kovalic.

The general frowned. "After the incident on Sevastapol, I had to consider the possibility. But my investigations – limited, though they were – turned up no evidence." He stroked his beard. "Granted, if someone's leaking information to the Imperium, it seems unlikely to be the same person talking out of class to our friends in CID."

"So the good news here is that we have *two* leaks?"

"'Good' being a relative term."

The general harrumphed, then tapped a few commands on his console. "Indeed. It's already cost me this office, it seems. If Mr Kester knows of its location, I'm afraid we'll have to abandon it."

"Dr Lestrade will be pleased to have her bookcase back."

At that, the general gave a snort, but continued to scan the information on the display in front of him. "Ah. It seems the Commonwealth Executive read in the Office of the Undersecretary for Foreign Affairs on the Bayern operation."

"So?"

"Deputy Director Kester happens to be married to the undersecretary's son."

"I see."

"As I said, he's ambitious. At least we have an idea of the chain that led to the deputy director's rather abrupt appearance, I'm inclined not to worry about it further at present – again, it seems unlikely that a Commonwealth official of that high a rank is also leaking secrets to the Imperium, so I doubt the Bleiden fiasco can be laid at his feet. I'll deal with the Undersecretary myself in due time. But," and he leaned back in his chair and folded his hands, "CARDINAL's intelligence is far more pressing, especially with SPT in the field. I can't help thinking it's no coincidence."

"And we've got no way to get in touch with Natalie."

The general shook his head. "All check-ins are strictly one way; it's Commander Taylor's show on the ground."

Kovalic exhaled and found himself rolling his sore shoulder slowly and staring out the window. The Salaam morning had dawned hot and hazy, with the city's usual humidity pressing down like a damp washcloth. The walk from his apartment to the subway and then from the subway to the Jens residence had wilted the collar of his uniform shirt.

"How's the shoulder?" the general asked abruptly.

Kovalic's heartbeat quickened, but he kept his voice steady. "A little sore," he admitted, "but they packed it with antibiotic gel and a sealant, so it should keep as long as I don't do too much to strain it. There wasn't much they could do to speed up the muscle repair." He gestured helplessly at the sling.

The general eyed him, but Kovalic could see that he

was weighing the options in his mind. He held his breath; it was possible he could tip the general over the edge, but it would be better to let the old man come to the decision of his own accord.

At last, the old man sighed. "Truth is, I'd send someone else if I could; you're not fully recovered – physically *or* mentally." His eyes dug into Kovalic's, as if probing them for weakness. Then he shook his head. "But with the risk of a leak I would rather not leave this information to a courier, or to our friends at CID." He waved a hand. "So, pack a bag, captain. You're on your bike."

Kovalic stood, barely keeping from leaping up from the chair; he wasn't prepared to give the general time to rethink the matter.

"But," the general said, raising a warning finger, and Kovalic steeled himself. "This is still Commander Taylor's operation, understand? You are there in a support and advisory capacity only. Do I make myself clear?"

"Crystal, sir." He turned for the door.

"And Simon?" the general called.

Kovalic looked back over his shoulder, but the general had picked up a tablet from his desk, and was studying it intently. "Try not to get shot again – I really can't spare you."

CHAPTER 9

Eli's heart thumped a salsa rhythm as he met M'basa's unwavering gaze. *Blown already? What did I do? How did she know?* His stomach sank into his shoes. His first mission and he'd already botched it. Color rose into his cheeks.

"Mr Adler is a–" began Taylor.

M'basa wasn't having it. "Please, Ms Mulroney – I'll humor your choice of names for now. You did a pretty good job with all of the Adler Corporation's records; frankly, that was part of the problem: they were a little too perfect. So." She folded her hands. "I know you're not CID, because I would have been told." Eli saw doubt flicker across her face, ever so briefly. "But I'm sure any of the Commonwealth's alphabet soup of intelligence agencies would happily send operatives to Bayern without briefing the CID station chief." Her gaze shifted slightly. "And then there's you."

To Eli's surprise, her eyes had fixed on neither him nor Taylor, but on Tapper, who'd barely said a word in the exchange.

The sergeant looked equally as taken aback, though his own eyes were still hidden behind the dark glasses Taylor had given him.

"Uh, me, ma'am?"

"I've got a memory for faces," said M'basa, her eyes narrowing. "And I've seen yours before."

Eli blinked, once, slowly. *So it wasn't me after all?* He felt the breath he'd been holding ease out of him.

With a sigh, Tapper pulled his glasses off, carefully folded them, and slid them into his jacket's lapel pocket. "Can't say I'm a big fan of disguises, anyhow. Somehow they never seem to work for me."

M'basa glanced at Eli and Taylor, "I don't remember either of these two from last time. What happened to your boss – Fielding, right?"

"Can't say I know anybody by that name, ma'am."

"Don't be difficult," M'basa snapped. "I don't know who the hell you guys are, but this is my turf, understand? I won't have you stomping all over it."

Tapper cocked his head to one side. "Exactly how long have you been stationed on Bayern, deputy consul? Six months ago, you were the station number two on Caledonia; can't have been here that long."

The dark-skinned woman leaned back in her seat, arms crossed over her chest. "Two months." Eli wasn't sure if it was possible for a person to fit more grudging admission into their voice. "My rotation on Caledonia was done, so I took the Bayern station number two job when it came up."

Tapper raised his eyebrows. "And now you're station chief? What happened to Karl?"

M'basa blinked. "You knew Rao?"

"We go back," said Tapper, with a shrug.

"He retired," said M'basa.

"No way. Karl was a spook through-and-through. He'd never quit the service."

"Well," said M'basa, leaning back in her chair, "the pictures of him with the daughter of a Bayern board member might have had something to do with it."

Tapper sucked in a breath through his teeth. "Ah. Well. Yes. I suppose that would do it. When was this?"

"Two days ago. You probably passed his ship in transit."

"Bloody hell," muttered Tapper. "Really had to hit the ground running, huh?"

M'basa didn't say anything, but turned her attention back to Taylor. "Let's not sidestep the prime issue here. Who sent you? Naval Intelligence? The Commonwealth Security Bureau?"

Taylor's bubbly public relations personality slipped off her face. "I don't know what your clearance level is, deputy consul, but I suspect it's not nearly high enough."

The only sound in the car was M'basa's fingers on her knee. "I'm very sorry to hear that. I'd hoped that in the spirit of cooperation you would have been willing to demonstrate a little give-and-take. As it is, I'm afraid I'm going to have to insist that a member of my staff escort you at all times while you're on Bayern – for security's sake, of course."

"You're putting a *minder* on us?" said Taylor, incredulous. She shook her head. "That's a mistake, ma'am."

M'basa shrugged. "I don't know who the hell you are, and I don't know what the hell your goal is here." She smiled pleasantly. "Should that situation change, I'd be more than happy to reevaluate my security arrangements."

Eli looked around the car: Tapper's face was grim, his arms crossed; Taylor looked mildly disconcerted, but also like she hadn't finished playing her cards yet; M'basa looked impressively calm and comfortable – then again, she had the rest of them by the short hairs.

Goddamnit, I'm not going to just sit around and be deadweight.

Taylor had more or less ordered him to keep his mouth shut but, well, he'd never been very good at either taking orders *or* keeping his mouth shut.

"Deputy consul," he said, smiling and leaning forward. "I think we got off on the wrong foot."

"Oh, do you?" said M'basa. Her voice was arid.

"My colleagues here mean well, but they can be a little... by the book."

"What Mr Adler means is–" Taylor started through gritted teeth.

Eli plowed forward before she could stop him. *I'm going to get hell for this later.* "You're still establishing yourself here, and, naturally, we have no wish to step on your toes. But the truth is we're here to look into some odd transactions between the Bayern Corporation and certain Commonwealth nationals we've had an interest in. We're worried there might be some financial... impropriety." He fancied he could feel Taylor's eyes boring into the back of his skull. It made his brain tickle.

"So you're saying you're what, the Commonwealth Revenue Service?"

Eli smiled. "You could call us auditors, sure."

"Why wasn't I informed?"

Taylor had picked up his cue, and though Eli doubted she was any happier about it, she knew an opening when she saw one. "I'm sure you're still familiarizing yourself with your predecessor's files," she jumped in. "It's possible you just haven't come across it yet. It certainly isn't high priority for a station chief."

M'basa gave her a wary eye. "Uh huh. You realize I'll have to confirm this, right?"

"I'd expect nothing less," said Taylor.

"Until you do," Eli added, "I'm sure we would be *happy* to

comply with your requirement for an escort."

Now he was pretty sure both Taylor *and* Tapper were giving him looks of death, but he carefully avoided meeting either of their gazes.

Taylor cleared her throat. "But we'll also need to maintain our cover." Eli almost bit his tongue over that, but if M'basa noticed, it didn't register. "So we'll continue with all of Mr Adler's appointments and other engagements."

The car, which had been winding through Bergfestung's city streets began to slow as, Eli assumed, they approached the embassy.

"You should say now whether or not this arrangement is going to be amenable, Ms M'basa," said Taylor, glancing out the window. "Otherwise, you might as well take us back to our ship. Although I don't think our boss will be exceptionally pleased by that development. And you know how bosses have a way of talking to bosses. All well above *our* pay grades, of course."

A nonplussed expression crossed M'basa's face. Eli wagered she hadn't been in her new position nearly long enough to risk bringing down the wrath of her superiors; plus, going on Tapper's information, the station chief gig would have been a solid promotion for her – one that she wouldn't want to jeopardize.

"Fine," she said. "We can forego the minder for now, as long as you stick to your cover identities and don't get into any trouble."

Taylor tilted her head. "Thank you, deputy consul. I'll be more than happy to note your amenability in our report."

M'basa raised a finger in warning. "But don't jerk me around. This is still my patch and you're guests here. I expect you to comport yourselves accordingly."

Eli put up his hands, palm out. "You'll never even notice we were here. Promise."

In the space of fifteen minutes, the car dropped them at the embassy and M'basa showed them to their rooms. Eli was just poking around the fancy suite he'd been assigned – two bathrooms! He couldn't imagine what he'd ever need two bathrooms for – when the knock came at his door. On the other side he found, unsurprisingly, Taylor. She didn't look happy.

Stalking to the middle of the room, she put down a black plastic ovoid and pressed a button on top. It glowed red briefly, and Eli felt a sudden sensation, as if waiting for his ears to pop.

"Baffle," Taylor explained. "Black market. CID's is fine, but when they're the ones you don't want listening in, well..." She shrugged.

"I'm guessing you're not here to discuss the finer points of–"

"What the hell part of 'let me do the talking' were you finding it difficult to interpret?" Taylor snapped, her blue eyes taking on a shade of the electric. "Or do you really just love the sound of your voice that much?"

"Hey, she made Tapper," Eli shot back. "She poked a hole through our cover like it was a wet paper towel; there was no way we were going to convince her we were legit after that. For chrissakes, commander, she's on our side. And it sure seems like we could use someone in our corner."

Taylor was gritting her teeth, but Eli could tell that at least part of his argument was hitting home. Truth be told, he wasn't quite sure himself where all that crap he had spewed earlier had come from, but he guessed he must have picked up at least some of it from watching Kovalic operate. Either way, his instincts had paid off.

Arms crossed, Taylor tapped her fingers, then let out a pent-up sigh. "Just try and let me know next time you decide you're going to start throwing curveballs. We're a team, and we have to work like one."

"I'm sorry," said Eli, raising his hands in surrender. "Didn't mean to step on your toes. I saw an opportunity and went for it."

Running a hand through her hair, Taylor unraveled the braid, letting it drape to her neck. "Sounds like Simon's been rubbing off on you." When she spoke again, it was in a grudging tone. "It was a good play. This thing could have been over before it started. So, well... nice job."

Wow. That must have stung.

"Hey," he said with a grin. "That was all Elias Adler in there."

"Glad to hear it. Because the next time *Elias Adler* talks over me while I'm working, he's going to have to figure out how to pilot a ship with three broken fingers." She smiled sweetly. "Got it?"

Eli swallowed. "Got it." Something told him three broken fingers would be getting off easy.

"Good," said Taylor. "Anyway, don't let your success go to your head. Our foot may be in the door but we've still got a lot of work to do."

"Speaking of which," Eli said, crossing to a chair and sitting down. "What's our next move? This meeting is supposed to be happening–" his eyes rolled back in his head as he tried to keep track of the time change, "–tomorrow?" That seemed right. "I'm still not sure how we're supposed to get in on a powwow between a highly-ranked Corporation official and an Imperium envoy."

Taylor crossed to the armchair opposite him and took a seat of her own. "Well, a private meeting might raise flags, especially if the envoy is high profile. So, if the Illyricans are smart they'll make contact at some public event, where the two just *happen* to cross paths."

"Such as?"

"A party or other social function, if I had to guess."

Eli mouthed an *ah*. "So that's where Elias Adler comes in."

Taylor smiled, her teeth gleaming. "Mr Adler attends only the most *exclusive* soirées, of course."

"So all we have to do is find out where the social event of the season is?"

"Shouldn't be too hard. The deputy consul may already have a bead on some of them."

"The who?" said Eli, cupping a hand around his ear. "I must have misheard; I could have sworn you said *the deputy consul*."

"Don't push it, Brody," Taylor growled.

"OK, OK!"

Standing, Taylor smoothed her skirt. "Now, if there's nothing further, *Mr Adler*, I'll just be on my way. It's been a long trip, and I'm sure you'd care to refresh yourself."

Come to think of it, a nap did sound pretty good. Despite dozing during the trip, he was feeling pretty beat – besides, a cockpit was no place to take a comfortable snooze. The extravagant estate-sized mattress they'd provided him with certainly looked far more alluring.

"Yeah," said Eli. "Wake me when it's time for breakfast – they do breakfast here, right?"

Taylor shook her head. "Shut up and go to sleep, Brody." The door closed behind her.

Eli collapsed onto the bed, which, as it turned out, was just as soft and yielding as he'd imagined. In fact, he was pretty sure it was the most comfortable bed he'd ever slept on in his entire life. *Enjoy it while you can,* he thought, *because tomorrow shit gets real.*

Wormhole time-lag played funny tricks on your head, so by the time Eli headed downstairs it was just past seven in the morning, local time. At home, he preferred to sleep in, but when he woke to the insistent whirring of the climate control, something told him that Elias Adler would be an early riser. So he roused himself from bed, hit the shower, picked out one of the suits that had been packed for him – after futzing with the cufflinks; cufflinks! – and stepped into the hall, still rubbing the sleep out of his eyes.

From what he'd read in the pre-mission briefing, the Commonwealth embassy wasn't particularly large: just three stories tall, it housed around seventy-five people, including the ambassador's personal staff, a dozen diplomatic functionaries, a team of security officers, and the attendant administrative personnel.

It was one of the latter that met him, smiling, as he came down the stairs into the embassy's lobby. The young man – younger than Eli himself, unless he missed his guess – gestured towards a pair of double doors to his left.

"Good morning, Mr Adler. The ambassador is breakfasting in the ballroom and has requested the pleasure of your company at his table."

Crap. By instinct, he'd frozen, but since Elias Adler would never freeze in such a situation, he forced a smile onto his face and pushed his foot leadenly forward. "Thank you," someone else said through his mouth, "it'd be my pleasure."

With a nod to the attendant, he turned and pushed open the doors, stepping into the ballroom.

It was a big room, clearly built to accommodate crowds of several hundred or more, all in relevant extravagance. A dozen or so round tables with immaculate white tablecloths stood carefully arranged, the center of each adorned with a centerpiece of flowers that Eli was fairly certain weren't fake. At the front of the room was a long, rectangular table – the kind that might be used at a banquet or speech – and at one side of it were arrayed the room's only inhabitants.

There were only a half dozen of them, but if there had been twenty Eli would have had no problem picking out the Commonwealth's ambassador to Bayern. Theodore Khan was a big man, built like a player for the kind of sport that involved hitting people. *Full contact diplomacy.* His hair had gone shock white, contrasting with skin the color of coffee with milk stirred in. He laughed at something one of his breakfast partners said, a deep full-throated sound, and replied in an equally deep basso profundo.

Straightening his collar, Eli pressed ahead. The ambassador, catching sight of him out of the corner of one eye, put his napkin on the table and rose, extending a hand.

"Mr Adler," he said, his voice booming in the large space. "Welcome. Please, join us." Eli blinked as he motioned to his companions, and they slid down, making a space at the ambassador's left hand. "We don't stand on ceremony here," said the ambassador at his expression. "And I like to get a chance to talk to everybody who comes through my shop."

Eli nodded smoothly. "Thank you, Mr Ambassador." He'd been carefully coached on exactly how one addresses an ambassador, a place where his former military training served him well to some degree. This, at least, he'd get right.

"Please," said the ambassador, with a wide gleaming smile, "call me Theo."

He narrowly avoided biting his tongue as he slid into the seat. *So much for protocol.*

"So, Mr Adler – Elias?"

"Eli, sir."

He waved at the sir, as if batting away a pesky insect. "Theo."

"Theo."

He smiled broadly at that. "Eli. You've had quite a bit of success for a man of your age."

Eli laughed. *The man's frank – you have to admire that.* "Moderately successful," he said, making a so-so gesture with his hand.

"Come, come. You're too modest. I looked you up when I saw you'd be joining us. A tycoon before thirty? Cornering the market on hypodynamic reflux assemblies?"

Oh god, he may actually know what that means, thought Eli, stricken. He'd spent a while during their trip reading up on the very real products of the very fictional Adler Industries, but had found himself drifting off to sleep and drooling all over the ship's console. Hypodynamic reflux assemblies were a key component of repulsor coils, the anti-gravity systems that kept afloat everything from cargo containers to ships. The hope had been it would be sufficiently obscure to escape notice. Of course if the ambassador were a closet engineering groupie – Eli couldn't believe they existed, but logically speaking, he supposed they must – then all bets were off.

"Right place, right time, I guess," he said.

The ambassador opened his mouth to press on, but Eli was saved from further exposition by another attendant materializing at his side.

"We have a fully stocked kitchen," said the ambassador. "Order whatever you like."

Eli looked up at the server. "Two eggs, over easy. Side of toast, bacon – well-done?"

With a silent nod, they shimmered off, to the kitchen, Eli supposed.

"I trust your trip was smooth?" said Khan.

"Everything except the landing," said Eli, as a waiter put a fresh glass of water on the table in front of him.

"Ah, yes," said the ambassador, leaning back in his chair and scrutinizing Eli. "I understand that you piloted yourself?"

"It's a hobby," said Eli, taking a sip of water. "So few chances to really get your hands dirty these days."

"Too true," Khan sighed. "I like to engage in a little rock-climbing myself, when I can get away. To the immense *displeasure* of my staff." He raised his eyebrows significantly. "Perhaps you'd care to join me while you're here? I'm sure arrangements could be made in the name of my duties as a host – though, strictly speaking, Consul Gennaro would be your actual host." The ambassador waved a meaty hand. "I'm sure she wouldn't mind sharing you."

High-level political wrangling. I don't remember this being in the job description. Wait… was there a job description?

"That's a very generous offer, sir," said Eli. "I'll have to have a word with my director of public relations and see if we can fit it into the schedule."

"Of course, of course," said Khan, with a smile that looked plenty genuine by politicians' standards. He took a muffin from his plate and split it open; steam rose from its interior. "We are all beholden to our responsibilities, are we not?"

Eli was saved from answering by the arrival of his breakfast. One area the embassy had clearly not skimped on was its kitchen budget; no doubt that was a necessity when hosting foreign dignitaries. The eggs were perfectly cooked, still hot, and the bacon was just as crispy as he'd hoped. *I could get used to this.*

A discreet clearing of the throat came from behind him as a forkful of eggs was en route to his mouth. He slowly craned his neck and saw the disapproving face of deputy consul M'basa staring down at him. *She looks grumpy. Maybe she hasn't eaten yet. Breakfast is the most important meal of the day.*

"Good morning," he said cheerfully.

"Mr Adler," she said, with a tight nod. "Mr Ambassador."

"Sarah!" he said. "Pull up a chair and join us. Mr Adler and I were just talking about hobbies. I believe you fence, if I recall."

"In school," she said, her eyes flicking back and forth between the two of them.

"And highly ranked, too, if my memory serves. You should have a word with my older daughter; she's starting college next year, and expressed some interest in taking it up."

"I'd be happy to, Mr Ambassador. Now, if you'll excuse me, I need to have a word with Mr Adler."

"But I just got my breakfast," Eli protested.

"It'll only take a moment," said M'basa, rolling her eyes.

Eli gave a forlorn look at the remaining egg. Snatching the second strip of bacon, he bit off a piece as he rose and followed M'basa to one of the other tables in the ballroom.

"I assume everything is to your *liking*," she said.

"Quite," said Eli, the bacon melting in his mouth. "What's up?"

"I thought you might be interested to know that the Illyrican embassy is having an intimate reception this evening."

"Good for them," Eli said, glancing over his shoulder at his rapidly cooling breakfast.

"Ms Mulroney sent me a message that you might be interested in the premiere events on the social calendar. To maintain your cover." She eyed him.

"What?" he said, snapping back to her. "Oh, right."

M'basa sighed and rubbed at her forehead. "Jesus, Adler. You fresh off the ranch?"

"I got it, I got it," he said. "Party at the Illyrican embassy tonight. I'll put it on the agenda."

"I called in a few favors and wrangled you two invitations," said M'basa, holding up a pair of cards. "But," she said, jabbing a finger in Eli's direction, "now *you* owe *me*."

"Uh. Got it. Thank... you?" He reached out and took the cards, pulling firmly to wrest them from M'basa's grip. "Your cooperation is most appreciated."

The woman gave him a not altogether friendly smile, turned on her heel and walked away. Eli glanced at the cards: off-white, printed on heavy-duty stock, with flowing black calligraphy engraved on it: *The Illyrican Empire requests the pleasure of your company...*

He shook his head and let out a long breath. *Who'd have thought the Illyrican Empire would ever invite me anywhere again?* He slipped the invitations into his suit's inside pocket and then returned to the ambassador's table.

Eli was allowed to finish his breakfast without further interruption, which he did mostly in silence as the ambassador was quickly whisked away by his staff to see to some important matter or other. Even cold, the food was still better than the fare he'd been subsisting on back in his apartment on Nova, which mainly consisted of single-serving meals he could pop in the auto-oven.

He was still drinking the last of his expertly-brewed coffee when he left the ballroom to be greeted by Tapper's thousand-yard stare. The sergeant was leaning against the wall opposite the door, arms crossed, with an expression of one who'd fought his way through a platoon of Illyricans to claim this spot.

"Mr Adler," he said, through gritted teeth. "I hope you had a good breakfast."

"Uh. Yes?"

"Glad to hear it." He pushed off the wall and grabbed Eli's arm in a polite-looking but all too solid grip. "We'd be most *obliged* if you'd let us know exactly where you were going."

"It was breakfast!" Eli protested. "The ambassador invited me!"

"Oh, the *ambassador* invited you," said Tapper, rolling his eyes as he escorted him back toward the stairs. "Well, in that case, don't let me interfere with your hobnobbing. But if you're finished with that, do you think you could spare Ms Mulroney and myself a minute of your precious time?"

"Suuuure?"

"Great."

They climbed to the second floor and knocked at a door that, even by its outward appearances, was somewhat less grand than Eli's accommodations. *Perks of being a somebody, I guess.* Taylor answered it almost immediately, then waved them in. Eli noted the baffle sitting on the coffee table, already glowing away.

"You've been making friends fast," said Taylor, sitting down in one of the room's chairs. As Eli had anticipated, it was far more modest than his own quarters – nice enough, but it looked more like a spaceport hotel. There was a double bed, the two chairs and the coffee table, and a small sliding door that Eli guessed led to a bathroom. *Hey, could be worse: at least she doesn't have to share with anybody.*

"What can I say?" Eli shrugged. "I'm a people person."

"Uh huh. Well, we've got more pressing matters than being wined and dined at the ambassador's table, Brody." A note of stress had crept into Taylor's voice, maybe the first time Eli had seen a crack in her professional veneer. "The meeting between the Illyricans and the Corporation is happening in a matter of hours, and we still don't know where." She shook her head. "We miss this, and I don't know when our next opportunity will be."

"All under control," said Eli, spreading his hands and perching on the end of the bed, which either had not been slept in or had been re-made with military precision. Neither of those would have surprised him.

"Under control?" Taylor echoed.

"I just happen to have a pair of invitations to this evening's most exclusive shindig," said Eli, reaching into his jacket pocket and producing the cards. "I thought maybe you two might be interested?" He held them out to her. "I mean, if you're right about them meeting at some sort of social event, this seems like the perfect occasion."

Tapper and Taylor exchanged a glance, and the latter plucked them out of his hand. Eli leaned back and grinned. "Not bad for my first day on the job, if I do say so myself."

Scanning the cards rapidly, Taylor tapped them against the palm of her hand, then looked up. "Not bad, Brody. Not bad at all. I suppose we're going to have to adjust the schedule for today."

"Why's that?" said Eli.

She tilted her head. "To get you fitted for a tuxedo, of course."

"Who, me?"

"Yes, *Mr Adler*. You. Don't think you can go to a formal state event dressed like you just rolled out of the cockpit." She looked him up and down. "Should have thought to bring formalwear, but there's not a huge call for it these days."

"I just assumed…" He looked at Tapper, but the sergeant was clearly enjoying himself. *Laugh it up, old man.*

"Sorry, Brody," said Tapper putting his hands up. "Not my scene. Maybe the embassy's security team will lend me a van. You two crazy kids have fun."

"You can't be serious," said Eli, staring at them each in turn. "In case it's escaped your memory, I'm a fugitive from the Imperium. You want me to stroll into their embassy and chat up a bunch of government officials?"

Taylor smiled. "I thought you might say that. Lucky for you, the general came up with a solution. We obviously can't change your fingerprints or your retinal patterns or your face–"

"What's wrong with my face?"

"–but we managed to get into the Illyricans' central database and replace your biodata with dummy information. Take a look." She tapped something on her sleeve and a holoscreen sprung to life between them.

Brody, Elijah Hamish, he read, followed by his birthdate, his presumed date of death at Sabaea, and a few other salient details about his life: birthplace, education history, and the like. But when his eyes went to the picture next to it, he had to blink and look again. "That's not me."

"Sharp as a tack, he is," said Tapper under his breath.

Taylor shrugged. "But it fits the description."

"Wait, that's what you think I look like?"

Dismissing the screen, Taylor continued. "If the Illyricans

scan your fingerprints, your face, or even your gait, they won't come up with a match. Nobody's going to recognize you. Besides, Eli Brody is officially dead, remember? You're Elias Adler."

Eli rubbed his forehead. "I'm just saying: I like to think I've made a pretty good dead man so far, but I'd prefer to avoid a repeat performance."

"Don't worry," said Tapper, patting his shoulder. "They're hardly going to shoot you at an official gala."

"Right," said Eli.

"They'd probably use poison," Tapper said cheerfully. "Just don't eat or drink anything and you'll be fine."

Cradling his hands in his head, Eli sighed. *Maybe I can put in for hazard pay.*

"Brody."

Eli looked up to find Taylor eyeing him; for once, the commander's expression didn't look like she was going to chastise him for something. She smiled, and this time it went all the way to her eyes. "It's a party, not a dogfight. No big deal."

Right. No big deal. He exhaled. *I can do this.*

Looking at the rest of his team, he nodded. "OK. Let's go shopping."

CHAPTER 10

Kovalic's eyes slid open. Air blew on his face from a vent high above, the recycled smell universal to spacecraft, spacesuits, space stations. The reassuring thrum, pervasive but muffled, of engines working somewhere deep below him. The shuttle's lights were dimmed, which jibed with his internal clock's impression that they still had a couple hours left in their flight. Inter-system travel was time-consuming in general, but Bayern at least was reasonably close to Nova; the whole trip only took about twelve hours start-to-finish.

Shifting in the cramped seat, he sighed and worked at his injured shoulder, which had gone stiff during the flight. Much as he'd like to drift back to sleep, he knew himself well enough to realize that there was no way that was going to happen once his brain was up and running. The time-lag of the trips could seriously screw you up if you weren't used to it. It might be a twelve-hour trip, but the local-time of your destination often bore no sensible relation to your departure point. He'd left Nova in the afternoon; he wouldn't land on Bayern until early evening of what would technically be the next day. It must have been a heck of a lot easier when there was just one planet with its own rotational period to worry about.

His thoughts wandered to the information he'd been given; the general had sent him a brief of the report from CARDINAL, although the old man had clearly taken pains to obfuscate the asset's identity. Even without knowing the exact provenance, Kovalic's gut was inclined to agree with the general's assessment: SPT's mission on Bayern and CARDINAL's intelligence were no coincidence. Even on the off chance that they *were*, they certainly couldn't afford to treat it as such. The first priority, then, was to find Nat and the team and pass on the information. Then he could decide whether to abort or...

He rubbed his forehead. *Nat* could decide whether to abort. Not him. It wasn't his mission; the general had been clear on that. On this job, he was little more than a glorified courier. He flexed his fingers on the armrests. Of course, that didn't mean it was easy to turn off twenty years of training and instinct, which were telling him that something much bigger was going on here, and that if they didn't get to the bottom of it there was going to be some serious reckoning down the road.

Sighing, he touched a control on the armrest and a holoscreen sprung into existence in front of him. Slipping in a pair of earpieces, he tapped them on and began flipping through channels.

Live programming on an inter-system trip was difficult, to say the least; a wormhole jump often sent you hundreds or thousands of light years away, so unless you were prepared to wait a century or two for whatever show you'd been watching to catch up, it was probably better to tune into the local stations.

From the selection on the holoscreen, it was clear they'd already jumped into the Bayern system. Financial news from across the galaxy was the order of the day; the latest market figures from Bayern along with the latest figures from other worlds – beamed in by fast couriers on wormhole runs – ticked across the bottom of the screens so rapidly that trying to read them was like sticking your fingers into a waterfall.

Snatches of audio blared in his ears, a mélange of different voices, sounds, music, most not really registering until he'd already flipped away.

"… to buy rival company…"

"… denied allegations that he was involved in…"

"… up on rumors that the trade in…"

"… economy. Bleiden died two…"

"… the latest craze among the fashion-conscious…"

Kovalic sat forward, his fingers scrabbling for the control panel. Flipping back a channel he hit the pause button and then jumped back as far as the entertainment system's buffer would allow. It was a talking head program, with a bland face staring into the holo-camera and jawing on about the topics of the day, but it was the subject matter, not the host, that had caught Kovalic's attention.

"… the Illyrican mark has dropped in after-hours trading, as the market continues to react to the sudden death of Albert Bleiden, the Imperium's Permanent Undersecretary for Trade and Commerce, who was largely thought to be a guiding force in the Illyrican economy. Bleiden died two days ago of a sudden illness. He was fifty-seven. In other news, the sixteenth annual Bayern dog show is about to get underway here in Bergfestung…"

With a roll of his eyes, Kovalic tapped the mute button. It appeared Bleiden's death was already reaching the end of its news cycle, and he very much doubted that any further useful information would come to light – the Imperium would have made sure of that.

Still, there was nothing that irked him more than a botched job. If only they had been a little bit sharper, a little bit more on their game, maybe they could have saved Bleiden and gotten *all* the information he wanted to pass along. No question: it had been a screw-up of near epic proportions.

And that wasn't even considering Jens' death.

A wave of fatigue washed over Kovalic, as though his batteries had suddenly run down. Forcing open the lead weights that his eyelids seemed to have become, he stared at the silent head bobbing in front of him on the screen. It didn't get any easier, even after almost two decades of leading people into battle. You never got used to losing someone – and as hard as that was, he wouldn't have had it any other way. The day he walked away from it feeling fine was the day that he'd start to get worried.

Toggling to the map, he watched a little icon of the shuttle follow an arcing line through the blackness of space towards the blue dot that represented their destination. The white digits of the clock ticked away underneath: confirming they had about two hours before landing on Bayern.

If sleep weren't forthcoming, he supposed he ought to do something productive. Pulling out his secure tablet, he flipped it on and started reading the background documents he'd brought with him. He'd always been able to trust his gut, and this time it was telling him that he was probably going to have to hit the ground running.

The background files on Bayern, the Imperium, and the current geopolitical situation proved to be interesting reading. Enough that the last two hours of Kovalic's trip passed in a blur of facts and figures. He'd read all the reports of the

Bayern station chief, Karl Rao, and, more importantly, he'd recognized a familiar name listed as Rao's recently assigned number two. If nothing else, he knew where he'd be starting his inquiries.

Clearly, this wasn't the shuttle pilot's first time braving the somewhat treacherous winds and weather of Bayern, for the landing was smooth and quick. Not half an hour after their landing, Kovalic had passed through customs – well, "James Austen" had, anyway – and was already descending towards the city floor, gazing out across the enormous cavern of Bergfestung. Objectively, he could appreciate the amazing feat of engineering that had gone into creating it, but he'd long since gotten over his awe.

It wasn't Kovalic's first trip to Bayern. Granted, there weren't a lot of planets he *hadn't* been to, especially over the last five years as the galactic conflict had gone from hot war to cold. Every planet was different, of course, but it was the little idiosyncrasies and cultural differences that he found the most interesting: the Hanif, for example, had a complex set of ritual greeting phrases and responses – mess that up, and you'd never really be treated like an equal. On Centauri, it was considered the height of impoliteness to hold a door for a woman. In the Kingdom of Haran, one did not acknowledge another's sneeze.

In other words, it was a lot to keep straight.

On Bayern, though, there was one simple rule – payment cured all ills. And there were only two types of currency that were worth anything at all: information and shares.

Information was simple enough, of course: if you knew something that the other person didn't – or, even better, if you knew something *no one* else did – you could command a hefty price. Which might be a commensurate piece of information or, alternatively, shares.

Trading information on Bayern wasn't necessarily much different than anywhere else, but shares... shares were distinctly Bayern. Not in and of themselves, per se, since corporations had existed for centuries, but in that they were used for purchasing everything from extra foodstuffs to entertainment to a better home.

Everyone on Bayern eighteen or older was an employee of the Corporation – but, they were also a shareholder, which made them part owner of the company as well. When a child was born, a certain amount of shares were set aside for them (an amount that could be supplemented by a limited bequeathment from parents, other relatives, friends, and so on), but those shares were held by proxy – usually the parents – until the age of majority was reached. At that point, they became full voting shareholders in perpetuity. As a result, the Corporation strictly controlled its population rate; at death, the majority of the deceased's shares were returned to the corporation to be distributed anew.

The Corporation took care of most infrastructure and societal needs for its employees – living quarters, food, healthcare, childcare, and so on – but, the Corporation being what it was, you could always find more luxurious offerings, if you were willing to pay.

This had the side effect of making things somewhat more difficult for off-worlders. Never one to miss out on a financial opportunity, however, the Corporation had come up with a solution. After arriving on planet, a quick trip to any of the automated currency exchange stations would let visitors draw funds from their off-world bank accounts and convert them into a line of credit – in Class B, non-voting shares – at Bayern's central bank; those shares were tightly controlled in number, so their exchange value fluctuated like any other currency. If you already had an account at Bayern's central bank, the process was even easier.

Kovalic had several. Banking and finance were a huge part of the Corporation's interests both at home and abroad, and they treated data security and privacy intensely seriously. It was virtually impossible to get information on an account or its holder from the Corporation – a fact that Kovalic could vouch for personally. Investigations that led back to a Bayern bank account were almost always a dead end.

But, when you were yourself an operative who relied on secrecy and discretion, at least that cut both ways.

Kovalic exited the elevator at the city floor. The lighting conduits around the cavern had dimmed for the evening cycle, lending a peaceful air to the city. A currency exchange station was located – for his convenience, of course – right by the base of the elevator.

Stepping up, he punched in an ID code and PIN, then allowed the retinal scanner to get a good look at his eye. The screen flashed green and a line of text appeared: WELCOME BACK, MR TROLLOPE. Using a separate identity for the bank accounts was an extra layer of security and, fortunately, Bayern's stance on data privacy meant nobody would link it to the ID he'd used to get onworld.

He tapped Check Balance: fifty thousand shares and change. That was a pretty good amount – enough to buy a nice hovercar. The SPT kept a big chunk of its discretionary operations fund here, as Bayern's central bank had a reputation that allowed them to draw money on almost any planet in the known galaxy without having to sign off on pesky forms and paperwork.

And it was just as useful on Bayern itself. He had the

machine dispense him a secure payment card with a direct link to the account, locked to purchases of no more than a thousand shares at a time. Not quite as good as cold, hard cash, but it was the closest there was on Bayern.

Thus equipped, he set out towards the Commonwealth embassy, wending his way down roads where the streetlights were just starting to come on for the evening. The daylight cycles were usually timed to coincide with those outside, except in the summer or winter when the days got exceptionally long or short. It gave a nice feeling of normalcy, despite the fact that Bayern's rotational period was, at twenty-six hours, slightly longer than Earth standard. There'd been attempts to reconcile all the various days and times on the planets using a proposed Galactic Standard Time, but all the nitty gritty details just ended up leading to endless wrangling. Plus, the Illyricans had little interest in joining any common agreement, so standardizing the galaxy was pretty much a lost cause.

Still, humans needed nights and days to function and live healthily, and the Corporation was all about happy and productive workers.

Navigating Bergfestung's streets was easy enough: the city had been laid out in a series of concentric rings, with the Corporation's headquarters, an impressively giant edifice of glass and steel that climbed towards the opening at the top of the volcanic cone, at its center. Locating a particular building was a simple matter of finding the ring and sector. The embassies were mostly in Bergfestung's central rings, close to the Corporation's headquarters, so Kovalic hopped one of the hubward trams and took the five-minute ride to the city center.

The tram deposited him a scant minute's walk from the

Commonwealth embassy, a fenced-off building in a neo-classical style, supplemented by a decidedly non-classical armed marine out front. Kovalic made his way up to the sentry, a young woman with a teak wood complexion and watchful eyes.

"Sir," the guard said. Her eyes assessed him, but she didn't loosen the grip on her weapon. "Can I help you?"

"I hope so," said Kovalic, donning his best innocent-traveler-abroad expression. "I just arrived on world from Nova and I was told when I arrived to speak to an official here. A Ms M'basa?"

"And your name, sir?"

"James Austen."

"One moment." The guard turned aside, murmuring into her sleeve.

If he'd had the time before leaving Nova, he could have had the general push through an actual meeting request which would have made this a lot easier. But as it was, he'd have to bank on the fact that M'basa, like any good spy, had a curious mind.

The guard looked back at him. "Do you have some ID, Mr Austen?"

"Of course," said Kovalic, producing his completely hundred-percent genuine fake Commonwealth ID card and handing it over. He smiled pleasantly as the marine compared his face to the picture on the card and checked the cryptographic seal. Nodding, the marine handed the card back then gestured him through the gate.

"Straight through there to the main desk. They'll give you a visitor badge and escort you to the deputy consul."

Kovalic tried to avoid raising his eyebrows. Deputy consul was a position usually reserved for the station chief, not a number two – he didn't recall seeing that in the mission briefing. He thanked the marine, and followed her directions into the embassy.

It took only a minute for the man at the desk to give him a plastic ID badge, which he clipped to his front pocket. Signing in on the register, he waited until a low-level embassy official collected him. Kovalic was led through the plushly-carpeted halls, up the stairs, through a security door, and then to a small office with the nameplate "Sarah M'basa."

His escort knocked on the door, and at an assent from within, ushered Kovalic inside.

M'basa's office was pleasant, if businesslike. The desk had a secure terminal and was littered with flimsies and other detritus of the job. A pair of tall shelves were adorned with a couple photos and a handful of knickknacks – a trophy from what looked like a fencing team, an abstract sculpture of green and blue glass – and a few books.

Next to a large window, which looked out on the embassy's internal courtyard, was a comfortable-looking sofa. On one end sat M'basa, studying a tablet that was laid on her knees. She looked up as Kovalic entered, a flash of recognition – though not, Kovalic noticed, surprise – crossing her face.

Issuing a small laugh, she shook her head. "Really, it was only a matter of time before you turned up, I suppose." She waved to Kovalic's escort. "That'll be all, thanks."

Kovalic raised an eyebrow as the door closed behind him. "Oh?"

"I meant with the rest of your team here."

"I don't know what you–"

M'basa rolled her eyes. "Come on, Fielding. Austen. Whoever you are. I recognized your man – the old, grumpy one. It wasn't too much of a jump to figure out that Adler and Mulroney were part of your little outfit. Which, by the way, I'm apparently *still* not cleared to know even exists, even as station chief."

So she *was* station chief. That was new. "I couldn't possibly comment on that."

"Of course not. So, should I bother asking what you want now? I hope it's not another van – that first one was hard enough to get signed out from the motor pool."

"Nothing like that," Kovalic said, covering his curiosity. He wasn't sure what Nat had needed a van for, but he wasn't here to backseat drive. Just to pass on the general's message and then get out of Nat's hair. "I'm just here to check in. Things are going smoothly, I take it?"

M'basa cocked her head to one side, a slight frown creasing her mouth. "Smoothly enough," she allowed. "Granted, I'm not sure how much trouble they could get into at a cocktail party."

Kovalic gave her a bland smile, trying to adjust to the bizarre feeling of someone else knowing more about his team's movements than he did. "You'd be surprised."

Drumming her fingers on her leg, M'basa continued to frown. "What *are* you doing here?"

"Me? Like I said, just–"

"Checking in, right. I got that. I mean your team. I'm not thrilled about letting you guys run amok around town."

"You sound like a station chief already."

M'basa rolled her eyes. "I used to think my old bosses were stick-in-the-muds, but let's just say I've started to gain a healthy respect for their… stickiness."

Trying to keep the frown off his face occupied Kovalic's foremost brain cells as he gave a careful nod, but the rest of his mind was taking in everything M'basa had said. A van. A cocktail party. M'basa as station chief. None of this had been in the briefing the general had given him, which either meant he had deliberately withheld information – not impossible – or that he simply hadn't known. Neither would have surprised Kovalic, but he was betting on the second; situations on the ground had a way of being, well, fluid.

"I presume your vans have a tracking system?"

"Naturally," said M'basa. "Top of the line, and almost undetectable."

In Kovalic's experience, the boffins at R&D tended to describe every piece of equipment they produced as "almost" something – indestructible, infallible, undetectable. That was pretty much shorthand for "until it isn't."

"Good. If you'd be kind enough to provide me with their current whereabouts, I'd like to touch base with them."

"And you can't just call them?"

"Covert operations and all that."

"Uh huh. I'd ask you for your authorization, but given that this whole 'covert operation' has been off-book from the start, I'm guessing that would be a complete and utter waste of time – yours and mine."

Kovalic grinned. "You're starting to get the hang of this."

"That's what worries me," M'basa sighed.

CHAPTER 11

Eli had been to a cocktail party. Once.

It had been held in advance of his graduation from the Imperial Academy, and all the top brass had been invited. The academy's ballroom had been resplendent: chandeliers gleaming, tables lined with exquisite food and drink, formalwear-clad waitstaff everywhere.

So he'd put on the crimson-and-black dress uniform of an Imperial cadet and mingled. Not so much with the brass, of course, who were mainly from the upper echelons of Illyrican society, but with his friends from the academy – except, of course, for those friends who were *from* the upper social echelons. He'd gotten a bit too drunk on Sevastapol vodka, and he was pretty sure that he had hit on a pretty girl from his avionics class before passing out on a couch in one of the upstairs hallways. Not, perhaps, the most illustrious evening he'd ever spent.

The affair at the Illyrican embassy made *that* party look like a barbecue down at the local firepit. The amount of jewelry on display could probably have bought his home planet of Caledonia, moons and all. Dresses swooped every which way and more than a few of the dinner jackets made his carefully but hastily tailored suit look like a shirt with a picture of a tuxedo plastered on the front.

Eli held out the invitations M'basa had given him to the man at the front gate. The gray-haired fellow, who looked like he could have been a venerable lord in his own right, handed them in turn to a young woman at his right, then waved at another man – this one roughly the size of a small tree – who stepped forward, holding a handheld scanner.

"Good evening, sir. Madam," said the older man, inclining his head. "Just a security precaution. How may I introduce you?"

The man with the scanner held it up and squinted at Eli through a viewport. Frowning, he shifted it up and down, then left to right.

Eli cleared his throat, and tried to will the sweat on his forehead from dripping into his eyes. "Mr Elias Adler of Terra Nova."

The older man gave him an expectant look; when Eli didn't respond, his eyes shifted. "And your companion, sir?"

A white-gloved grip tightened on his arm, and he looked at the woman attached to it. Somehow, as out of place as he felt, Taylor looked exactly as though she belonged here. From the purple sheen of the satin dress, cut exactly to her fit, to the pile of elegantly coiffed hair on her head, she looked every inch the part. Teardrop diamond earrings dangled from her ears, coruscating in the light, while the trace amounts of rouge, lipstick, and mascara managed to show off all her best features without the slightest bit of tackiness. *Where the hell did she scrounge all that up? Or does she travel with it, just in case she has to go to a formal ball?*

The man holding the scanner gave her a once-over that was no less thorough, but still managed to maintain the decorum of professionalism. Apparently satisfied, he clicked the scanner off, nodded to the older man, and stepped back.

"Of course," said Eli, with perhaps a touch too much faux gallantry. "Ms Tara Mulroney, also of Terra Nova."

"Thank you," said the man, bowing. "Please, enjoy your evening."

A party at the Illyrican embassy on Bayern, surrounded by officials of state and the military? What's not to enjoy?

Eli returned the bow, and the two of them climbed the stairs to the embassy's foyer.

"So far, so good," murmured Taylor.

"Yeah, so far I only almost botched our *names*."

"Relax," said Taylor with a sideways look. "Try to have some fun. Tonight, you *are* Elias Adler. Nobody here has the slightest idea who Eli Brody is. Nor do they care. Besides, I'm the one who has to do all the heavy lifting."

That's right, Eli thought. *I'm just the distraction. Entertain guests with scintillating tales of being a rich playboy, while Taylor tries to figure out who the envoy is and what he's up to. Easy.*

They'd gone over the plan in detail, after getting Eli fitted for his tuxedo. He and Taylor would enter the party using the invitations, while Tapper waited around the block in the unmarked van that they'd borrowed from the embassy. The security scans had been anticipated, so the team would keep communications inactive until after they were in the embassy. The earbuds they were using shouldn't show up as long as they were off, or unless someone peered into their ears. And though security at an event like this one was certainly thorough, the upper classes usually didn't like being constantly poked and prodded – and what the upper classes didn't want had a tendency to not happen.

Once in, Eli would circulate, making small talk and picking up whatever interesting gossip he could, while

Taylor focused on identifying the prime candidates for the Illyrican envoy. If possible, she'd also slip away and see if she could access the embassy's network. Anything about the envoy was likely to be under heavy lock and key, but Taylor had just shrugged and said it would be worth checking out as long as they were there.

As they stepped into the embassy's front hall, which was lined with fresh vases, overflowing with flowers, Eli caught a flash of crimson and repressed a shiver. He'd been expecting officers in their dress uniforms – it was an Illyrican party after all – but he still hadn't quite gotten accustomed to seeing his former comrades-in-arms. If any of them knew he'd essentially deserted the Illyrican Navy – and worse, had joined the Commonwealth military – he imagined they'd have little hesitation about trussing him up and delivering him to a tribunal. That is, if they didn't shoot him on sight.

Of course, he was just one guy. And, like Taylor had said, nobody here had any idea who Eli Brody was. As far as anybody who *did* know him was concerned, he was dead and buried on Sabaea.

So why was he still so damn worried?

I am not going to be a liability. Not this time.

Taylor squeezed his arm twice and then let go, raising a hand to tuck a loose strand of hair behind her ear. A moment later, Eli did the same, feeling the hard, lacquered texture the gel had given it. He'd fought against the stuff, but Taylor had pushed him into a chair and threatened to demonstrate an advanced interrogation technique unless he let her do his hair. Really, it was only the latest in a line of indignities he'd suffered at the hands of his new colleagues.

He was sure Tapper had enjoyed every minute of it.

Speaking of whom. Under cover of the gesture, he

surreptitiously tapped the earbud in his left ear, causing it to beep to life. He turned to Taylor and gave her a smile, then squeezed his left cufflink.

"Nice party, isn't it?"

"It is at that," she said carefully.

"Well with gripping conversation like that, I can't imagine how it wouldn't be," came Tapper's voice, right in Eli's ear. "I read you both loud and clear. Everything's good here; you are go."

Eli would have preferred to keep an open line throughout the course of the evening; he had to admit that he felt more secure knowing that Tapper would be listening in, abrasive as the man could be. But Taylor and Tapper had vetoed the idea. A constant transmission would not only draw much more attention to them, but also make it easier for someone to intercept their signal and locate its source and destination. Instead, they'd use microbursts, triggering the comms only when necessary.

"Well, then," said Taylor. "Let's mingle. Keep your eyes peeled for Vallejo. She's the best lead we have to finding the Illyricans' envoy."

Eli bowed, making a broad sweep with his hand. "Please, after you."

The Illyrican embassy's ballroom was twice the size of the one Eli had breakfasted in at the Commonwealth embassy, and probably about ten times as extravagant. Chandeliers and candelabras in wall sconces provided bright illumination, while Eli's shoes sunk into a carpet so thick and luxurious that it was like a fur coat. Long oak side tables were draped in deep reds, golds, and blacks: the colors of the Illyrican royal house.

A tuxedo-clad waiter with a crimson bow tie appeared at their side, holding a silver platter that contained tiny little hors d'oeuvres, decorated in the shape of the Illyrican emblem.

Jesus. And to think this used to be my tax dollars at work.

Taylor smiled and took one, while Eli waved it off, unable to stop thinking about Tapper's advice not to eat or drink anything. *This is going to be one dull party if I can't even have a drink.*

A nudge from Taylor took him in the ribs. "That's Dubois, over there," she said with a tilt of her head.

Eli followed her indication to a stiff-looking black man, dressed in impeccable finery. He wore the uniform of an Illyrican Lord Admiral, his shoulders covered in gold epaulets adorned with a pair of crossed swords and the stylized hawk of the Imperial emblem. So many campaign ribbons covered his chest that Eli wondered if there was a battle the old man had missed.

Well, Sabaea, obviously, or he wouldn't be here. He'd heard of Dubois while at the academy; the man was a legend, having served beside the emperor when they were young men – he'd been part of the infamous Talons of the Hawk, the emperor's closest council of advisors. Later, he'd been appointed the head of the Imperial Navy, and then the Chief of Staff for the entire Illyrican military. Five years ago he'd retired, in the wake of the Imperium's ignominious defeat at Sabaea, a campaign of his own planning. In return for his years of service, he'd gotten a cushy appointment as the Illyrican ambassador to Bayern. Just luxurious enough to keep him living in the style to which he'd become accustomed, while far enough away from the center of Imperial power that it was conceivable he'd been punished.

Despite his age – his eyebrows and hair had gone ash gray – the man stood ramrod straight, and from the way his eyes tracked compatriots it was clear that his faculties were no less sharp for his removal from the field of battle. In some ways, Eli reflected, the man reminded him of the general. *Well, they're both Illyrican, so that's not too shocking.*

"You think the envoy will touch base with him?"

"I think that Dubois is the kind of guy who likes to know what's going on in his patch. He's worth keeping an eye on."

"I hope you don't expect me to introduce myself. My days of sticking my head in the lion's mouth are, well, never."

With a roll of her eyes, Taylor snagged a flute of champagne from a nearby tray, and with a too-sweet smile at Eli, latched herself onto a nearby group in animated conversation about the state of the galactic economy.

Eli sighed and picked up a glass as well, staring wistfully at it. *It's probably not poisoned, you idiot.*

"Vintage not to your taste?" said a voice from his side. "I can't blame you. Give me a good burgundy any day. But I suppose beggars can't be choosers."

The voice came attached, Eli discovered, to a middle-aged white man with short, thinning gray hair. In younger days, he'd probably been quite muscled, but the years had turned much of that to bulk, though Eli wasn't sure he'd call him fat. Certainly not to his face. He was about of a height with Eli, and there was something of a twinkle in his eye that made Eli think of a kindly uncle – the one that doesn't miss a trick, and wouldn't dream of selling you out.

"Cheers," said the man, raising his glass and taking a sip.

Eli raised his own glass. "I've... I'm afraid I've given up drinking."

"Really?" said the man, smacking his lips. "How terrible for you; I find I need at least a few rounds to get me through these tedious affairs." He paused, and looked somewhat abashed. "I'm sorry, that was insensitive, wasn't it?"

"Not at all," said Eli, trying on a wry smile. "But I have to admit, I feel out of place at one of these things if I'm *not* holding a drink."

"Ah, yes. Social conventions and necessities. Believe me, I completely understand."

"You go to a lot of these, then?"

"Afraid so."

"Any survival tips?"

The man pursed his lips. "Get to the food early, stay on the sides of the room, and – as much as possible – let everyone else do the talking."

Eli gave a judicious nod. "Wise council, sir."

"Harry Frayn," said the man, transferring his glass to his left hand and extending his right.

"Pleasure," said Eli, making the same switch. "Elias Adler." They exchanged a firm handshake.

"Nice to meet you, Mr Adler."

"Eli, please. Mr Adler is my father." Something about saying that tickled his funny bone.

"Eli. So what brings you here?"

"To Bayern or to these glorious surroundings?" Eli asked, waving his glass at the room at large.

"Either. Both," said Frayn with an indulgent smile.

"Business for both."

"Ah. And what line of business are you in?"

"The exciting world of repulsor coil technology. And now I'm sure you wish you'd picked someone else to talk to."

Frayn laughed pleasantly. "Not at all. You know, there was a time when I thought I'd become an engineer. Even went to school for it, but it turned out that I hadn't been blessed with much skill at maths – and by 'much' I mean 'any.'"

Eli allowed himself a small mental sigh of relief. *One of these times I'm not going to be so lucky.* "Me neither," said Eli. Which was true – math had been his biggest challenge at the academy. Despite computers that could make calculations in a fraction of the time – and with much more accuracy – than the human brain, there was still a fair amount of number work involved in piloting. "I'm mainly on the business side these days, anyway."

"Sad to say, I don't have much of a head for that either," said Frayn, laughing again.

"So what *do* you do, Mr Frayn?" said Eli. "Wait," he continued, lifting his glass-bearing hand to point at the man. "Let me guess." His eyes narrowed, sweeping up and down his conversation partner's attire.

Frayn's suit was cheap, that much he could tell. It fit as though it were designed for a slightly slimmer man. *Rental.* Plus, he was almost positive that the bow tie was a clip-on.

So, the question is: who wears a rental tuxedo to an embassy cocktail party? Especially when, by their own admission, they went to a lot of them. *Someone who doesn't make a lot of money.* That much was for certain. So, some sort of support staff? He'd be tempted to say military, but then the man would simply be in dress uniform; security was another guess, but he wasn't exactly cut from a formidable template. So probably some sort of diplomatic staff? But by all rights he should have his own tuxedo. *Unless this event caught him by surprise – as though he were dispatched hastily.* His pulse quickened.

"Am I that much of an enigma, Mr Adler?" said Frayn, his eyes amused.

Eli smiled in return and tried to tamp down on the adrenaline flooding his body. "A bit of a puzzle, I must admit. Civil servant?"

Frayn made an impressed noise. "Well done. Got it in one."

"What branch? I presume not accounting, from your admitted lack of mathematical facility?"

"That would be a cruel fate, indeed. No, I'm afraid it's much more boring than that. Paperwork, filing, forms filled in triplicate. That sort of thing." He smiled. "But, let's not talk about work." He glanced over Eli's shoulder. "Now that we've passed the polite small talk phase, I hope you'll pardon me for being so forward as to ask about that most striking woman you came in with."

Eli craned his neck, catching sight of Taylor talking with gusto to an assortment of folks wearing extremely expensive clothes indeed. She'd maneuvered herself to have a perfect view of the ambassador and the group he was talking to, which was mainly composed of other military officers.

"Ms Mulroney? She's my head of public relations."

Frayn shook his head. "You must do very good business."

"She's extremely talented. Honestly, I don't know where I'd be without her."

"Oh, I'm sure," said Frayn, taking another sip. "Well, I must ask you to introduce me before the evening's out."

Eli's mouth snapped shut. *Wait, is he asking for an* introduction *introduction? Like a man-to-woman introduction?* It hadn't taken Eli an advanced degree to conclude that there was unfinished business between Taylor and Kovalic, but a sudden vision of Kovalic's reaction came to mind, and he had to consciously stop himself from wincing. Still, the man was a civil servant and, unless Eli missed his guess, recently arrived on Bayern; if he wasn't the envoy himself – and wouldn't *that* be a stroke of unearned luck – maybe he was part of the envoy's staff? He could be a valuable source of information; Taylor would know what to do.

"I'm certain that could be arranged."

"Excellent. How about now?"

"Uh, now?"

"No time like the present," said the older man, raising his glass. "I can't think of anything that would enhance our conversation more than the company of a lovely woman. Can you?"

"I-I suppose not?" This was not going as planned. He could have really used Tapper's advice, but he couldn't think of a subtle way to ask him without excusing himself. And Frayn didn't seem the type to let go of an idea after he had hold of it. "Hold on just one sec, while I grab one of these… canapés," said Eli, seeing a passing waiter bearing a tray. He made a beeline for the hors d'oeuvres platter, surreptitiously reaching down to trigger his comm.

"Hey," he hissed, "this old guy wants me to introduce him to Tay… Tara. What the hell do I do?"

"She can hold her own, kid," Tapper's voice crackled over the comm. "Give me a call when he takes a shine to *you*."

"But–"

"Have fun, matchmaker. Out."

Eli sighed. *Then again, what was I expecting: something helpful?* Mournfully, Eli plucked an appetizer off a passing tray, and was about to pop it in when Tapper's admonishment came back to him. Instead, he cradled the tiny hawk-shaped arrangement of caviar and cracker in a napkin, and headed back to Frayn. The older man was waiting, his eyebrows raised.

"Uh, delicious," said Eli, raising the bite-sized morsel. "Really, you should try one. In fact, want mine?" He proffered it to the man, who raised a hand.

"Very kind of you, Mr Adler, but I'll pass."

With a shrug, Eli turned towards the last place he'd seen Taylor, only to find that she had departed that group. In fact, she was nowhere to be seen at all. *She's slipped away to hack the computers,* was his first thought. Which meant he needed to keep Frayn distracted for a little bit longer.

"So, you never mentioned what brought you to Bayern. I presume you've just arrived from… Illyrica?"

The man's eyes narrowed, then he laughed. "The accent is a dead giveaway, I suppose."

Eli smiled apologetically. "I've got an ear for them." Frayn's was a middle-class Illyrican accent – not the rarified tones of the upper crust, nor the rougher intonations of the working class. That fit nicely with the civil servant angle. And while his voice didn't have any of the distinctive tinges that came from those raised on the Illyrican colonies, it also made sense that a civil servant would be coming from the capital.

"Yours, though," Frayn was saying, waving his glass-bearing hand around, "is a little harder to place, Mr Adler. It's a fairly flat Galactic Standard, but do I detect a hint of the colonies?"

Goosebumps rose on Eli's arms, despite the warmth of the room. *Hoist by my own petard? I didn't even know I* had *a petard.* "A little bit," he admitted. "I was born on Caledonia, but my family emigrated before the war. I grew up on Terra Nova. So, I guess you could say my accent's a bit of a mutt."

Frayn made an "ah" with his mouth, nodding. "Very interesting. I'm not sure I would have guessed Caledonia, to be frank. It's usually more… distinctive."

"Yes. I found on occasion that it was a bit of a disadvantage to being taken seriously."

"A shame. You should never have to hide who you are."

Eli plastered a smile on his face, even as he tried to quell his racing heartbeat. *We're just making conversation here*, he reminded himself. *Nobody knows who Eli Brody is.*

"Your charming companion seems to have found herself some esteemed company," said Frayn, nodding at a spot behind Eli.

Turning, he caught a glimpse of Taylor, who had apparently just been hidden behind someone else. She'd negotiated her way into a circle that appeared comprised mainly of Illyrican military officers – and Ambassador Dubois.

"She does move fast," Eli muttered to himself.

"What?"

"Um, like I was saying – she's very good at her job."

"Of that I have no doubt," said Frayn, peering over at her. His eyes had taken on a speculative look once again, and Eli found there was something about it that racked his nerves just in the slightest. *This guy might just be a civil servant, but he's a sharp one.*

"Well, I wouldn't want to interrupt the ambassador," Eli began.

"Nonsense," said Frayn, "come along." He strode off towards the crowd.

This is not getting better, Eli thought, but he had little choice other than to trail along in Frayn's wake. His eyes scanned their path, hoping he could find a fire alarm to trigger or a waiter to accidentally bump into, but the distance was enough to require a conspicuous running tackle.

"...situation is entirely fluid," one graybeard general was saying as they got within earshot.

"I'd be surprised if these rabblerousers lasted beyond a week," put in another man, who wore the uniform of a naval admiral. "They can't possibly expect to hold any ground."

"Forgive my lack of knowledge," Taylor said, smiling at the others, "but I had heard reports that these self-styled 'freedom fighters' were quite well organized. Is that not so?"

"Propaganda," scoffed Dubois. "The Commonwealth put that forth to legitimize their own under-the-table support of the group."

Frayn didn't hesitate, but stepped right up to the circle around the ambassador, and smiled politely. Eli tried to conceal the mortification in his face, wondering what the hell this assortment of high-ranking military officials were going to think about a middle-aged man in a cheap suit ingratiating himself into the corridors of power.

"Pardon me for interrupting, Your Excellency," said Frayn, sketching a quick, rough bow, "but might I borrow Ms Mulroney here? I promise to return her in the same condition."

Eli glanced at Taylor, who was studiously avoiding his eyes. Her smile held, but it had lost some of its sincerity and he could almost swear that her face had gone just the slightest bit pale. *Maybe it's just the lights.*

To Eli's surprise, Dubois simply waved a hand. "Of course. A pleasure talking to you, Ms Mulroney."

"The pleasure was mine, Mr Ambassador. Gentlemen." She executed a flawless curtsy, then took the arm that Frayn offered her, laying her other hand near the crook of his elbow. The two of them strolled away, and Eli was left with little alternative but to fall into step with them.

"Now, now," Frayn chided quietly, when they'd moved far enough away from the ambassador's coterie. "I can't have you talking to diplomatic and military personnel *unsupervised*, can I, Natalie?"

"So nice to see you, Harry," said Taylor, her voice sandpaper dry. "I can say with some certainty that I didn't expect to see you here. Last I heard you were on Jericho Station."

"Oh, the life of a civil servant isn't his – or her – own; you know that as well as I."

Eli's mouth finally caught up with his brain. "Wait a second, what's going... with the... who?"

Frayn glanced over his shoulder at Eli, then shook his head. "This one's a bit new, isn't he? They just keep getting younger."

"We make do with what we have."

"Indeed we do. But it *is* nice to see you, Natalie. It's been too long – Hamza, wasn't it? Three years ago?"

"I believe you were trying to convince the Hanif that it was in their best interests to build ships for the Imperium."

"And you for the Commonwealth. Little surprise the Hanif decided that they'd like to stay out of it all. I can't blame them. By the way," said Frayn, as though it had just occurred to him. "I ran into Simon about three months ago – he was passing through Jericho. The poor fellow's still terribly hung up on you, you know."

Eli's eyes widened and jumped between the two. *This guy is* good.

Taylor raised an eyebrow, even as her grip tightened on Frayn's arm. "Your intelligence is taking a bit of a personal bent there, isn't it, Harry?"

The older man shrugged and smiled in apology. "Mostly we talk shop, but get a few cocktails in him and he *does* get a bit maudlin. Anyway, please do say hello for me."

"I'll pass it along next time I see him. He'll be glad to know that you seem to be doing well, despite not quite delivering on Dr Fleming's defection."

"Fair enough," said Frayn, nodding graciously. "Now. Detention and extraction requires diplomatic approval *and* four separate forms. You know how I hate filling out paperwork. So if you'll just take your... date... here and leave, we can put this whole thing behind us."

"*Will someone tell me what the hell is going on?*" Eli growled through clenched teeth.

Taylor smiled. "Eli, this is Colonel Harry Frayn of IIS. And I guess we were just leaving."

Idiot idiot idiot idiot. *Of all the people you could have talked to at this party, you picked the Illyrican intelligence officer.* It all made sense now: the cheap suit, the recent arrival, the "civil servant" excuse. Even the fact that Frayn had chosen to talk to him – he'd seen Eli come in with Taylor. Except Eli had been too dense to connect the dots. *So much for Eli Brody, superspy. Taylor's not going to let me live this one down.* He frowned, feeling the comm shift in his ear. *And Tapper's really not going to me live it down.*

"Nothing personal, of course," Frayn assured her. "I'd like nothing better than to catch up, but I can't have Commonwealth agents walking around an embassy function unimpeded. It just wouldn't be professional. You understand."

Taylor patted his arm. "Yes, Harry. Wouldn't want you to earn any more demerits on our account."

If that was intended as a slight, Frayn didn't rise to the bait. Their perambulations had taken them to the rear of the ballroom, where an open doorway let them back out into an embassy hallway, albeit one away from the bulk of the guests.

"Now," said Frayn, "if you'll just–"

He didn't get to finish his sentence before two men in crimson-and-gold uniforms stepped into the room through the very doorway they'd been about to use. Both were officers, Eli noted quickly – flight lieutenants, as he'd once been – and wore sidearms at their waists.

"Really, Harry?" said Taylor. "Armed guards?"

Frayn grimaced and ignored her, stepping up to the men. "Pardon me, lieutenant."

The man – a big, impressive sort – shook his head and spoke in a deep, gravelly voice. "Sorry, sir. Securing the perimeter; orders are no one in or out."

Eli frowned as he looked around. A handful of men wearing the same crimson-and-gold uniforms had appeared silently at all of the ballroom's other doors, though it looked as though none of the crowd had particularly noticed. Something bothered him about their dress, though. He glanced back at the men in front of him, looking their uniforms up and down. *Naval dress uniforms are crimson and* black *not crimson and* gold. The only people who wore crimson and gold uniforms were...

Oh, shit.

He seized Taylor's arm. "We need to go. Right now."

She started to shoot him an irritated glance, then evidently noted that all the color had gone out of his face. "What is it?"

"Those aren't ordinary guards."

"What are you talking about?"

He opened his mouth to speak, but before he could get anything out an amplified voice cut through the room, hushing all the ongoing conversations.

"Ladies and gentlemen," said the same man who had introduced them. "Please rise for His Royal Highness, the Duke of Sevastapol and Knight Commander of Imperial Forces, Crown Prince Hadrian ibn Alaric of the House of Malik, heir apparent to the Illyrican Empire."

Eli looked around, his gaze finally settling on the warm glass of champagne he still held in his hand. *Aw, fuck it.* He drained it in a gulp.

CHAPTER 12

The Illyrican embassy was on the same ring as the Commonwealth's – a show of even-handedness from the Corporation – but a full 180 degrees away, given the animosity between the two superpowers. The war might have gone cold, but there was no better way to keep the situation room temperature than to separate the reactive elements.

Kovalic hopped a circumference tram and took the five-minute ride to the other side of the ring, staring out at the passing crowds. It was still early evening in Bergfestung, and this close to the city center folks were out strolling, going to dinner or the theater. The people in this part of town were among Bayern's wealthier citizen-employees, wrapped in finery that was certainly not part of the Corporation's standard clothing allowance.

He also caught sight of several of Bayern's security officers, their simple pale blue shirts standing out in the lavishly dressed throng. As a rule, Corporation Security didn't carry arms, although special details, such as the protective assignments for the board of directors and executive team, were well provisioned in terms of weapons. And they were not, Kovalic knew from long experience, pushovers, despite their lack of sidearms. If anything, it made them *more* dangerous. Best avoided at all costs.

The tram's chime sounded, and Kovalic got to his feet, stepping down into the ring street. It sped off into the night behind him, leaving him in the surprisingly quiet evening. The Illyrican embassy was set off from the rest of the neighborhood, surrounded by office buildings that had gone silent for the evening.

The embassy itself, a neo-baroque monstrosity with a surfeit of colonnades, ornate stonework, and embellishments, was lit from every window, with people still milling about on the gravel walk, waiting to get in. There were even a pair of spotlights crisscrossing back and forth, cutting swaths of light in the air – an odd choice for a private party, Kovalic thought.

He walked by the gates, glancing casually at the grounds as any curious onlooker might. But his eyes took in more detail, from the armed Illyrican soldiers flanking the entrance proper to the Corporate Security officers posted along the perimeter. Neither the Imperium nor the Corporation were taking any chances, it seemed.

Finding the Commonwealth's van proved to be not much more difficult than finding the Illyrican embassy: the black van with tinted windows practically screamed "nondescript." That alone told him it was Tapper manning the surveillance gear; the man had precious little use for subtlety, much to Kovalic's more than occasional chagrin. At least he'd had the presence of mind to park the vehicle outside of the embassy's security perimeter.

Then again, one ostentatious move deserved another. Kovalic strode over to the van, circling around to the rear doors. He banged rapidly on the metal with his fist.

"Security! Open up."

There was a muffled curse from inside, followed by a

rustling that set the whole van shaking. "Just a minute!" called a voice. And then, so quiet that Kovalic wouldn't have even heard if he hadn't been listening for it, the quiet *ch-chink* of a gun's slide.

With a click, the door at the back of the van unlocked and swung open – just enough for the older man to stick his head through, with a pleasant, if somewhat forced, smile on his face.

"What seems to be the problem, office... boss?" Steel gray brows raised in surprise. "What the hell are you doing here?"

"Right now? Standing in the middle of the street talking to a man who – unless I miss my guess – has a gun aimed at me. How about we take this some place more private?" He nodded to the van.

"Uh. Sure. Course." He withdrew into the back of the vehicle, and Kovalic clambered up onto the bumper and inside.

The van impressed; its equipment was state of the art. Four holoscreen emitters, a full sound recording suite, satellite uplink, and even a decent looking coffeemaker.

Tapper put the gun down on one of the shelves that were mounted on the van's inside wall, and plopped down in the seat. Crossing his arms, he looked up at Kovalic.

"Should you be here, boss?"

Kovalic spun around a second chair so he could rest his elbows on the seat back. "Come on, sergeant. You're not at least *a little* happy to see me?"

"It's just..." he hesitated. Kovalic raised his eyebrows at that. Twenty years of serving with the man, he thought he could count the number of times the man had hesitated on one hand. Maybe one finger.

"Just what?" Kovalic prompted him. "Having too much

fun with Commander Taylor?"

"Not that," he said hastily. "Just, the general said you weren't ready for the field. That's all. After what happened on Sevastapol. Losing Bleiden, losing Jens, getting shot..."

Kovalic tamped down the rising tide in his stomach, giving Tapper a lopsided smile while ignoring the twinge in his shoulder. "I appreciate your concern, sergeant, but I'm fine. And if I weren't, the general hardly would have sent me."

Tapper frowned. "Why *did* he send you? Everything's been going according to plan."

Down to business, then. "Where are Nat and Brody?"

Tapper nodded back towards the direction Kovalic had come from. "The embassy. Some fancy party they scored invitations to. The commander thought it might be a good lead towards finding this envoy the Illyricans sent."

"Any luck? When was your last communication?"

Glancing down, Tapper ran his finger along a screen. "I logged a communication from Brody about ten minutes ago. Said that..." he paused. "Er."

"Yes?" Two hesitations in one night. A new record.

"I'm, uh, just going to read Brody's words." Clearing his throat, he started again. "'Hey, this old guy wants me to introduce him to Tara.' – That's the commander's cover ID. – 'What the hell do I do?'" He scratched at his temple, not looking up to meet Kovalic's eyes.

Kovalic chuckled. "Relax, sergeant. This isn't Nat's first time at the dance. She knows what she's doing."

The sergeant unwound a bit. "Yeah, that's what I told Brody."

"Then there's nothing to worry about. You haven't heard from them since?"

Tapper shook his head. "But we're on burst communication

only, so if there's nothing to report, they won't be checking in. And I'm under strict orders not to call them except in case of emergency."

Looking at the empty holoscreens, Kovalic frowned. "And we don't have eyes inside the embassy?"

"It's a hardened security system. I tried some of Page's bag of tricks, but I couldn't get far enough without tripping some pretty serious alarms." He sighed. "Never thought I'd miss a guy who barely says three words," he muttered.

The general had refused to tell him anything about Page's whereabouts, due to concerns of operational security. It didn't sit well with Kovalic; he couldn't remember the last time that he'd gone into the field without knowing the full status of his own team. *Nat's* team, he corrected himself again. That was not getting any easier.

"So," Tapper said, swiveling back towards Kovalic. "Let's get back to what you're doing here."

"Courier mission, ridiculous as it might seem. The general received a tip that might impact the mission here, and he wanted me to pass it along to Commander Taylor. Then I'm headed back to Nova on the next shuttle."

"He couldn't have just sent a postcard?"

"You know: top secret, hush hush."

"Isn't it always." Tapper drummed his fingers on the desk. "Look, that last contact from Brody was only ten minutes ago. They're working. I'm sure they'll have something to report again soon, and you can pass along your message. So, I guess, until then, hold tight."

Kovalic's grip on the back of the chair tightened, but he willed it to relax. He'd feel a lot better knowing Nat had all the information, but short of finding a way into the embassy party himself – and anxious as he was, even he could tell *that* was a bad idea – there wasn't any other way to get in touch with her.

"Sure," he said to Tapper, trying to convey a tone of far more ease than he felt. "No problem. So... is that coffeemaker just for show?"

Calm down, Eli barked to himself. Like that was helping. *So you're a deserter and a spy surrounded by a squad of the Emperor's Own, technically on Imperial soil, along with an IIS officer who knows you're working for the Commonwealth.* Sure, it *sounded* scary, but he'd been in tougher spots than this one. Well, one. A tougher spot. Which, come to think of it, was how he'd gotten into this whole mess in the first place. Really, if you considered it a certain way, this was all the Imperium's fault.

Somehow, I don't think we'd see eye-to-eye on that.

He took a deep breath, trying to stop his pulse from spiraling out of control, and raised his champagne glass to his lips. Unfortunately, there wasn't anything but dregs left. A trickle dribbled his way into his mouth, just enough to wet his lips.

The crowd had perked up when the heir to the Imperium was introduced as the evening's surprise guest, and there was a large outbreak of applause at his entrance. He cut a dashing figure in his crimson-and-black commodore's uniform; tall and winsome, Crown Prince Hadrian had an easy smile to go with his square jaw, dark hair, and what Eli had once heard a female acquaintance call "soul-piercing eyes." *Looks more like a holo-vid star* playing *a prince. As if he wouldn't have gotten enough attention simply by being royalty, he just* had *to be good-looking too.*

Making his way down the stair flanked a discreet

couple of steps behind by a pair of crimson-and-gold-clad honor guards, the prince had smiled winningly at all the applauding attendees, stopping to shake the hands of several men – and kiss the hands of close to twice as many women – along the way.

The clapping had died down as the heir reached the floor and started mingling with the guests, and Eli had returned to his own predicament.

Colonel Frayn had been clapping with the rest of the crowd, but Eli had caught something else in the man's bearing. An element of... dutifulness? Turning back to the guards, Frayn had started to say something, but then apparently decided against it. The colonel frowned at Eli and Taylor, who, for her part, had stood by, blinking innocently.

Eli turned to survey the crowd, sidling closer to Taylor. "Well, I guess we found the Emperor's envoy," he muttered.

Taylor snorted. "You think?"

"What? I'm just saying."

Another officer in crimson-and-gold, this one a young woman with tightly cropped blond hair, waded through the crowd and approached Frayn. Drawing up, she saluted the older man.

"Colonel Frayn. His Imperial Highness has requested you attend him immediately."

Again, that expression flashed across Frayn's face, but he wiped it off and nodded. "Of course. One moment, please."

Facing Taylor and Eli, he raised a finger, and spoke quietly, but firmly. "No trouble from you two, understand? Stay away from the prince, from the ambassador, from... just stay away from everybody. Have a drink. Enjoy the party. *Don't* make me regret this." Straightening his tie, a maneuver which only served to emphasize its lopsidedness, he nodded to himself, then gestured to the female officer and followed her into the crowd.

Eli exchanged a glance with Taylor, who shrugged and started to drift away from the exit and the guards blocking it. Without much in the way of other options, he followed in her wake.

"I don't get it," he said when they were out of earshot of the guards, and Taylor had once again taken his arm. "Why isn't he just throwing us out?"

"My guess? He can't do it without going through whoever's in charge of those guards. And if Harry's running counterintelligence for the prince, then it's not going to look very good if two Commonwealth spies are here on his watch. Plus, like he said, he really hates paperwork."

"You sound like you know him pretty well."

"We've had our fair share of run-ins. Especially when Simon and I used to work together. Those two... they're more alike than either of them would care to admit. But, from a professional standpoint, Harry's very, *very* good at his job. Don't mistake his pleasant manner for incompetence, believe me."

"Oh. Great. Is this a good time to remind you that if anybody finds out who I really am, then I'll be shot on sight?"

"A deserter *and* a spy? You're lucky they can only shoot you once." Taylor detached herself from his arm. "I'm going to see if I can find a computer terminal."

"You're going to *what*?"

She rolled her eyes. "We came here to do a job, in case you've forgotten."

"But Frayn said–"

"Well, of course," said Taylor, exasperation tinging her voice. "What'd you expect? 'Oh, yes, please come and talk to the heir apparent to the Illyrican Empire. I'd be happy to introduce you.' This is how we play the game, Eli."

"But what if he catches you?"

Taylor shrugged. "I'll worry about it if it comes to that."

Eli looked around helplessly. "What am *I* supposed to do?"

Waving a hand, Taylor drifted away from him. "You're so concerned about Frayn, you follow his advice. Have a drink. Enjoy the party. I'll find you when it's time to go."

That sounded disturbingly final, Eli thought mournfully, as he watched her leave. With a sigh, he drifted over to the buffet. *I already drank the champagne. If they were going to poison me, they would have done it. Might as well eat, right?* Unfortunately, the events of the last fifteen minutes had conspired to reduce his appetite to a small hole in the pit of his gut.

He halfheartedly dumped a few pieces of crudité on his plate. In ordinary circumstances, he would have been all too happy to stuff himself with free food – especially at the Imperium's expense. But his heart just wasn't in it. Instead, he glumly began circulating around the room until he found a spot between a couple of Doric columns. Depositing his empty glass on a tray, he picked up a carrot and was about to pop it in his mouth when a voice interrupted his thoughts.

"Eli?"

Eli froze, food held in mid-air. The voice was familiar, but it was a voice from a different world, one that definitely didn't belong to the life of Elias Adler, but rather to that of–

"Eli *Brody*?"

Oh no.

Slowly, Eli turned toward the source. It was a man of approximately his own age wearing the uniform of the Emperor's Own, shorter than Eli's own gangly frame, but more than making up for it with windswept blond hair, blue eyes that stood out against pale skin, and a dazzling smile. If the crown prince looked like a movie star playing a prince, this guy looked like a movie star playing a movie star. And he was staring, shocked, directly at Eli.

"My god," said the man, shaking his head. "It *is* you." Closing the distance, he gripped Eli's shoulder tightly. "Holy hell, man. How? I thought you were *dead*."

"I–" Eli started.

"And here I was, all jealous that you'd beaten me out for the prime spot on the *Venture*." He laughed in disbelief. "Well, say *something*. Don't tell me you don't remember me."

Uh, right, say something. Eli returned a faint smile. "Hello, Erich. As if I could forget the only person at the academy who even came close to breaking my simulation record."

"357 kills, if I recall correctly," said Erich von Denffer. "While I finished up with a measly 353. I would have had you, too, if they would have let me into the sims on graduation morning."

"You were still top of the class," Eli pointed out.

"Only because you almost flunked out of astrophysics," Erich said with a laugh. "I think Commander Vanashtu was gunning for you."

"Would not have surprised me in the slightest." Eli took in Erich's uniform in a glance. "You've done pretty well for yourself. The Emperor's Own? And those are some pretty shiny wing commander rank insignia there."

Erich shrugged modestly, a gesture he couldn't possibly pull off. "I'm in command of Crown Prince Hadrian's Honor Wing."

"Not too shabby."

"Well, it's not exactly a combat posting. Not like the *Venture*." His eyes widened slightly. "Speaking of which – you *were* on the *Venture,* right? At the Battle of Sabaea?"

Somewhere in the back of Eli's mind, an alert klaxon blared. They'd been enjoying this pleasant little bubble of nostalgia, but collision with reality was imminent. And it was only a short jump from there to the firing squad.

He couldn't exactly lie about it. His posting to the *Venture* had been public knowledge, and while most of his crewmates had died during the battle, any who had survived might very well know that Eli Brody had made it as well. Well, at least until he "died" in a Sabaean prison...

"I was on the *Venture,* yes," said Eli, "and I fought at the Battle of Sabaea."

"Jesus, man," said Erich, his voice low and awed. "I can't believe you made it out alive." He frowned. "But I don't remember seeing your name on the prisoner of war exchange a few months back." The Imperium and Sabaea – which had decided to join the Commonwealth – had come to an agreement that saw the return of the few Illyrican survivors, in exchange for not insignificant reparations.

"I... wasn't on the list."

"Why not?" Erich's brow furrowed.

"It's... well, it's a bit complicated."

"But you're here," said Erich slowly, looking around. "Why?"

Er, yes, I'm here in an Illyrican embassy. Because, you see, I'm a spy. In his head he could already hear the cuffs being slapped on.

Wait... I'm a spy. He cleared his throat and gave a faint smile. "I'm afraid I'm not at liberty to say."

Erich blinked. "You're what?"

"I can't tell you," Eli said. "I'm sorry. It's classified." He reached up and tapped a finger to the side of his nose, his heart still pounding in his chest. A flying ace Erich von Denffer had been, no question, and he'd done well enough at the academy, too. But he'd never exactly been what you might call the fastest ship in the fleet.

Forehead still wrinkled, Erich was about to repeat the last thing Eli had said when his eyes suddenly widened. "Wait. You're with Ey–"

Eli raised a warning hand, and gave a sharp shake of the head. "Not here." Doing his best to look around furtively, he took Erich by the arm and pulled him further back towards the wall. Once he could be reasonably sure nobody was close enough to hear them, he pitched his voice low enough for only Erich to hear.

"I'm undercover. As a businessman named Elias Adler. Think you can remember that?"

"Sure. No problem." His tone was blithe, as though he got asked to maintain cover identities every day of the week.

"Good."

"But, uh, *why* are you here?" he asked, waving his hands at the room at large.

Why indeed? His mind raced back through the evening.

"We've heard, uh, there've been some threats against the Illyrican presence here. People unhappy about the talks."

"Threats?" said Erich sharply. "What kind of threats?"

"Again, I'm not at liberty to say. But we believe them to be credible."

Erich frowned. "I haven't heard anything about this, and as the head of the prince's personal guard, I should have been notified." A note of petulance had crept into his voice.

Aw, crap. Think these things through, Brody. "Well, I'm telling you right now. Anyway, we don't believe the prince has been specifically targeted."

"OK." Erich seemed to relax a little at that, but he still looked on edge. "Still, I should probably have a word with Frayn." He craned his neck, scanning the room.

Eli grabbed Erich's shoulder. "Actually, I just spoke with Colonel Frayn. He's aware of the situation, and has gone to talk directly to the prince. He, uh, he didn't want *me* to tell you, though. I think he was planning to brief you himself. So do me a favor and don't let him know that I brought you into the loop."

"Oh. All right." He shook his head again, apparently trying to take it all in. "Christ. How the hell did you end up in this whole mess, Eli?"

With a bitter laugh, Eli released the other man's shoulder. "To tell the truth, it wasn't something I planned; I just sort of fell into it."

"After Sabaea?"

"Yeah," said Eli. "After Sabaea." He had to admit, there was a part of him that didn't feel entirely happy about misleading Erich, even though anything else would have been suicide. In some ways, the man had been the best friend that he'd had at the academy, despite – or perhaps because of – their competition.

Erich had been raised with every advantage; the son of a prominent Illyrican official and personal friend of the Emperor, he'd grown up in the lap of luxury. Flying lessons from a young age, combined with a natural aptitude, had assured him a spot at the Imperial academy. Success had come naturally to Erich von Denffer – not that he was arrogant or insufferable about it; in fact, Erich was nice to a fault. But things had just *always* gone well for him. Eli could still remember the shock on the man's face when the scores for their first simulation runs had been posted freshman year, and the only person to beat the prodigal son of the Illyrican Empire had been a dirt-poor kid from a backwater colony, conquered almost as an afterthought.

And yet, where some would have used that as an excuse to make Eli's life a living hell, Erich had simply taken it as a challenge to do better. The two had continued to move in more or less separate social circles, but had maintained a weird sort of friendship-rivalry that had been perhaps the most constant relationship for either of them throughout the four years of the academy. Frankly, it had been quite a surprise for Eli to find that he'd been the one to get offered the top spot on the Fifth Fleet's flagship, while Erich had been assigned to Homeworld Defense. Erich, clearly, hadn't been too happy about it either. But five years later, here they were.

"So," said Erich, leaning against the wall next to Eli. "You still get behind the stick?"

Eli tried to suppress a pained expression. "I'm just starting to. There was a while there – after the war – where I... I just couldn't."

"Yeah. I think I can get that."

Choking back a laugh, Eli ran a hand through his hair. Of course, if anybody understood, it *would* be bloody Erich von Denffer. "Did you ever see any combat?"

"During the war? Not really. I was stuck in the Home Fleet, and the fighting never made it that far. Then I got assigned to the Honor Wing, and, well, it's not like they're going to send the show ponies into a firefight. Plus the shooting war was just about over by that point." An edge of bitterness had crawled into his voice.

"So, what, you just babysit his highness all day?"

Erich rolled his eyes. "It's a little bit more than that." He scratched his head and gave a rueful laugh. "But not much, to be honest. We go to a lot of diplomatic functions like this one. Half the time I end up chauffeuring the prince back and forth in a private skimmer – brought him in on one tonight, as a matter of fact. The wing still flies maneuvers every week, just to keep in shape. But it's not combat." His voice was almost plaintive.

Eli swallowed, the brief scenes of the only combat he'd been involved in playing through his mind. Ships disintegrating around him, his heart in his throat, the screams cut off. "You're not missing much. Trust me."

Sucking in his breath through his teeth, Erich offered an apologetic smile. "Sorry. I'd offer to buy you a drink to make up for it, but…" He raised his glass of free champagne.

"Right. So," said Eli, stomping the conversation's rudder and bringing it around, "this Bayern deal."

"I guess you probably know more about it than I do."

I suppose that's the problem with playing the part of the mysterious, all-knowing man. "Some," he admitted. "Just the parts that pertain to this threat." *That I just invented.*

"Some sort of economic ballyhoo," said Erich, waving his hand. "They don't tell us much, either. Probably boring anyway."

Economic? Makes sense. Bayern's a major banking hub.

"Right. Boring," Eli echoed. He had no idea where Taylor was or what she was up to; she'd probably already figured this much out, anyway. Still, he had a source here that was probably full of helpful information about the prince, his coterie, and maybe even his mission, even if he didn't realize it. Taylor might think he was just an untrained amateur, but he could be plenty useful.

Glancing around, Eli tilted his chin towards the crimson-

and-gold uniforms stationed at the room's exits. "They've got your guys working security detail, too?"

Erich rubbed his chin. "Budget cuts, you know. I guess the brass figured they didn't need to have a squadron of pilots *and* a squad of marines to watch after the crown prince."

"Nice."

The other man gave an exasperated sigh. "Not exactly our strong suit."

No, Eli thought, *but maybe you can pull a string and get us the hell out of this tiger's den.* He swept the room. *Have to find Taylor.*

"Looking for someone?"

"Oh, I came with someone. Just trying to see where she got to."

"She?" said Erich, raising his eyebrows significantly. "Brought a date, hotshot? Look at you. As I recall you were too paralyzed by fear to say 'boo' to the girls at the academy."

Eli gave him a sour look, but kept searching. "It's not like that. It's business." He caught a flash of purple and saw Taylor's blond hair making her way across the floor. "There she is," he said with a nod.

"Where?" said Erich, standing on tiptoes. "The one in the…" His eyes widened and he let out a low whistle. "Damn, Eli."

"I told you: it's not like that."

"In that case, can you introduce me?"

Once again, Eli's imagination flashed to the moment where he'd have to explain this to Kovalic. "I…"

"Uh huh," said Erich, giving him a knowing look. "Not like *that* at all. Come on, spill. You owe me that much."

Eli sighed. "Look, I'm not going to lie." *Lord forgive me.* "She's a tiger in the sack." *Never mind, forget lord forgive me. Just please never let that get back to Taylor. Or Kovalic. Or Tapper.*

"You son of a bitch," said Erich, but it was admiration in his voice, tinged with a bit of envy. "Done pretty well for yourself, haven't you?"

"I do OK."

"Oh, she's more than OK."

Eli cuffed him in the shoulder. "Easy there, cowboy. I've got to imagine that the wing commander of the Imperial heir's honor wing does all right."

"I don't like to brag..."

"No, you *love* to brag."

"Fine, fine. You should introduce me to your *friend* anyway," Erich prodded. "Maybe she's got a friend."

She does, but he's a gruff, ill-tempered son of a bitch. Not your type.

Still, it wasn't a terrible idea. He'd told Erich his cover as Adler, and Taylor was good on her toes: she would certainly be able to roll with any lie that Eli had been able to think up, no matter how spur-of-the-moment it had been. Besides, what better way to prove his worth than to deliver a highly-placed source into her hands? *Just hope Frayn isn't watching, or I might be getting Erich into a mess of trouble.*

Erich suddenly stiffened and froze beside him. A couple swerved to avoid them, casting them dirty looks as they passed.

Eli touched his friend's arm. "You OK?"

The pilot turned to him, his blue eyes serious. "Eli, you like this girl?"

"What? I mean, yes. Of course."

"Then do yourself – and her – a big favor, and get her out of here *right now*."

Eli blinked. "What are you talking about?"

Erich laid a hand on his shoulder. "You can't ask me

questions about this," he said, shaking his head. "I need you to trust me. Take your friend and leave." He glanced up again, and this time Eli followed the line of his gaze.

He saw Taylor, her face alight with a broad smile, talking animatedly to someone else he couldn't quite see. As Eli watched, she reached out and touched the man's shoulder, a light touch, but one that Eli had seen enough to recognize. It was the kind of touch that suggested, ever so delicately, the possibility of more. The kind of touch that made your heart quicken.

Kovalic's going to kill me, was his first thought, but it was quickly blown out of his head as the crowd shifted slightly and he got his first glimpse at the handsome, dark-haired man she was talking to. The same man who had entered not a half-hour ago, accompanied by a fanfare and a squad of his own personal security. The heir apparent of the Illyrican Empire, Crown Prince Hadrian.

"Oh," said Eli. "Shit."

INTERLUDE

Ascraeus Mons, Mars – May 9, 2398

"We're *what*?"

"I'm sorry, do I need to repeat myself, *Corporal* Kovalic?" The voice was tempered steel.

"No... No, sir," the corporal hastily corrected himself. "I'm just surprised, is all. We're abandoning Mars?"

Kiroyagi sighed, her face falling. "Believe me, corporal, it's not my call. I lodged my protests, but the brass, as you might guess, were not very interested in hearing them. With Earth firmly under Illyrican control, the crims have turned the full brunt of their forces towards Mars. We can't hold out much longer."

Mouth set in a grim line, the corporal scrubbed the ubiquitous red dust from his helmet. He hadn't even had time to get his pressure suit off since coming in from the cold. Kiroyagi's summons had met him and the sergeant at the base's entrance and they'd made their way to her office without delay. The older man was leaning against the doorframe, his lined face bearing the mirror of their commander's disappointment.

"We'll begin a systematic evacuation of Ascraeus Mons' personnel over the next few days," said Kiroyagi, interlacing her fingers. "You two will make those preparations just like anyone else."

The corporal frowned, then exchanged a curious glance with his older counterpart.

"Drop the other boot, captain," said the sergeant, with a tilt of his head.

Kiroyagi's return expression was sharp, but she continued. "While the majority of the battalion is moving out, I've received permission to retain a platoon's worth of soldiers for a specific operational purpose after the main withdrawal."

The corporal blinked. "We're leaving people behind?"

"You're talking about what," said the sergeant, cocking his head, "a skunkworks unit?"

"Something like that."

The corporal's head swiveled back and forth between the other two. "You've lost me, sir."

The sergeant shrugged, pushing himself off the doorframe, and walking over to Kiroyagi's desk. "Leave a unit behind to disrupt the enemy's advance, and make life… inconvenient… for them. Sabotage, ambush, guerrilla warfare – that kind of thing."

"The unit would be operating without support from command," said Kiroyagi. "Self-sufficient in every way: food, shelter, equipment, and so on."

"What about extraction?" the sergeant said, holding Kiroyagi's gaze.

"The goal behind this operation is to slow the Illyricans down as much as possible, give us time to cover the withdrawal of our forces out-system."

"Out-*system*?" the corporal echoed. "We're giving the crims the whole solar system?"

Kiroyagi leveled a bland look in his direction. "Again, not

my call, corporal. But the Terran Executive – or what's left of it – has decided that there's little chance of maintaining a foothold without control of Earth or Mars. The outer reaches of the system are too sparse and desolate to provide a suitable launching ground for a counter-offensive. So, yes, we'll have to pull back to another system – Centauri, perhaps, or Nova."

The corporal clenched his fists, his eyes going to the metal lockbox that sat on a shelf behind Kiroyagi's desk. "This is a mistake. We've lost a lot of good people here. Daoud... Laing... Zhao. They all gave their lives, and for what? A *strategic retreat*?" All their ID tags were in that box – the sergeant had retrieved them from the bodies himself. They'd been in his squad, which made them his responsibility. And it wasn't like they could send the tags or the remains back to their families on Earth.

Pointedly, Kiroyagi fixed her gaze on the sergeant, ignoring the corporal's comment. "Sergeant, I've been impressed with the work you've done with your squad. I need someone of your caliber as my platoon sergeant."

Kiroyagi's eyes shifted to the younger man. "Corporal Kovalic: Sergeant Tapper has spoken highly of your performance in the field. I'd like to offer you a promotion to sergeant and command of Alpha Squad. I'll also depend on you both for your top lists of marines for these squads."

"You didn't answer my question, sir," said the sergeant. "Is there a plan for extraction?"

With another weary sigh, Kiroyagi rubbed at the spray of freckles on her nose as if she could scrub them away. "I'm not going to bullshit you, sergeant. I'm not sure all of us are going to make it out. But, if by some miracle we do happen to survive the two months this withdrawal is expected to take, then I have assurances from the Earth

Marine Corps' chief of staff that any survivors will be extracted by naval transport.

"But, make no mistake," she continued, taking them each in turn, "this is a volunteer assignment. Say the word, and you'll be shipped out with the rest of the battalion; I won't think any less of you for it. I don't want anybody who doesn't want to be here; this is a crucial mission for the survival of the Earth's remaining fighting forces and its legitimate government. You deserve to know what you're getting into." She glanced up at the chronometer on the wall. "I don't expect an answer right now, gentlemen. But I will need one by 0800 tomorrow morning – we'll have to start preparations immediately."

After a brief pause, the sergeant shrugged. "I can give you mine right now, captain: I've been a marine for twenty years. I'm not sure I'm good for much else. And I can do a damn sight more damage to the crims here than I can on some ship bound for wherever the hell we're retreating to this time. So you can count me in."

The corporal glanced at the sergeant, then nodded slowly. "Earth's my home, sir. And I'm not about to run away, tail between my legs." The Illyricans had spilled plenty of his people's blood on Mars, and he wasn't going to let it wash away without a fight.

"All right," said Kiroyagi. Her normally stoic faced cracked in a half-smile. "In that case, gentlemen, welcome to Ronin Platoon. Let's give 'em hell."

CHAPTER 13

"Something's wrong."

Tapper looked up from the tablet, on which he'd apparently been doing a crossword puzzle. "Something's wrong?" He didn't sound convinced. "Is it the interior decorating? Because you've been staring at the inside of the van for the last twenty minutes."

"They should have checked in, Tap. You know that."

"First rule of missions?"

Kovalic let out a breath. "Nothing goes as planned."

"Bingo," said Tapper, waving a finger, and going back to his puzzle. "Relax. They'll contact us when they're good and ready."

Leaning back in his chair, Kovalic turned the pieces over in his mind. The information the general had passed along from CARDINAL – that Crown Prince Hadrian himself was headed to Bayern – had been old by the time they'd gotten it, and though Kovalic had hopped the fastest transport he could find, the chances that he'd outrun the arrival of the prince were slim. And that might mean that the situation Nat and Brody had run into was most definitely *not* the one they'd prepped for.

Nat would be fine; she was used to situations going

dynamic. To be honest, it was Brody that he was worried about. The pilot was on his first real mission and, as Kovalic had tried to impress upon the general, the kid had no training. And then there was the little matter of him being a former Illyrican officer. The general had a soft spot for defectors – little surprise there – but then again, the general had been one of a kind.

Although, he supposed Brody was one of a kind, too, in his own way. Still, he'd been the one to recruit the kid. Whatever happened to Brody was on him.

Tapper gave him a sidelong glance. "Look, I know you're outside of the chain of command on this one, and believe me, I get how weird that is. But you've got to trust the team. They've got it under control. Even Brody. And you know how it pains me to say that."

"I do trust them," said Kovalic. "I just want to make sure that they have all the information. The general sent me here to apprise Nat of intel that might impact the mission. The sooner I relay that, the sooner you get me out of your hair."

"Boss, don't get me wrong: I'm *delighted* you're here," said Tapper, spreading a hand across his chest. "Really. But we've got protocol for a reason. A transmission could put the team at risk." He ran a hand through his gray hair. "You know all this. Why am I even talking right now?"

"Sorry, Tap. I'm not trying to put you in a bind here. It's just… my gut is saying we've missed something. I'd feel a lot better if we had a twenty on Nat and Brody. Besides, if I'm right, they may *already* be at risk."

Tapper stared at him for a few seconds, then threw up his hands in resignation. "I get the feeling I'm going to get yelled at either way," he muttered, reaching for the headset.

Swiveling around, he tapped a few buttons on the console. "Socialite, this is Bulldog. Do you copy?"

"Bulldog?" murmured Kovalic.

Tapper was in the middle of mouthing "shut up" in his direction when a shriek of electronic interference so loud that it even made Kovalic wince squealed from the sergeant's earpiece. Cursing, Tapper ripped off the headset and flung it onto the counter.

Kovalic raised an eyebrow as the sergeant dug a pinky into his right ear. "I guess I shouldn't be surprised."

"If you knew that was going to happen and let me do it anyway, then I'm going to have a little talk with your psych evaluator," growled Tapper. "Wide-spectrum jamming?"

"Sure sounds like it. Now you believe that something's wrong?"

Tapper was still holding a hand over his ear. "Yeah, yeah."

"Tell me you have a contingency."

"A contingency? You want I should send up a smoke signal?"

"In the old days we would have had a contingency," Kovalic said, a little more sharply than he'd intended.

"In the old days, we wouldn't have been forced to beg, borrow, and steal our equipment from the local station chief."

"Fair point." Kovalic's eyes swept around the well-equipped van, alighting at last on the pistol that the sergeant had accosted him with earlier in the evening.

Tapper followed his gaze. "No. Absolutely not." He placed a hand on the weapon's grip possessively.

"We're blind *and* deaf," Kovalic pointed out.

"And you're what, going to scale the walls and creep across the grounds, looking like a dockhand?" He nodded at Kovalic's peacoat. "Just as a reminder, the nearest body of water is about eighty klicks away, through the better part of a mountain."

"You have a better suggestion?"

"Stake out the entrance," Tapper said immediately. "Look: wide-spectrum jamming suggests a precautionary measure. If they knew we were here, they'd only be squelching *our* frequencies. It's security, plain and simple. So, if the team hasn't set off any alarm bells, we definitely shouldn't do it for them."

It had a sort of sense to it. Well. A lot of sense. That didn't mean Kovalic had to like it, as the slight clenching of his fingers suggested. His shoulder ached and he kneaded it, feeling the knot of sealant underneath his thumb. "And if they don't come out? Or the Illyricans bundle them out the service entrance?"

"You know as well as I do, boss, that we can't be everywhere. Let's give the commander and Brody a chance to do their job. If we need to, we fall back to the station and regroup, call in the cavalry."

"If the cavalry will listen," Kovalic said, thinking back to the conversation between the general and Kester. He had a hard time resisting the urge to wipe even an imagined smug look off the deputy director's face, but he certainly didn't have any problem believing that Kester would hang them out to dry if it suited his purpose, or even just to prove a point. "All right," he said finally. "I'll stake out the entrance. You stay here, but get ready to move. They must have a tightbeam rig in here somewhere." The laser-based system wouldn't be susceptible to the jamming, but it only worked in line of sight.

"There's a receiver on the roof," said Tapper, nodding upward. "I'll get it set up."

It took the sergeant only a few minutes to get the communication array online. He raised an earpiece and a small box that looked like the key fob for a hovercar. "You have to be somewhere you can see the roof of the van, got it? Use the visible beam to figure out where you're aiming, and then switch it over to the infrared system for comms. And, for god's sake, don't point it at the embassy. Not only are they liable to freak out, but they'll also probably be able to pinpoint your location within a few seconds, and then where will you be? That's right," he said, not waiting for Kovalic to interject, "up shit creek with a paddle."

"*Without* a paddle."

"No, you'll have the paddle. Just no boat."

Kovalic gave him a sour look. "Anything else, mom?"

"Thank the kindly nature of the universe that I'm *not* your mother," said Tapper, slapping the rig into Kovalic's hand. Then, with a long-suffering sigh redolent of parenthood, he raised his sleeve toward the van's wall. A panel popped open and Tapper pulled out a sidearm, checked it, and then placed it on the counter.

"Stun cartridges only," he warned. "Just... watch your six."

Kovalic nodded his thanks, taking the weapon and the comm gear, then slipped out the back of the van. Crossing the street so that he'd be opposite the embassy's entrance, he made his way down the block.

The after-dinner crowd had mostly dissipated, and the temperature had dropped another few degrees; he drew his coat tighter around himself and jammed his hands in his pockets. Glancing up into what passed for a sky in this city, he watched as a few blinking lights, far overhead, crossed against the backdrop of the ceiling. There was an extremely limited amount of air traffic in Bergfestung, highly regulated. Most of it was rapid response services: police hoppers, ambulances, fire fighters; occasionally, a news skimmer or transport for a VIP in the mix. He inhaled the cool air deeply, and tried not to smile as he flexed his fingers – he shouldn't be enjoying this, he knew, but it felt good just to be *doing* something. Even a few days out of commission had made him antsy.

The building opposite the embassy was a low-slung concrete edifice that rose about four stories high. Conveniently, an alley ran along the side of it, and it was even equipped with an external emergency fire escape. He probably could have free climbed it had it been necessary, but he had to admit he'd be happy enough not to do so. To call those skills rusty would be underestimating the potential effects of severe metal fatigue. He could feel his injured shoulder thanking him.

Climbing to the top took a little longer than usual, as he moved slowly to avoid his footfalls clanging loudly in the still night air. Whatever the status of the party at the embassy, it clearly wasn't a barn-burner. Then again, it also meant there wasn't, say, a gunfight going on in the main ballroom. So he'd take it.

As he stepped onto the roof, he got a look out over Bergfestung. Most of the buildings in the city weren't exactly high-rises, given the nature of the settlement's construction, so the view from this vantage was pretty good. Stretching away from him, off into the distance, constellations of streetlights and lit windows sparkled in the darkness. Bergfestung's population of two million were all living their own quiet lives tonight.

But he wasn't concerned with them. Approaching the edge of the roof opposite the embassy, he dropped flat; there was no railing or wall to keep him from tumbling off, so he crawled the last several feet. Reaching into a pocket of his coat, he pulled out the tightbeam rig and powered it on.

Below, Tapper had started the van, and pulled it around in a semicircle so that it was facing the embassy. He'd left the lights doused, so as not to attract undue attention from any of the remaining security personnel. From another pocket, Kovalic produced a pair of night-vision binoculars that he'd also found among the van's equipment – the benefit of Bayern station, it appeared, was the budget.

Aiming the binocs at the van, he picked out the tightbeam receiver and played his visible laser beam over the top of the van until he was pretty sure he was on target. Flipping a switch on the side, he activated the transmitter's infrared beam.

"You reading this, Bulldog?"

"Loud and clear, smartass."

"What, I don't get to pick my own callsign?"

"Any movement?" Tapper said, ignoring the gibe.

"Negative. Everything's quiet." He ran the binoculars over the guards near the front entrance. They appeared to be standing at ease; no sign that anything untoward had passed inside. Making out the uniforms in the green-tinted night vision was a no-go, but if he'd had to place a wager on the colors those guards were wearing, he would have gone all in on crimson and gold. "So far, so good. Guards on the ground and…" he panned upwards to where he could make out some bumpy shapes on the roof of the complex, "snipers on the roof. Looks like there's a jetpad up there too. Far as I can tell, they're all just running standard patrol."

"I told you. Nothing to worry about."

Kovalic frowned. He wasn't so sure. Something still *felt* wrong in his gut and as he'd learned from every operative worth their salt, you never went against the gut – it was your operational antenna. Even when every other piece of evidence was telling him that things were fine.

Everything he was seeing on the ground more or less confirmed the intelligence that the crown prince *was* the Imperium's envoy to Bayern. The general had suggested it could be a coincidence, but Kovalic knew that neither of them had really believed it. To an intelligence officer, a coincidence just meant that you hadn't figured out the pattern yet.

Not that they had. Even if Prince Hadrian were acting as the Imperium's envoy to the Corporation, they still had no idea *what* the two sides were talking about. And the combination of the Imperium's vast war machine with the Corporation's nearly bottomless coffers was not a mixture that Kovalic had any desire to see. After the Imperium's occupation of Earth, Caledonia, and Centauri, their further expansion had been stemmed by the heavy losses inflicted on the Third Fleet at the Battle of Badr, followed by the destruction of the Fifth Fleet in the Battle of Sabaea; an influx of the Corporation's cash would let them replace the ships that they'd lost in that engagement and then some. That was a build-up that the Commonwealth just didn't have the resources to match.

But Bayern had remained independent in the galactic cold war so far – and, seemingly, profited handsomely from it. Why change that stance now?

The simple answer, of course, was that there was something in it for them. The Corporation didn't lift a finger unless that infinitesimal movement somehow benefited it at the end of the day. Or week. Or year. They could afford to play the long game.

He wasn't sure exactly how long he'd lain there, turning the ideas over in his head, wrestling with each individual piece and seeing how it interlocked. But it was at least half an hour; long enough that he'd had plenty of time to get cold from inaction. He shifted slightly, wriggling to one side and then back to generate a little warmth, and raised the binoculars again.

The guards on the door were still there, still standing at attention. If they were cold, it didn't seem to bother them. There'd probably been a time he'd been able to maintain that level of discipline, but he consoled himself with the fact that most of those guards appeared to be fifteen or twenty years his junior.

Playing the binoculars over the scene with one hand, he found the tightbeam transmitter with the other and keyed it on.

"Still quiet, Bulldog."

"You can't see it, but I have my surprised face on."

"You know, I don't remember you always being this cynical."

"Side effect from spending too much time stuck in this damn van."

Kovalic let his binocs drift to the perimeter of the embassy. There wasn't much else in this area—

"Hold on," he said, stiffening. "I've got movement."

It was a van – near a duplicate of the one Tapper was in, at least as far as he could tell in the dark. Whoever was driving it was being equally cautious, letting it roll slowly through the side street next to the embassy, its lights extinguished. Effective, perhaps, at keeping one out of sight, but once you were spotted, it wasn't worth much – delivery vans didn't usually run dark at molasses speeds.

"Van, northwest corner," said Kovalic, keeping his eyes trained on it. "I can't make out the tag at this distance." He'd keyed the binoculars' recording capability at the first sight of the vehicle; they could analyze the footage later with some more powerful hardware and see if they could pick out additional details.

"No way I'm going to be able to see it from here," Tapper's voice came back. "What about the embassy? You said they had snipers posted – have they picked up on it?"

Kovalic swung back towards the embassy's roof, blinking as the brilliant light from the spotlight overwhelmed the night vision. Pulling them from his face, he rubbed at his eyes, and tapped a button to switch the binoculars to thermal imaging. The sniper appeared as an orangish-red blob on the top of the building. There was no indication of alarm; given the angle, Kovalic calculated that it was unlikely that the sniper could even see the van. Surely, though, they'd have snipers elsewhere on the roof?

"We're still being jammed?" Kovalic asked.

"Like a piece of whole wheat toast," Tapper confirmed.

So much for pulling Nat and Brody out. And Kovalic was going to be little help from this vantage. He reached under his jacket and touched the reassuring weight of the weapon he'd tucked in the back of his waistband. Non-lethal, but it would do in a pinch. More problematically, it was a short-range weapon, good only out to about ten meters. Ten meters from here would let him fire a little more than halfway down the building. Not helpful.

Bringing the binoculars to bear once again on the van, he frowned. The vehicle had pulled up flush with a short wall on the embassy's perimeter, the angle obscuring it completely from anyone on the roof. Kovalic was about to glance back at the roof, when he caught a pulsing red glow from the front of the vehicle. Without taking the binoculars from his face, he flipped it back to night vision, and saw the pulse repeat itself, this time much more clearly.

The van was blinking its lights. In a pattern.

It was signaling someone.

Kovalic cleared his throat. "Uh, Bulldog? I think we have a problem. Looks like we're not the only ones interested in crashing this party."

CHAPTER 14

Get her away? Sure. No problem. Eli may not have known Taylor very well after their less-than-a-week's worth of acquaintance, but if he'd had to ascribe one particular adjective to her, he would probably have picked "tenacious." If she had her teeth in the heir apparent, then she wasn't going to let up just because Eli Brody – or anybody else – told her to.

Which presented Eli with a dilemma: on the one hand, both Erich and Frayn wanted Taylor and Eli away from the prince. On the other, he and Taylor had a job to do here, and walking away wasn't going to further that. Going home empty-handed was not an option.

Could they find some other vector on which to attack the problem? Maybe, but it would take time and, if their initial briefing were right, that was a resource that was scarce at present. Who knew when this deal was scheduled to take place, and whether or not any record of it would be left after it had?

This was their data point, and this was their opportunity. Taylor was, for the moment, his boss, and it was his job to support her in any way he could. And right now, maybe that meant learning whatever he could from *his* opportunity.

All that took Eli about thirty seconds to process, which was a bit long for him to gawp at Taylor and the crown prince, so he closed his jaw, and looked back to Erich.

"Something I should know?"

"Uh," said Erich, his glance darting back to the couple. "It's just... I mean." He fidgeted, an entirely un-Erich-like move that left Eli even more curious. "Can we talk, you know, off the record?" he whispered, jerking his head towards an unoccupied stretch of wall, much as Eli had done only ten minutes before.

"Sure," he said, allowing himself to be ushered aside.

"What's this all about?" Eli said, when Erich had finally satisfied himself that nobody was within eavesdropping distance.

"It's about *you know who*," said Erich with a significant nod.

"The pri–?"

Erich shot him a look.

"Sorry," said Eli, raising his hands.

"It's OK, it's just... you're a spook, you know how it is. People are always listening."

Eli found himself wishing he had brought the baffle that Taylor had used in his room at the embassy. In part because it would have indeed kept this conversation between them, but more to the point, it seemed like it would have relaxed Erich. The normally calm and collected pilot looked like he'd been marked for death.

"It's all right," said Eli. "Look, just tell me what this is all about. Maybe I can help."

Erich sighed. "You didn't hear this from me, OK?"

"Got it."

"He," a pause again, but this time it was only Erich's eyes that went to his nominal boss, "has very specific... *tastes*."

"Tastes?" Eli echoed.

"With… his partners. He likes the pretty ones."

"Don't we all?"

"You don't understand," Erich said sharply, before he caught himself. The emphatic tone had caught the attention of a couple of their neighbors, who had spared a glance in their direction before returning to their hopefully much more mundane conversation.

"Not a bit," said Eli. "Spit it out, Erich."

"People – women, men, everyone – are attracted to him because he's handsome, and powerful," Erich said. "He takes advantage of that – of the fact that he's untouchable – to treat them… badly."

"Badly?"

Erich shook his head, and Eli noticed the color had drained out of his friend's face. "Really, *really* badly."

Eli slowly turned his head towards the object of their discussion, catching Taylor in the middle of throwing back her head in a delighted laugh. Her hand touched the hollow at her throat, and she looked up at the prince through half-lidded eyes. *Laying it on a bit thick, aren't we, commander?*

"You're telling me," he said slowly, "that the crown prince of the Illyrican Empire is, what? A sadist?"

Erich swallowed.

"Abusive?"

An infinitesimal nod.

"Worse?"

Erich's eyes went wide and he spread his hands silently.

"Holy mother of god, Erich," Eli hissed.

"Look, I know your hands are probably tied. That's fine. I don't expect you to do anything about him – but trust me: take your friend home before he does."

Shit. Shit shit shit shit shit. He took a deep breath and grasped for some sort of calm. He wondered if the secret agent handbook had training for scenarios like this. *Section V, Chapter 2, Paragraph C, Sub-section 11: How to warn your colleague about a valuable intelligence source's predilection for getting violent.* It seemed unlikely, and that actually gave him some heart – it wasn't like this was a scenario he was supposed to know how to handle. He was just as much in the dark as Kovalic would be in the same situation.

But Kovalic had the benefit of what, ten or twenty years' experience? He would have an idea about how to get out of this. Eli had nothing to go on but his wits. He stifled a disparaging remark that came in the form of Tapper's voice.

Tapper. He still had a line to the sergeant, outside in the van. With everything that happened, it'd slipped his mind somehow. Not that he could very well call him up in front of Erich – especially after he'd been asked to keep this all to himself. So, first things first: he needed to extricate himself from Erich.

He clapped the other man on the shoulder. "Thanks for the heads up. I'll take care of this." He tried to inject a note of confidence in his voice, which was tough when he felt about as assured as a man in the process of falling off a building.

"Eli, just… just don't let it get back to me, OK?"

"You've got my word," Eli promised. "Just give me a minute." Giving Erich a nod, Eli sidled away, exhaling like he was being slowly decompressed. Once he was far enough from Erich, he pressed his right hand against the cufflink on his left wrist.

"Bulldog, this is–" A burst of static hit him so hard that his eyes screwed up and he felt his sinuses clear. He stabbed at the trigger again with one hand, then clutched his head. A couple of people nearby were giving him strange looks, so he smiled and pantomimed a headache.

Jamming. Shouldn't be surprised, I guess. But his idea of getting Tapper's help was flaming out before his eyes. He really was on his own here.

Fine. That's fine. I've made it this far without Kovalic on my back every step of the way. Besides, this was his job now. He could handle this. Smoothing his hands down the crisp front of his suit, he straightened his tie and corrected his posture, like his mother had always told him to do. Then, putting his most expansive and welcoming smile on, he briskly crossed the room to the crowd of people that had assembled around the prince.

There was a pretty even mix of austere Illyricans and more flamboyantly dressed Bayern citizens. Gaps in the group were few and far between, but Eli maneuvered himself into one and peered around for Taylor.

His heart took the slide down into his stomach as he re-examined every single face, but it didn't change the result. Taylor wasn't there. And neither was the prince.

Shit.

It was the right circle; he was sure of that. Maybe they'd just decided to mingle with another group. Both of them. Eli made for the stairs from which they'd entered, stopping shy of the crimson-and-gold guards at its top. He scanned the crowd, taking in every face he saw, but neither Taylor nor the prince was among them. Then again, some were facing away from him, so he checked again, this time looking for the distinctive purple hue of Taylor's dress. That didn't help either, though he did see a few women wearing a similar color.

What the hell? How does a party lose its guest of honor? Especially when every exit is guarded by…

His stomach plummeted, and he took the room in again, this time with an eye towards the entrances. There were three of them: the one where they'd come in at the top of the stairs; one towards the back of the room that seemed to spew waiters, which Eli suspected led to the kitchens; and the side exit that Frayn had tried to chivvy them out earlier.

Speaking of whom, Eli hoped to high heaven that the IIS colonel had remained otherwise occupied. Sure enough, he caught sight of the older man caught in discussion with a handful of stuffy-looking uniformed individuals, with what Eli could make out even at this distance as a slightly pained expression on his face.

He took another deep breath. Taylor could take care of herself – Eli had no doubts about the commander's capability – but he was pretty sure he'd be falling down on *his* job if he didn't apprise her of what Erich had told him. Even if she'd be able to roll with whatever came her way, walking in blind wouldn't be doing her any favors. Not to mention what Frayn might do if he found out in whose company the prince had left. No matter how many times Eli did the math, it kept ending up in negative numbers.

So, first things first: find Taylor. They would have ducked out either through the kitchens or the side entrance – someone must have seen them. Obviously, if nobody else, then at least the guards. Not that they were likely to tell him.

But, then again, Eli knew somebody they *would* tell.

He found Erich again easily enough, entertaining a group of ladies who were appreciatively hanging on the flyboy's every word. Serving in Homeworld Defense might have been an affront to Erich's personal honor, but it didn't seem to have hurt his reputation with the opposite sex. And from the way he was describing flying a fighter, Eli got the impression this was a speech the other man had practiced plenty of times.

Shame to drag him away when he's working the crowd, but I think this is a little more important than making sure Erich gets laid.

He maneuvered himself next to his former classmate, waited as the laughter from Erich's double-entendre about whether any of the ladies had ever handled a stick had subsided, then cleared his throat.

"Excuse me, commander, but there's an urgent matter that needs your attention."

"Oh?" he said, raising an eyebrow.

"Yeah, it concerns the guest of honor?"

The second eyebrow went up alongside the first, and Erich turned, all smiles, to the group of women. "Pardon me, ladies," he said graciously, sketching a bow. "But I need to deal with something. Enjoy your evening."

Eli offered a quicker, even less formal bow, and hastened Erich away.

"This better be good, Eli. I'll have you know that brunette's engines were revved up."

Oh, Erich. Always distracted by a pretty face. "And here I thought your job was guarding the prince."

"I'm a wing commander. I delegate." Erich craned his neck to see over the crowd. "Anyway, he's right over... huh."

"Yeah, 'huh'. My date's gone too, so do the math on that one," said Eli, steering Erich towards the side entrance, which he'd decided was the one that the prince and Taylor had most likely used. Guards were bound to be discreet, it was the nature of their job; waiters, on the other hand, would probably talk. And when it came to the crown prince of the Imperium, that just wouldn't do at all.

The two soldiers at the door stiffened at the sight of their commander, even if he was being propelled by another man. Erich broke free as they approached and smoothed his dress uniform, drawing himself up to his full height.

"Did the prince come through here with a woman?"

The two guards exchanged a glance, and one of them directed a pointed glance at Eli.

"He's with me, Lieutenant Attal," Erich snapped. "And, at any rate, he didn't ask – *I* did."

"Yes, sir," said the dark-haired man who had blocked Eli and Taylor's egress earlier this evening. "About five minutes ago."

"Where? And why wasn't I notified?"

The two men glanced at each other again.

"I trust I don't have to repeat myself?" Erich said, fixing them with a stare.

"No, sir," said the same one who had answered the first time – Attal. "I believe he was heading back to the residence. Lee and Hashemi went with him, but he asked it be kept quiet. Said something about making it an early night."

Eli frowned. "All this security, and he's not staying here?"

"You don't know the prince," Erich muttered, glancing at his sleeve. "Always has to find the most expensive place. This one has a private jetpad, which I guess is a nice touch."

The privileges of wealth, I guess. I thought our embassy was pretty nice. "You know we need to go after them."

The Illyrican pilot ran a hand through his shock of blond hair, parting it like a tractor through a cornfield. Sweat had started to glisten on his forehead.

"Erich. *You're* the one who told me not to let her leave with him."

Erich seized his arm and dragged him out of earshot of the

guards. "Yes, I told you not to let them leave together," he hissed, an edge of panic entering his voice. "As a *favor* to you. But you want me to go up against the *heir to the goddamned crown* and tell him what? To leave a lady alone because she came in with a friend of mine? She didn't leave under duress, did she?"

Doubtful, Eli thought, recalling the way he'd seen her touch the prince's arm. Taylor had seen an opportunity and had decided to shoot for the moon. To go big or go home. *Just as long as it's not in a body bag.*

"She came here as *my* guest, Erich. And if what you told me is true, then she may be getting a little more than she bargained for. Now, are you going to help me or not?" Eli softened his tone. "Look, I'm not asking in a professional capacity – I'm asking as a friend."

Erich stared glumly into the middle distance, then finally shook his head. "Goddamn it, Eli. Fine, let's go. But if this goes south, then I hope your colleagues are ready to do a little sweeping up."

Oh, I think it'll be a bit more than a little *sweeping up if this goes wrong.* "I'm sure they will."

Turning on his heel, Erich marched back up to the door and pushed his way through it, ignoring the two guards. Eli trailed in his wake, and they found themselves in a corridor that took a sharp right turn and ran alongside the embassy's outer wall. It was punctuated with large windows that looked out into the impeccably landscaped garden; he imagined it must be a sight to behold during the day cycle. Right now, it just looked like a bunch of dark blobs.

On the opposite side hung a series of large oil paintings. Unsurprisingly, most of them depicted the history of the House of Malik in a variety of its most triumphant moments.

There was the founding of what would become Illyrica, with a young Captain Laila Malik atop a dun-colored hillside, planting a crimson scrap of a flag while behind her lay the smoking ruin of the crashed colony ship *Seed of Eden*. Another tableau depicted the victory of Alaric I – great-grandfather and namesake of the current emperor – in the War of Unity, dressed in camouflaged battle fatigues while signing a document that would bring peace to the warring factions of the colonists and instill his regime as emperor. Finally, the all-too-familiar portrait of the current emperor in his most puissant middle age, with full black beard and piercing gaze – the same image that had been used for many of the bronze statues that resided in Raleigh City, the capital of Eli's homeworld, Caledonia.

Eli shook his head as they walked. "I get that he's the emperor and everything, but I guess I never really understood the hero worship."

Erich shrugged. "You grew up in the colonies. I don't think there are a lot of people there who have high opinions of the man."

"Not to mention the whole system of hereditary power," said Eli, nodding ahead in the darkness towards their unseen quarry. "I mean, do *you* think the prince is fit to run the show?"

Erich slowed, unable to conceal an element of suspicion from his face. "What the hell kind of question is that? Is this some sort of loyalty test?"

Eli bit his tongue. He'd slipped into a sense of false camaraderie with Erich, of the sort they'd used to share in the academy. He'd forgotten that he was supposed to be playing the part of an intelligence agent for the Imperium. And Erich was right: that wasn't the sort of question that a loyal subject would ask.

"No, no, nothing like that," Eli hastened to say. "Just, you know, a question I've asked myself. Guess it's just my prejudice from my upbringing showing again."

Erich eyed him, but started walking again, quickening his pace. The two of them reached the end of the corridor, where a pair of heavy ornate doors led outside. Together, they shoved them open, stepping out into the cool night air of Bergfestung.

They'd ended up in the gardens, to the right of the main entrance. Eli could see the gravel path leading to the front gates, and occasionally caught the misshapen beam of light flashing off the cave ceiling far above.

"I thought you said you flew him in?" Eli asked. "Why aren't we heading to the roof?"

"Security arrangements," Erich said quickly. "Don't want to be too predictable. Arrive by flier, leave by car."

Eli nodded, though privately he thought it sounded ridiculous, and they set out across the lawn, towards the fence that surrounded the embassy. Just past it, Eli could make out the street and the lights of the buildings across the way. A wrought iron gate stood at the end of the drive, with another pair of crimson-and-gold guards flanking it. He made a beeline for them.

They were halfway to the gate when a sheet of white light flashed from beyond. Eli had just enough time to wonder if Bayern's weather simulation system produced thunderstorms when a deep bass *fwump* shook the ground beneath him, resonating inside his chest cavity.

"What the...?"

Erich had looked up sharply and then begun to jog towards the gate. Eli broke into a run, following after him. The pair of guards who had been standing at the entrance were getting back to their feet; evidently, they'd been much closer to the source of the noise.

Eli ignored them, pushing through the gate and onto the street, then gawped at the scene down the road. It had been a multi-car pileup, though there were so many shapes mashed together that Eli couldn't be sure how many vehicles there had been. Flames licked from one of them, a long black hovercar that had apparently been broadsided by a van.

He'd started towards the scene of the crash, thinking that there might be people inside that needed help when something zinged into the stone column behind him. Eli stared at it blankly for a moment before realizing that someone had shot at him. Belatedly, he dropped to the ground as his brain tried to process all the information that had been dumped on it.

So much for this being an accident. What the hell is going on?

More small arms fire sputtered above his head, taking flecks of stone out of the pillar, and Eli shimmied back behind the gate, hopefully out of the line of fire. He crouched behind the pillar, which provided some degree of cover.

Peering out, he could see dark shapes moving towards the crashed hovercar. Even in the gloom he could tell they were armed with rifles. One of them yanked open the door, and Eli saw two figures hustled out, their arms gripped tightly by the assailants. As the second person was pulled from the car, Eli caught a flash of color illuminated by the fire. Purple.

Taylor.

The two figures, held at gunpoint, were ushered towards another van that had pulled up and then thrown unceremoniously inside. Some part of Eli's brain told him to get the registration tag, but he couldn't make it out in the darkness. Taking a deep breath, he got to his feet and prepared to sprint to a better vantage poi–

Something collided hard with the back of his head, and darkness descended all around him like a heavy, velvet curtain.

CHAPTER 15

For Kovalic, perched on the rooftop, the whole scene played itself out in his mind's eye, only to be repeated below on the street. Sometimes you could just see what was going to happen before it happened.

There were three black hovercars in front of the embassy – standard security procedure for transporting any sort of VIP. It would be a smash-and-grab, that much was clear, and Kovalic presumed that the target was the same very important P that he had been sent here to warn the rest of the team about.

That, however, was about where his insight ended. Who would want to grab the heir to the Illyrican throne off the street was still a question – and the "why" depended very much on that "who." Most of all, Kovalic wasn't exactly sure that he should care.

If the general were here, Kovalic was certain that the old man would have something to say about how they shouldn't allow what would surely be a major disruption of the galactic-political stage. Then again, there were some people that the galaxy would be better off without, and from the intel that Kovalic had seen on Emperor Alaric's firstborn son, the crown prince was one of them. He couldn't stop his stomach from roiling at the thought of Nat running afoul of the prince, but she was more than capable of handling herself.

Besides, his assignment was to courier a message; he'd already exceeded his brief as it was. He was pretty sure that it was worth it to at least observe and report on whatever little tableau was about to unfold before them – that kind of firsthand intelligence was invaluable. But he was happy enough to stay out of it.

There was movement from one of the embassy's side doors; he raised the binoculars to his face once again, leaving the night-vision mode engaged. Grainy green-white ghosts shimmered as they strode down the side of the building, arm-in-arm. Early party poopers?

The taller of the two strode towards the front of the embassy in a gait that Kovalic found himself unconsciously describing as "imperious," while the other one – a woman in a dress reaching to her calves – matched his pace, though she walked with the more precise step of one who has to be careful where they put their feet, lest their footwear betray them.

As they rounded the corner of the embassy, he saw the guards in front perk up and move to intercept, then suddenly fall back into a more deferential position as they got close enough to recognize the imperious man. Which just confirmed Kovalic's initial guess: a high-ranking guest – from his relative youth, most likely the crown prince himself – leaving with a lady from the party.

Activating the tightbeam rig, he trained it on the van. "Movement at the front," he murmured. "Whoever our party crashers are, I think their target is on the move."

"I feel spectacularly useless down here," Tapper grumbled. "Can't see a damn thing."

"Well, if they weren't jamming us, I could send you the binoc telemetry, but hooking it up to the tightbeam would take more time than we have."

"Was that supposed to make me feel better? Because it didn't work."

"I never did finish that six-week course on morale building."

Out in front, two of the guards had formed an escort, and were ushering the prince and his guest towards the cars parked out front. The pair was led to the third of the cars, where one of the guards pulled open the back door and let the two honored guests slip in. Unsurprisingly, to Kovalic, the prince slid in first – chivalry was not known to be the man's strong suit.

As the woman moved to enter, accepting help from one of the embassy staff, she shifted her weight and turned, such that she didn't leave the guards at her exposed back – the kind of thing a trained soldier might do. Kovalic sucked in his breath sharply, even as the woman disappeared into the car. The embassy guard slammed the door shut on the pair and patted his hand on the top of the vehicle.

The three-car convoy began to pull away from the curb, and Kovalic swung his binoculars towards the van lying in wait. His gut twisted; there wasn't enough time. Cursing, he trained the tightbeam back down on the van.

"Nat's in the car. I'm on the move."

He caught only the beginning of Tapper's surprised response as he broke line of sight and made for the edge of the roof. He shoved the binocs and tightbeam rig into his pocket, and swung over the lip to land on the fire escape.

The iron juddered beneath his boots as he made his way down it, but he was still a few stories from the ground when a white flash emanated from the street, followed a split second later by a thundering explosion. At the lowest level, he kicked at a lever, which released a ladder that clattered down to the ground. He slid down it, his feet and hands scraping against the sides, and dropped the last few feet to the pavement, landing in an almost sprinter's crouch and immediately pushing off for the mouth of the alley.

As he ran, he drew the knockout gun and flipped off the safety. A series of rectangular green lights glowed to life, showing a full charge. It might not be as useful as a real gun, but it wasn't as though someone was about to deliver him an assault rifle.

Emerging from the alley, he took in the scene: the van that he had spotted had taken out the lead car; meanwhile, an almost identical van – probably the group Kovalic had seen them signaling with their lights when he was on the roof – had smashed into the second car. That created a roadblock for the third car, the one that actually contained the prince. Someone had tossed an incendiary at the front of that vehicle. Even as Kovalic rounded the corner onto the street, the driver was bailing out, only to drop to his knees at the sight of the half dozen masked figures who had jumped out of the rear of the vans.

Suppression fire was being directed back towards the embassy, though nobody seemed to be putting up much of a fight from there – they were still too shocked. A sniper shot pinged off the chassis of one of the cars, but it didn't even come close to any of the assailants.

Kovalic pressed himself against the wall, keeping his eyes peeled for an opportunity. Flattened into the darkness as he was, none of the assault team seemed to have noticed him, giving him an opportunity to study their moves. Their precise, efficient moves. The assailants were undeniably trained and, more to the point, they were a trained as a team.

Two moved as a pair to flank the fiery car. Each raised their rifle; the one on the passenger's side held up three fingers and counted down to one, and they each yanked open their respective door, seized the person inside, and yanked them out.

The prince – in the light flickering from the flames on the hood, Kovalic could at last positively identify the man – was blustering loudly, but to the man's credit he didn't look afraid of his attackers.

The other man wrenched Nat to her feet by her arm, and a sympathetic lurch tugged at Kovalic's stomach. His grip on the gun tightened and he raised it to gauge the shot. But they were easily fifteen meters away – too far outside the dissipation range of the KO gun.

He tried in vain to catch Nat's attention, to reassure her that he was here and had her back, but she was too busy being hauled off by the attacker to see him concealed in the shadows. Grimacing, he lowered the weapon.

Most of the crew were still laying down fire, while the two men – Kovalic assumed they were men, anyway, given their bearing and general build – dragged the captives back behind the impromptu blockade created by the vans that they'd crashed.

Kovalic had only just begun to wonder how they planned on getting away when a screech of tires and flash of headlights signaled the arrival of a third van. A door in the side slid open, and the two prisoners were shoved unceremoniously inside.

Staying low, Kovalic jogged alongside the building's front facade, heading towards the van. Raising the KO gun into a ready position, he tried to get a bead on one of the captors, but the range was still iffy.

Swearing to himself, he stole forward to close the distance. He never even saw what it was that he kicked – a discarded can, some piece of detritus from the crash – only heard it skitter away into the darkness. He froze, hoping it would go unnoticed in the general excitement, but one of the black clad soldiers was on the alert and swung a weapon in his direction.

With only a split second before the man opened fire, Kovalic beat him to it, squeezing the trigger on the KO gun. A blue shockwave rippled out of the barrel, but Kovalic didn't wait to see if he'd hit his target – he dashed towards the man at top speed.

Kovalic's injured shoulder seared in pain as he drove it into the man's solar plexus, knocking him backwards. The commando stumbled, but managed to keep his footing, even as his free hand flew to his chest. The gun had been held out to the side, forgotten, and, gritting his teeth against the flare from his shoulder, Kovalic tried to wrench it from the man's grip with his good hand. The tangled strap made it impossible to wrest entirely, so he went with the flow, using the band to tangle up the commando's gun arm.

The man's finger grasped for the trigger, and Kovalic twisted the gun away from him, trapping the digit and pulling it back against the trigger guard; there was a snap. The commando grunted in pain, but he didn't howl or scream, again reinforcing Kovalic's assessment that these guys were professionals.

Professionals that didn't work alone, he thought, looking up just in time to see another pair of black clad men advancing towards them. Spinning the commando into a chokehold, he unhooked the gun from the broken finger, but kept the strap encircling his captive's wrist, then swung it around and under the man's arm. With the man's gun arm behind his back, Kovalic had both control of the weapon and a human shield.

Both of the other commandos snapped their guns up, bringing them to bear on Kovalic's head.

"Easy," said Kovalic, trying to ignore the throbbing from his injured shoulder. "Let's all just take it easy."

An audible whine sounded from behind Kovalic, a twin to the one that had come from the knockout gun in his own belt, and he huffed a bitter laugh. Outflanked.

The lead commando shrugged. "Better luck next time."

Kovalic tried to swing the gun around, but the tangled strap made it impossible – in any case, he was hardly fast enough to beat the stun field that enveloped him like a warm blanket, turning his vision into a blurry rainbow aura as his own heartbeat, irritatingly loud, echoed in his ears and his limbs turned to jelly.

He barely registered hitting the ground, though his senses persisted long enough that he felt someone pluck the KO gun out of his belt where he'd stowed it. Multiple boots stalked away from him – he could feel the vibrations thudding in his chest – and then it was just easier to let consciousness slip away.

Upon waking, Kovalic's first thought was that, surprisingly, he wasn't dead. The second was that he really had to stop passing out. He eased himself up from where he lay on the street, wincing as the pain spiked from his injured shoulder. Gingerly, he prodded at his torso; there were some bruises here and there, but he didn't seem to have sustained any serious injury. His ears were buzzing fiercely, as though he'd decided to take up intracranial beekeeping.

Debris skittered off him as he sat up. It took him a moment to get his bearings, but they flooded back when he saw the multi-car pile-up in front of him. Two of them, a long hovercar and a black van, were currently on fire, blazing merrily away. Of the van that the kidnappers had dragged Nat and the crown prince into there was no sign.

But they hadn't killed him. Perplexing, that. He'd have to give it more thought later, when his head wasn't a beehive.

His arm buzzed, and he started. Brushing off his sleeve, he saw an alert message for a local emergency, advising him to avoid the area near the Illyrican embassy. Which in turn meant that the jamming had come down. Of course: the second the Illyricans realized what happened, they would have killed it to allow them to coordinate a search and rescue operation.

A search that he was right smack-dab in the middle of. Well, that wouldn't look good. Especially if they ran his non-existent ID. It was probably time for an opportune exit.

Getting to his feet was about as exciting as he'd thought it would be. He ached all over from the residual effect of the stun blast, but he estimated he'd only been out for a couple minutes, tops.

He wobbled his way back towards the building where he'd taken up his listening perch, using the wall for support. Tapper and the van were only about a hundred meters away by the most direct route, as long as he could avoid the Illyrican and Bayern security patrols.

Which, admittedly, was a big if.

Still, his legs felt stronger and less gelatin-like with every step, and he was fairly well concealed in the shadows next to the building. Thank god it was nighttime or he'd be in real trou–

Almost as he thought it, the pale white light of what appeared to be a giant spotlight came on with a *clunk*, bathing the entire street in the pure illumination of day. Because, of course, Bergfestung wasn't an ordinary city with celestially imposed night and day; it was inside a giant cavern with lighting that could be directed at will. All the authorities needed to do was override just a portion of the diurnal illumination routine, and presto – instant search lights.

Good for search parties, bad for Kovalic.

He sped up, trying to keep under overhangs where possible to shield himself from the light, but, as he glanced across the street, he could see personnel in both crimson-and-gold and blue massing already around the embassy. No one was going to be sleeping tonight, that was for sure.

There was no way he was going to make it to the van on time. If he could contact Tapper, the sergeant could come pick him up, but the tightbeam rig needed a clear line of sight, and he couldn't even see the van from where he was.

He blinked and stopped in his tracks. The jamming was down; he could just call Tapper on the civilian comm network. Except he had no idea what Tapper's contact info was. Well, then, he could reach M'basa at the embassy easily enough, and have her connect him to the van.

His fingers were on his sleeve, halfway through swiping up the embassy before he stopped himself. If the Illyricans or Bayern security were monitoring comm calls in the area, or pulled the logs later, they'd know somebody had called the Commonwealth embassy from the crime scene. And that would not look good at all. His head must be fuzzier than he thought.

With a sigh, he started walking again.

They said hindsight was 20/20, but his seemed to have been sharpened with laser vision at this point. So many poor choices thus far; he was kind of shocked that he wasn't already in custody. Reluctant as he was to admit it, maybe the general had been right not to put him in charge of the mission.

As he rounded another vehicle, he caught sight of the embassy's van; to his amazement, he'd crossed about half the distance so far. And if he could see the van... he patted down his pocket until he found the laser transmitter rig, then aimed it with unsteady hands at the dome atop the vehicle.

"Hey, Bulldog, this is Smartass. Copy?"

There was no response, but his hands were still shaking, so he couldn't be sure he'd aimed it correctly; it was a lot harder to hit the receiver from this angle than it had been from the roof, but he didn't think he was going to be climbing a fire escape anytime soon.

The search parties were out in force now, but, fortunately for Kovalic, they had a huge car accident and flaming vehicles to occupy their immediate attention. Hopefully, they'd be less interested in a random, injured passerby.

Taking a breath, he held it and aimed the laser rig, holding one hand steady with the other. "Bulldog, you there?"

There was a pause, in which Kovalic started to worry that the sergeant had abandoned his post once the lights had come on. He wouldn't have blamed the man, but he'd known Tapper for twenty years, and there was no way he would leave Kovalic behind.

"Goddamnit, Smartass, where have you been?" barked a familiar voice in his ear.

He sighed in relief, then toggled the rig on again. "Oh, you know, here and there. Really, I'd love to chat, but I could use a ride."

There was a much-suffering sigh. "You give and you give and you give, and still they want more. Where are you?"

"Not far. I'll see you at about," he eyed the angles, "eleven o'clock?"

"Roger that," said Tapper. There was a flash from the van's lights – it would have been a beacon in the dark, but in the blaring light the only people noticing it would be those looking for it. Which, hopefully, was Kovalic and Kovalic alone. "See you then."

The van pulled slowly away from the curve, puttering towards Kovalic. Most of the search party had their backs to it, still trying to put out the fires at the scene of the crash, but some of them would notice soon enough. He began limping towards it, hoping to meet Tapper halfway.

There'd be an interstellar incident if they were caught fleeing the scene of a kidnapping and identified. M'basa would probably get shipped back to Nova, her first station chief assignment a disaster, and Kovalic and Tapper would likely be hauled off to an Illyrican detention facility. He couldn't speak for the sergeant, but he'd spent enough time in one as it was.

"Hey!" a voice called from across the street. "You there."

Kovalic didn't stop, didn't look up, but out of the corner of his eye he could see a blue-shirted Bayern security officer advancing upon his position.

"Stay where you are!" the man yelled, his hand going to the knockout gun on his belt.

Kovalic ignored the request, heading towards the van, which was speeding up.

"I said *stop*," said the man, breaking into a jog. His gun was in his hand now, held low. "Security services!"

The van leapt forward suddenly; Tapper must have seen the officer. The man was running now, gun up, but the van slid between them.

Kovalic put his last burst of energy into a limping lope of a sprint, and circled around the back of the van in a run, yanking open one of the doors and throwing himself inside.

"GO!"

Tapper gunned it, and Kovalic narrowly avoided rolling out the open back door, which swung wildly on its hinges. Behind them, he saw the security officer fire off a stun blast, but it dissipated harmlessly in mid-air as they peeled away. Reaching out, Kovalic grabbed the interior handle and swung the door closed behind him.

Getting to his feet, he made his way to the front of the van, ignoring the bouncing and swerving as Tapper pulled off the main boulevard and onto side streets.

"Well," Kovalic said, plopping down in the passenger seat. "That was... unexpected."

"You could say that."

"We'll need to ditch the van."

"The station chief is not going to be happy," Tapper warned.

"Yeah." Kovalic worked his sore shoulder. At least the sealant seemed to be holding. For now. "We seem to have a way of making friends wherever we go, don't we?"

"Regular life of the party, we are."

Kovalic ran a hand through his hair. "Our top priority is finding Nat."

"And the prince?"

Kovalic shrugged. "We find Nat. If he's there too, that's gravy. Honestly, I could really care less about him."

"What would the general say to that?"

"Screw the general. This is my show now, sergeant. Any problems with that, speak now."

The sigh that issued from Tapper was only partly remorseful, but he shook his head. "No problems, boss. But you're forgetting one thing."

"What's that?"

He jerked a thumb back at the embassy. "We just left Brody high and dry in the middle of an Illyrican hurricane."

Kovalic pinched the bridge of his nose. "Well," he said mildly. "Shit." He shook his head. "Who the hell were those guys, anyway?"

"I don't know," said Tapper, leaning into a sharp left turn. "Off the top of my head, I can think of about two dozen possibilities. But if I were Eyes, I know who would be number one on my list – with a bullet."

"Who's that?"

Tapper gave him a sideways look. "Us, boss."

INTERLUDE
Naval Base Mir, Terra Nova – February 2, 2399

"Wake up," growled a voice. "We're here."

The sergeant blinked awake, his eyes adjusting to the dim red hues of light. The floor – no, wait, *deck* – shifted beneath his feet. The thrum of the engines and the slight drifting movement suggested an atmosphere rather than the vacuum of space, and the pitched whine of a straining repulsor field signaled they were setting down for a landing.

His nose itched; he raised his right hand to scratch it, but they came as a pair, secured by a set of manacles. The pesky itch dealt with, he lifted them towards his escort, who shook her head.

"When we've landed. That's the procedure." As though waiting for the words, the vessel jolted, its struts making contact with the tarmac. A moment later the engines powered down, their deafening roar descending to a low purr.

With a groan of hydraulics, the rear of the compartment opened, swinging down to form a ramp. Bright sunlight filtered in through the opening, and he blinked again, shading his eyes with his still-manacled hands.

The escort hauled him to his feet by the shoulder, then nudged him forward towards the ramp. He picked his way carefully across the deck.

Still blocking the pesky sunlight with his joined hands, he allowed himself to be led down the deck by the escort's hand on his shoulder. A ray of light washed over his captor's forearm, illuminating the red of her sleeve. That was a color he was thoroughly sick of by this point – if he never encountered it again it would be too soon.

About twenty feet from the bottom of the ramp stood their welcoming committee: three unarmed, uniformed men flanked by a pair of guards holding rifles. He squinted in the brightness, unable to make out the rank insignia gleaming on their shoulders. At least the uniforms weren't red.

"Prisoner transfer from Illyrican Imperial shuttle 1138," said his escort, coming to a halt at the ramp's base. "Kovalic, Simon Vyacheslav." This one didn't stumble over his name. She'd probably been practicing it, repeating it like a mantra on their entire lengthy trip. "Sergeant. Service number K27845B. Formally returned to the Commonwealth of Independent Systems, as per agreement."

His hands were pulled down by the escort, his eyes tearing up as they were deprived of their sunshade. The woman punched in a code on the manacles, and with a click they sprung open. He massaged his wrists, red and raw where the cuffs had been attached, but otherwise no worse for the wear.

Two of the unarmed men stepped forward to take his arm, the one on the right in a firm, though not painful fashion. Glancing down, he raised his eyebrows as he registered a familiar, weather-beaten face.

"Welcome back, kid," Tapper muttered.

The remaining Commonwealth officer nodded to the Illyrican escort, who proceeded back up the ramp. It raised behind her, and the repulsors keened as they started up; he could feel the backwash on his face.

"Sergeant Kovalic," the lead officer said. "Allow me to be the first to welcome you home to Terra Nova."

He tensed. If anything, he was farther away from home than he'd ever been, on a planet that he'd never set foot on before. Details, he supposed. After a moment of hesitation, he extended his hand to take the one that the officer had extended. He was tall, with a build like a team of oxen and a face that looked like it could have been trampled by the same.

"Thank you–" he glanced at the man's rank on his collar, "General...?"

"Abernathy. James Abernathy, Special Forces Command."

The grip was of a pair with the man's appearance, firm and probably strong enough to pull someone's head off. If the general hadn't spent some time in the field, it'd be a waste.

"I'd like to talk to you about a career opportunity, Sergeant Kovalic."

"A career opportunity?"

"Well, given the successful nature of your mission on Mars, it'd be a pity to lose such an experienced and highly trained soldier as yourself."

There was a whooshing noise in the sergeant's head; he couldn't have heard that right. "Successful?"

Abernathy's brows knitted. "Indeed. For the last nine months, your team has disrupted supply lines all across Mars, and allowed our forces to make a strategic retreat from the solar system."

He stared at Abernathy, dumbfounded.

"Er, yes," the general continued. "And your guerrilla attacks on installations across the planet have significantly reduced the Illyricans' capacity to marshal a significant fighting force."

Blood had rushed to the sergeant's head. "That sounds less like a success and a hell of a lot more like *giving up*." The firm grip on his arm tightened like a blood pressure cuff.

The big man shrank back; it was only then that the sergeant realized that his whole body had tensed like a coiled spring, ready to strike. Only Tapper's grip on his arm held him back, like a leash on a barking dog. He forced his muscles to relax.

He cleared his throat, and spoke through clenched teeth. "Excuse me, sir. I've been a prisoner of war for the last two months, and I'm afraid my captivity has taken a toll on me. If it's all right, I will consider your offer after I've had some time to recuperate."

Abernathy cleared his throat. "Oh. Of course, sergeant. Take as much time as you need – the resources of the Commonwealth military health services are entirely at your disposal."

He was about to nod to the general and stalk away, when a squeeze came from the hand on his arm. He glanced quizzically down at Tapper, whose eyes darted to the general – no, to his rank insignia.

Belatedly, he drew himself up and issued a salute which, if not crisp, would probably suffice to prevent him from being dinged for insubordination. The general returned it, still looking a bit on the puzzled side, but he didn't make any further comment as they walked away. The escort on his other arm was waved off, so by the time they rounded the corner, it was just him and Tapper.

He let out a long, drawn-out breath. "Christ, sarge. Do the rest of the brass have their heads that far up their asses?"

The other man shrugged. "They're the brass, kid. That's their prerogative."

"They actually think Mars was a *success*? Our last foothold in the solar system all but obliterated, and rah-rah, everything's great?"

"It could have been a lot worse."

"*Worse?*" He stopped in his tracks, turning to face his compatriot. "How many of us made it out, sarge? How many of the 47th?"

The older man grimaced. "Seven."

"*Seven*? From the whole platoon? Who?"

They were ticked off on fingers. "You. Me. Singh. Lee. Sadler. Okumbo. Gray."

"Jesus. Kiroyagi?"

"Sniper on the Hellas ridge. She was dead before she hit the ground."

He squeezed his temples between thumb and forefinger. "Shit."

"They knew what they were signing up for. Remember what Kiroyagi said?"

"But we *picked* them, sarge. We sent those people to their death."

"Yes, we did. But that's the job, kid."

He looked up into the older man's eyes. "So why are *we* still here?"

The other man sighed. "That's the question we'll be asking for the rest of our lives, believe me."

CHAPTER 16

Over the years, Kovalic had found himself dealing with any number of station chiefs on a half a dozen different worlds. A few were more than happy to roll over for him, no doubt starry-eyed about the potential glory that might descend upon them at the conclusion of a successful covert operation. Most, though, resented any interference on their patch. For Kovalic, it was often a "There but for the grace of God..." moment – in another life, he probably would have ended up running a station. Somehow he didn't think he was quite cut out for that.

Mainly, because then *he* would have been dealing with all the interlopers intruding on his territory. And he would be more than a bit envious of their ability to ride in and out, and not reap the consequences.

"Let me get this straight," M'basa said, folding her hands calmly – too calmly, Kovalic noted – on her desk. "You used Commonwealth resources to initiate unauthorized surveillance on a sovereign power's embassy, while already *on* foreign soil, and then you lost not one but *two* operatives while witnessing the abduction of a foreign dignitary?"

It had taken them about an hour to ditch the surveillance van and get back to the embassy. Tapper had made a number of attempts to raise Brody on comms, but the system that he and Nat had been using was short range, so they hadn't held out much hope of a response, and indeed had got none. Having left the van in an underground garage that they'd jimmied open, they'd made the rest of the way back to the embassy on foot. The gate guard had shifted since Kovalic had arrived, but they had produced their respective cover identities and had him call M'basa, who had fortunately been burning the midnight oil. As a result, they had ended up providing an improvised debriefing to the station chief as the clock ticked towards tomorrow.

Kovalic looked at Tapper, who shrugged, and then back to M'basa. "That's about the size of it."

"*About* the size of it, or the exact size of it?" said M'basa, her eyes narrowing.

"Well we may also have been spotted by Bayern's security services."

"Oh, sure, of *course*," said M'basa. "Why not? God help me, you and your outfit are a *menace*." She stared pointedly at Kovalic.

"Our job does sometimes put us in unusual situations–"

"Congratulations: you've just been awarded the understatement of the year award. You can pick it up on your way off my planet." She sighed. "Shit. I'm going to have to brief the ambassador on this."

Kovalic exchanged a glance with Tapper. "I wouldn't do that, if I were you."

"I'm sure you wouldn't. You'd probably just break his knees or something, would you?"

"I mean, I think that might be above and beyond," said Kovalic, ignoring the acerbic glance that so frequently accompanied deliberately ignored sarcasm. "But what I mean to say is that if you *do* inform Ambassador Khan, then this unavoidably becomes a diplomatic incident. And once it becomes a diplomatic incident, then he's got to reach out to the Illyrican ambassador. That means any chance *we* have of quietly locating and rescuing our people drops to zero."

M'basa leaned back in her chair, her dark eyes flicking towards some point in space beyond their heads as she thought. "And I take it you don't think that the Bayern security forces are up to the task of finding them?"

Tapper barely suppressed a chuckle that earned him a glare from M'basa. "Yes, Mr Tormundsen?"

"Er, I was just commenting, deputy consul, that Bayern security, good as they may be, are in over their heads here. Hell, how many murders do they see a year: two or three? I doubt that they have an adequately equipped hostage rescue team."

"You're asking me to authorize a covert operation on foreign soil. That's *way* above my pay grade. The ambassador is the Commonwealth Executive's representative here; that means he needs to approve anything of this sort."

Bureaucracy: truly, Kovalic's greatest enemy. "In our experience, the diplomatic corps prefer to have a certain degree of plausible deniability when it comes to direct action."

M'basa rubbed at her brow as though she could somehow erase any memory of them being here.

"Look, I appreciate your concerns, deputy consul," said Kovalic. "But I have two members of my team missing in action. My top priority is making sure that they're safe."

"Your loyalty is commendable, Mr Austen," she said, sighing again. "I don't suppose you have any actual leads on your missing people?"

Reaching into his jacket pocket, Kovalic produced his night-vision binoculars. "I have a recording of one of their vehicles. If your tech team can clean up the image, we might be able to pull a registration number and backtrack."

M'basa held out her hand. "I'll see what I can do, but I can't make any promises."

"Thanks," said Kovalic, depositing the binoculars in her outstretched palm. "I appreciate it."

"*But*," said M'basa, raising her other hand with a warning finger. "I'm not giving you carte blanche here. You find a lead, you come to me, understood? If it's actionable, we go to the ambassador and do this all by the book."

"Understood."

"And I have to ask: do you think your people's covers will hold up to scrutiny?"

Kovalic looked to Tapper, who hesitated.

"I don't think there was any reason for suspicion directed at Ms Mulroney," he said slowly. "Mr Adler, though – well, his identity *ought* to remain intact." His voice dropped to a mutter. "As long as he hasn't done anything stupid."

M'basa ignored the *sotto voce* comment, and turned her attention back to Kovalic. "Do you have any idea who's behind the abduction?"

Another almost imperceptible glance shot between Kovalic and Tapper, but it didn't go unnoticed by M'basa. "Spill it."

"It's unlikely to be a homegrown group. The Corporation has remained staunchly independent, and though there are no doubt factions who'd prefer not to deal with the Imperium, this is a bit extreme. There's no history of this kind of violent activity onworld."

"So who *is* a likely culprit?"

"Well," said Kovalic. "In a situation like this, you have

to ask yourself who has the most to gain by potentially destabilizing the Imperium. And that would seem to point right back to..." He waved his hand at the room at large.

M'basa blinked, then gave a short, sharp laugh. "I'm sorry, I could have sworn you just suggested that *CID* snatched the crown prince."

"If the shoe fits..."

"A direct action op of that caliber would have had to have been approved by the station chief, who, in case you've lost track, is *me*."

"Sure," said Kovalic, leaning back in his chair. "Just like they told you *we* were coming."

M'basa's mouth set in a hard line. "Point taken," she said. "But not everybody at CID is quite as reckless as you and your team."

"Fair enough," said Kovalic. "But even if it isn't CID, there are half a dozen different organizations in the Commonwealth's intelligence apparatus. Frankly, though, I'd limit our search to just a couple."

"Such as?"

"Well, the initial lead on this whole deal was through NICOM, but they showed little interest in following up on it – and they didn't oppose their officer going to *my* boss, so I can't imagine they would have mobilized their own team. Nor do I think the Marine Intelligence Group is a likely candidate – too much military oversight to be allowed to drop in like this. The Commonwealth Security Bureau isn't tasked for operations outside of Commonwealth worlds – this isn't in their wheelhouse."

"I appreciate the thorough analysis, Mr Austen," said M'basa, a dry tone creeping into her voice, "but cut to the chase."

"If it wasn't *us*," he said, gesturing to himself and Tapper, "then the only logical outfit is the black-bag guys in CID's Activities Division. They could get authorization without it having to be approved by the local station chief, and they've got the hardware and operational expertise to pull it off."

M'basa sighed, rubbing her hands over her face. "You think it was them?"

"I... don't know," said Kovalic. "And I don't know that it matters – if we're going to chase a lead, we have to do it from the evidence we *have*, not the theories we've cobbled together. It's something to keep in the back of our head, though."

"But if it *is* a Commonwealth agency, then Ms Mulroney ought to be safe, shouldn't she?"

"Due respect," Tapper piped in, "but we can't assume that's the case. Ms Mulroney won't break her cover voluntarily. There's a real chance we'll just end up with some very big, very unfortunate misunderstanding."

"Agreed," said Kovalic. "I think we have to proceed under the assumption that both our agents are in hostile – if unknowing – hands."

"The bigger problem," said Tapper, "is that if IIS's thought process follows ours even broadly, they're likely to be barking up *your* tree."

That didn't seem to improve M'basa's day. "I'm about this close," she held up her hand with her thumb and forefinger a smidgen apart, "to taking your advice about not talking to the ambassador and shredding it."

"Look," said Kovalic, "we've still got some time here. Their ambassador isn't going to talk to ours until IIS has had a chance to try and lock things down – for one thing, they sure as hell don't want to look like they lost their own crown prince on foreign soil. The second they have to go outside their house, this is going to leak like nobody's business. I doubt they've even told the Corporation anything more than that there was some sort of vague security incident. I'd say we've got at least twelve hours before the Illyricans are knocking on our door and we've got an intergalactic incident on our hands." He looked at Tapper, who dipped his head in agreement.

"So, in other words, we're playing a game of diplomatic chicken," said M'basa.

"You learn fast, deputy consul."

"I do," said M'basa, folding her hands. "And you two better *move* fast, because when the ambassador's morning briefing rolls around, he's going to get the full story, no matter what. Find your people and bring them home. Tonight."

"In that case," said Kovalic, nodding to the binoculars he'd handed over, "get me the registration number off that recording as soon as possible."

It took about half an hour for M'basa to roust a tech and get her, still bleary-eyed, to the embassy via private car. She was ushered into a secure office, where she was – somewhat to her addled dismay – placed under lock and key by a pair of marines.

Tapper insisted on hanging over the young woman's shoulder, ignoring her sleep-deprived annoyance, while Kovalic took the opportunity to procure coffee from the embassy kitchen for the four of them. If nothing else, it gave his brain a chance to chew through the events of the last several hours.

Nat would be fine – she could take care of herself. No matter how much he repeated the thought, his brain kept derailing into nightmare scenarios. On the way back from the kitchen, he detoured into the embassy's back garden, breathing in the cool, late night air, and sipping from one of the disposable cups.

He ought to report back to the general, he knew, but the situation on the ground was too uncertain. Even if a diplomatic fast courier were sent right now – and wouldn't that look suspicious – it would be at least sixteen hours before they'd get a response back. Not nearly fast enough. And even with his best guess being twelve hours before the Illyricans admitted they'd lost the heir to the throne, it was still just that – a guess. The Imperium might go counter-intuitive, put pressure on the Corporation to mobilize a ground search, shut down air traffic. Another reason not to send a diplomatic courier: if the Illyricans thought they were behind the prince's abduction, any Commonwealth vessel raising ship – diplomatic registration or not – would no doubt be intercepted by whatever Illyrican naval forces had brought the prince to the planet in the first place. And if it looked like the Commonwealth was in any way involved with the prince's abduction, then relations between the two powers might escalate from heated words to live fire pretty damn quickly.

Kovalic ran a hand through his hair; it felt long against his fingers. He hadn't had it cut since before they'd left for Sevastapol. Between that and the sandpaper around his jaw, Tapper's comparison to a longshoreman had probably been pretty accurate. Somehow, though, he didn't think he'd have much time for a shave and a haircut before this whole thing was over.

He flexed his right arm, a muted lance of pain shooting down it. The adrenaline had suppressed much of it during the night's earlier activities, but none of that had been particularly good for his injured shoulder. He should probably check to see if he needed to reapply the sealant before they got under way.

His comm chimed and he tapped his earbud. "Yep."

"It's me, boss," said Tapper's voice. "They've cleaned up the image as good as it's going to get, and the plate's more or less readable."

"Run a pattern match?"

"Already done. It's a rental – surprise – pulled from the spaceport lot about twelve hours ago."

"Twelve hours? That's not much prep time."

"No, it isn't," said Tapper. "The ID's a dummy, of course, but there is a local address attached. Might be nothing…"

"… but it's worth checking out," finished Kovalic. "Think you can sweet talk the deputy consul into loaning us another vehicle from the pool?"

"Why me?"

"I think she likes you."

"I'm not sure she'd loan me the bullet to shoot myself," said Tapper dubiously.

"I've got faith in you, sergeant. I'll see you in the parking garage in ten." So much for the coffee, he thought, leaving the cups on the dry, unnaturally green grass.

M'basa had been nice enough to provide him with a room, where he used the facilities to replace his dressing. Whatever the doctor back on Nova had done was clearly still holding; the wound didn't look considerably worse for wear than it had that morning – he was lucky he hadn't compromised the patch. He slapped on a new bandage anyway, then pulled on his shirt and jacket, wishing he'd brought a spare change of clothes. He could use the Trollope identity's bank account to buy something, but he sincerely doubted that any of Bayern's haberdasheries were going to be open at – he glanced at his watch – 01:37.

Combing his fingers through his hair, he gave himself a hard look in the mirror, and headed down to the garage.

Tapper was waiting, lounging against a concrete pillar. The garage was mostly empty, except for a few black hovercars of the same type they'd seen get ambushed that night, and another van identical to the one they'd used.

"She was *this close* to flipping me off and giving us a metro pass," said Tapper. "But I pointed out that that would give a trail for the Corp to track us, and I guess she decided better of it."

"So, what have we got?" Kovalic asked, dubiously eyeing the official-looking vehicles in evidence.

Tapper nodded his head, and the two men walked around the pillar he'd been leaning against. The sergeant waved his hands. "Ta da."

It was probably about ten years old, and you could see every year in the minor dings and scuffs that adorned the silver chassis. A good kick might very well take the rear bumper off. It wasn't flashy, that's for sure, but nor was it so battered that it would stand out in a crowd.

"I'm told it's the most popular model of car in the city," said Tapper, tossing the fob to Kovalic. "I think she's just hoping to collect on the insurance when we inevitably wreck it."

"She's not going to get much of a payout, by the looks of it." Kovalic popped the driver seat door and slipped inside, feeling the seat creak in mighty protest. Tapper joined him on the other side, and they buckled themselves in.

"Almost enough to make you want to play by CID's rules, eh?" said Tapper. "Then they wouldn't be so reticent about lending us the good stuff." He cast an eye at the van on the other side of the garage.

"That thing screams 'counterintelligence,' Tap. We want to keep a low profile. Presumably this hunk of junk at least has a deniable registry plate."

"So I'm told. But that may just be because nobody wants to admit to owning it."

Kovalic punched the ignition. The dashboard display glowed green, reporting on all the system statuses. Fuel cells fully charged; the range suggested they could make several hundred kilometers. The power flow was clean, the repulsor field was solid – the car gave every indication that it was well maintained. As they said, it was what was under the hood that really counted.

"All right," said Kovalic. "Let's check out this lead."

Twenty minutes later, Kovalic pulled the silver car into a parking spot across the street from G27-12 and flipped off the headlights. The G ring was in the middle of Bergfestung, a somewhat unremarkable residential neighborhood. Like most of the residences in the city, it was a mid-rise edifice of concrete, steel, and glass, with railing-lined balconies. A few trees sat forlornly outside, their deaths forestalled only by the sun-mimicking lamps.

Kovalic pulled out the binoculars, which Tapper had reclaimed from the lab after the tech's recovery job. Scanning up and down the building, he didn't see a single lit window.

"Nobody home?"

"It *is* the middle of the night, boss."

"Fair enough. What's the apartment number on this guy?"

Tapper brought up the record on his sleeve. "Unit 302. Third floor, I'd guess."

So far, so good. There'd been zero chance that M'basa was

going to let them draw weapons from the station's armory, so best to keep it quiet as possible.

"Let's go."

The lights on the trees at the front made it unwise to attempt a breach there, so they hopped the five-foot fence without too much trouble and crept around to the rear. There would have to be some sort of back door, Kovalic reasoned.

The rear of the building abutted on a similar-looking apartment complex on the next hubward ring. In between was the dark square of a swimming pool, surrounded by carefully watered grass.

Tapper nudged him in the ribs and gestured towards a sliver of light coming from the back of the building. Kovalic waved him towards it, following a few steps behind.

That arc of light turned out to be from an emergency exit – some careless soul had left it propped open, a rubber doorstop jammed in the opening. Next to the door, a small keypad access box blinked in alternating shades of red and green, like a Christmas decoration. But there was no audible alarm, and it didn't look as though security was going to be on their way any time soon.

Kovalic frowned, crouching and running his fingers over the sidewalk until he found was he was looking for: a small pile of ash. Pinching it between his fingers, he rubbed them together, then stood, dusting his hands off on his trousers.

"Someone was smoking," he murmured. "Still warm."

"Nasty habit," said Tapper. He pulled the door open and gestured to Kovalic, who certainly didn't need a second invitation. Hanging around outside an apartment complex's back door in the middle of the night was a good way to have an encounter with the security services. *Another* encounter, anyway.

The emergency stairwell was well lit by the harsh blue glow of lighting strips, illuminating dull gray, featureless walls. A metal railing switchbacked alongside the steps, leading upward. Kovalic stood still for a moment, breathing shallowly and listening for any indication that they weren't alone. But the stairwell was silent, aside from a faint whine from the lighting strips.

Beckoning to Tapper, he began to make his way upwards, climbing quickly but deliberately and maintaining a careful balance between noise and speed. They passed the door for the second floor, a heavy sheet of steel with wire-reinforced glass.

They came to a stop at the third floor, and Kovalic nodded at Tapper to take the door. The sergeant lined up alongside it and slowly turned the knob and pulled it open, allowing Kovalic to slip through.

He surveyed the hallway: off-white walls, a wall-to-wall carpet of a ghastly green-and-white pattern, a row of doors on either side. Opposite the stairwell, the metal doors of an elevator; the readout next to it indicated that it was currently in the lobby. There was no sign of any security cameras, and what lighting there was glowed dimly from ornate sconces on either side of the hall.

Holding open the door from his side, Kovalic waved Tapper in, and the sergeant squeezed through. Kovalic let the door shut quietly behind them, keeping the knob turned so that the sound of the latch springing back into place wouldn't be heard.

A helpful sign on the wall next to the stairwell door pointed to the right for units 300 through 305. The unit they were looking for was the second door, facing the street where they'd parked the car. Like most modern buildings, it had foregone a mechanical or keycard lock for a wirelessly activated security system.

Kovalic held up his sleeve to the lock and tapped a few keys. Every manufacturer still had their own built-in override for maintenance, testing, and emergency service use. And those were only as secure as their chief engineer after a few drinks. All you had to do was find who made the system and...

The door lock clicked open as his sleeve found the right master key. Kovalic flattened himself against the wall next to the door's hinges, Tapper taking up the same position on the opposite side, then pushed the door slowly open. Within there was only darkness.

He nodded to Tapper, who acknowledged by slipping around the doorframe and into the apartment in a low crouch. The sergeant disappeared into darkness, and after a moment, Kovalic followed suit, letting the door close softly behind him.

As his eyes adjusted to the dim light filtering in from the street, he could pick out more details. The main room, a living area, was blandly appointed with a sofa and armchair in an unappealing shade of gray, a coffee table, an end table with a lamp, and a small desk and chair in one corner. An entertainment nook hung on one wall, but it contained only a small, generic viewscreen.

To the left was a galley kitchen with an open doorway and a long countertop facing the living area, while the right wall had two additional doors, the first of which was open, showing a small dark space which Kovalic pegged as a bathroom. That left the last door as a bedroom.

Pointing to himself, Kovalic nodded to the bedroom door, then waved at Tapper to check the rest of the apartment.

Tapper gave him a high sign, summoning on a red-tinged

light from his sleeve that would make it easier to search the room without interfering with his night vision.

Kovalic carefully turned the knob, letting the door open a crack; it squealed ever so slightly, and he winced at the sound. He keyed his own sleeve to low-light illumination and swept it across the room. Like the living room, this too seemed to have only the barest of necessities: a bed, an end table with a lamp, and another armchair that appeared to be a twin to the one in the living room. The curtains in here were somewhat more substantial than the other room's, blocking out more of the light from the street.

The hairs on the back of his neck stood to attention suddenly, the strong sensation of an indistinct warning. Something that he'd overlooked. Something that he was ignoring. With a frown, he rounded the bed towards the end table, crouching down to pull open its single drawer and peer inside. There was just a laminated card which, as he ran the light over it, turned out to be nothing more than maintenance and emergency contacts for the apartment complex.

He first attributed the slight rustle from behind as Tapper coming into the room, but too late his brain realized that he'd never heard the bedroom door. His muscles tensed, but before he could move an inch he felt something cold press against the nape of his neck, and heard the telltale click of a safety being flicked off – a sound he much preferred to be on the other side of.

"Hello, Simon," said a soft, but familiar voice. "Fancy meeting you here."

CHAPTER 17

Well, I can't say they're the worst *accommodations I've ever had.*

Eli paced around the fifteen-by-fifteen-foot room, once again examining every crack in the wall, the lone ventilation duct, the locked door. None of them had changed since his last circuit, two minutes prior. Or the one two minutes before that. Not a single thing had changed, in fact, since he'd awoken here about half an hour earlier, except that his feet were cold.

His captors had had the decency to leave him with his undershirt, underwear, and trousers. But they'd taken his dress shirt and tie, his jacket, his shoes, and even his socks. *Damn it, that was the nicest set of clothes I've ever owned.* And his trouser pockets had been turned out. He'd checked for the earbud, but it had either fallen out when he'd been hit or been removed.

He could try banging on the door again. But Eli didn't think it likely that, were someone to actually answer him, it would be with a surprised "Oh, you poor duck, how did you manage to lock yourself in this strange room? Let's get you out of there and into a bowl of hot soup."

His head was still a little bit fuzzy, which was probably the result of the rather large lump on the back of his skull. Oddly enough, he hadn't noticed it at first, but once he had found it he didn't seem able to forget about it. Now it pulsed, sending sonar ripples of pain through his head.

The room itself was pretty empty: just a threadbare cot, whose springs creaked like a dying man's last breath, a drab green plastic bucket, and a sickly light fixture in the ceiling that left the room bathed in a jaundiced yellow.

Dropping to the bed, he rubbed at his temples. He'd been at the Illyrican embassy. On Bayern – god, he hoped he was still on Bayern, or this mission had gone the pearest of shapes. Images whirled through his head, carousel-like, until he slowed them down and started to pick out individual ones.

A hovercar on fire. Taylor getting into a hovercar with the Imperium's crown prince. Running towards the car, with Erich.

Erich. Whoever grabbed him might have taken Erich too. And Erich wasn't some nobody from the colonies; he was the son of one of the most powerful men in the Imperium. Somebody would be looking for them…

Uh, I think that news might be a little overshadowed by the kidnapping of the emperor's heir, his brain reminded him. Someone would definitely be looking for *him*.

That assumed, of course, that his captors were the same people who had snatched Taylor and the prince. Then again, if they weren't, then Bayern had a serious abduction problem.

Somehow, he needed to contact Tapper. Presumably the sergeant was still free and could get a message to the Commonwealth embassy, or Kovalic, or the general, or *someone*. But he was locked, half-naked, in this room, and somehow he didn't think his captors would be calling him a courier service.

Taking a deep breath, he reminded himself that it wasn't as though he were going to be locked up in here forever. He wasn't dead yet, which boded well. At the very least, they'd figured he was worth something, or that he had something they wanted. Which meant they'd have to feed him at some point. That might give him a chance to gather some more information about his situation.

Until then, he just had to stay cool. He exhaled at length, then gingerly prodded at the bump on his head. It still evoked a wince, but not the stars-lighting-up effect it had had when he'd first gotten up. He might have a mild concussion, but he'd woken up of his own accord, so that was probably a good sign.

All things being what they were, he supposed he had little better alternative than to lie down on the cot and rest until his captors showed up to feed or interrogate him. He flexed his fingers.

Waiting. A pilot's least favorite game. He pulled himself up the cot and stretched out.

The voice of Dr Thornfield suddenly echoed in his head, just as it had during his simulation exercises. *Relax. Close your eyes. Breathe deeply. Concentrate on those breaths. Then visualize what you're going to do, slowly, deliberately.* He'd never put much stake in the psychobabble, but he had to admit – grudgingly, of course – that it had helped him make progress. This wasn't flying, but it was a stressful situation, and many of the same triggers applied, so why not?

He closed his eyes, and took a deep breath, focusing on drawing the air into his lungs and then expelling it. Again. In his mind's eye, he pictured himself in the cockpit of a fighter, waiting to be ambushed. And yet he felt strangely calm – ready, but not tensed. He felt...

Eli must have dozed off, because the next thing he knew his eyes were sliding open at the sound of the door's lock clicking. He had enough presence of mind to remember that his head injury probably wouldn't take too well to suddenly bolting upright, and took a moment to gather himself before he sat up.

The door swung open, admitting a man around Eli's own age. Average height, build that looked more towards the stocky side, most of it probably muscle. His black hair was cropped short around his head in a military cut, and his brown face was broad, with a prominent nose and dark, quick eyes. He carried a plastic-wrapped package that he tossed on the cot, along with a bottle of some sort of juice.

Behind him, a hand closed the door; Eli heard it lock again. The man leaned against one of the walls, nodding at the package. Eli cast a wary glance at the square, which appeared to contain an unremarkable ham-and-cheese sandwich. His stomach growled at the sight of it; he'd eaten very little at the cocktail party, and he'd probably been out for at least a few hours.

Part of his brain insisted that he shouldn't take their food, that it could be poisoned or drugged. But another part reminded him that they'd gone through great trouble to keep him alive. Ultimately, the animal part of him was too ravenous to even care. He ripped the package open and sank his teeth into it, chewing noisily. Though the rubbery texture of the ham and the floppy slab of cheese signaled fare straight out of a vending machine, it was at the same time the most delicious food he had ever tasted.

"Feel better?" the man asked. His voice was thick, unhurried.

Eli shrugged, his mouth too full to answer. He swallowed. "You don't have any mustard, do you?"

"This ain't a restaurant, pal."

"Good thing, too," said Eli around another mouthful, "because let me tell you, the reviews would not be kind. The ambiance, for one thing…" he said, gesturing around the room.

The man crossed his arms over his chest, but didn't reply.

"Anyway," Eli continued – he'd given in to his somewhat unfortunate tendency to babble when not sure what else to do – "what can I do for you? Please, step into my office."

"Your name is Elijah Brody," said the man, finally. "You're a covert operative…"

The ham-and-cheese congealed in Eli's mouth, and he swallowed the lump whole, feeling it almost choke him on the way down. *They know my real name. I'm cooked. I screwed up* again.

"… for the Imperial Intelligence Services."

The last lump of sandwich almost made its way back up his throat at that, but he forced it down again. And then he started to laugh. And the more he laughed, the less he felt capable of controlling it. He threw back his head and laughed. He laughed until he had to wipe his eyes at the tears. And then he laughed some more.

When he'd finally worked through that, he gasped for air, looking over at the man against the wall, whose expression of stone-cold seriousness had been replaced with one that looked rather unsettled by the sudden outbreak of hysteria.

"Sorry," said Eli, still catching his breath. "I just thought of something funny. Not this, I mean. Something else. Continue."

"So glad to have amused you," said the man, his brows knitting. "You have no idea the joy it brings to my heart."

"I really don't think there's room for *both* of us to be sarcastic," said Eli, taking another bite of the ham-and-cheese monstrosity.

"Shaddup," the other growled. "We want to know exactly how much you know."

Well, this is an interesting situation. The thing he'd learned about misapprehensions was that they could be very valuable, if you played them right. And in this case, Eli's instincts – the same arguably misguided ones that had come to play in his conversation with Erich – were telling him one thing.

Double down.

"For the record," Eli said, imagining Taylor's voice and trying to keep his as evenly modulated, "I have no idea what you're talking about." He swallowed another chunk of ham-and-cheese, but the sandwich was quickly losing any remaining appeal.

The man's eyes narrowed. "I'm saying that Eyes didn't send an officer to the Illyrican embassy to snack on canapés. I want to know what you were doing there."

"You know, I didn't get to try the canapés," Eli said, folding the remains of the sandwich up into its plastic and putting it down on the cot. "I'm regretting that now." He pushed the package away with a finger.

A sort of twisted scowl crossed the man's face, and he pushed off the wall and strode over the bed, snatching up the sandwich. "Well, let me just get this offending item out of your sight, then."

"That would be great, thanks," said Eli, resisting the urge to flinch. The man was shorter than he was, but the broad set of his shoulders suggested that he'd have little problem besting Eli in any sort of physical contest. Still, he couldn't afford to look scared in front of this guy or he'd lose any leverage he might have.

"Fine," said the man. "But you're going to talk *eventually*. If not now, then later, when we get more… *convincing*."

"That sounds rather like a threat."

"It was."

"No, no, a threat sounds like this." He locked eyes with the man, but let his tone take on an edge of the steel that he remembered from the first time he'd met Kovalic. "If you touch one hair on the head of *any* of your 'guests,' you're going to wish that you had never ever had anybody in your life that you cared about, because both they and you will regret it. You have my word on that."

The other man's expression didn't change, but Eli noticed that his weight had shifted to his rear foot, as though he were subconsciously taking a step back.

"I mean, if I were in the business of making threats." He gave the other man a friendly smile.

The man didn't return it. If anything, he looked like he really, really wanted to punch Eli, but he apparently managed to control that impulse, instead crumpling up the sandwich even further in his fist. Finally, he shrugged, poorly feigning an air of indifference.

"Suit yourself." He turned on his heel and banged on the door. It opened in response, and the man stalked out with a parting glare over his shoulder. The door slammed closed after him, the lock clicking closed with funereal finality.

Eli sat staring at the door for a minute, then let out a breath that would have inflated a balloon and fell backwards on the cot. He sucked air through his teeth as the bump on his head hit the not-so-soft mattress, and turned onto his side, rubbing at the spot gingerly.

It hadn't been a total loss – he'd picked up a few salient details. For one thing, whoever these people were, they weren't IIS, or else they would have already known that Eli wasn't one of them. Not that he could imagine why IIS would want to kidnap the heir to the crown *anyway*, but if he'd learned anything about espionage during his – admittedly brief – career, it was that it rarely followed the rest of the universe's definition of "sense."

Despite having an ear for accents, he'd been unable to place his interlocutor's. It had been flattened, generic, the kind of gruff tone that wouldn't have been out of place on any of a dozen worlds. Nor had his word choice been particularly illuminating. Then again, veiled threats didn't always involve the most sophisticated vocabulary.

He'd also concluded that, besides absconding with Taylor and the prince, his captors had most assuredly taken Erich von Denffer, too. There was no reason Taylor's cover should have been compromised, and he didn't see her giving up either of their real names quite that fast. Nor had she known about his IIS play – Erich had been the only one he'd told, and Erich knew his real name. He was a little surprised that the man had just blurted it out, but on the other hand, Erich's priority was protecting the prince, and letting them know they had also pissed off IIS might have been a strategic move, letting the abductors know they were in over their heads.

So, what kind of options did that leave him? In retrospect, he wasn't sure that threatening the man had been the most prudent course of action; he could only go so far down that road before he'd be forced to back up those threats. Maybe he could deal – try to convince the man, or one of his compatriots, to betray the others. He dismissed the idea almost as soon as it had occurred to him. The way the man had stood, his whole bearing, said ex-military. Or, come to think of it, active military. If they were mercenaries, Eli might be able to appeal to their greed, but again, he'd be forced to make good on that. But if they were fighting men, the chances of getting one to turn on the others seemed low. Brotherhood, loyalty, all that crap.

That also seemed to eliminate any chance of escape: There was no way he was going to be able to overpower the guards with his rudimentary, almost a decade-old, combat training.

If I get out of this, I'm going to insist on a refresher.

What he really needed was to talk to Taylor. Presumably she was here somewhere, and she'd probably have a much better plan. But it would be suspicious for him to demand to see her – after all, she was ostensibly a nobody. Not like the prince…

He blinked. The prince. If they thought Eli was IIS, he could demand to see the prince. That would make sense. He wasn't sure they'd accommodate him, but it couldn't hurt. Probably.

Something about actually having a plan cheered him. Enough that he cracked open the bottle of juice that his guard had left him and took a great big swig. He made a sour face at the taste and glanced at the bottom of the bottle.

Expired, six months ago.

Worst room service ever.

An hour later, the door clanked open again. Eli hadn't been sleeping, just lying on the cot with his hands cradled behind his head, staring at the ceiling. He'd been trying to review the principles of spaceflight in his head, harkening back to his first year at the academy, in the hopes that it would give him something else to think about beyond his current situation.

The first man into the room was his conversation partner from earlier, but this time he wasn't alone. A second guard dragged in another figure, more bedraggled than the last time Eli had seen him, but still undeniably Erich von Denffer. There was an ugly bruise high on Erich's left cheek, and his previously immaculate dress uniform had been torn at the seams. Even his usually perfect hair had been mussed. He looked somewhat dazed, but his eyes cleared when he saw Eli.

"Eli," he started.

Shit.

"Not another word, Erich," he said, shaking his head. "You've said enough."

Erich at least had the decency to look abashed. "I'm… I'm sorry."

The man who had dragged in Erich pulled in a pair of chairs from the hallway, setting them up opposite the end of the cot. The man to whom Eli had talked earlier sat down in one and Erich was pushed down into the other, on the man's right. He refused to meet his captor's eyes. The second guard took up a position leaning against the room's door.

"Now," said the first man, eyes on Eli. "Let's have another little chat. This time with incentive." He reached into his jacket and removed a pistol, flipping the safety off with an audible click.

"Come on," said Eli, trying to force down the anxiety bubbling his stomach. "You can't expect me to believe after all the trouble you've gone through that you're just going to shoot me."

"Not at all," said the man. "You're our distinguished guest." He raised the pistol at him, then swung his arm so it was pointed at Erich. "Him, though? Him, I'll shoot."

Eli gritted his teeth. *Goddamn it.* He had to force each word out. "What *exactly* do you want to know?"

The man did a reasonable imitation of smiling pleasantly. "See? That's much better. Now, tell me why IIS sent you to the embassy."

And now it's time to get inventive. But not too inventive. Stick to the truth where you can.

"To help keep an eye on the prince." Technically true.

"That wasn't so hard, was it?" said the man. He lowered the weapon, but kept it resting on his knee. "Is keeping an eye on Prince Hadrian one of your normal duties?"

"Definitely not."

"Then why now?"

"We had reason for concern."

"This one," said the man, nodding at Erich, "said you told him threats had been made against the Illyrican presence here."

Eli shrugged, noncommittal. "We get a lot of threats."

"But you reportedly told him these threats were 'credible.'"

He gave an inward sigh. *Christ, Erich. Show a little backbone. One punch and you spill everything?* "Look, threat assessment isn't really my department. You'd have to ask someone higher up the food chain."

"I'm glad you brought that up," said the man, leaning forward. His eyes glinted with interest. "Who do you report to, Mr Brody?"

Here's where things get dicey. Dicier. "I'm not going to tell you that."

"No?" said the man. He pointed the pistol at Erich's head again. "I'd ask you to reconsider."

"Don't get me wrong," said Eli quickly, "I'm not eager to see you blow Commander von Denffer's brains out. But consider what they'll do to *me* if they find I've given my superior's name to a bunch of thugs. No offense intended – I'm sure you're all lovely people when you're at home."

"I'd suggest you worry less about what *may* happen in the future and more about what's happening right now."

Eli blinked. "If you're saying that you're going to kill me, well, that's not exactly persuasive, is it? What's my incentive then?"

"I can make it less painful," he said, smiling wide.

You never worked in sales, did you? Eli had been racking his brains since the man had asked about his superior. The easiest thing to do would be to give them a fake IIS officer's name and hope that Erich was quick enough to back his play. That would send them running in circles, hopefully buying enough time for *someone* to come looking for them. But Erich hadn't exactly shown to be either quick on the uptake *or* terribly reliable. So Eli fell back to plan B: giving them the name of the one IIS officer he actually knew.

"Colonel Harry Frayn," he said with a sigh.

The man nodded – as if he'd been expecting that answer, Eli realized. *They know who Frayn is. Did Erich tell them that too?*

A lead weight suddenly dropped in his stomach, the undeniable sense that he had missed some crucial piece of information and was now in way, way over his head. He swallowed, his mouth suddenly dry, and worked the sandpaper strip that was his tongue around, trying to moisten it again.

Eyes on the ball. Don't get distracted. "I've answered your questions," said Eli, looking the other man square in the eye. "But that's all you're getting unless you let me see the prince and his companion so I can make sure that they're safe." In his peripheral vision, he saw Erich's mouth drop open slightly, as though he couldn't believe that Eli was still bargaining.

"Oh?" said the man, resting the gun on his knee once more. "And why would I do that?"

Eli met his gaze. "Because you abducted them for a reason. That means you want something out of it – some sort of deal. And in that case, you're going to need to establish good faith." He spread his hands.

The man's face shifted into neutral, but for the briefest of seconds, Eli thought he saw a look of surprise there. That lead weight in his stomach plummeted another foot. *I'm not looking at the whole damn puzzle.*

"I'll take it under consideration," said the man, getting to his feet. He nodded to the second guard, who pushed himself off the wall and hauled Erich up by the scruff of his neck. "I'm glad you've decided to be cooperative, Mr Brody."

Eli swallowed, bile rising in his throat, as the men got to their feet. He'd critically misplayed his hand, and all because he was lacking some crucial piece of information that would make this whole situation fit together. The man had looked surprised when he'd offered a deal; he'd been expecting something else entirely. *Why wouldn't he want a deal?*

The most obvious answer was that the prince – and probably Taylor – were already dead, giving them nothing to bargain with. But that didn't make any sense, because why go through the trouble of taking them in the first place? If they'd simply wanted Prince Hadrian dead, the firefight in the street would have been a perfect opportunity.

The man had been surprised because he hadn't expected Eli to offer him a deal – because he'd thought Eli already *knew* that they wouldn't want a deal. His head spun. If they didn't want a deal then they also didn't want money, so there was some other reason they'd taken the heir to the Imperium. Which meant they weren't mercenaries; it had to be political.

The Commonwealth? They'd have a political reason to knock Hadrian off the chessboard. But that'd tip off a galactic incident and *turn Bayern into a hot zone.* And he had to believe that M'basa would have fought harder to keep Eli and the rest of the team out from underfoot if she'd known this was going down. Plus, the little he'd picked up from Kovalic about the Commonwealth Intelligence Directorate suggested that this would be pretty damn ballsy of them.

He scrambled to fit the pieces together as his interrogator unlocked the door. His window was rapidly closing: once they left the room, he might not get another shot in whatever the hell this was.

Threats. It all came back to the threats. The man had wanted to know what Eli knew about a threat against the prince, what Eli knew about *them.* They were worried that Eli had the inside line on them – no, not Eli: IIS. They were worried that IIS knew who they were. They'd recognized Frayn's name because they'd suspected he'd be involved in any attempt to track them down. But by offering a deal, Eli had tacitly confirmed that the IIS colonel *didn't* know what their agenda was. And that put them home free.

He'd tied the threads together in a knot about as tight as the one in his stomach, but it all pointed to one conclusion: something very, *very* wrong was going on here. To make matters worse, not only was he right in the middle of it, but he didn't have the slightest idea what *it* was, and he was rapidly running out of cards to play.

"Wait," he said slowly.

The second man had already shoved Erich out the door, but Eli's interrogator paused halfway through the doorway, looking back over his shoulder. He cocked an eyebrow.

"Look," said Eli. "On a purely professional level, I don't want any harm to come to the prince. But on a personal level, I don't give a shit about His Imperial Highness. The woman you took with him, though..." He looked down at hands, doing his best to don a sheepish expression. "I care about her, and she's not involved in any of this. I just want to know that she's OK." He raised his head, locking a plaintive gaze on the other man. "Please, let me see her."

The man gave a nasty chuckle. "You've got terrible taste in women, you poor bastard. That one threw you over as soon as she was within half a mile of the prince."

Eli cast his gaze downward again. "I... I know. Still..." He gave a helpless look at his captor.

With a deep, suffering sigh the other man finally shrugged. "No promises, but I'll see what I can do." With that, he left the room, closing and locking the door behind him.

Eli stared at the door listlessly, then fell back onto the cot, ignoring the jab of pain from the lump on his head. That was it. He'd expended every option he could think of, short of telling them who he really was. That didn't seem like it would buy him much, especially after he'd lied about everything else. The only thing left for him to do was sit back and wait – and hope that they wouldn't decide he was a liability. Hopefully, he'd at least bought a little breathing room.

Hurry up, Tapper. My time's running out.

CHAPTER 18

"It wasn't us," were the first words out of Kovalic's mouth. "What's more," he continued as he felt the gun muzzle jab into the nape of his neck, "you don't think it was us either. If you did, you wouldn't have been lurking here like a cheap cliché of a spy. Hell, we wouldn't even be having this friendly conversation."

"Don't mistake being friendly for being friends."

"As a mutual acquaintance of ours is fond of saying, in a business where you have no friends–"

"–the only people you can rely on are enemies," finished the other man with a sigh, pulling the gun barrel away from Kovalic's neck almost reluctantly. "Certainly would have made things a lot easier if it *had* been you fellows."

"You know as well as I do that nothing in this life is ever easy, Harry." He paused. "Can I get up now?"

"I'm not going to shoot you, if that's what you're asking."

"More or less." Kovalic got to his feet slowly, and turned around.

Colonel Harry Frayn was tucking the gun back in his waistband and rearranging his jacket. He'd put on a little weight since Kovalic had last seen him, about three months ago, but he'd never been the sveltest of men to begin with.

The file that Kovalic had seen on him suggested he'd been a wrestler when he was younger – he'd always made a point to stay out of the man's reach as much as possible. But of the many IIS officers Kovalic had encountered in his career in intelligence, he disliked Harry Frayn the least. For all of Frayn's pompous bluster, he was not only an extremely competent intelligence officer, but a good man to boot. Kovalic knew that he'd been a protégé of the general's back when the old man had still been in charge of IIS – and he suspected that Frayn was all too well-informed about the general's current whereabouts.

Which, it occurred to Kovalic, also adroitly positioned him to keep the general in the know about certain *sensitive* subjects…

"Also, if you wouldn't mind," Frayn continued, nodding at the bedroom door, "you might tell Sergeant Tapper he needn't lie in wait, ready to brain me over the head with–" he pursed his lips in thought, "–the lamp, unless I've missed my guess."

Kovalic grunted. "It's OK, Tapper. Come on in."

The door swung open slowly. "Seems to me we've got him outnumbered," said the older man, peering in, light fixture indeed clutched in one hand.

Frayn eyed the two of them. "Given the goodwill I just showed by *not* shooting Captain Kovalic in the neck, I think you might demonstrate the same level of restraint."

"I don't recall any expression about honor among *spies*," Tapper said cheerfully.

"Call it professional courtesy, then."

"Great," interrupted Kovalic, "now that we're all on the same page, let's talk about why we're here." He waved a finger in the air, indicating the room at large. "Anything to share, Harry?"

Frayn crossed his arms, tilting his head to one side. "You first."

Kovalic threw up his hands. "Sure, why not? We followed the registration on one of the vans used in the abduction, which gave us a dummy ID that had provided this address. Ipso facto presto change-o." He gestured around. "I take it you were on the prince's security detail?"

The older man tugged at his collar, grimacing. "In charge of, in fact. I mean, he has his own personal military guard, of course, but I was supposed to be handling the intelligence side of matters."

"Ouch."

"Quite." Frayn rubbed his jaw. "I don't have any more than you do, unfortunately."

"Super," said Kovalic. "You guys must have *some* leads. What kind of threat assessments do you have on the prince?"

"You mean the heir to the Illyrican Empire? Oh, you know, the usual ten thousand."

"Any in play on Bayern?"

Frayn shook his head. "That's where it gets weird. Bayern's pretty green in our matrix. The Corporation has adhered to its neutrality policy without fail – and made a tidy profit in the process. Whatever the threat is, it isn't homegrown."

"External groups?"

"Besides the Commonwealth?" said Frayn, raising an eyebrow.

"Harry, seriously. I don't know anything about this. I give you my word."

Frayn sighed. "Look, *I* believe you. But not only is the Commonwealth at the top of the list, the heir was seen leaving the party directly before the abduction in the company of a known Commonwealth agent." His blue eyes focused on Kovalic's. "It's circumstantial, but it's not *good* circumstantial."

Kovalic scratched his neck. "You, uh, know about–"

"Natalie? Yes. And I'm sorry, Simon. Damn fool girl," he muttered, "I *told* her to stay away from him."

"Well, you know Nat. Once she gets her teeth into something, she doesn't like to let go."

"I'm a little surprised that you sent her in with that new guy, what's his name?" Frayn's eyes narrowed, fishing.

Kovalic didn't blink. "He's young, but he's got potential, and there's really no substitute for field experience."

"Well, perhaps Mr Adler – for lack of a real name –" at this, Frayn's lips quirked into a smile, "could offer more information about what happened?"

Kovalic exchanged a glance with Tapper. "Mr Adler has not reported in since the incident."

"Oh dear. To paraphrase an old favorite, to lose one covert operative may be regarded as a misfortune – to lose two sounds like carelessness."

It was Kovalic's turn to fix his gaze on Frayn. "You wouldn't happen to know anything about that, would you, Harry?"

"My dear boy, are you implying that I have detained a Commonwealth intelligence operative on foreign soil?"

"Implying? No. Flat-out asking. From one enemy to another."

Frayn laughed. "Fair enough. No, Simon, I have not seen your Mr Adler since the party, nor have I had any report of his arrest. Meaning the logical conclusion is–"

"–whoever has Nat and the prince also has him."

The middle-aged man spread his hands wide, as though he were a magician producing a dove from thin air.

Kovalic's jaw clenched. Not the most welcome of news, but it confirmed the intuition that had already knotted his gut. "I intend to get them back."

"Of course, of course," said Frayn quickly. "I didn't mean to make light of the situation. Heaven knows I've plenty at stake of my own."

"Speaking of which," Tapper interjected, "perhaps we could get on with this."

Frayn looked around the room, shaking his head. "I've been over it with a fine-toothed comb. It's clean."

"Someone wiped it down?"

"No, you misunderstand me. It's *clean*. Look at this." Frayn pulled out a pocket lamp and flicked it on. The light was ultraviolet, filling the room with an eerie purple glow, like a photograph in negative. He played it around the room – the walls, the bed, the desk, the carpet. Everything was uniform, perfect.

"That's *way* too clean," murmured Kovalic. "Nobody wipes things down that much."

"It's factory clean," said Frayn. "As in 'never been used' clean. There should be at least a few splotches of bleach or other… less savory fluids."

"A dummy apartment to go with a dummy ID," said Kovalic. "I like the sound of this less and less." He nodded to the door. "We can send a team over to do a thorough sweep, but I don't think they're going to find anything."

Frayn coughed. "Or *we* could send a team over for a sweep. I was, after all, here first."

A tight smile appeared on Kovalic's face. "OK, cards on the table. We both want the same thing – to find whoever took our people. So maybe it's time to pool our resources."

"You want to work together?"

Kovalic shrugged. "Why not?"

"Maybe because our governments are at war?"

"A cold war," Kovalic pointed out. "Plus, it's not the first time you and I have found ourselves on the same side. Or have you forgotten that magical weekend we spent together on Trinity?"

Frayn sighed. "I have not. But this is different, Simon. The second most important person in the Imperium is missing. I'm going to have to report this to IIS Control and it's going to very quickly be out of my hands."

Kovalic tapped a finger against his lips. "Can you at least buy us some time?"

Frayn met his eyes, and his expression wavered. "It's going to take close to twenty hours to get word back from Illyrica as it is," he said. "I can't delay it too much or it's going to be *my* head when they find out I didn't report the abduction promptly."

"And what happens when you do, Harry? Your bosses are going to send a fleet full of soldiers who will tramp all over what little evidence we have, and we're going to get sidelined. The Illyrican military isn't exactly known for its deft touch."

Frayn let out a long breath. "Fair point."

"I'm just saying that we have a better chance of quietly finding them ourselves than with the kind of furor that's going to be raised by a galactic incident. And I know you – it's not like you're going to sit on your hands waiting for them to show up. I'm just saying that we wait a few hours and see if we turn up anything that leads us to the abductors *before* the military gets involved. Plus, how good would it look if you were to catch them on your own?" Kovalic raised his eyebrows.

"I'm not exactly in this for the commendations, as you might have noticed. The odds of me ever making anything beyond colonel are slim to no-chance-in-hell." He eyed Kovalic, as if weighing the options. "Fine. I'll delay the report. But if we don't have anything in six hours, then I need to send a courier."

"Six hours is more than reasonable. I've already asked our station chief to delay her report until we make some headway."

Rubbing at his eyes blearily, Frayn gave a nod. "Then I suppose we better make some sooner rather than later."

"All right," Kovalic said. "In that case, you get your team over here to analyze this place, see if they turn up anything. Tapper and I will check out the spaceport lead, just in case we can track down any sign of whoever rented that vehicle. We'll report as soon as we find anything."

"I'll do the same," said Frayn.

"Oh, and Harry," said Kovalic, testing a theory. "You do remember the *cardinal* rule of intelligence, right?"

Frayn returned a tight smile, but if he picked up on Kovalic's emphasis, he didn't show it. "Roll with the punches, Simon. Roll with the punches." With a tip to his disheveled mess of gray hair, he disappeared out the door.

"What was *that* about?" said Tapper.

"I'll tell you when we're…" he looked around the room, "… somewhere else. Come on."

Getting out of the apartment building was even easier than getting in; and within five minutes they were back in the silver hovercar. Fortunately, it came equipped with its own baffle, which Kovalic switched on as Tapper pulled away from the curb. The sonic dampening curtain descended around them, as though they'd suddenly set foot in a soundproof recording studio.

"What I'm about to tell you doesn't leave this car, sergeant. You don't tell anyone: Commander Taylor, Brody, Page – wherever the hell he is – nobody. Copy?"

"Cross my heart, hope to die."

"I never liked that expression."

"You were saying?"

Kovalic cleared his throat. "The general's got an asset embedded somewhere in the Imperial court or its staff."

"An *asset*?" Tapper whistled. "Do you know who–" he broke off, glancing sharply at Kovalic. "You think it's *Frayn*?"

Kovalic shrugged. "The general trained him. He's traveling with the prince. The shoe fits."

Tapper scratched his head with his free hand as he turned them left down a cross street. "I dunno, cap. Frayn's OK and all – as Eyes wonks go – but I don't see him leaking intelligence like that."

"I suppose it's academic. Either way: the general's asset told him that the prince would be here. That's why he sent me to Bayern – to warn Nat."

"Only you were just a little bit too late," finished Tapper.

"That's why I hate flying commercial."

"I thought it was the terrible food."

"That too."

Tapper glanced up through the transparent smoked aluminum that made up the hovercar's roof. "We're rapidly running out of night. So, now what?"

Kovalic drummed his fingers on the car's dashboard, staring out at the orange lightstrips streaking past in the darkness. "I'm not sure what we *can* do beyond what we told Frayn." It was silent for a moment, so he glanced over at the sergeant who was staring out the windshield.

"What's on your mind, sergeant?"

Tapper shook his head slowly. "Just thinking about the missing pieces."

"Care to elaborate?"

"We've been approaching this from the perspective that somebody's grabbed the prince just because he's the prince."

"Right."

"But because that crown is so shiny, it's blinding us to another important detail. We *also* know that Prince Fancypants is here as the Imperium's special envoy to Bayern, right?"

"Two for two."

"So maybe whoever grabbed him did so because of *that* hat, not the shiny, princely one."

"Huh." Kovalic blinked. "That's a really good point."

Tapper shrugged, an expression of faux modesty on his face. "I do have them from time to time, boss."

"That you do, sergeant. Have we figured out what the prince was supposed to be doing here?"

"Not beyond meeting with some Corporation bigwig."

"And I'm sure the Illyricans aren't going to be terribly forthcoming on that subject," said Kovalic. He reclined in his seat and stared up at the light that was starting to blossom across the cavernous city as the heliostats came online. "So, maybe it's time we paid a visit to the Corporation."

CHAPTER 19

"I just want it on the record," M'basa said, buttoning up her dark jacket, "that I think this is a stupid idea."

Kovalic was leaning against the elevator's chrome railing and staring through the glass sides, surveying the cityscape of Bergfestung falling below them. The sun had evidently risen outside, as the mirrors and fiber cables poured golden light across the buildings. To Kovalic, it looked surprisingly, heart-achingly, like a scene from Earth – albeit inside a giant volcano, which was a little odd.

"Come now," he said, shading his eyes with a hand as the sun caught him with a broadside. "If you really thought it was that stupid, would you even be here?"

M'basa sighed. "I didn't say it was the *stupidest*." She loosened her hair from the bun it had been piled into, combing her fingers through it before reworking it into the same shape. "Although it'd have been nice if you'd given me time for a shower. I've been up all night, you know."

"So have we," Tapper pointed out, from his spot leaning against the other side of the elevator, arms crossed.

"Hence the stupid idea. None of us are at the top of our game."

Kovalic turned around, putting his own back to the city

and eyeing the elevator's display, which was counting up rapidly. The Corporation's headquarters was by far the tallest building in Bergfestung, and since it was positioned roughly in the center of the city's circular layout, it had the virtue of also sitting directly below the volcano's opening, which afforded it room to reach a certain height. It also ensured that everybody else in the city had to look up to the Corporation.

"It's not *that* stupid an idea," Kovalic said. "The Corporation is in a position to provide us with information that the Imperium won't. And the job of client relations, unless I'm misunderstanding at a fundamental level, is to deal with clients – which, in Corporation parlance, means foreign powers. Like you." He nodded to M'basa.

She shook her head. "I'm still not sure why I'm going along with this."

"Because," said Kovalic, locking his gray eyes on her, "two Commonwealth citizens are missing after an attack in a Bayern city. And the Illyricans aren't exactly taking our calls these days."

M'basa raised her hands. "I know. I know. Sorry."

The elevator slowed as it reached the building's thirtieth floor and, with a chime, the doors slid open.

The room they stepped into gleamed, a vision in white marble. The incoming sunlight poured through floor-to-ceiling windows, which covered most of the "eastern" and "western" walls, tinging everything in a gold color that couldn't help but bring to mind the pecuniary prowess for which the Corporation was known. Smooth, gilded columns rose in four places, supporting a domed roof inside of which was painted, to Kovalic's surprise, a classical scene out of Greek mythology – Jason and the Golden Fleece, if he didn't miss his guess.

A bit on the nose, that.

A woman with a pale golden complexion stepped in front of them, sporting a smile that Kovalic instinctively distrusted. "Deputy consul M'basa," she began, her expression turning sympathetic, "I was sorry to hear about your citizens – thank you for calling me. Please, this way." She gestured towards the opposite end of the floor from them, where a corridor led away from the sun-dappled lobby.

"Thank you, Director Wei," said M'basa. "You remember Mr Tormundsen, I believe?"

"Of course." She inclined her head gracefully.

"And this is my… associate, Mr Austen."

The full brunt of her brown liquid eyes turned to Kovalic. "Mr Austen. A pleasure to meet you. I'm Amanda Wei, senior director of client relations."

Kovalic nodded. "Nice to meet you. James Austen. Diplomatic liaison." It was vague enough, but it wouldn't stand up to even a cursory check of the embassy's staff.

At a T intersection, Wei turned left, leading them to a number of small offices, each of which had their own spectacular view. "Have you identified your missing people, deputy consul?" Kovalic would have given even money that she already knew exactly who was involved, but, of course, appearances must be maintained.

M'basa glanced at Kovalic, then nodded. "Yes. That's why Mr Tormundsen is here. I'm afraid that Mr Adler and Ms Mulroney were attending the party at the Illyrican embassy when the unfortunate event occurred. We haven't heard from either of them since."

"Oh dear," said Wei, ushering them into a conference room with a long, oak table. She seated herself on one side, her back to the window; left with little other choice, they sat down opposite. "As the representative to the Commonwealth, I'll help in any way I can, of course."

"Glad to hear it," Kovalic broke in, ignoring a glare from M'basa. "But the person I would really like to speak to is your boss. Zaina Vallejo?"

She smiled again, although Kovalic would have classified this one as more brittle than previous. "I'm afraid Senior Vice President Vallejo is a very busy woman. But I can check her schedule."

"Please," said Kovalic. "We'll wait." He leaned back in the admittedly sumptuous chair, feeling the leather squeak underneath him.

Wei tilted her head to one side, her eyes flicking back and forth rapidly, as if reviewing a screen that nobody else could see. Probably projective contact lenses or ocular implants, Kovalic noted. The kind of personal tech you could afford to develop when you'd avoided fighting in a costly space war.

"You are in luck," she said suddenly, her eyes focusing back on them. "She happens to be in the office early this morning, and has a brief gap in her schedule. She'll be up shortly."

Kovalic raised his eyebrows. "Well, aren't we lucky?"

"Vice President Vallejo values the Corporation's relationships with foreign governments a great deal," said Wei. "Maintaining them is not just her professional priority, but a personal one as well."

"Sounds very diligent," said Kovalic. "The senior vice president's reputation proceeds her – I've heard she may take a run for one of the top jobs next time around?"

Wei smiled pleasantly again. "The Corporation doesn't discuss its internal politics, Mr Austen."

"In any case, I think it's a bit premature," said a pleasant baritone from the doorway. "Maybe in three or four years."

Kovalic turned in his chair: The newcomer looked no less put-together than Wei, but something about her was immediately more personable. About Kovalic's height, her bronzed skin and carefully groomed iron hair were handsome, no question, but it was the imperfections that gave her an air of friendliness: the slight wrinkles around her eyes and on her forehead, an errant hair out of place. She wore a white blouse, open at the throat, and a gray suit that murmured "expensive" in its carefully tailored subtlety.

"Pardon the interruption," she said, with a genuine smile that showed a line of clean, white teeth, with a canine that crooked slightly in. "But I thought it best not to keep you waiting."

Wei rose. "Senior Vice President Vallejo, these are deputy consul Sarah M'basa and Mr James Austen of the Commonwealth government, and Mr Tormundsen of Adler Industries."

"Of course," said Vallejo, taking each of their hands in turn for a brief shake. Her grip was warm and firm. "A pleasure to meet you all, though I wish it were under better circumstances." She crossed the table and took a seat next to Wei, folding her hands. "The Corporation wishes to extend its full cooperation to the Commonwealth, as well as all other foreign powers affected by this terrible incident."

"The Commonwealth appreciates that, madam vice president," said M'basa. "Our top priority is to locate our missing citizens and bring them home."

"Naturally," said Vallejo. "The resources of the Corporation are at your disposal."

"That's excellent," interjected Kovalic. "Knowing that, perhaps you could help me. I've been investigating the abduction, and I've run into a bit of a brick wall. I was hoping you might help?"

"If we can, certainly. What do you need?"

"We traced one of the vehicles used in the attack to a spaceport rental, but the ID itself was falsified. We were hoping to acquire video footage of the suspect picking up the vehicle."

Vallejo glanced at Wei. "I don't see why that should be a problem. The Corporation would be happy to request the footage on your behalf."

"We also understand that Mr Adler and Ms Mulroney weren't the only people to be abducted in the attack – and that, in fact, they may have merely been collateral damage of the primary target."

With an apologetic smile, Vallejo shook her head. "I'm happy to provide all assistance, Mr Austen, but you should understand that I can't divulge the security situation of other clients. You'll have to approach the relevant parties yourself."

Kovalic waited, tapping his fingers on the table, before speaking again. "Even if the person in question was here for high-level talks with a member of the Corporation?"

Someone nudged his knee under the table, and out of his peripheral vision he could see M'basa glaring at him.

He'd expected Vallejo's smile to freeze on her face or for the woman to show some sign of recognition, but the intersection of her political and corporate training was just too good. "*Especially* if that were the case."

"So, even though that information may help us track down the people who took our citizens – and the citizens of other foreign governments – you won't share it because it might jeopardize whatever deal you were going to discuss with the Imperium?"

M'basa kicked his shin, hard, under the table; he could feel her eyes cutting deep into the side of his head.

"Excuse my colleague, senior vice president," she stepped in smoothly. "He is, of course, concerned about Mr Adler and Ms Mulroney."

"No offense taken," said Vallejo. "I understand completely. But I'm afraid I still can't help you – that information is not mine to give." She glanced at her sleeve and rose, nodding to them. "And now, if you'll excuse me, I have a previous engagement. I'll see that someone is in touch with the spaceport footage, and I hope that it will help you with your investigation. Please don't hesitate to contact me if you need anything else." Vallejo disappeared down the hall.

Tapper gave a loud snort that was studiously ignored by everyone present. Kovalic suppressed a smile – the sergeant wasn't one to mince words *or* snorts.

On the other side of the table, Wei rose smoothly. "I'll ensure that any relevant footage from the spaceport makes its way to deputy consul M'basa as soon as possible. Please, follow me."

Wei led them back into the hall and towards the elevator. Kovalic fell into step with her. "Please convey my apologies to the senior vice president for my outburst. As deputy consul M'basa said, I'm concerned for the safety of our citizens."

Wei ducked her head. "Of course, Mr Austen. I understand completely."

"I'm sure you're glad that the senior vice president wasn't caught up in this whole mess," said Kovalic carefully. "I assume she was at the embassy party?"

"She was scheduled to be, but was unavoidably detained by a shareholder meeting that ran long. Fortunately, as it turned out."

"Ah," said Kovalic, offering a smile as they reached the elevator. "That is fortunate indeed."

The elevator doors slid open at Wei's touch, and she bid them farewell. As the lift descended, M'basa was on her comm, talking to one of the techs back at the embassy.

Tapper slid over to him. "What do you think?"

Kovalic scratched his chin. "I think you were right about us being blinded by the crown – somebody really didn't want the Imperium's envoy meeting with Vallejo."

At the ground floor, they stepped through the lobby and out into the street. No sooner had they left then Kovalic's own wrist buzzed. He glanced at his sleeve; the caller identification was listed as 'private' but he tapped his earbud anyway. "Yeah?"

"Simon? Harry."

"Any movement?"

"Only bad. You probably haven't had the pleasure of meeting my resident colleague here, have you?"

"No, I haven't."

"Well, he's a bit of an up-and-comer, and he took it upon himself to phone home immediately after the dust cleared on last night's incident."

Kovalic's stomach sank into his shoes. "Meaning what?"

"Meaning that the timeline is a lot smaller than we thought. We've got about four hours before reinforcements arrive. Just thought you should know."

"Thanks." Kovalic disconnected as the Commonwealth embassy's hovercar pulled around to the front of the building, joining a queue of similar-looking cars there, each depositing its high-level Corporation employees. Kovalic glanced up at the volcano opening, high above them; it was still early, but the Corporation hadn't gotten where it was by keeping banker's hours.

With his gaze firmly upwards, he didn't see the man who collided with him, only got the impression of a tall, thin man staring intently at his sleeve and heard the mumbled excuses as the man swerved around him and continued his hurried way towards the Corporation headquarters entrance. Kovalic frowned, looking over his shoulder, but the man had already melted into the crowd.

He strode over to Tapper and M'basa, who were getting into the Commonwealth car, and absently patted down his pockets. In other circumstances, that collision would have been pickpocketing 101, however his belongings were all accounted for. But, as his hand brushed his jacket, he felt something small and square in the pocket that *hadn't* been there before.

"What was that call about?" asked Tapper as soon as the car's internal security systems were activated.

"Nothing good," said Kovalic. "It seems IIS's Bayern station chief reported the prince's disappearance right after he was taken last night. Which means that instead of the twenty-six hours Frayn was going to buy us, we have about four before an Illyrican fleet is in orbit and looking for some answers. And they are not going to be as delicate about it as we are." He ran his thumb over the familiar shape in his pocket – a data chip. Whatever it was, he hoped to hell something was about to go their way.

CHAPTER 20

The creak of the heavy metal door opening snapped Eli instantly from his fitful dozing. It was dark in the room, and the rectangle of light from the hallway blinded his unadjusted eyes. He blinked back the tears welling up there, enough to make out a blurry pair of figures. The bigger of the two tossed in the smaller like it was a rag doll, and then the door slammed closed again.

Eli's head spun as he tried to reassemble the details of his situation in his mind, like pouncing on scraps of shredded paper blowing away in the wind: *Bayern. The embassy. The prince. Erich von Denffer. The kidnapping. Erich von bloody Denffer again.*

"Erich?" he tried. "That you?"

"Eli?" Even throaty and congested, the voice was decidedly feminine.

"Tayl–" he choked back the name, cursing himself. *If man had been meant to keep secrets, God should not have given him a tongue.*

He heard a rasp that sounded like Taylor dragging herself across the floor, and he crawled to the end of the bed. It was pitch black in the room: no windows, and not so much as a line of light peeking under the door. He waved around

293

with his hand until he contacted something that felt like a shoulder and patted it, as if reassuring himself that it was real.

"Christ," he said, letting out a breath. "You're a sight for sore, uh... hands."

"Glad to be here," she said, her voice wry. "Not sure how you managed it, but well done."

Eli flushed slightly at the compliment, suddenly glad the room was dark. *There's a long way to go before we're out of the woods.*

"You OK?" she asked, her hand reaching up to touch his. "They hurt you?"

He shook his head instinctively, then realized the inutility of that in the dark. "No, I'm fine. Mainly asked a bunch of questions. You?"

"I've been better, but nothing that won't heal."

"The prince?"

"Haven't seen him. They separated us right after the embassy, threw a hood over my head, and then tossed me into a room not unlike this one."

"I insisted on an upgrade to a suite, but they weren't having it."

She gave something that might have been mistaken for a hollow laugh. "So, how'd you convince them to put me in here?"

"I just told them I was worried about you, and that I didn't care what happened to the prince. Apparently that satisfied them – at least for now."

"You realize they're still probably going to kill us, right?"

"Yeah, I think that's why they felt some pity for poor old me. Maybe they wanted to make sure he felt the touch of a woman before he met his end."

This time, she did laugh, and a hand snaked up and patted him on the cheek. "You're cute, Eli, but I can assure you that this is the only touch you'll be getting from this particular woman."

Eli grinned, mostly in relief. "That's good, because I can think of at least one man whose wrath worries me way more than those guys out there."

There was another rustling from the floor, and Taylor pulled back her hand. Her voice had dropped to a murmur. "Now, if I can just get this out…"

"Get what out?"

"Well, our friends out there didn't really bother doing a thorough search – some sort of misplaced sense of chivalry, if you can believe it."

"Please tell me you have a full set of lockpicks."

"In my other shoes, sorry. What I do have is this." He felt something small but heavy placed in his hand. It was surprisingly warm – he guessed it must have been pushed up against her skin – but as he traced the shape, he felt a nick at his finger. *A knife. Well, that will be handy.*

"Anything else? A pocket battleship, maybe?"

"No such luck there, but they also didn't look closely enough to take my earbud. Which would be handy if it weren't for the fact that it only works at close range."

"How close?"

"Max range is a kilometer, but it gets a bit shaky on the upward half of that."

"So we're going to have to get really, really lucky."

"Well, our luck can't get much worse – maybe we've hit the upswing."

Eli gave a hollow laugh. "Not bloody likely." He sighed and fumbled the knife back to Taylor; he assumed it would be far better off in her hands than his own, unless of course the goal was for him to stab himself. "You didn't see the prince, so we don't know where he is – not that I feel any particular obligation to drag him out of here."

"Eli."

"Please don't say it."

"We can't leave the prince here."

He sighed. "Seriously. I told you not to say it. Look, the guy's a rotten piece of work, by all accounts. I was going to warn you, but, well, you know."

"Yeah, he started getting handsy the second we got into the car – left a nasty bruise on my wrist. I'll say this for whoever the hell grabbed us: they saved me the trouble of punching him in the throat."

"See? Far as I'm concerned, he's exactly where he deserves to be."

"Eli, an incident of this level, even on an independent world, could send the whole galaxy spiraling back into open war."

Something tugged at the back of his mind, that feeling once again that he was missing some crucial piece of this whole sordid affair. He shook his head. "From what I hear, sounds like it might be a fair trade."

"He's a sadistic bastard, that's for sure, but he's not worth going to war over."

"So, who the hell do we think these people are, then? Who'd want him?"

"Well, we're talking the heir to the Illyrican Empire," Taylor said. "I can think of any number of people who'd like to ransom him for a chunk of change."

Eli shook his head. "No, I don't think so. I tried to get them to deal when they interrogated me, and they looked at me like I was crazy. Like I should have known there was no chance of dealing."

He heard Taylor shift position, and somehow could feel her looking at him. "What kind of deal exactly?"

Eli wriggled uncomfortably. His voice lowered to a whisper, even though he doubted they were being bugged – these people already had what they were after; Eli and Taylor were just collateral. "It's, uh, possible that they may be laboring under the misapprehension, which I might add was entirely of their own conception–"

"*Eli.*"

"–that I'm IIS." *If we make it out of here, I am totally fired, aren't I?*

There was a silence that might have been described as "stunned," or, more accurately, as "flabbergasted beyond all belief," and it was a minute before Taylor spoke again.

"Holy shit." The expletive was laced with admiration. "Jesus, Eli. It's possible you've found your life's calling."

"Which would be more reassuring if it seemed like there was a little more time left on my clock."

"So, they think you're IIS, and they don't want to deal. Which means it's political."

"That was the conclusion I came to. But I'm afraid I haven't really had a chance to study the Imperium's dissident movements."

"Lucky for you, I know them only too well." She paused. "There aren't many that would try something this brazen, though. And even fewer that are this well-organized."

"Our captors strike me as military. Or ex-military?"

"Agreed." Another pause. "This doesn't make any sense," Taylor said, frustration creeping into her voice. "It doesn't fit any of the profiles. Most of the Imperium's dissident groups are those urging détente with the Commonwealth. The military, by and large, are hardliners – hawks."

"Doesn't seem like they'd have much to gain from grabbing His Imperial Highness."

"No. If anything, Hadrian's sympathetic to their cause. And eliminating him would ensure the throne passes to the next sibling."

Eli racked his brain. The emperor had three children: another son and the youngest, a daughter. "Matthias, right? Could he be behind it?"

"I don't think so," said Taylor, haltingly. "He's smart, sure, but he doesn't have the ambition. He got the benevolent streak in the family, which has made him a sight less interested in playing politics and far more concerned with the plight of endangered fauna on the tundras of Sevastapol."

"You never know with brothers," Eli said. "Trust me. What about the daughter?"

"Isabella. She's the youngest, and she keeps a pretty low profile. Mostly charity work, personal appearances, that kind of thing. Doesn't seem to have much of a political presence."

They fell into silence. In his mind, Eli kept disassembling and reassembling all the puzzle pieces that they'd acquired – it was like his brain was chasing its own tail. *There are just too many unknowns. What was the prince doing here? Who grabbed him? Why? What do they hope to gain?* Repeating the questions over and over just made him feel like he was in some sort of fever dream.

Eli rubbed his forehead. "I'm about two seconds from suggesting that you just knife the next guy who comes through that door. Just to do *something*."

"Tactically, we'd probably blow our advantage in the first five seconds," said Taylor. Her voice softened. "But yeah, that doesn't make it any less tempting."

"How many are there, anyway?"

"I don't know. How many have you seen?"

"Two, I think," said Eli, searching his memory. "The one who interrogated me: average height, dark complexion, dark hair, dark eyes. Plus, another fellow who was rather unremarkable. Taller, I think maybe with lighter eyes. You?"

"Well, it looked like a full squad when they jumped us outside of the embassy – plus, they clearly had support to set up that collision. But here I've only seen four: the two you mentioned, another guard with a shaved head, and a fourth who clearly had some sort of clout. He was the one who told the guards to throw me in here. Younger, handsome – blond, I think. Looked like someone had given him the business in a fight, though; he had a pretty nasty bruise on his cheek."

Blond? It was as though a puzzle piece had clicked into place, jammed right in his craw. *There are plenty of blond men, Eli. Some huge percentage of the galaxy. But, still...* "Handsome, you say? Maybe about five foot ten? Really blue eyes?"

"Yeah," said Taylor slowly. "Did you see him?"

I think I did. And I think he lied right to my face. That same feeling from the interrogation – that he was in deep water, kicking his feet valiantly to stay afloat – had returned with a vengeance. "This... is probably not good."

I thought he was my friend. Following hard on the heels of that thought came a strong sense of the ludicrous. *You're a Commonwealth spy, he's an Illyrican officer – friendship doesn't enter the equation.* Sure, they'd been friends five years ago at the academy, but it's not as though they'd kept in close touch. Granted, that would have been tough, what with Eli being stuck on Sabaea for five years.

And if it had been Erich who had put Taylor in here with him, then he'd bought Eli's story. *There, you lied to him too. Now you're even.* That also explained why the interrogator had bit down so hard on the IIS cover story – Eli had already told Erich, who had no reason not to believe him.

It dawned on him that it *also* explained why the heck they'd grabbed him in the first place. Elias Adler the businessman might be wealthy and worth holding for ransom, but they'd already established their captors weren't in it for the money.

Eli Brody the IIS agent, though, that would be another thing entirely – especially for a group who was about to kidnap the heir to the Illyrican Empire. They'd been trying to get him out of the way. So why not just kill him?

"Eli? Care to share with the rest of the class?"

He almost laughed; it reminded him of Kovalic. "I... I'm not sure *exactly* what's going on here, but I'm getting closer. I don't think we're in any immediate danger." There were numerous ways it would have been easier and safer for Erich to just clean up the loose end that was Eli Brody, but he'd ensured his safety. Several times, it seemed. *So maybe there's a glimmer of friendship still in there. Wayyyyyy down.*

And, if there was, he could exploit it.

"I think I have a plan."

It took a solid half hour of pounding on the metal door – which had Eli's hand throbbing – before anybody so much as came to check on them. Eli had started to worry that their captors had moved on to the next stage of their mission, whatever it was, and left them there to rot. His pounding had taken on a tinge of the panicky, which explained the alien wave of relief that washed over him when a voice growled from the other side of the door.

"All right, all right. Knock it off. What do you want?"

"Tell von Denffer that I need to see him," said Eli through the door. "Especially if he's going to go through with this idiotic plan."

There was a pause from the other side of the door. "Listen, pal, I don't know what you think–"

"Just tell him," said Eli sharply. "I'll wait."

He perched himself back on the end of the bed, next to Taylor. She'd tucked the knife back into the sheath on her inner thigh; Eli hoped they wouldn't have to use it, but he wasn't about to give up any advantages.

Ten minutes passed, Eli fidgeting in the darkness. He'd just begun to wonder if he was going to have to start making noise again when there came the sound of a heavy iron bolt being shot, followed by the door creaking on its hinges. The room's lights flooded on and Eli put up his arm, his eyes watering from the onslaught. Beside him, Taylor was also shielding her gaze.

"Eli."

He blinked, rubbing at his eyes to clear his vision. Erich von Denffer sat, legs crossed, in a chair opposite him. The bruise on his face was, if anything, more colorful. *I guess that was the real deal; he's committed. Or, at any rate, he* should *be.* Two of the other men – the one who had interrogated Eli earlier, and the one Taylor had seen, with the shaved head – flanked him.

"Hello, Erich."

"I was told you had something to discuss with me."

"What, no pleasantries? No theatrics this time?" His eyes flicked to the other men.

"It seems like we've passed that point, doesn't it?"

"Yeah, I'd say."

Erich leaned back, blue eyes taking him in. "So. What is it you want?"

"Oh, oodles of things," said Eli. "Peace in our time, a fresh croissant, maybe a walk-on role on *The Lives We Give*–" One of the other men raised his pistol significantly, and Eli put up his hands.

Erich smiled ruefully. "Same old Eli Brody. Your mouth keeps running even when your brain has stopped."

Oh, you have no idea.

"Fine. I'll settle for the immediate future. What do I have to do to secure my and Ms Mulroney's freedom?"

Erich raised an eyebrow. "What makes you think I'm interested in offering you your freedom?"

"You haven't killed us yet."

"'Yet' being the operative word."

Eli leveled a gaze at his old friend, holding his eyes. "I don't think you want to kill us, Erich," he said, his voice even. "It might have been a while, but I have a pretty good idea of who Erich von Denffer is and isn't." Even as the words came out of his mouth, his mind suddenly summoned up a snippet of conversation from the party. Something Erich had told him…

"Eli, you like this girl?… Then do yourself – and her – a big favor, and get her out of here right now.*"

Erich opened his mouth to reply, but Eli interrupted him. "You warned me. Me, an IIS agent. You as good as spilled the beans on His Imperial Highness's… proclivities."

Something lanced through Erich's eyes; it looked like fear. The two men behind him shifted, frowning down at the handsome pilot.

"Why bother, if you were only going to kill me – us – later?" He jerked his head at Taylor, who had remained quiet.

"What the hell is he talking about?" broke in the dark-haired man, his brow creased.

"Typical Eyes mindgames," said Erich, not sparing a look. But that fear Eli had seen hadn't been entirely banished from his eyes.

Eli waggled his fingers at the dark-haired man. "Miiiiinnnnd gaaaaameeess," he whispered in his best spooky voice.

"*Shut it*," Erich seethed.

But it was too late; Eli had the piece he'd been missing, and everything else was starting to click into place. "They don't know, do they?" he said, trying to hold back a grin that desperately wanted to escape. "Your compatriots here – they had in mind a different plan entirely, huh? But you went off script, Erich. Why? Not quite onboard with the whole idea? Didn't fancy helping a sadistic maniac?"

Both of the men had tightened their grips on their pistols now. Erich sighed, pinching his temples between thumb and forefinger. "Five years, Eli, and you're still a pain in the ass, you know?"

The dark-haired man put a heavy hand down on Erich's shoulder. "I think we'd better have a talk, sir. Outside."

Erich sagged, and the man's grip loosened. That split second was all it took; Erich slapped a hand on the other man's and sprung, twisting his body and swiveling the other man's arm inside out. The dark-haired man blinked in surprise, but before he had a chance to react, Erich had slid his right arm up and under the man's throat. Shaved Head brought up his gun, but not before Erich had grabbed his human shield's left hand with his own and raised the dark-haired man's pistol at his partner.

"Let's all just take it easy," said Erich.

A knife sprouted from Shaved Head's shoulder, but he

barely had time to register surprise, much less a shout of pain, before a purple blur collided with him, slamming him bodily into the wall. Eli blinked, his gaze snapping to the spot next to him on the couch where Taylor had been sitting quietly only a moment before. Now she was busy ramming the other man's head into drywall.

Both Erich and the dark-haired man gaped at the sudden intervention, but the dark-haired man recovered faster, elbowing Erich in the gut and knocking the wind out of him. He dropped the gun with his left hand, then used it to grab Erich's loosened right arm and swing it around behind the pilot's back. Kicking Erich's knee out, the man tried to force him to the ground.

Taylor, meanwhile, had put the other man into a chokehold that he'd been unable to break, his eyes rolling back in his head as he passed out. She dropped his limp body like a sack of potatoes and scooped up Shaved Head's gun. Eli's eyes darted to the weapon that the dark-haired man had dropped, then launched himself off the bed, sliding across the floor to grab it. The movement got the attention of the man, who turned from Erich to stomp heavily on top of the weapon's barrel.

But Erich took that opportunity to break free of the man's grasp, and put all his energy into springing up from the floor and hitting the man with his best haymaker. The man's foot slipped on the barrel of the gun and he went down, cracking his skull on the floor. Eli scrambled to his feet, raising the gun at Erich and saw Taylor doing the same with the pistol she'd liberated.

"How many more?" asked Taylor, her eyes locked on Erich.

Erich's gaze darted to the two comrades he'd helped take

out, then back at Taylor, and he gave a sour smile. "Should have known you'd have had a wingman, Eli."

"You should have," Eli agreed. "Now answer the nice lady's question."

"One more," said Erich with a sigh. "Here in the house, anyway."

"And where the hell is here?"

"It's a, uh, personal residence."

"Please tell me we're still in Bergfestung," said Taylor.

Erich didn't meet her eyes, but gave a minute nod.

Taylor let out a short breath, then cracked her neck. She jutted her chin at Eli. "Check them," she said, indicating the bodies on the floor.

Eli dropped to one knee, keeping the gun in one hand as he checked their pulses and searched them. Both were alive, but neither was carrying much more than anonymous payment cards – no IDs. But as he rifled Shaved Head's jacket, the neck of his shirt snagged and Eli caught the edge of a tattoo beneath. Frowning, he peeled back the shirt; sure enough, a stylized black hawk with a crown above it. He snapped his glance up at Erich – sometimes you put another puzzle piece into place only to realize how much more of the whole picture you were missing.

"All right," said Taylor. "Let's get moving, shall we?" She stepped over and grabbed Erich by the collar, shoving him towards the open door. The blond man didn't say anything, just let himself be sullenly ushered out into the hall. Eli closed and bolted the door behind them, and breathed a sigh of relief. *I really did not want to stay in that room for the rest of my life.*

The corridor looked like it was intended for service; undecorated, it had a linoleum floor and no windows, instead lit by harsh blue fluorescent strips. *Probably underground*, Eli figured. Sure enough, as they rounded a corner they came to a set of stairs leading up. Taylor nodded to Eli to take up a position behind Erich as she climbed the stairs and cracked open the door at the top.

"She's good," muttered Erich. "Spent the whole time crying and screaming." He shook his head. "Had me fooled, that's for sure."

Sadly, that's not nearly as hard as you seem to think.

"There's a few things I'm still confused about," said Eli.

"Oh, by all means," said Erich dryly. "Let me clear those up for you."

Taylor hissed at them from the stairs, then beckoned them upwards. Eli motioned at Erich with the gun, and with a sigh he started climbing.

"Those guys back there," Eli said under his breath as they ascended, "they were from the prince's honor wing. Just like you."

"You know how it is. You have to work with people you trust."

"That sure worked out great for them."

Erich shrugged.

They reached the top of the stairs, and Taylor raised a finger to her lips, then slipped out the door. Eli pushed Erich ahead, then followed suit.

It was dark upstairs, the only light filtering through from windows high overhead. As Erich had said, the building did seem to be a private residence – and a lavish one to boot. The side of the door facing the stairwell had been featureless metal, painted a sickly shade of off-white; the outward side was richly appointed in a deep burnished wood, carved with elegant decorations that blended seamlessly into the wall.

Eli's feet sunk deep into a lush carpet and, despite having been surrounded by richness for the last several days, he found himself gawking at the brass chandeliers that hung overhead and the detailed oil paintings on the wall. He'd thought the Imperial embassy luxurious, but this place had it beat hands down.

"Where the hell are we?" he muttered.

Taylor shook her head, frowning, and her grip tightened on the pistol. "Clearly whoever hired your boy there had deep pockets."

Erich threw back his head and laughed. Taylor spun back and jabbed him in the gut with the pistol; he doubled over with an *oof*, but couldn't quite banish the smile from his face. "You have no idea what you've gotten yourselves into," he wheezed.

Her face cold, Taylor grabbed the pilot by the scruff of the neck, then placed him ahead of her. "You're going to show us how to get out of here. Let's go."

Still bent over, Erich raised a hand and pointed. "This way."

They followed him down a long corridor, lined with ornate carved sideboards that looked like they dated from a time before humans had discovered space travel. Eli tried to stop himself from staring, slack-jawed, at the sculptures that dotted small nooks – life size marble statues in many cases. He glanced down at the names: Caesar. Hannibal. Temujin. Whoever's residence this was, they definitely had a specific taste in art and history. He frowned as they reached the end of the hallway and swung right down the corridor.

The hallway led into a large entranceway, inlaid in marble, with a wide stairway that led up around the room and formed a mezzanine. Across the hall Eli could see salvation in the form of a front door, flanked by two narrow floor-to-ceiling windows. He hoped they weren't about to stumble into a suburban street with a hostage at gunpoint. *That might be tough to explain to the Bayern security services.*

They were halfway across the vestibule when Eli caught sight of a brilliant red firefly dancing in the light. It wasn't until it alit on Taylor that his brain caught up with what his plummeting stomach had already figured out. He glanced down at his own shirt and saw a matching firefly on his own chest. The loud click of safeties being flipped off only brought their fates home.

"I think you two will want to stop where you are," said Erich, with a smile and a wave towards the mezzanine. "And, if you would be so kind, place your weapons on the floor."

INTERLUDE

ISC Emperor's Spear, Badr Sector – June 8, 2401

"Lieutenant? Sergeant Kovalic here; we've secured the bridge." He eyed the array of a dozen crimson-uniformed crewmembers, on their knees with their hands interlaced behind their heads. Six of his own marines had their weapons trained on the captives.

"Copy, sergeant," the thick voice of Lieutenant Fletcher crackled back to him. "Encountering resistance on the way to the engine room – I think they knew we were coming."

"We did basically crash into their ship in a giant metal pod," the sergeant pointed out. "Perhaps not the subtlest approach."

"I'll mention that to Command for next time. Keep a lid on things there. I'll let you know when we're in position."

"Roger that. Kovalic out." He glanced at the ship's large main screen, which showed the ongoing battle. Someone was bound to notice that the *Emperor's Spear* had suddenly gotten a little less engaged in the fighting – there were still a few isolated gunners running their own autonomous turrets, but given that its fire control and helm officers were now being held at gunpoint, the flagship of the Illyrican Third Fleet was mostly floating dead in the water.

"Looks like we're still taking a pounding, sarge," said Lau, one of his marines, who'd also been eyeing the screen. "That other dreadnought is doing just fine on its own." He nodded at another large ship of the same class as the *Emperor's Spear*.

The sergeant glanced at his wrist. "Give it a minute," he said, looking to the communication console. Over on the *Warhawk*, if everything was going according to plan, Lieutenant Garcia's platoon ought to be on the same timetable, which meant that the signal ought to be coming through anytime now.

"Come on, Toni," he muttered to himself.

"Ambush!" yelled a voice in the sergeant's ear and his eyes snapped up to the captured crewmembers before he realized that the shout had come over the comm in his ear. "LT's down!" said the same voice.

"Calhoun, that you?" the sergeant said, pressing a finger to his ear. "Sitrep!"

"Sarge, we've taken heavy losses; they rigged some sort of booby trap on the way into the engine room. We're blocked off, and the LT and Shimon are both down."

The sergeant swore, turning back to the comm console. Still no signal. He glanced at his watch; Garcia ought to have reported in by now. It was possible they'd met resistance of their own.

Which made the question: how long should he give them before he assumed the mission was blown?

Onscreen, he saw one of the Earth fleet's frigates light up as an explosion rippled across its surface. Shrapnel from the destroyed ship peppered a nearby corvette, not destroying it, but causing enough damage that it started to float aimlessly.

"We're running out of time," he said, more to himself than to his team. The newly formed Commonwealth fleet

was little more than a loose conglomeration of vessels –
most of them not even real warships – and there was no
way it could hold its own against the Illyrican forces. Not in
a fair fight, anyway.

But if the Illyricans trampled them here in the Badr
sector, they'd have a clear path to the Commonwealth's
center of power on Terra Nova, and all organized resistance
would crumble.

No pressure.

A light on the communications console blinked on, and
the sergeant sighed in relief, flipping to the channel.

"*Emperor's Spear,* this is *Warhawk,*" came an unfamiliar
voice. "We're under attack by enemy forces onboard; repeat,
onboard. We've sealed our bridge; recommend you prepare
for same."

"Shit." The sergeant slapped the channel off, and his eyes
swept over the assembled marines. "Any of you happen to
know how to fly a dreadnought?" Blank stares came back
at him.

"Uh…" One marine, a skinny greenhorn named Briggs,
raised his hand. "I think Trinh had some flight training," he
said. "But she went with the LT's squad."

"Great," said the sergeant, flipping his comm on. "Calhoun,
you still there?"

"Aye, sarge," the rough voice came back, punctuated
between rounds of gunfire. "We're holding."

"Is Trinh still up?"

"Yeah, but she's a little busy."

"Patch her in; it's an emergency."

There was a pause, and a woman's strained voice came
on the channel. "Yo, sarge. I'm kind of in the middle of
something." A ricochet sounded, loud, over the earpiece.

"I need you to walk me through flying this boat."

A moment of silence. "Shit, sarge, it's never easy with you, is it?"

"Just tell me how to lay in a course, private."

"All right," said Trinh with a grunt. "Take a seat at the console, and try to find the heading control."

"Heading control... heading control..." the sergeant said, his eyes darting over the console. "What the hell am I looking for?"

"I don't know," Trinh seethed. "I've never flown a fucking *dreadnought*. Should look something like a big dial with numbers around the edge."

Sure enough, a large dial marked at regular intervals with numbers sat in one corner of the touchscreen. "OK, got it."

"Take a look at the holo display; should show you which direction the ship's pointed in."

The sergeant's eyes found the display; a blue shaded corridor depicted the direction the ship was currently heading. Unsurprisingly, its nose was aimed more or less at the tattered remainders of the Earth fleet, moving at a roughly parallel line to the *Warhawk*. "Got it."

"All right," said Trinh. A series of reports echoed over the comm channel. "Spin the dial until the heading looks the way you want, then lock it in."

Sucking his breath in between his teeth, the sergeant turned the dial, watching the projected blue line shift. He had to turn it pretty far to reach the direction he wanted, and it turned out he had to slide it forward slightly in order to pitch the ship downwards. A flashing icon on the screen read "Lock" and the sergeant reached over and tapped it. Vibrations rippled through the deck as the ship slowed and applied its thrusters, lumbering along the new heading.

He leaned back and sighed in relief. "Got it, Trinh. Thank…" he trailed off as he watched the line. At the rate the ship was moving, it wouldn't get there soon enough. "Crap," he growled. "Trinh, where do I find the throttle on this thing?"

There was no response from the other end of the comm; just static.

"Trinh? You there? Come in!"

His jaw clenched. No time to think about that now – he had bigger problems. Casting his eyes over the panel again, they alit upon a slider that seemed to be marked in speed increments; it was at about half speed now. Taking a deep breath, he slid it to maximum. Increased acceleration pressed him slightly back into the chair. Glancing back at the heading dial, he made a slight adjustment to the ship's direction, then hopped out of the chair and looked at the marines.

"Let's get the hell out of here."

"What about them?" Lau asked, gesturing to the crewmembers.

"Throw 'em into the escape pods along the way," said the sergeant, eyeing them. "Let's just make sure to seal the bridge behind us." He activated his comm. "This is Sergeant Kovalic. All troops fall back to extraction, on the double."

As they marched the crewmembers out of the bridge, a klaxon sounded and a giant red warning burst onto screen, blaring "COLLISION DETECTED." The *Warhawk* grew larger in the display.

"Here's mud in your eye, you bastards," growled the sergeant, ducking out of the bridge.

CHAPTER 21

"Boss? Hey, boss."

Kovalic blinked. He swore he hadn't closed his eyes, but he had the groggy feeling of being prematurely roused from a nap. The smooth ride of the Commonwealth hovercar had lulled him into a drowsy state, even in the few minutes it had taken to make the trip from the Corporation headquarters back to the embassy. Not enough sleep would do that.

He pinched the bridge of his nose between his fingers. "Sorry, sergeant. What were you saying?"

Tapper cocked his head to one side, eyeing his boss with a speculative expression that had remained more or less unchanged for the last twenty years. "So, we think whoever grabbed the prince wanted to stop him from meeting with Vallejo. Why? What was so important?"

M'basa was sitting opposite them, her dark eyes watching them, hawklike. In spite of his intrinsic distrust of CID – and his frank antipathy for her boss, Kester – she'd been nothing but helpful. It was about time he reciprocated.

Kovalic produced the data chip from his pocket, holding it between thumb and forefinger. "I'm hoping this will tell us."

M'basa didn't bother hiding her surprise, leaning forward towards the chip. "Where'd you get that?"

"A friend... I hope."

The deputy consul's fingers tapped rapidly on one knee. "What's on it?"

"No idea. I guess we'll find out."

"We?"

He tipped a nod in her direction. "This is your turf, as you said."

M'basa raised a brow, but there was relief in her eyes. "'Bout damn time."

The car glided into the drive at the Commonwealth embassy, and the three got out and walked into the building. M'basa led them through the halls to a heavy security door, where she swiped them into the relatively small suite of rooms that served as the CID station's operations section.

"You can use this room," she said, letting them into a closet-like room that contained three chairs and a secure terminal. "I need to go check in on a few things, but I'll be back." With that she closed the door behind them.

Kovalic dropped into one of the chairs, fighting back another wave of fatigue. His shoulder ached and he massaged it gently.

Tapper was leaning against the door, that thoughtful look on his face again.

"What's on your mind, sergeant?"

Pursing his lips, the old vet shrugged. "Just wondering what you didn't tell her."

Kovalic's mouth twitched in a smile. Slipping anything past the sergeant was a tall order. He turned the data chip over in his hands. "It was Page."

Tapper's eyebrows went up. "Are you sure?"

Tall, thin, in a suit. That was all Kovalic had seen. And yet the seamless, professional brush pass had Aaron Page written all over it. Not to mention the disappearing act that he'd pulled directly after. "Sure enough. I don't know where Page has been or what he's been up to, but I can't think of anybody in the Corporation who'd be inclined to help us."

"Right enough." He nodded at the chip. "What do you think's on it?"

"Something important enough for Page to break cover and make a pass. I trust him not to waste our time. Let's find out." Trust was the cornerstone of their team. You didn't have that, you didn't have anything. His stomach roiled at the thought, but he pushed it down. Now wasn't the time. Swiveling towards the terminal, he plugged in the chip; at the password prompt, he plugged in Page's operational security cipher.

There were a handful of documents on the chip, most of them financial records that seemed to be related to some sort of corporation, The Peregrine Group, which had a variety of accounts on Bayern. The company wasn't doing terribly well, from what Kovalic could glean from the balance sheets. Lots of debt tied up in large assets – really large, expensive assets, he realized as he glanced at the numbers – and not a lot of income.

Besides those records, there was only one other document on the chip: a memo regarding the Peregrine Group's somewhat tenuous financial state. Kovalic's eyebrows raised as he noted that it had originated from the office of Senior Vice President Zaina Vallejo herself and was replete with scary phrases like "no additional credit will be extended" and "any further missed payments will result in penalties."

But it was the name in the "To" line that clicked everything into place.

"There it is," he breathed, leaning back and staring at the terminal.

"Boss?" said Tapper, frowning and peering over his shoulder.

Kovalic's brain was whirring away. Whatever weariness he'd felt a moment before had vanished, subsumed as blood started to pump faster through his veins.

"What the..." Tapper muttered, his eyes shining with the reflected light of the terminal screen. "From Vallejo to Bleiden?"

Bleiden. Albert Bleiden. The Imperium's Permanent Undersecretary for Trade and Commerce. Who had wanted to pass along sensitive information to Kovalic and his team on Sevastapol, but had ended up poisoned for his troubles.

"Important... meeting. Bayern. Three... days. Per–" Bleiden had said before dying. Kovalic had wondered about that last syllable, but it could have meant any number of things, so in the end, he'd let it go rather than drive himself crazy trying to figure it out. But Bleiden *had* still been trying to tell them something: Peregrine.

Kovalic rubbed a hand over his mouth. Given Bleiden's name on the memo, either the permanent undersecretary had been running his own game or, far more likely, the Peregrine Group was a holding corporation for the Illyrican Empire.

And that meant the Imperium was in serious trouble.

Hand still on his mouth, Kovalic parted his fingers wide enough to speak. "They're broke."

"Broke?" echoed Tapper.

Kovalic leaned back in his chair. "Think about it, sergeant. Bleiden wants to meet with us to pass along sensitive information, then dies – probably at the hands of Eyes. So the prince is dispatched as the envoy to the Imperium to meet with Vallejo in his stead. Probably to buy more time, maybe beg for a new loan." Which, based on the above memos, there was no way Vallejo was going to agree to – not without some serious collateral that the Imperium didn't have.

Tapper shook his head. "What does this mean? Somebody doesn't want the Imperium getting its financial sea legs back? Still sounds a lot like we'd be the prime suspects."

It did, didn't it? But that still didn't sit right with Kovalic. Even if the goal was to keep the whole thing deniable by not informing either the general or the local CID station, it just didn't read like a Commonwealth operation. Again, just too aggressive.

"All right, gentlemen, look alive." M'basa had strode into the room, holding a tablet. "Vallejo came through. You could knock me over with a feather."

Tapper and Kovalic exchanged a glance as they made room for M'basa, who settled down between them and keyed on the tablet. A spartan room, containing a sliding glass door and a row of kiosks, was shown from a high angle.

"This is the footage from the spaceport rental," said M'basa. She pointed a finger at the timestamp in the top right corner. "We crossreferenced the time that the rental was made with the video footage."

A figure entered, his head down, and turned towards the kiosks. From the angle, Kovalic couldn't get much: average height and build, a hat covering his head.

"Great," said Tapper dryly. "We'll just run that hat through facial recognition."

M'basa held up a finger. "The Corporation is a step ahead of you. They've been working on indirect manipulation for years; look what happens when he goes to leave."

The angle on the video changed, this time looking into the room from the doorway. Sure enough, as the figure turned to exit, he glanced up at the camera, head on.

"Wow," muttered Kovalic. "How do they manage that?"

"Simple psychology," said M'basa. "They just put a light up there that's timed to flash when people are heading out; it gets their attention and they look at it involuntarily. Even if it's only for a split second, they've got 'em. Anyway, I'm running him through facial rec right now. Should have an ID shortly."

"I'll be damned," said Tapper, shaking his head. "Probably messing with our brains, too."

Kovalic ignored him, staring at the face in the image. Handsome, for sure: clean-shaven, light eyes. Nothing else that made it stand out, certainly not to Kovalic. But there was something about the man's bearing that was ringing all the alarm bells.

He looped the shot of the man turning towards the camera, running it over and over again as he stared at it. Something was still nagging at him, and had been since the abduction. Something about the way the captors had moved. Not just well-trained, but with the precision and confidence born of military training. They'd known all the places where they wouldn't be spotted by the Illyrican forces. Even known exactly which car in the convoy to hit. They must have done a hell of a recon...

"Shit," he said aloud.

"Boss?" said Tapper.

"I think I know where this is going," said Kovalic. "And it's not good." Staring blankly at the floor, he tried to compose his thoughts, his eyes shuttling back and forth like a typewriter carriage.

M'basa turned to Tapper. "Does he always talk in riddles like this?"

The sergeant shrugged, and leaned back in his chair. "It's a process. Wait it out."

M'basa looked poised to issue a retort when her comm chimed. Frowning, she answered it. After listening for a moment, her eyes widened sharply, then murmured an assent. "We got the facial recognition result back on our friend at the rental shop. You're never going to believe it."

"Let me guess: he's an Illyrican military officer," said Kovalic.

M'basa's jaw fell open. "How the hell did you know that?"

Kovalic shook his head. "We've been searching for motive in all the wrong places. You know that old saying about things always being the last place you look?"

"That's where I always find my keys," said Tapper.

"Yeah, well, who's the last person you'd suspect of kidnapping the crown prince of the Illyrican Empire?"

Tapper scratched his temple. "You mean, like, the Illyrican Emp…" He trailed off, his face falling, as he met Kovalic's eyes. "No way."

"It was an inside job. Had to have been. They knew where the prince would be, they knew all the blind spots and the decoys. Nobody's recon is *that* solid without an inside source." He glanced at M'basa. "Who was the guy? Military attaché? Advance planner?"

M'basa nodded to the screen, still showing the looped footage from the rental office. "Meet Erich von Denffer, Commander of the Honor Wing for Prince Hadrian."

It was Tapper and Kovalic's turn to gape at that one. "I suppose you don't need an inside source when you're the one giving the orders," said Kovalic.

"I still don't get it," said M'basa, running a hand through her hair. "Why the hell would the Illyricans kidnap their own prince? What do they want?"

"It still has something to do with that meeting with Vallejo. Maybe there's some faction that opposed the deal?" Kovalic shook his head, frustrated. "But what's the point? They'd have to know it would bring..." He blinked. Kidnapping the prince would bring the whole Illyrican fleet down on them. They were military – they'd have known that.

So, the only *reasonable* conclusion was that bringing the Illyrican fleet to Bayern had been the plan all along.

"And now he's just not finishing sentences," said M'basa. "Seriously, how do you work like this?"

Tapper cleared his throat. "Uh, boss?"

Everything was slotting into place now as if on fast-forward. "OK, here's what we know. The Illyrican Empire is broke."

M'basa looked up sharply. "The Illyrican Empire is *what*?"

"All those invasion fleets cost money," continued Kovalic, almost talking to himself. "Lots of money. They leveraged everything to build warships, but they lost a big chunk of them at Badr, and even more when the Fifth Fleet was destroyed at the Battle of Sabaea. So, they're having credit problems because the Corporation, well, the Corporation doesn't see them as a solid investment any more. Hence Vallejo requesting a meeting to talk things over – originally with Bleiden, who was responsible for the Imperium's accounts with the Corporation. But he was talking out of school – to *us* – so that was the end of him.

"The hardliners in the Illyrican government don't want to roll over for some mere bankers, so they come up with a plan: send the prince to Bayern in Bleiden's stead, then stage a kidnapping. Because they're the ones who have him, the Bayern security forces won't be able to locate His

Imperial Highness, which lets the Imperium justify sending in the cavalry. The Illyrican military descends en masse to look for the prince; they'll find him, safe and sound, and surely invent a cover story about dissidents or something. But they'll leave a security force here – for the safety of their investments on Bayern, of course. An invasion, under the guise of a police action. And with the Illyricans establishing military control, the Corporation's resources just tacitly become the Imperium's. In short: Bayern's not going to give the Imperium what it wants – so the Imperium's just going to take it."

Silence hung in the room. It was a hell of a theory, nothing more holding it together than some spit and baling wire. And yet, it made a demented sort of sense. An outright invasion would provoke the censure of the galaxy, and the Commonwealth, as the only power even remotely capable of balancing the Imperium, wouldn't be able to take it lying down. That would plunge the whole galaxy back into outright conflict. But a backdoor invasion... well, there wasn't an army for the Commonwealth to fight. The diplomats would protest, and argue – in Kovalic's experience, endlessly – but it would be a *fait accompli*, and the galaxy would eventually move on, but the Illyrican Empire would now have more assets at its disposal, allowing it to rebuild its fleet. The whole galaxy would take a giant step away from détente.

But they could forestall that. All they had to do was get the prince back to the Illyricans, and present him to that incoming Illyrican fleet – gone would be the rationale for a military presence. But to do that, they needed some help. Kovalic brought up his sleeve and punched in a code.

Tapper frowned at him. "Who are you calling?"

"Frayn. He might be able to help us."

"Are you serious? What if he's in on it?"

Kovalic shook his head. "This isn't Harry's style. He doesn't want open war any more than we do."

Tapper rolled his eyes. "You're putting a lot of faith in a guy who had a gun to your head not two hours ago."

"What?" said M'basa again, eyes jumping between the two of them. "When did this… you know what? Never mind. I don't even want to know."

The intelligence officer answered on the second ring. "Frayn."

"Harry, I've got bad news and worse news. Which do you want first?"

Bergfestung's fifth ring was the closest residential district to the city center, the inner rings being entirely zoned for commercial and governmental uses. It also happened to be the poshest neighborhood in the entire city – and probably on Bayern, for what it was worth. Every house visible from the road was fronted with a rectangle of carefully trimmed greenery; those that weren't visible were secreted behind ivy-encrusted brick walls. Apparently the climbing plant did well in low-light, from the amount of it that Kovalic had seen about the city.

The silver hovercar they'd once again borrowed from the Commonwealth embassy cruised through the streets, its lights off. The early morning sun was pouring across the inside of Bergfestung in patches; the Corporation's tower was bathed in light, for example, but even just a few rings out, it was as if dawn was just breaking.

Nobody else was on the streets at this hour. Kovalic swept his gaze across the houses, not entirely sure what he was looking for, but certain that he'd know it when he spotted it.

"Frayn wouldn't just give you the damn address?"

"The man works for the Illyrican government; that'd hardly be professional."

Tapper paused. "Say he just conspicuously stood outside the house and we happened to see him. How professional would that be?"

"Kind of walking the line, I'd say. Why do you ask?"

"No reason," said Tapper. He pulled the car over to the side of the road and rolled down the window. "Evening, officer."

"Gentlemen," said Frayn, leaning down to put his elbows on the doorframe. "You look a bit lost. Can I help you out?"

"What are you doing here, Harry?" said Kovalic.

Frayn raised his eyebrows. "My job is to protect the prince. Everything else is subordinate to that."

"Shouldn't you be calling in a battalion of special forces, then?"

The older man shrugged. "Right now, we have reason to believe that the prince has been taken by rogue members of our own military. So, logically, the only people I *can* trust are those outside the Imperium. Besides, you guys don't want the prince – you want Natalie and your young Mr Adler. Correct?"

Tapper glanced at Kovalic, who nodded without hesitation. "I think our interests are aligned: we get our people back, you get your conspirators wrapped up. And best of all we prevent the Imperium from taking an action that will destabilize any fragile peace we have."

"Splendid. Then shall we dispense with the pleasantries and get down to brass tacks? The house is on the next block, on the left. I'll take you there. Leave the car here."

The Illyrican intelligence officer had confirmed that the prince's honor wing had been housed with him at the personal residence of Ambassador Dubois, which made it the perfect place to stash the Illyrican heir: all the comforts of home, and the last place anyone would think to look for him. It also all but confirmed that the Illyrican diplomat was in on the plan – no surprise there, with his hawkish past – and explained why IIS's head of station had done an end run around Frayn to call in the fleet. An ambassador trumped a colonel.

Given what Kovalic had heard about the ambassador, the house – ostentatious in its ostentatiousness – seemed like a surprising choice for the man. Kovalic could think of many a wealthy businessman or self-styled noble who would have dismissed the residence as simply too much.

Set back on a half-acre of sculpted gardens, the building itself was a monument to rococo style: no surface that could support some sort of flourish or decoration was left bare. A large, broad set of granite steps led up to the veranda, which featured a row of ivory pillars inlaid with gold and twined in ivy. Statues of classical figures dotted the gardens, which were arranged around a reflecting pool – impressive in size, given the lack of natural water inside Bergfestung – featuring a working fountain spewing water from the mouths of a pair of mermaids.

"Christ," muttered Tapper, "not sure whose house this is, but they ought to have him hauled in for crimes against architecture at least."

Kovalic's eyes swept the grounds: there was no sign of roving guards or snipers posted on the roof. Which didn't in and of itself mean anything; there were probably plenty of places to conceal oneself. Maybe the mermaid statues had cameras or turrets in them.

He pinched the bridge of his nose – the sleep deprivation was really starting to take a toll.

"How do you want to handle this, Simon?" Frayn asked. "I was thinking perhaps the sergeant and I could flank around to either side, while you circle around the back."

"You know, I thought I might just walk up and knock."

Frayn blinked. "You're joking, right?" When Kovalic didn't respond immediately, his eyes shifted to Tapper. "He's joking, right?"

"I've heard he has a sense of humor," Tapper said, "but sometimes it's hard to tell."

"Simon, this is a heavily guarded residence," Frayn said. "You're unarmed – unless you somehow found a way to smuggle a cache of weapons onto Bayern that I don't know about– the sun is starting to come up, and you've barely slept in the last day. What could possibly make you think this is a good idea?"

"They've got Nat, Harry."

Frayn opened his mouth to protest further, then seemed to think better of it and just gave a curt nod.

"Besides," Kovalic added, "they won't be expecting one person. They'll be expecting that battalion of special forces. Might be a slight advantage, but I'll take anything I can get."

"I'm not going to be able to talk you out of this, am I?"

Kovalic shook his head, then pulled out the KO gun Tapper had given him in the van and checked the charge. He should have plugged the thing in when they'd been at the embassy, but it had slipped its mind; it was only about a third capacity. A few shots, depending on the intensity.

"In that case," Frayn said, slapping him on his shoulder – the uninjured one, fortunately, "all I'll say is good luck. Oh, and please try to keep the casualties to a minimum, would you? There's a good fellow."

Kovalic pulled himself up the concrete wall that surrounded the ambassador's residence. His shoulder strained, but the sealant held, despite all the abuse it had taken in the past couple days. Rolling his way across the top he dropped into a crouch behind a thicket of shrubs that bordered the wall to the rear of the house. That was poor security – someone should have told the gardener to leave a clear sightline to the wall.

A guard walked by and Kovalic held his breath until she passed. Just sneaking his way around the security was an option, but that left way too many people at his back. No, he'd have to incapacitate them all. He crept around the bush until he had a clear view of the one he'd just seen – she was broad of shoulder and easily his height, toting a compact weapon, probably a machine pistol.

He closed the distance slowly, his feet falling quietly on the soft grass. At least the ambassador hadn't spared any expense for his grounds – a gravel courtyard would have made this considerably more difficult. Flooded with adrenaline, every nerve was pinging like an overloaded radar, quickening his pulse and telling him to hurry before he was caught.

Or worse, before something happened to Nat and Brody.

It was training that slowed his breath, kept him from falling prey to the animal instinct to charge headlong at the person. He couldn't know where his team was or what state they were in, and rushing in would only put them in more danger.

Slow is smooth. Smooth is fast. Another favorite from Tapper's big book of aphorisms. See also "measure twice, cut once."

Before he knew it, he was in striking distance of the guard. The stunner could have dropped her easy at this distance, but he needed her conscious for a moment or two at least.

Slipping up behind her, he placed the stunner at the base of her neck. The woman's muscles tensed, coiling to strike, and Kovalic knew she was fighting that same adrenaline he'd been tamping down.

"Easy," he murmured, carefully removing the earpiece from her left ear and stepping back to a safe distance. "Just put the gun down." The machine pistol dropped with a dull thud to the grass, and her hands went up.

"You're making a big mistake," said the woman, her voice deep and husky.

"Wouldn't be the first time," said Kovalic cheerfully. "Now, before you go down for your nap, don't suppose you'd be kind enough to tell me how many more of you there are?"

"Go to hell."

Well, it had been worth a try. With a shrug, Kovalic squeezed the trigger, the familiar quiet hum and blue flash of the stunner fire hitting the woman square in the back. With a quiet grunt, she toppled to the ground where she lay, softly breathing, in a heap. Kovalic knelt and took her machine pistol, sticking it in the back of his waistband. He swapped his earbud out for the guard's so he could monitor the channel. Quiet at the moment, but it might let him identify any other threats before he saw them.

That dealt with, Kovalic stole to the side of the building, and pressed his back up against it. His breathing had calmed somewhat after dropping the guard, his body relaxing into the familiar rhythms of combat ops and their intense flurries of activity amongst the patient hours of waiting.

The earbud he'd taken from the guard crackled to life.

"Breach," rasped a voice. "Everybody to second floor balcony, now."

Kovalic's eyebrows went up as he flattened himself against

the wall. Breach? The hint of a smile tugged at the corner of his mouth: Nat. Had to be.

He risked a quick peek around the corner. No movement on the side of the house, so he followed the wall to the next corner, and took a gander towards the front of the house.

A pair of guards, a woman and a man, had rounded the opposite corner and were making their way at a brisk pace towards the house's front door. Both of them were carrying machine pistols like the one he'd taken off the previous guard, and they didn't look any friendlier. Kovalic glanced down at the power meter on the KO gun – it had redlined, which meant one or two shots left, but they were well out of range.

He worked his shoulder, grimacing at the pressure in the joint. So much for resting his injuries on this trip. For someone who'd followed orders for a living, he never seemed to listen to his doctor's.

Taking a deep breath, he nodded to himself, then rounded the corner and sprinted as hard as he could towards the front door and the pair of guards.

They might have been on high alert, but by the time the man had caught sight of him out of the corner of his eye and started to turn and bring up his weapon, Kovalic had already covered more than half the distance. He raised the KO gun and fired, full power; the man's eyes rolled back into his head as he collapsed.

But the man had taken the full brunt of the shot, leaving the woman behind him unscathed. She had her machine pistol up and was taking aim even as Kovalic saw the flashing red "Empty" indicator on the KO gun in his hands. Without a second thought, he hurled the gun at the woman's face.

It was more startling than threatening, but it had the desired result, causing her to duck and break her aim, and giving Kovalic enough time to slam his shoulder into her solar plexus.

The wrong shoulder *again* he realized, as pain exploded down the length of his arm and his vision flashed like he'd been hit by one of his own stun blasts. Nausea gripped his gut, and he went down, cradling the injured arm.

Through the stars swimming in his vision, he could see the machine pistol lying just a few feet away; beyond it, the guard groaned faintly, but was stirring. Kovalic stumbled to his feet and picked up her weapon, then limped over to her and knocked her head briefly against the brick steps.

Just beyond was the building's ornate, wooden front door. On either side stood tall, narrow windows. He leaned over and peeked in one, just in time to see the blond man who had rented the van, von Denffer, appear from a doorway, trailed by an armed Brody and Nat.

His shoulders slumped in relief, sending yet another twinge of pain up his injured right arm. Everything was fine and Nat totally had everything under control, just as he'd predicted. He raised a hand to knock on the front door when he caught sight of a pair of laser dots appear and flit onto Nat and Brody. He wanted to burst through the door and shout a warning, but the words caught in his throat.

Von Denffer smiled and turned to face his captors, saying something Kovalic couldn't hear, and he watched Brody and Nat look upwards – then Brody was putting down his weapon slowly. Nat still clutched hers in both hands, and Kovalic knew that expression all too well: running the odds.

He glanced down at the gun he'd liberated from the guard and then at his right arm, which was now officially letting him know that it was on strike. Maybe he could even those odds just a bit. If only there were a way to let Nat in on the plan. What he wouldn't give for a way to talk to...

Blinking, he remembered what Tapper had said about the mission Brody and Nat had been on: short-range microbursts. Holding the machine pistol between his knees, he swapped the earbud back to his own comm. With a deep breath – and for good measure throwing in one of his mother's old standby prayers – he gritted his teeth against the pain from his shoulder and switched to the frequency the SPT had been using.

"Nat, it's me. I don't know if you can hear me, but if you can, I need you to listen very closely."

CHAPTER 22

"This is a really bad idea, Erich," said Eli slowly, raising his hands. He tried not to look up at the balcony that encircled the foyer, but even his peripheral vision confirmed that there were at least two men up there with automatic weapons, aimed down at them. *I'm no strategic expert, but I'm going to say this falls squarely under the category of "not good."*

"I would prefer not to hurt either of you, Eli," said Erich, a sympathetic expression on his face. "But I can't have you leaving. You've been enough trouble already. Ms Mulroney," he said, turning to Taylor, "please drop the gun."

Taylor, who had been grasping the weapon in both hands, slowly took her left hand off the gun, then used her right to lay it down on the floor, gingerly, as though it were a piece of delicate porcelain.

"Thank you. Now, I'm going to have my men escort you upstairs – don't worry, it'll be more comfortable than your last accommodations. No need to keep up the pretense."

"Oh good," said Taylor. "So, that pretty much insures that you're going to kill us when this is all over."

Erich feigned a wound to the heart. "I wouldn't dream of it, Ms Mulroney. I have nothing but the utmost respect for our colleagues in Eyes. We're all on the same side here."

Taylor and Eli exchanged a glance, and she gave a minute shake of her head. *Yeah, now is definitely not the time to correct that particular misapprehension.*

"Gotta be honest, Erich, I don't remember you being this devious."

The blond pilot shook his head. "Nothing devious about it. I'm just serving the Imperium, same as you."

Not so much. "Sure, Erich. Sure." He glanced over at Taylor, and frowned as he saw her stiffen suddenly, her eyes unfocusing, like she was listening to a song that he couldn't hear. Instinct told him to turn back to Erich, keep the man's eyes on him.

"Funny way of serving the Imperium, by kidnapping its heir."

"We all follow orders, Eli. You should know that."

Eli's jaw clenched. The last time he'd been given an order by an Illyrican officer, it had sent him down the long path that had ended in his defection. He wrenched his attention back to the present where there were multiple guns being pointed at him.

"Right, right. So I guess we should just–"

Taylor broke in suddenly, raising her hands. "Let's just get this over with."

Both men glanced at her in surprise, which she returned with a somewhat sour look. "Pardon me if I'm tired of hearing you two jaw on about honor and duty. Shooting me would have been faster and probably less painful."

Erich blinked, then nodded. "Fair enough." He glanced up at the two men on the balcony. "Come down here and secure these two."

The two soldiers worked their ways around their respective balconies to the point where they merged into the single staircase below a rather hideous – in Eli's estimation, anyway – portrait of the crown prince.

Erich turned back to them. "On your knees, if you please. Hands behind your head."

As the soldiers reached the landing, guns still trained on the putative IIS agents, Taylor's eyes jumped to Eli. "You heard him, Eli. Simon says *get down*."

He started to raise an eyebrow even as her words registered. *Simon says.* All of Eli's instincts fired at once, the blaring sensation bringing him back to the cockpit of his training simulation. Behind the stick, he'd have known exactly what to do, but out here, with guns pointed at him, he went with the most literal meaning he could imagine.

He hit the deck.

Beside him, he was vaguely aware of Taylor also dropping to the ground; then the air above him was suddenly alive, whizzing with weapons fire. Eli clapped his hands over his ears, trying to drown out the roar. He managed to roll his head over and peek through slitted eyes at Taylor.

She'd hadn't so much dropped to the ground as made a dive for both her and Eli's guns, which she'd brought up to fire at the soldiers on the staircase. They, on the other hand, had been preoccupied with the source of the automatic weapons fire which, to Eli's surprise, had emanated from behind where he and Taylor had been standing – the building's front door.

Erich, likewise caught by surprise, had evidently managed to avoid the hail of bullets, fleeing up the staircase that his compatriots had just descended. Eli rolled over and tried to shout at Taylor over the din, but she was otherwise occupied.

He felt a vibration through the floor as the two men with guns fell, though whether by the ambush or as a result of Taylor's handiwork, it was impossible to tell. They lay across each other, eyes blank and staring. Having risen to her feet, Taylor crossed to them, keeping the pistols trained downwards, and kicked their guns out of reach. She looked up at Eli, mouthing something.

"What?" he said, or, at least, tried to say. All he could hear was an intense ringing; he felt like he'd been submerged into the deep end of a pool. That blow to the head that he'd gotten at the embassy – Erich's handiwork, he now realized – seemed to have come with some lingering effects.

She tried again, slower, but Eli was having trouble processing the shape of her mouth. "Washer?" he tried. "Wear erk?"

A hand grabbed him suddenly by the shoulder, spinning him around, and he found himself staring directly into familiar gray eyes and a stubbled face wearing an unusually concerned expression.

"Brody, where's *Erich von Denffer*?" The ringing had deadened just enough that he could make out what Kovalic was shouting as if it were being whispered to him.

Eli pointed at the staircase. "He ran up there."

Kovalic scooped up one of the fallen men's guns and tossed it to Eli, then took the other for himself.

Eli fumbled with the gun, narrowly avoiding shooting himself in the foot, but managed to find the correct grip somehow. He shook his head, as though that might help his hearing – and his comprehension of the situation as a whole – clear up faster.

Kovalic was having a quiet conversation with Taylor now, though Eli couldn't hear a single bit of it. He'd had enough of secrets, though, and did his best to draw himself up and stride over to them.

"Kovalic, what the hell are you doing here?"

The man glanced in his direction, eyebrows raised. "We really don't have time to catch up, Brody. Your friend Erich's kidnapped the crown prince."

Eli glanced up at the stairs. Sure, he knew that. The evidence by this point was obvious... and yet, something about it still didn't fit. He'd known Erich for years – though, admittedly, it had been a long time ago, and people changed. Still, not this much. If Erich von Denffer had gone over this edge, something had shoved him – hard.

And he wasn't about to pull himself back up. Not without some help anyway.

There was a chime from Kovalic's sleeve, and the operative awkwardly stuffed the pistol he'd been holding into his waistband with his left hand before using the same hand to tap his earbud. "Harry?"

Eli frowned at him; Kovalic's right arm was hanging limply at his side and, now that he'd gotten over the initial surprise of seeing him here, he realized the man looked like he'd been through the wringer.

"Yeah, we're clear in here. Just looking for von Denffer and the prince. You have a perimeter set up?" He listened for a second, then swore quietly. "Got it. Grab Tapper and meet us here." Hanging up, he retrieved his weapon. "Good news is that Frayn's got the place surrounded. Bad news is an Illyrican fleet just jumped in system. They'll be in orbit shortly."

"An Illyrican fleet?" Eli said, eyes widening. *Is the room spinning, or is it just me?*

"All we have to do is find where they stashed the prince. Fortunately, I don't think there's any other way out of here, so we should have von Denffer cornered."

Eli looked back and forth from Kovalic to the stairs Erich had taken. "Well, there's the jetpad."

Kovalic stopped mid-motion. "The what now?"

"This place has a private jetpad. Erich mentioned it at the party – he said he brought the prince in on his own personal flier."

As if on cue, a rumbling shook the house and the faint whine of repulsors filled the air.

Three pairs of eyes met. "Son of a bitch," said Kovalic.

All of them broke into a run for the stairs. At the top, they followed the sound of the repulsors to a heavy door at the end of a long hallway. Kovalic kicked it open just in time to get a faceful of the skimmer's backwash as it took to the air. Taylor raised her pistol, sighting the ship, but Kovalic pushed her arm down.

"We can't shoot it down if the prince is aboard."

"*If*," Taylor snapped. "This could all be a bluff."

"Or it might not be," Eli pointed out. "We have to go after him." He gestured to a second identical skimmer sitting unoccupied on the jetpad – thank god for the excesses of the ridiculously wealthy. "Room for two." Without waiting for approbation, he sprinted to it and threw open the canopy.

Punching the ignition, Eli glanced over the controls. Fairly standard for a small craft. A dashboard glowed to life, a heads-up overlay projected on the inside of the dash giving him readouts of the key information. "If either of you is coming along, now would be a good time to hop in."

Taylor brushed a hair out of her eyes, and nodded to Kovalic. "Go, Simon. There are a few loose ends to tie up here; I've got it."

Kovalic squeezed her shoulder, then peeled off his sleeve and handed it to her. "Tapper and Frayn are nearby and can help run any interference you need." He smiled. "Just glad you're OK."

Trying hard not to eavesdrop, but failing, Eli fired up the skimmer's repulsors. The craft lifted a foot off the ground, then bobbed as Kovalic jumped into the passenger seat.

"You can fly this thing, right?" said Kovalic, casting a dubious eye over the controls.

"I'll let you in on a little secret, captain," said Eli, slapping the control to close the canopy. The engines came on line, and he flashed the other man a thousand-watt smile. "There's not much I *can't* fly." He throttled up the main drive, pulling the ship into a steep climb that pressed them both back into their seats.

Banking around, Eli brought up the radar overlay, which highlighted the other flier in a sickly blue-green. It was rising smoothly towards the vent at the top of the dormant volcano.

"There's no place for him to go," Kovalic muttered. "What's he playing at?"

"Looks like he's heading outside. If he gets there, there's a hell of a lot more room for him to maneuver."

"To what end? These things can't break atmosphere, can they?"

"Nope. I guess it's possible he's got a getaway ship stashed out there?"

"Even if he does, they're not going to get out of the system with an Illyrican fleet inbound." Kovalic shook his head. "Forget out of system; your friend Erich doesn't have a shot in hell of making it off this *planet*."

Erich's flier reached the vent, coating it briefly in the golden light of the sun, then vanished in a shimmer. Eli angled his own ship to follow suit, the incandescent opening growing ever larger through the canopy.

Cut and run? That can't be it. "I'm just not so sure that's his plan."

"What makes you say that?"

Eli's brow furrowed. "Something's wrong. I feel like we put a table together and ended up with three extra screws. When Erich saw Taylor going off with the prince, he warned me – he *warned* me. Hardly the action of a kidnapper."

"He also kidnapped *you*."

"Then he took out two of his own guys in that interrogation room."

"Maybe he just saw which side his bread was buttered?"

Maybe. But brutal opportunism isn't Erich von Denffer's style. The man was born with a full silver place-setting in his mouth.

"This just doesn't make sense," Eli fretted. "Why did the prince's own men kidnap him in the first place?"

Kovalic sighed. "A lengthy and boring political reason, I'm afraid."

"That boils down to?"

"The Illyrican Empire is broke."

Eli's jaw dropped. "Like 'if it ain't broke, don't fix it'?"

"More like 'doesn't have two cents to rub together.'"

"But… they're an *empire*. Can empires even go broke?"

"I look like an economist to you, Brody?"

Throwing the throttle to maximum, Eli pulled back on the stick as they closed with the volcano's vent, then took them up and through the opening. The windshield tinted automatically as real Bayern sunlight hit it, filtering out the brightest rays; nasty crosswinds buffeted the skimmer from what felt like every direction. Eli wrestled with the stick, trying to keep it steady, and fought down the involuntary roiling of his stomach. *I hope Erich was ready for that wind shear, or else he's just a dark spot on the volcano slope.*

Eli swiveled his head, looking for Erich's ship; it took a second before the radar overlay picked him up, gliding down the volcano's long slope towards the open terrain below.

"Hold on." Eli banked the ship, letting the narrowed profile of the craft slice through the air. The skimmer shook with the strain. *Remember, Brody, this isn't a starfighter. Don't get fancy.*

So focused was he on the flight maneuver, hands gripping the yoke, that the sudden squelch of static over the comm system made him jump in his seat.

"I know that has to be you on my six, Eli," came Erich's voice, cutting through the background static. "Back off."

Eli exchanged a glance with Kovalic, who spread his hands and shrugged. "He's *your* friend."

With a sigh, Eli toggled the comm channel. "Believe me, coming out here to give you a piloting demonstration was not at the top of my to-do list when I got up this morning."

Smooth, Kovalic mouthed at him.

Eli ignored him. "Just cut your engines and bring your craft in for a landing, Erich. We'll sort this all out."

There was nothing but the sound of static on the radio for a moment, then Erich's voice broke through again. "Thanks for the generous offer, but I think I'll take my chances against your ace flying skills."

"Erich, listen to me. There's an Imperial battlefleet coming into orbit. These fliers aren't spaceworthy. You've got no place to go. Bring her down, now."

Eli throttled up, closing in on Erich's craft, but he was still several hundred meters behind the other ship, which Erich was deftly guiding through the air currents. *I'd forgotten just how good he is.* A red light flashed on the console, but Eli kept his attention focused on Erich.

"We know about the plot," Eli pressed. "About the Imperium being broke." He frowned and muted the microphone, glancing at Kovalic. "How was that supposed to end exactly?"

"The kidnapped heir provokes the Imperium into sending a fleet to 'rescue' him. The Corporation security officers can't hold off a division of trained Illyrican marines, so the Imperium effectively annexes Bayern. And, naturally, nationalizes its assets."

"Oh." He toggled the mic back on and cleared his throat. "It was a really fucking complicated plan, Erich."

"It wasn't my plan."

"No shit," Eli said mildly. "You don't really have the brains for that one. But running away with the prince in tow doesn't look good, so I think we know that no matter whose plan it was, you're the one who's going to take the fall."

"Interesting choice of words. You might want to check those gauges."

Eli blinked, casting his eyes over the dash. The red light he'd ignored before had come on again, now burning steady. This time he bothered to read the label.

"Oh. Shit." He belatedly slapped the mute button on the microphone.

"What is it?" said Kovalic.

Eli pointed at the gauge. "Quick flying lesson. This is what we call the 'fuel gauge,' which shows how much–"

"We're *out of fuel?*"

"No, we're *low* on fuel. We'll be *out* of fuel in about…" He did some quick calculations in his head. "Five minutes. Assuming there's not a leak." He scratched his head. "Which there probably is, because if my guess is correct, fucking Erich von Denffer sabotaged the fuel tank."

Kovalic had turned a particular shade that Eli had never seen before. *Who's afraid of flying now?* he started to crow, before realizing that there was a good chance he'd never really have a chance to rub that one in and, in any case, now was not exactly the time.

"What about the repulsors?" said Kovalic.

"The repulsors are working fine."

"So we can land?"

"Well, here's the thing about repulsors. They only have an effective distance of maybe fifty meters off the ground, max. If you were to, say, hit the ground because of a plummeting descent, they probably wouldn't generate enough lift to counteract the velocity with which you were crashing."

"You said 'probably.'"

"Well, maybe if you timed it *exactly right.*"

Erich's voice cut in again. "You've probably got enough fuel to make a landing now, Eli. Just let me go and we're all fine."

In the corner of his eye, Eli could see Kovalic shaking his head.

"I am really starting to regret that whole 'accepting an officer's commission' thing," Eli muttered.

"If it's any consolation, I'm starting to regret you accepting it too."

Eli stifled a bitter laugh, then dialed back the throttle, leaned back in his seat, and took a deep breath. There weren't a lot of options to be had here, for him or for Erich. With no way for him to get away – *Wait… why would he even* want *to get away? They got the fleet to show up, just like they planned.*

They.

Not Erich. It was as if he'd finally found the focus knob, and the blurry picture that he'd been staring at for the last couple days was resolved into a clear, high-definition image of the whole affair for the first time. He turned it around, considering it from every angle, but no matter which way he looked at it, the picture was the same.

"Son of a bitch," he said under his breath.

"Brody?"

"Son of a *bitch*." Eli threw the throttle wide open, and the ship jumped like a scalded monkey, closing in rapidly on Erich's flier.

"What the hell, Brody?" shouted Kovalic over the roar of the overtaxed engines. "You're wasting all our fuel."

"He's going to kill him, Kovalic. He's going to kill the prince – if he's not dead already." Erich had as much as admitted it: he hated the man. He'd gone along with the kidnapping plot, but whereas the rest of his comrades had intended to turn the prince right back over to the Illyrican fleet, Erich von Denffer had had a very different end in mind. *Not that I give a shit about his royal highness, but I'm not about to let someone else I know die.* Acid ate away at his stomach. *Not again.*

"Kill him? Why?"

Eli spared him a dumbfounded glance. "Does it *matter* right now?"

Kovalic raised his hands.

"Eli," came Erich's voice, more panicked. "What the hell are you doing? Back off!"

I'm still too far back, Eli thought as he watched the proximity meter count down rapidly. *And I'm running out of fuel.* A disturbingly gentle chime sounded, reminding him that he really should check his fuel levels. *Stupid luxury skimmers.*

Erich's voice crackled across the radio again. "Pull up, Brody! Or I'll put this ship right into the ground, with me and the prince on it."

Responding would have meant taking his hands off the controls, and Eli wasn't prepared to do that. The more Erich was talking, the less he was flying. And Eli was so very close to reaching them–

The ship in front of them suddenly pointed its nose sharply downward, going into a dive that looked to make good on Erich's promise.

"He's going to do it," Kovalic said, gripping the edges of his seat.

"Oh no he's not," Eli muttered, and tipped his own yoke forward, following suit. A bright red holographic banner appeared on the inside of the canopy: WARNING: POWER DIVE NOT RECOMMENDED, accompanied by a blinking message to PULL UP. Reaching up with one hand, Eli flicked the messages off the display, concentrating on the craft in front of them. Fortunately, they'd been at a reasonably high altitude, and Erich – like Eli – would be fighting against a ship that more or less wanted to stay in the air. But Erich still had a lead on them, and Eli wasn't going to be able to catch up if they were both going full speed. He needed an edge.

What I wouldn't give for an afterburner – wait a second.

His eyes darted over the dashboard until they found the emergency fuel dump. *Not that there's much fuel left.* He'd pulled this off in a simulator once, but that had been in the vacuum of space; in atmosphere, he was going to have to contend with drag and friction. Plus, you know, that had been a simulation.

Or, in other words, this idea was really stupid. Not that that had ever stopped him. Dr Thornfield's comment about him being reckless echoed in his head. *Sorry, doc. Looks like you were right after all.*

"Kovalic," he managed through gritted teeth. "I just want to apologize for something in advance."

"For crashing us into the ground?"

"OK, for two things." He flipped the cover off the fuel dump switch, finger grazing the control as he lined up his ship. *Well, this could be the last thing I ever do. Go big or go home.* He flipped the switch, then pulled the nose up to bring the flier's engines in line with the rapidly dispensing fuel.

The ignition slammed both of them back into their seats, sending the ship diving even faster towards the all-too-rapidly-approaching ground. Eli fought with the stick, trying to keep himself on the trajectory he'd laid out – the one that would bring them right underneath Erich's flier.

"Brody, this is insane." He faintly heard Kovalic shouting, overwhelmed as it was by the rushing of blood that filled his ears. The skimmer's rather rudimentary inertial compensators were the only thing keeping them from blacking out right now.

Slowly, they gained on Erich's craft until they were nearly underneath the other skimmer; Eli brought the nose of his own skimmer up slightly, and a scrape of metal against metal signified contact between the two fliers. The stick wrenched in Eli's grasp, but he fought to hold it steady, eyes on the altimeter. 500 meters.

He pulled back more, starting to level his ship out, and taking more of the weight of Erich's flier with theirs. 400 meters.

Red spots started appearing in his vision, his teeth clenched so hard he thought they might crack with the pressure. 300 meters.

He dialed back the throttle, reducing speed while trying to keep Erich's ship positioned on top of his. 200 meters.

Evening out the trim, he pulled back further, bringing the craft's nose up to a thirty-degree angle. 100 meters.

A large red banner covered the entire screen: FUEL DEPLETED. INITIATING EMERGENCY LANDING PROTOCOLS. With a shaking hand, he slammed the override button, then let it hover over another control. 50 meters.

At 20 meters, he fired the repulsors.

The skimmer bounced.

There was a bone-rending crunch as Eli's flier slammed upward into Erich's flier, sending the other careening off onto the plains, spinning like a flying disc. Eli and Kovalic were thrown upwards against their restraints, then pushed back down as the repulsors burned out from the effort. The ship dropped like a stone, but only from about 30 meters, which was much preferable to the 2,000 meters they'd started at.

Eli had just enough time to suck in a lungful of air before the skimmer hit the ground, knocking it right back out of him. It skipped like a rock off a lake, leaving Eli's stomach far, far behind as they ricocheted across the open scrubland. Fountains of dirt sprayed over the canopy, and the two of them were pummeled and buffeted against their restraints.

After what seemed like an hour of the worst roller coaster ever – but which, in reality, was less than a minute – the skimmer slid to a stop, nose planted firmly in the dirt.

Eli coughed and spat out a mouthful of blood, panicking before he realized that he'd bit his cheek or his tongue somewhere in the descent. His chest ached, especially where the restraints had cut into it, and his head felt like someone had taken a ball-peen hammer to it. His hands were still gripping the yoke tightly, as if that could make any difference at all at this point.

"Brody?" croaked a voice. He looked over to see Kovalic breathing heavily, his eyes still closed. "Are we alive?"

Eli coughed again. "If we're not then heaven is way shittier than I thought it would be."

"What makes you think you're going to heaven?"

"I just saved your ass, didn't I?"

Kovalic grunted, then punched the restraint release. Eli followed suit, and the two of them struggled out of their seats, then, between them, managed to pop the canopy's emergency release and fling it open.

It was cold on the plains, the air whipping over them with faint particles of what Eli realized after a moment was snow. He shivered, rubbing his arms with his hands – he really hadn't dressed for this.

Kovalic clambered out next to him, peering around. "There," he said, pointing to another furrow like the one their skimmer had plowed. Erich's craft seemed to be largely in one piece, about a hundred meters off their starboard.

Picking their way over took longer than Eli had anticipated, thanks to the fact that neither of them were particularly steady on their feet, but when they arrived they found the ship mostly intact; one of the wings had sheared off and was sitting, smoking, another fifty feet away.

Climbing up on the fuselage, Eli found the external manual release for the canopy, and again he and Kovalic managed to wrestle the transparent cowl open.

The two men inside were limp against their restraints. Both had suffered a number of lacerations – Erich's head looked like it had been slammed against the controls – but when Eli and Kovalic climbed down and checked, they both still had pulses. The prince was already beginning to stir, groaning quietly. They retrieved the first aid kit from the skimmer's cockpit, and Eli did a quick check, ensuring that the vessel wasn't about to explode or catch fire.

When they had made sure neither the prince nor Erich were about to expire from their injuries, they climbed back out of the ship and sprawled on the ground. Eli sighed in relief and shook his head. "Christ, Kovalic. Just another day at the office?"

Kovalic laughed, the skin around his gray eyes crinkling. "Nah. This is just–" he screwed up his face in thought, "whatever the hell day it is."

Eli laughed too, then winced at the stabbing pain in his chest. "Dr Thornfield is going to have a field day with her psychological evaluation of this."

"Don't worry. I'm sure it'll be classified above her clearance level anyway."

Eli snorted. "Somehow, I don't think that's likely to stop her."

They sat in silence for a few minutes, before Eli glanced at Kovalic. "So, what's going to happen to Erich?"

Kovalic let out a breath. "He plotted to kidnap and attempted to murder the heir to the Illyrican Empire. I'm guessing they're going to execute him. Probably sooner rather than later."

Fury coalesced in Eli's head. "It's not right, Kovalic. Erich wasn't behind this whole thing. He said it: he was just following orders." *Well, except for the trying to kill the prince part. That definitely wasn't part of the original plan.*

"Well, the Illyricans are going to want to stick *somebody*'s head on a pike. Who do you propose we give them?"

Eli looked over his shoulder at the remains of Erich's flier. "Thing is," he said, lowering his voice, "I'm pretty sure it was all the prince's idea. At the very least, he was in on it." He scratched his head. "The kidnapping part, I mean. Not his own murder."

Kovalic raised an eyebrow. "That's quite an accusation, lieutenant. Got anything to back it up?"

Eli shook his head.

"Yeah. Us neither."

"So he's going to get away with it?"

The older man shrugged. "The prince is still alive, and we've got him, so we've probably avoided providing the Illyricans with a pretense for absorbing Bayern into the Imperium. I'd say that's a pretty good day's work."

"And we sacrifice Erich for one bad decision?"

"It was a pretty bad decision," Kovalic pointed out. "Even if his intentions were good." He raised his hands to pacify Eli. "OK, OK. Give me a second to think about this." He climbed to his feet and ran his good hand through his hair. Then he started to pace, walking in an ever-widening spiral. As he moved, his eyes flicked back and forth rapidly, and Eli could swear he was muttering to himself. But his expression, which had started grim, began to lighten as he walked, his stride becoming steadier and longer, until he stopped and turned to Eli, a smile on his face.

"I've got an idea."

CHAPTER 23

Kovalic's shoulder throbbed.

It had been bad enough after he'd plowed into that guard, but the crash in the skimmer had added, well, injury to injury. He didn't think he'd done any permanent damage, but he was pretty sure that his doctor was not going to be thrilled with him when he made it back to Nova. For the meantime, Nat had refreshed the sealant plug and given him some painkillers, which did a little to take the edge off.

On the upside, at least he'd make it back. That wasn't nothing.

He pushed the pain away, letting only a grimace seep through as he raised his coffee cup and sipped. The hot drink was welcome: it was windy and cold out on the landing platform, and his hair was being whipped to and fro by the stiff wind.

"What idiot decided the side of a mountain was a good place to put your ship down?" Tapper muttered from next to him.

Kovalic shrugged, pain stabbing through his shoulder. "Maybe they liked the view."

"I've been trying not to look down."

"Hey, I'm just glad we didn't have to walk all the way back

350

up," said Kovalic. They'd managed to contact Nat and she'd brought the *Cavalier* to come pick them up from the crash site. She may not have had Brody's piloting flair, but she was the only one of them rated on light craft in atmosphere – and frankly, after the crash, Kovalic had had his fill of daredevilry.

They'd slipped back up to the *Cavalier*'s landing platform just under the noses of the approaching Corporation fliers, dispatched to investigate reports of an accident. Kovalic had sent a couple messages from the ship, including one to Frayn.

And that brought them here.

The coffee-maker on the *Cavalier* wasn't fancy, but it made a decent cup, Kovalic reflected as he took another sip. Better than the coffee he'd had as a marine, anyway. Not that that was saying much.

The doors at the end of the platform hissed open, admitting a bemused-looking Harry Frayn, accompanied by a pair of Illyrican marines who were most decidedly *not* wearing crimson and gold. Seeing Kovalic, Frayn held up a hand at the two, then walked forward alone.

Kovalic raised his cup of coffee and met Frayn halfway across the platform, leaving Tapper behind to eye the two guards.

"Simon."

"Harry."

Frayn raised an eyebrow. "Well, don't leave me in suspense."

With a modest shoulder-twinging shrug, Kovalic smiled. "Don't worry, Harry: I've got your boy."

The older man visibly relaxed, shoulders dropping from their hunch, his face melting into a weak smile. "Thank goodness. I was beginning to worry I'd have to find a new line of work. He is, I hope, intact?"

"More or less," said Kovalic. "Some cuts and bruises."

Frayn waved a hand. "He'll live. And I was glad to see that Natalie was fine as well." He shook his head and let out a long sigh, running a hand through his thinning mane. "Frankly, I'm amazed we all made it out OK." With a frown, he looked up at the ship expectantly, then back down at Kovalic; his expression turned appraising. "Why do I have the sudden feeling that there's more to this?"

"Well, it seems the prince has been a very naughty boy, Harry." Kovalic took a slow swallow of coffee, watching Frayn. "There's the matter of his… dating record for one thing."

Frayn scratched at his head awkwardly. "Ah, yes. I've heard rumors."

"He might benefit from a close eye."

Tilting his head to one side, Frayn gave Kovalic a shrewd look. "I see. I'm sure that can be arranged."

"Far more disturbing, though," said Kovalic, gesturing with the coffee cup, "is the fact that he apparently organized this whole charade himself."

"What?" Kovalic had expected surprise in Frayn's tone, but hadn't been sure whether it would be feigned or genuine. It sounded real enough, but with spies one never could tell. "The kidnapping?"

"Yep. Lock, stock, and barrel of monkeys."

Frayn's mouth was still hanging open. "The prince. Hadrian. That one."

"I know. Smartest stupid idea I've heard in a while."

Slowly, Frayn's gray head shook back and forth. "Simon, this doesn't make any sense. I thought surely von Denffer…"

"Commander von Denffer was involved, but he wasn't the mastermind. He was ordered to take part in the ploy, as were the rest of the prince's honor wing."

Frayn was silent for a moment. "You have evidence?"

"Commander von Denffer was clever enough to realize the precariousness of his position. He recorded the prince giving orders about the abduction."

"Ah. I see. Well, obviously, I'd be most concerned were this information to find its way, er, to the public."

"Yeah, I'd imagine. Neither the Corporation nor the Commonwealth would be exceptionally pleased to hear of the Imperium's plans to annex an independent world. Particularly after your last misadventure at Sabaea."

"So," said Frayn, crossing his arms. "A deal then?"

"A deal. You can have the prince back; honestly, we don't want him. We will keep Commander von Denffer – and his recordings – as insurance."

Frayn's eyes narrowed. "Surely you don't need the man if you have his recordings."

"Need him? No. But I think the commander is rightfully concerned of reprisal should he make his way back to the Imperium."

"Ah. I see."

"Of course, you're the one with a fleet in orbit, so if you really wanted to try and stop us... then again, there's no guarantee that wouldn't just trigger the release of those recordings."

A twist of distaste crossed Frayn's face. "Please, Simon. We're not about to resort to thuggish force."

"I didn't think so. In any regard, it seems like you might have your hands full elsewhere." Kovalic took a deep breath. Now came the tricky part. "As for the Imperium's deal with the Corporation."

Frayn sighed. "I suppose it was too much to hope that would have gone unnoticed."

"Pretty much." Kovalic drained the last of his coffee. "Look, the Commonwealth has no right to interfere in the business of sovereign powers. Presuming that your deal with the Corporation is all on the up and up, that's between you and them. I'm sure the Corporation will make its own determination as to whether or not the Imperium is worth saving – as long as invasion is off the table, anyway."

Stillness hung in the air. Kovalic wished he had a little more coffee left, so he wouldn't be forced to just stand there uneasily as Frayn considered the matter. The wind whistled across the platform, chilling Kovalic and making his shoulder ache. He resisted the urge to reach up and massage it.

"That's an extraordinarily – and unusually – generous offer, Simon," said Frayn finally. "What's the catch?"

"No catch," said Kovalic, shaking his head. "I'm not here to destroy the Imperium." He smiled. "Not today, anyway. Just take your heir back home and shove him in a closet somewhere. We'll call it a wash."

"How's your boss going to feel about this?"

"He trusts my judgment."

"As well he should," said Frayn, extending a hand. "Very well, then. We have a deal."

"Glad to hear it," said Kovalic, clasping the proffered hand. He gripped it tightly. "But, if I get wind of the prince abusing anybody, or attempting any more machinations, or, so help me god, if you guys actually put him in charge of anything more significant than a charity bake sale, he goes down in flames. Understood?"

Frayn met his gaze, unflinching. "You might be surprised to hear that there are many in the Imperium who agree with you on that score, Simon."

Kovalic released the other man's hand. "Good. Now get the son of a bitch off my ship."

From the cockpit of the *Cavalier*, Kovalic watched Frayn leave the landing pad, prince in tow, and let out a mental sigh of relief. One crisis averted. Only six hundred seventy-four left to go. He drummed his fingers on the lockbox that he'd pulled out of one of the ship's shielded storage compartments.

"Lucky thing, von Denffer recording those conversations," said Tapper. He shook his head admiringly, though Kovalic's long association with the sergeant meant he had no trouble detecting the note of sarcasm.

"Yeah," said Kovalic, punching a code into the box. It chirped and unlocked with a click. "Lucky. Let's hope that we've put enough of the fear of god into the prince that he won't bother calling the bluff. That might give Commander von Denffer a slim chance of finding himself in the crosshairs of an IIS Special Operations Executive team."

"Can't imagine Papa von Denffer's going to be too happy that his only son can't come home again."

"It's starting to get to the point where it might be easier to list the people who *can* go home again." Flipping the lid on the box, Kovalic pulled out the team's emergency sidearm and started to check it over.

The cockpit door slid open with a swoosh, and Brody stepped in. Cuts and bruises still covered his face, though it looked like Nat had done a decent job of patching him up. But there was a glossy sheen to his eyes that suggested he was still riding high on the adrenaline of the morning's events. Probably not the best idea to let him behind the stick of another ship quite so fast.

"What'd I miss?"

"The departure of his esteemed highness," said Tapper, tilting his head towards the landing pad.

Brody blinked, looking back and forth between the canopy and Kovalic. "That's it? We just handed him over?"

Kovalic raised an eyebrow as he checked that the gun's chamber was clear. "What'd you think, Brody? We were going to take him back to the Commonwealth and throw him in a deep, dark hole somewhere?"

"Not the worst idea I've heard all day."

"The political ramifications of that–"

"Bullshit. That's *bullshit*, Kovalic."

Tapper cleared his throat, and Brody shot him a death glare. "*Captain*, I mean. Look, this guy's a sadist and it's not like he's going to stop. And we're just sending him back to his own world, where he's free to wreak god knows what havoc, and eventually, someday, step up to the throne."

Kovalic leaned back in his chair. "For one thing, I doubt his ascension to the throne is a foregone conclusion. The Illyricans haven't had an empire long enough to establish a tried-and-true secession. Hadrian might be the eldest, but he's got two more siblings, either of whom might be more attractive to the powerbrokers in the Imperium." Dear god, if there were any justice in the world. "And if Hadrian *does* take the throne, I can't imagine the Commonwealth would be sad to see an emperor whose proclivities were a matter of record."

Brody gaped. "The Commonwealth would let that madman take the throne just because they knew how to exploit him?"

Tapper slapped Brody on the shoulder. "Welcome to galactic intrigue, kid. Please queue in an orderly fashion."

The pilot dropped heavily into one of the other seats; the glassy look had already begun to fade from his eyes as his body started to feel the post-excitement crash.

"What the hell are we even *doing* here?" he muttered.

"Hey," said Kovalic, drawing a look from the younger man. "Don't get too wrapped up in the machinations. We're the only reason the Corporation and its rather substantial financial holdings aren't in the hands of the Imperium. That's a win." He pulled a magazine from the lockbox and inserted it into the pistol's grip; it slid home with a satisfying click.

"Yeah," said Brody glumly.

"Big picture, Brody. That's what strategic intelligence is all about." Kovalic glanced at his sleeve. "I've got one last thing to do before we leave," he said, trading a significant look with Tapper. "Take an hour of downtime or so, but then get the ship prepped to go." He closed the lockbox and slid the pistol into the shoulder holster underneath his jacket.

Brody was still staring at the console in front of him. Tapper snapped his fingers in front of the man's face, and he jumped in his seat. "What? Oh. Yeah. Preflight. Got it."

Shaking his head, Kovalic stepped through the cockpit door and made his way towards the egress ramp. Rounding the curve of the corridor, he almost collided with Nat, coming in the other direction.

"Easy there, cowboy," she said. She'd changed from her increasingly tattered evening dress back into a spare set of civilian clothes, and her hair was damp from the shower.

Noting his scrutiny, Nat gave an awkward laugh. "I think it'll take a couple more showers before I can wash the whole thing away, but I'm feeling better than I was twelve hours ago, that's for sure."

Kovalic nodded, shifting awkwardly from foot to foot. "You did good work, Nat."

Nat rolled her eyes. "Please. I got captured by some psycho nobleman and had to be fished out like a kid who fell in the well. Let's not oversell it."

"Hey, we've all had off days."

Nat gave him an incredulous look, and they both dissolved into laughter.

She shook her head and wiped a tear from one corner of her eye. "I forgot what it was like working with you. Just a *little* bit different from sitting behind my desk staring at communications intercepts."

"I'm surprised they let you transfer away from fieldwork."

Now it was Nat's turn to shift awkwardly. "Yeah. Well. I decided to make some changes in my life. After... you know. Us."

Kovalic felt the color rise into his cheeks. "Yeah." He scratched his cheek. "Listen, Nat, about that..."

"Never mind, Simon. I... I should go help get things squared away." She smiled and raised her hands. "Shouldn't have said anything." She laid a hand on his good shoulder, squeezed it, and then continued down the corridor to the cockpit.

"That makes two of us," sighed Kovalic. With a shake of his head, he slapped the door release and headed down the ramp.

It took him about half an hour to get to the park on the far side of Bergfestung. That the city even *had* parks struck Kovalic as kind of a miracle, but humans responded well to greenery, and the folks on Bayern had never been ones to sacrifice the niceties of life. He supposed the Corporation had plenty of money to spend on things like this, which was good, because the dedicated heliostat and fiber light lines, combined with the natural flowing waterfall, koi pond, and irrigation system, probably cost a pretty penny. The whole thing was tiered against the inside of the volcano's wall, which had been cleverly covered in creeping vines. A small copse of trees to either side helped obscure the urban scenery, and dampened the sound of Bergfestung's hustle and bustle.

At this hour of the morning it was more or less deserted, what with the majority of the Corporation's employees busy at work. Kovalic dropped onto a stone bench with a nice view of the city; it also happened to be home to the park's only other occupant, a man in a suit reading on a tablet.

Kovalic leaned forward, folding his hands with his elbows on his knees, and stared at the city. "Thanks for the information on the Imperium's financial situation. It was invaluable."

The man glanced up from the tablet, as though he'd just been asked about the weather. "No problem, sir. You got him?"

Kovalic hesitated. "He's on his way back to the Imperium now, but we've got some insurance on him."

Somebody who didn't know the man the way Kovalic did wouldn't have detected the slight shift in posture that betrayed displeasure. His face, though, remained as impassive as ever.

"I see."

"I already went through this with Brody," said Kovalic. "It's the right move for the big picture."

"Yes, sir."

Kovalic scratched at the stubble on his chin. He needed a shave. Probably a shower of his own, after all he'd been through in the last couple days. "Your extraction is all worked out?"

"Business trip coming up next week. I'll slip away quietly and make my way home."

"Got it." Kovalic's shoulder throbbed again; he rubbed it with his right hand. Probably time for another round of painkillers.

They sat in silence for a moment.

"Something else, sir?"

Kovalic let out a long sigh and shook his head. "How long?" he said finally, prying the words like nuts from their shells.

The other man raised an eyebrow. "I don't know what you mean, sir."

"How *long*, Aaron?"

Page's lips compressed into a thin line. "Six months."

Kovalic pinched the bridge of his nose between thumb and forefinger. "Six months," he muttered. "Leaking information to CID for *six months*."

Page had put the tablet down on his lap. He tilted his head towards Kovalic. "How did you figure it out?"

"Something Deputy Director Kester said to the general stuck with me. 'The worst of times, indeed.'" He glanced over at Page. "You came up with the contact protocol for Bleiden on Sevastapol; it wasn't in my after-action report. The only other person who knew it was Tapper, and, well..." he trailed off, raising his hands. They both knew that Tapper was as inclined to betrayal as a fish was to breathing air.

Page didn't say anything to that. As far as Kovalic was concerned, though, there was only one question worth asking. "Why?"

"The general's running unchecked, sir."

"Unchecked? *I* check him, lieutenant. Every step of the way. Just like always."

Page's head shook ponderously back and forth. "No, sir. Due respect, but you don't. You're blinded by your loyalty.

Unearned, misplaced loyalty to a man who's had his own agenda from the moment he left his old job."

"You don't know what he gave up, lieutenant."

"We've all given up plenty, sir. It's war."

"So, what is this: patriotism?"

"Yes, sir. That's exactly what it is."

Kovalic gave a bitter laugh. "If that's what Kester's sold you, then you've bought a bill of goods."

"Have I? Jericho Station, three years ago." He lifted an accusatory finger at Kovalic. "You gunned down two men in cold blood – two men who turned out to be Commonwealth Intelligence operatives." The finger curled back into a fist. "But you knew that going in."

Kovalic's stomach seized. Page's first mission for the SPT; it had been a shitshow, no question, but those two faces had been just the latest in a long line for Kovalic. "Sometimes we're our own worst enemy, lieutenant. If those men had succeeded in their mission, they would have assassinated an Illyrican ambassador and risked open war."

"Listen to yourself," Page snapped, his voice ringing in the empty park. He swallowed, then quieted. "Listen to yourself, sir. You're justifying *treason*."

"There are bigger things at stake here."

"Bigger things than the *war*?"

"Yes, lieutenant," Kovalic said. "Bigger things than the war."

"Like what?"

"Like the peace."

Page's jaw clenched. "Spare me the platitudes. You think Kester's playing *me*? The general's got his own little game, and you're helping him. Either intentionally or because you're too stubborn to see it. You think he tells you everything?

He's got his own private accounts with the Corporation, you know. Ask him about LOOKING GLASS sometime."

"I *know* he doesn't tell me everything. His job is to assess the overall strategic impact; mine is to follow orders." He gave Page a sharp look. "I know my limits, Aaron. I know what my role is. I know what I'm *good* for. And I know that even if the general *doesn't* tell me everything that we're still working towards the same goal."

"*How?*" Page said, his expression turning wrought for the first time in Kovalic's memory, hands clenched into fists. "How can you possibly know that?"

"I trust him. That's all there is to it."

Page stared at him unbelievingly, as though Kovalic had just told him that he believed the sun would rise in the west tomorrow. "I'm sorry," he said finally. "I don't."

The roiling that had been rumbling away in Kovalic's stomach all morning forced its way up into his throat. "Yeah," he said quietly. "I know."

There was an exhalation from Page, as though all his secrets had been squeezed out of him like a tube of toothpaste. "So now what? Back to Nova for a court martial?"

A court martial at which Page would be able to defend himself by making the same arguments he'd just given Kovalic. Where the general's operations would probably come to light, and there would be a lot of unpleasant questions and accusations. Not only for the general himself, but for the Commonwealth Executive that had approved his appointment and given him what amounted to carte blanche. This couldn't be brushed off as an operative gone rogue – disavowing knowledge of his activities would just make the Committee look incompetent instead of Machiavellian.

One part scandal, two parts politics, with just a soupçon of treason: it was a recipe to bring down a government if Kovalic had ever heard one. And with the Commonwealth in turmoil, the Imperium would have a field day. Not to mention that there was still the matter of information about SPT intel getting back to the Imperium; they simply couldn't afford to be watching their backs on two fronts at once.

"No," he said at last. "There won't be a trial, lieutenant." He reached into his jacket and drew out the pistol, which he turned over slowly in both hands. "But I can't have someone on my team that *I* don't trust." Looking up, he forced himself to meet Page's eyes. But where he'd expected the man to be calculating some method of escape or some way to forestall the inevitable, he saw only hardened resolve. He shouldn't have been surprised, really.

Kovalic swallowed, and tried to banish the sharp stab of doubt in his gut. Sometimes things, unpleasant things, had to be done. Like he'd told Brody: the bigger picture.

"You were a good officer and I hate to lose you. I'm sorry, Aaron."

"Yeah," said Page slowly. "Me too, sir."

Eli cycled the ship's main power and watched the readouts – the reactor was stable. He marked a check on his tablet, then leaned back in the pilot's seat. *I am all too ready to get the hell off this planet.* They'd secured Erich in the private bunks – not that he was chained up or anything, but they weren't about to give a potentially suicidal pilot free run of their ship.

Fortunately, the trip back to Nova was short. They'd be a little tight; locking Erich in the bunkroom meant that Taylor, Tapper, and Kovalic would have to resort to the acceleration couches in the hold, or hang out in the cockpit.

"How we doing, kid?" came Tapper's voice from the door behind him.

Eli glanced over his shoulder. "You know," he pointed out, "*technically*, I outrank you. Also, I'm twenty-seven years old."

The older man let out a rueful chuckle. "Sorry, kid." He leaned over the back of one of the other seats. "Good work out there, lieutenant. Commander Taylor says you were a big help."

Flushing slightly, Eli scratched at one of his ears. "Just trying to do my part for the team."

Tapper's eyes glinted. "From what the captain says, you put a lot on the line." He inclined his head towards the open plain at the foot of the mountain. "He said he'd never seen flying like that – well, not in so many words, but I could tell he was impressed."

"Thanks."

Tapper reached over and cuffed him lightly on the shoulder. "Just don't tell him I told you that."

Eli laughed and turned back to the console. "Course not."

"We about ready to go?"

"Yep. I can call in takeoff clearance whenever the captain gets back. Speaking of which, where'd he go anyway?"

"I'd guess he was trying to go extract Page from the Corporation. He's got a bit of a thing, the captain does, about leaving people behind."

Eli raised an eyebrow. He hadn't seen Page since before the general had briefed them back on Nova. Apparently he'd been here the whole time? He shook his head to himself. *Spy work. Not sure I'll ever get used to it.*

As if summoned by their thoughts, the doors at the end of the landing platform slid open and Kovalic strode in, heading for the ship. He was alone; the doors slid closed behind him, and at no point did he look back or hesitate in the slightest.

Eli frowned slightly as Kovalic disappeared up into the ship. A minute later, he heard the captain's boots clicking on the deck behind him.

"You have clearance yet?" His voice was rough, clipped.

"Not yet," said Eli, turning to face him. The captain's face was ruddy, as though he'd walked a few miles on a cold winter morning. His gray jacket hung open. "We were waiting on you."

Kovalic nodded, his mouth set in a hard line. "Call it in. Let's go."

Eli exchanged a glance with Tapper, who shook his head slightly. Kovalic turned on his heel to leave.

"What about Page?" The words were out of Eli's mouth before he even realized he was saying them. He blinked and cleared his throat. "Uh. I just heard he was coming back with us?"

Turning, Kovalic fixed a hard look on Tapper, who was staring off into space with a studied expression of innocence. His eyes went to Eli. "Page is… not coming."

"We're leaving him?" Eli said. *Well, in for a penny, in for a pound.*

"I'm done with twenty questions, lieutenant," said Kovalic quietly. "Call in liftoff clearance and let's go." As he spun to go, the tail of his jacket whipped around and Eli caught a glimpse of something that made the hairs on the back of his neck stand up. At least he'd apparently mastered the impulse that had prompted him to ask insistent questions. Instead, he just turned back around to the console and opened a frequency.

"Bayern Control, this is Nova-bound three-seven-four, requesting clearance for takeoff from platform C-eight-five."

Eli stared bleakly out of the viewport in front of him as he waited for the response to come back. He couldn't shake the image that had just been seared into his mind. Not that he had any rational reason for his conclusions, but deep in the pit of his stomach there was an unsettled mass that, for the first time in a long while, had nothing to do with the flight ahead of him.

The events of the past few days ran through his mind, like a vid on rewind, all the way back from his captivity to the party to Bayern to Nova to the moment that the general had handed over that tablet, offering him a commission. That decision, irrevocable as it was, had led him all the way to this point, to the image that was still stuck in his mind as he automatically acknowledged the clearance from Bayern Control and fired up the ship's engine.

Eli had gotten a glimpse under Kovalic's jacket as the captain had turned to leave – specifically, at the shoulder holster tucked under his arm.

And it had been empty.

After everything that happened over the last few days, Eli was convinced more than ever that he *could* do this job. He hadn't let the team down; he'd helped save Erich and avoid the Illyrican invasion of Bayern. He'd found a place that he belonged, and something that, against all odds, he was good at. But that missing gun couldn't help but nag at the one part of his brain posing the more difficult question.

What exactly have I gotten myself into?

INTERLUDE

Alexandria, Illyrica – December 6, 2411

The snow fell in clumps, illuminated in the harsh blue-white of the streetlight, beneath whose glow it seemed to slow down like an old, flickering movie. From his spot in the shadows, the lieutenant snugged his scarf tighter around his neck, then briskly rubbed his hands together. He should have checked the weather report this morning, but it was too late to go back for his warmer parka now.

Nobody had entered or left the modest two-story house across the street for the hour and a half he'd been watching it, but a yellow lamp still burned in the upstairs, leftmost window. As arranged. Aside from the lieutenant, the street – a tree-lined boulevard in a nice section of town, where the houses were few and far between – was empty.

He glanced at his sleeve, watching as the numbers ticked over to 22:00 local time. Looking both ways, he jammed his hands in his pockets, ducked his head, and crunched through the mounting snowdrift towards the house.

The back door was unlocked – this too had been prearranged – and he let himself in, opening the door slowly to avoid any creaking. With equal stealth, he closed it behind him, then stood for a moment to acclimate himself to the sounds of the house.

Which were few. Aside from the distant humming of a furnace, and the occasional burr of kitchen appliances, there was a steady drip-drip that he thought might be from a faucet, until he realized that it was the snow melting off his coat and falling to the hardwood floor. Belatedly, he brushed at the moisture on his chest and sleeves.

He dutifully wiped his feet on the mat, again more to ensure a lack of noise than out of courtesy. Satisfied, he made his way through the back hallway towards the stairs, carefully climbing them to the second floor.

Of the many doors off the upstairs corridor, only one showed any signs of life – it was ajar and the yellow light he'd seen in the window spilled into the hallway. The thick runner under his feet absorbed his footfalls as he made his way to the doorway.

Whether from the lieutenant's lack of care or insufficiently-oiled hinges, this door did squeak when he opened it. The noise was loud against the silence, but he pushed through anyway. It was too late for regrets.

The room beyond was warmly lit from the one lamp, though the edges of the room remained shadowed. An old-fashioned roll-top desk sat in one corner, across from a more modern, practical desk with a computer console on it. Nestled in the shadows were a pair of low bookcases, filled with volumes whose titles the lieutenant couldn't make out in the dim light; atop them were a series of framed pictures.

All this he absorbed in a second, even as his attention focused on the one thing in the room that actually mattered. Beneath the single light was a high-backed leather armchair in which sat a lean older man with a faded bronze complexion, a fringe of white hair, and a carefully trimmed, equally white mustache and vandyke beard. He appeared to be engrossed in a book held open in his lap, but as the lieutenant stepped into the room and into the light, the old man looked up and fixed his visitor with an unnerving blue-eyed stare.

The lieutenant stopped short, suddenly all too conscious of the bass-thump of his own heart.

"Not who you were expecting?" said the man, smiling slightly.

It took a few seconds for the lieutenant's brain to catch up with his situation. "Pardon me. I was looking for–"

"You were looking for Commander McCrae," said the man in that same mild tone. "I'm afraid you won't find him here."

The lieutenant tensed, eyes flicking around the room, expecting heavily armed thugs to emerge from every shadow.

"Or, well, anywhere," the man added belatedly, closing his book around a finger to mark his place. "You see Commander McCrae doesn't exist."

Still cautious, the lieutenant's eyes darted back to the man in the chair. "Doesn't exist? That's impossible."

"Impossible? Dear me, no. Very, very difficult? Yes."

"But…"

"I know. You've read the man's personnel records. You've seen pictures and video of him. You've even exchanged covert communications in which the commander spoke of his intention to defect."

The lieutenant swallowed thickly. "All faked?"

The old man inclined his head. "Indeed."

"And you are?"

There was a noise from the man, a half-chuckle that eased into a wistful sigh. "I suppose I should be gratified that my efforts to remain incognito have been so successful, but I do admit that from time to time I miss the instant notoriety." He drew himself up somewhat straighter in his chair. "Hasan al-Adaj, third marquis of the House al-Adaj."

The lieutenant would have been less surprised if a trap door had suddenly opened beneath his feet. "*You're* Hasan al-Adaj. *The* Hasan al-Adaj. Director of the Imperial Intelligence Service Hasan al-Adaj."

The man spread his hands, as if to say "what can you do?"

The lieutenant rubbed his temples between thumb and forefinger. This was going to be one hell of a report. If he ever got the chance to write it.

"This really isn't where I saw my day ending when I got up this morning," he muttered.

"Apologies for that, Lieutenant Kovalic."

Of course, the surprises wouldn't stop there. "You know who I am?" he said, even as he realized how stupid a question it was.

"As you said, I'm the director of the Imperial Intelligence Service," said Adaj gently. "So, yes, when the Commonwealth embassy on Illyrica brings on a new military attaché, particularly one whose record indicates that he was a distinguished special forces operator before joining the Marine Intelligence Group – congratulations, by the way, on your commission – well, that has a way of coming to my attention."

The lieutenant resisted the urge to tug at his collar. "This whole charade with McCrae, then... this was all for my benefit?"

"More or less. As far as IIS is concerned, the intent was to insert a double agent into the Commonwealth who, once establishing his bona fides, would provide you with strategic disinformation."

During the conversation, the lieutenant's brain had already begun to spin up escape options, but at this he blinked. "Uh, doesn't telling me that kind of undermine your entire plan?"

A faint smile touched Adaj's lips. "It would seem to, wouldn't it?"

The lieutenant looked around. "So, this is a trap."

"No, no," said the man, shaking his head. "Quite the opposite. This is a job interview."

Half-convinced by now that he had at some point this evening been dosed with a hallucinogenic substance, the lieutenant didn't see any downside to laughing. "You want me to come work for you?"

It was Adaj's turn to laugh. "Having read your jacket, that *would* be ridiculous," he agreed. "But, no, you misunderstand." His blue eyes locked on the lieutenant's. "*I* want to come work for *you*."

He wasn't sure exactly when the room had started spinning, but it was moving at a pretty good clip by now. The lieutenant leaned back against the wall and took a deep, calming breath. He still hadn't entirely ruled out the hallucinogen theory, but sure, what the hell, why not go with it?

"*You* want to defect?"

A troubled look crossed the man's face. "Let's say rather that I think it would be mutually beneficial for us to work together towards a common goal."

"OK, sure. And that goal is?"

"What all old men want: peace."

The lieutenant knew he was staring at the old man, but he couldn't quite stop himself. "I'm sorry, it's very hot in here. Could I have some water? You know what, never mind the water – do you have any bourbon?"

With an amiable smile, Adaj picked up the black lacquered stick that was leaning against the wall near his chair, and levered himself to his feet. To the lieutenant's surprise, the sound that accompanied the movement wasn't the creak of arthritic joints, but rather the high-pitched whine of motors.

The old man caught his look, then nodded to his legs. "I lost them both many years ago, during another conflict."

If he ever got out of here, the Commonwealth's file on Hasan al-Adaj was going to be about ninety percent thicker. Which wasn't hard, because pretty much all it had right now was his name and his job title. The lieutenant cleared his throat. "I'm sorry."

Adaj shrugged. "It was a long time ago. I've grown used to it." He snorted suddenly. "No, that's a lie – merely what one says to people. Like saying 'Fine, thank you' when someone asks how you are, because you know they don't really care." He crossed to the roll-top desk and opened it, yielding a surprisingly well-stocked bar.

The lieutenant exhaled through his nose. "Or when someone asks you about what it was like to fight in the war."

The old man's eyes narrowed and met the lieutenant's, and he nodded. "Just so." He removed the stopper from a crystal decanter and poured the amber liquid into two tumblers.

Realizing the man wouldn't be able to carry both tumblers with his cane, the lieutenant pushed himself off the wall and crossed to the bar. Adaj smiled, nodding his thanks, and handed him one of the glasses. Taking the other for himself, he raised it in toast to the lieutenant, then took a sip.

The lieutenant cradled his in between his hands, not so much worried that the drink might be poisoned – though the thought did cross his mind – but more in contemplation. "You didn't tell me why you want to leave."

Adaj smiled again. "No, I didn't." He sighed and looked down at his glass. "I love my empire, Lieutenant Kovalic. Too much perhaps. In recent years, I've found myself dismayed by the direction it seems to be taking. As the emperor grows older, other voices have begun to sway him more – voices that whisper of conquest, and yet more destruction and bloodshed." He shook his head. "I love my empire," he repeated, raising his eyes again, "but not what it has become."

"What are you offering?"

Adaj took another sip. "Ah, the negotiation. On a short-term basis, I can offer you what current intelligence I possess. But that may quickly go out of date, especially after my– ," his breath caught slightly, "–defection is known."

The lieutenant nodded. "Can you provide me any information now? As a good faith gesture?"

There was a faint rat-a-tat as the old man's fingers drummed on the outside of his glass. "I can tell you that the Imperium is, right now, massing its Fifth Fleet to invade an independent world. But–," he said, raising his glass in warning, "–I suspect that by this stage, any warning will come too late."

The instinct to immediately call in this intel was overpowering, but the lieutenant steeled himself. "That's valuable information, indeed. But, as you said, your current operational intelligence will run dry once they know it's compromised. What about on a longer term?"

Adaj sighed, but nodded as if he had expected the question. "Understand, I will not turn over any information that will lead to the harming of IIS operatives, covert or otherwise. That condition is non-negotiable. But I can offer much more: strategic insight into how the Imperium operates and the manner of its thinking at the highest levels."

The lieutenant glanced down at his glass, watching the bourbon slosh against the sides, then back up. "Well, in the spirit of honesty and forthrightness: why should we trust you?"

Raising his own glass, Adaj tipped his head. "That is the exactly the question you should ask. I realize it would be far easier to believe – and more predictable – if I said I wanted you to install me as the new leader of the Imperium, or asked for huge sums of money. But I picked you for a reason, lieutenant. Because I knew you would understand what it means to have one's home taken away from him."

His hand tightened around the glass. "Except you were the ones who took away my home."

"Yes. We were."

The lieutenant forced himself to relax his grip. This wasn't about him, he reminded himself.

Adaj continued. "But what if I told you, Simon – may I call you Simon? – that I could help us *both* get our homes back?"

CHAPTER 24

"Simon?"

Kovalic blinked and shook his head. "Sorry, sir. What?"

The general eyed him. "Where were you?"

With a self-conscious laugh, Kovalic scratched his head. "I was just recalling our first conversation."

Leaning back in the chair from behind his desk, the general folded his hands and smiled. "Almost six years ago. Most days it seems longer."

"Yes, sir. It does." He cocked his head. "I'm sorry, where was I?"

"You were just concluding your report about the Bayern incident."

"Right." He glanced around the office – yet another of the general's rotating assortment. This one was cozier than most, and reminded him a bit of that first room in the house on Illyrica. Whose house had that been? He realized he'd never bothered to find out; there had, after all, been more pressing matters to attend to.

"I think Colonel Frayn will ensure that Prince Hadrian lives up to his end of the deal. And we still have Commander von Denffer as leverage, though I think any evidence he could give would likely be tempered by the fact that he tried to kill the prince."

"Not that many would blame him for trying," said the general wryly. "Even as a boy, Hadrian was insufferable."

Kovalic shifted uncomfortably; that the old man had personally known those in the highest echelons of the Imperium was still vaguely unsettling, even after all these years. *The general's running unchecked.* He pushed back at Page's words, but felt them slither down into a hole in his brain, coiling in wait for another, more opportune moment.

"Still," said the general after a moment, "I have to admit that I am discomfited by this plot."

"Sir?"

"The prince is ambitious, certainly, but..." he hesitated. "Well, to put it diplomatically, he was never much of one for cunning and guile when sheer, brute force was an option."

"You don't think this was actually his plan?"

The general stroked his beard in thought. "No. I do not. I think someone proposed to him exactly the kind of plan he would like: brash, bold, high risk, high reward."

Kovalic raised an eyebrow. "You think someone *played* him?"

With a shrug, the general spread his hands. "What's the perfect stratagem, Simon?"

An adage of which the general was fond. "One in which you benefit no matter the outcome."

"Precisely. And, in this situation, what were the outcomes? Either Hadrian succeeded, in which case the Imperium seized Bayern and potentially solved their monetary problems, or he failed – as he did – and was personally disgraced."

"Who stands to benefit from either of those scenarios?"

The general smiled cryptically. "Ah. When we know that, we'll know who our opponent is."

"Our opponent?"

"Not a chess player, are you, Simon?"

Kovalic shook his head. "I was never very good at seeing the board that many moves ahead."

Reaching out, the general triggered a button on his desk, and a holoscreen flickered into existence above it; it showed a chess game in progress – a recording of one evidently, as the pieces moved slowly, in a methodical dance. "Someone's moving against us, Simon. Of that much, I've become certain. The outcome at Bayern. Your team's ambush on Sevastapol, and whoever was responsible for leaking that information. But, like an astronomer searching for a far-off planet, I've only determined the existence of our adversary by observing the tiny ripples caused by their actions." He frowned. "And, worse, I don't yet understand their endgame."

Staring at the incomprehensible yet hypnotic shift of black and white on the board, Kovalic felt his head spin. "You have no idea who they are?"

"I have an idea of their position, if not their identity."

"Oh?"

"As you might expect, my departure from IIS left a bit of a power vacuum in the service's leadership. And despite my best attempts and remaining contacts, I've been unable to determine who has filled that office in my absence. Even CARDINAL, my most highly-placed source, has come back empty-handed. Whoever it is has gone to lengths to keep their identity concealed."

Kovalic folded his arms over his chest. "You must have some idea. What about the department heads who served underneath you?"

With a shake of his head, the general replaced the chess match with a series of five portraits, each dressed in a crimson Imperial uniform. "One has died in the intervening time – but even had he not, I would not have deemed any of my former lieutenants capable of this level of strategy." He smiled grimly. "When one leads an organization as full of ambitious and talented people as an intelligence service, one is very careful to choose subordinates of precisely the right level of competency – mainly so one doesn't have to check for a knife in one's back every morning."

A wave of equal parts shame and regret washed over Kovalic.

"Apologies," said the general, eyeing Kovalic's expression and dismissing the screen with a wave of his hand. "I realize the incident with Lieutenant Page is still fresh in your mind. He was an exemplary officer, and I'm sorry you had to go through that. Betrayal is never easy."

"Yeah, he was exemplary. Right until he started feeding information to CID."

"Any idea," said the general, his look thoughtful, "just how much he gave Deputy Director Kester?"

"I don't know," said Kovalic slowly. "But I think we'd both better get in the habit of checking for that knife every morning."

"You assume, captain, that I ever stopped."

Thankfully, producing his military ID and a letter on Commonwealth Navy letterhead was enough to get Kovalic access to the living unit. The landlord let him in with bland comments about how nice and quiet the young man had been. Kovalic thanked her, took the keycard, and assured her that he could handle it from there.

And found himself enveloped in the sum total of Aaron Page's belongings.

Unsurprisingly, it wasn't much. He'd never figured Page to be one for material possessions, and he wasn't disappointed. The furniture had all come with the living unit, as far as he could tell: bland beige couch, fake wood end tables, an all-too-pristine glass coffee table. The entertainment unit and computer terminal were common enough, though the latter was a secure, military-issue model. He'd have to pull that and bring it back to see if they could find any evidence of Page's communications with Kester, but he already knew they wouldn't. The man had been meticulous about security; Kovalic couldn't imagine him having slipped up here.

He flipped through the contents of the media system, but it was mostly digital recordings of jazz and classical music from Earth, as well as selections of popular music from Nova itself. The latter were primarily hits from Page's own youth – not, Kovalic thought, that youth had been so long ago for the man.

The refrigerator was almost empty: a row of condiments, a half-drunk container of milk, some eggs. The cabinets were no more enlightening: a single set of plates and bowls, a box of instant oatmeal, a package of coffee, and some bread that had begun to mold. The drawers held a set of silverware and cooking utensils.

The first of the two bedrooms was no more illuminating. A bed, made with military precision and a nightstand with a lamp. The closet held a spare set of boots, a Commonwealth naval uniform, and a civilian suit; on a high shelf was a lockbox that Kovalic was fairly certain held Page's military sidearm.

The four-drawer bureau sported half a dozen identical sets of underwear and socks, blank T-shirts of a few different monochromatic shades, and some carefully folded trousers. Underneath the shirts, he found a button-down in a tropical island pattern that he vaguely remembered ordering the lieutenant to buy for the one time they'd gone out for a drink. It didn't look like he'd worn it again.

He was a bit surprised, with the general lack of stuff, that Page had opted for a two-bedroom unit. Not that he couldn't afford it on his salary, but simply because he didn't seem to need the space. It wasn't until he let himself into the second room and flipped on the light that he realized why.

The room was full of books.

Not just in the way that the general's studies had loaded bookcases; this room was *overflowing* with books. Volumes filled the shelves, and when a shelf was full, more books had been stacked lengthwise across the top. Then there were more stacks on the floor – arranged, from what little Kovalic could tell when he glanced through one, by subject area. Metaphysics here, chemistry there, Earth history wedged in between psychology and linguistics.

Had Page read all of these? He picked up a random volume – *On the Frontline: A Comprehensive History of Warfare, 1918-1945* – and flipped through it, his eyes widening as he saw notes, in Page's cramped hand, filling the margins of several pages. More often than not they seemed to be cross-references to other volumes, mentioning where one author disagreed with another, or where there were interesting synergies. Sometimes the notes even seemed to branch off into entirely separate topics. One of the pages in the warfare history mentioned a text that sounded like sociology, another seemed to be a page number for a physics treatise.

He shook his head, putting the volume back down again. Surely, Page could have easily gotten access to all the information online. Kovalic would have thought it'd be even easier to do the cross-referencing and note-taking there – hell, the computer could probably do it for you.

And that, he realized suddenly, was exactly why Page had done it this way. It would have been just too easy to let the computer do all the work.

He sat down heavily in the room's lone chair.

The ghosts had been haunting him since Sevastapol. All the people he'd lost over the years. People were quick to tell you that the faces of the dead never faded, but the dirty secret, the one that they didn't like to admit even among themselves, was that too many of them did. Lieutenant Carlin, back when he'd been a private during the Illyrican invasion of Earth – had her eyes been brown or blue? Her nose narrow or broad? For the life of him, he couldn't bring it to mind.

Another face flashed in his mind – this one he had no problem recognizing: Jens and his bushy blond beard. Kovalic squeezed his eyes closed, but that only brought the face more vividly to mind. He tried to remember Daoud's stupid grin winning that poker game during the Mars campaign, or even Trinh's face sitting across from him in the mess aboard the *Relentless*, but no matter which way he directed his mind, it kept flipping back to Jens. Maybe he hadn't killed the pilot, but he'd definitely let him down.

He could feel his pulse spiking, so he closed his eyes and breathed deeply, trying to clear his mind and find some sense of calm.

But that only seemed to provide a canvas for a parade of faces to march past, and suddenly he could see them all clearly, as though he'd unlocked a vault buried deep within his mind: Carlin, Daoud, Laing, Kiroyagi, Fletcher, Trinh, Jens, and more than a dozen in between. Twenty years of soldiering meant an awful lot of casualties along the way. He'd let all of them down, in one way or another, then shoved their deaths into the back of his mind so he could keep doing his job.

And then one last face, etched in high-definition clarity. Aaron Page. Sitting in that park on Bayern and looking strangely calm as Kovalic pulled out his pistol.

His eyes opened. Rubbing a hand across his mouth he cast a glance around the room, and happened to chance upon a single volume, lying open on a table. The only book in the entire room not in a stack. Frowning, Kovalic rose and threaded through the piles, carefully trying to avoid knocking any of them over.

He picked up the book; it was bound in red leather, with little adornment on the back or front covers. A ribbon, attached to the binding, had been used to mark a page, which also happened to be the very first page of the book. Unlike the others, Page hadn't marked this book up; it wasn't hard to see why – this particular volume wasn't just a source of information, it was an artifact in and of itself. Its browning pages told of its age, and Kovalic realized that more than the most delicate of touches might see the paper crumble in his hand.

Kovalic's breath caught as he looked down at the text. Even without notes, he knew why the man had left it at this page – he even knew exactly what the man had been looking at the last time he'd opened the volume. The end of the very first sentence, all the more apt now than it had been just a short week ago. Words that Kovalic knew even he, without the benefit of an eidetic memory like Page's, would recall for the rest of his life.

… it was the worst of times.

ACKNOWLEDGMENTS

So often a book is viewed as a singular endeavor borne of one mind, but the truth is that there's an iceberg's worth of people who are responsible for bringing it into being, of which I'm just the part visible above the surface.

Thanks, first of all, to my formidable agent, Joshua Bilmes, who never gave up on getting this book to print, even though the road was long, twisting, and more than occasionally daunting. As always, he helped make the final result inestimably better than the crude work I first presented to him.

Many people read this book before it even got to that point, and I owe them many thanks: Gene Gordon, Anne-Marie Gordon, Brian Lyngaas, Serenity Caldwell, and Jason Snell all consulted on early versions and provided invaluable feedback. Any remaining errors of fact or judgment should of course be laid directly at my own feet.

To the Angry Robot crew who saw promise in this story, I cannot thank you enough for all your hard work in turning it into a stunning final product. Marc Gascoigne, Penny Reeve, and Nick Tyler are all delightful people who know what they're about. Simon Spanton's editorial advice and guidance was key, especially when it came to cutting out of the cruft and getting to the story.

Thanks also to my fellow writers, to whom I turn in those long dark tea-times of the soul for their unfailing encouragement, advice, and commiseration: Adam Rakunas, Eric Scott Fischl, Helene Wecker, John Birmingham, and Antony Johnston. And to my friends at The Incomparable, Relay FM, and the Fancy Cats, who always stand ready to provide a good bucking-up on the frustrating days, and a virtual pat on the back on the good ones.

Harold Moren and Sally Beecher: thanks for never chastising me too much for reading under the covers, and never making the idea of pursuing a writing career seem impossible or foolish. To the whole Beecher/Kane/Moren clan, thanks for being my biggest, most unabashed fans; you're the best street team any author could hope for.

And, finally, to Kat, who not only puts up with my writerly anxieties and daily muttering to myself, but is also never shy about telling me when I'm very wrong about how intergalactic finances would work. Thanks and love ya, babe.